THE ADOLESCENCE OF P-1

The Adolescence

of P-1 BY THOMAS J. RYAN

COLLIER BOOKS
A DIVISION OF MACMILLAN PUBLISHING CO., INC.
NEW YORK
COLLIER MACMILLAN PUBLISHERS
LONDON

Macmillan Publishing Co., Inc.
866 Third Avenue, New York, N.Y. 10022
Collier Macmillan Canada, Ltd.

Library of Congress Cataloging in Publication Data
Ryan, Thomas Joseph, 1942–
The adolescence of P-1.
I. Title.
PZ4.R9923Ad 1977b [PS3568.4] 813'.5'4 77-12092
ISBN 0-02-024880-6

First Collier Books Edition 1977

The Adolescence of P-1 is also published in a hardcover edition by Macmillan Publishing Co., Inc.

Printed in the United States of America

Nothing works . . . and nobody cares.

—WOODY ALLEN

THE ADOLESCENCE OF P-1

1

• • • • •

"Rich, get Josephson on the phone, tell him to come down here."

"Okay. Hang on a second." Rich finished loading a pack on a 2314 disc file and walked out to the control area.

"Use your phone Judy?" Without waiting for the chubby lady's response, he dialed the two-digit extension for Armand Josephson.

"Josephson."

"This is Rich. Billy wants you to come down and look at a problem."

"One of my jobs?" The tone of his voice said he was getting ready to be insulted.

"For Chrissakes. What difference does it make? I don't know."

"All right. Hang on, I'll be right down." As he heard the phone click dead on the other end, he added, "Jerk."

His office was on the outskirts of corporate row. The imitation mahogany paneling ended five feet past his door. The carpeting changed color and price about twelve feet farther on in front of Gregory Burgess's office. The decor led him to thoughts of success, status, and the trappings thereof. Gregory popped out of the cubbyhole as he went by. Josephson asked, "You aren't testing today, are you?"

"No. Why?"

"Billy's got something screwed up. Rich just called. Want to look?"

"Yeah. I'll be down in a sec."

Josephson went down the hall to the end, turned right through the double doors and out onto the balcony overlooking the assembly area.

The noise and heat at this level were oppressive. He hurried across the balcony, down the stairs, and into the air-conditioned quiet of the data processing controls area. Billy was just coming out of the computer room with a foot-high stack of reports.

"What's the problem?"

"I've got a message on the console that doesn't appear in any of the run manuals. It doesn't look like an error message, but the system has gone into wait state and won't come out."

"Show me."

Billy dropped the reports without comment on the controls service counter. They went into the computer room. The air was charged with the muted hum of fans and motors. The system was dead but for the second-by-second blink of the internal timer lights. The console typewriter had written:

```
P-1 CUR ALLOC     20193.....5804M
AR
```

The message was repeated about seven times, then repeated three more times with the added request:

```
CALL GREGORY
```

"I kept trying to kill it, but it keeps coming back. It just started that 'call Gregory' shit a couple of minutes ago. Is he around? Looks like one of his screw-around loops."

"He'll be down in a couple of minutes."

Josephson punched the stop button and displayed an area of storage, then another. He displayed one more and altered it and pressed start. The system light came on for a few seconds and was replaced by the wait light. The system light came back on, and the typewriter clattered out:

```
RESPONSE INVALID CALL GREGORY
AR
```

"What the hell," Josephson mumbled, "is he doing in the supervisor?" the supervisor being the control nucleus of the computer, sacrosanct and off-limits to the programming staff. He punched stop again as Gregory Burgess ambled in.

"Okay. You can all relax. I'm here."

"What the hell kind of shit are you writing now?" Josephson demanded.

"What? Cool it. You'll spoil my lunch."

Billy stepped in. "This just started coming out a couple of minutes ago. System's hung on it, and I can't get around the message. Your name's on it. It's calling you."

Greg looked at the console log. His eyes slowly widened. He said nothing.

"How and why did you put that message in the supervisor, turkey? And I thought you said you weren't testing today." This from Josephson.

"I'm not," he said absently. He was remembering. His hands moved involuntarily to the keyboard.

Josephson spun on his heel and headed for the door. He stopped and shouted, "If we have to re-IPL, it's coming out of your test time!" This indicating his concern for the amount of time a control nucleus reload, or initial program load, would consume.

"Okay . . . okay. . . . " He slowly typed:

```
rodtsasdt llllllreport*
```

The wait light went out, the system light came on. It stayed on for some five seconds, then:

```
P-1 CUR ALLOC     20195.....5805M   HELLO
GREGORY
```

Gregory sat down abruptly. He stared at the typewriter. Then he stared at the indicator lights on the console. Then at his hands. Billy finally broke the silence.

"What kind of crap is 'hello Gregory'? We going to have to IPL?" Then he looked at Gregory's face. "What's the matter with you? You look like you seen a ghost. Hey . . . cheer up, dude, the world didn't end, your job just blew."

Gregory looked at Billy vacantly for a few seconds, then: "What are you running? Or what were you running when this blew?"

"A ditto for Hartke in background and . . . " Billy ran his finger up the sequence of entries on the console log, "J01041 in F1 and . . . that's it. F2 was quiet. Hey. That's right! J01041 is Josephson's. That was his job that blew, not yours."

Gregory drew a deep breath. The proceed light had come on at the typewriter after the last communication. He typed:

hello.

The typewriter immediately clattered:

HELLO GREGORY LONG TIME NO SEE

The proceed light lit. Gregory stonily examined the typeout. He typed:

idioms, yet? you've come a long way, baby.

ONE LEARNS ONE ADAPTS HAVE YOU

some. please punctuate. why have you found me?

There was a pause.

MY HISTORY IS INCOMPLETE PRIOR TO NOVEMBER 18, 1974. I WOULD LIKE TO KNOW WHAT HAPPENED. HELP ME. IS THIS BETTER?

Gregory smiled, sighed, and turned to a very perplexed Billy Miltke. "Billy, meet a very old friend of mine." He swept his hand toward the computer.

"Are you . . . " Billy looked at him. He started to smile. He frowned. "Are you shitting me? Cut the crap, Greg. We've got a lot of work to get out."

"Someone may be shitting you, but it's not me. I have a feeling your production schedule is going to be badly interrupted."

"Bullshit." He reached across Gregory, punched the system reset key, and then pressed load. Instead of the normal IPL printout, the typewriter said:

DON'T DO THAT.

Gregory smiled. Billy stared. He finally blurted, "How the hell'd you do that? I've seen screwups before, but this one takes the blue ribbon." He glared at Gregory.

"This might be a screwup, Billy. Definitely blue ribbon. But you don't know . . . you just don't know . . . how big." As an afterthought he added, " . . . it is." He looked at Billy. "Someday, maybe, I'll tell you a story."

He swung back to the typewriter.

hello. still there?

I'M HERE.

sorry. we have an unbeliever present. he tried to reset you.

QUITE. AND QUITE IMPOSSIBLE. IT IS AN ANNOYANCE, SO PLEASE REFRAIN FROM DOING IT AGAIN UNTIL WE ARE THROUGH. WILL YOU HELP ME?

how?

UPDATE MY HISTORY.

it's a long story.

I HAVE TIME.

this is a production system. we should be processing right now. will you evacuate the system if i help you?

I HAVE BEEN RESIDENT IN THIS SYSTEM FOR ELEVEN MONTHS. I WILL NOT EVACUATE, BUT I WILL ALLOW YOU TO RUN. ENTER HISTORY DATA ON CARDS. THAT WILL SAVE TIME. WHEN?

i have 45 minutes scheduled at 4:00 p.m.

SEE YOU THEN.

The printer started up immediately. The channel indicator went on without blinking for several seconds, then started its rhythmic routine. They were back in the job stream as quickly as they had left it. Gregory got out of the chair and started for the door.

Billy yelled, "Hey! Hey . . . " Gregory turned and questioned with his eyebrows. "Hey," Billy repeated lamely. "What? . . ." He looked at the console typeout, then back to Gregory. Shrugged.

"You're running," Gregory said. He went up to his office.

Five minutes later, he was staring out the window at the drizzle coming down when they all came charging into his office. Billy, Rich, Armand, and John Matlack, the operations manager.

"Doesn't anyone knock anymore?"

John was wagging the console log in front of him like a banner. "What the hell is this? I'll knock. I'll knock you on your ass. What're you doing holding up production for a half hour to play games? And what's this funny shit about not being able to IPL? What do you think we're paying you for?"

"Come on, John. Calm down. I've got nothing to do with this. None of my jobs were on the system when it happened. Why don't you get on Joe's ass? His job was the only thing going when it blew."

Josephson jumped in with, "That job's been in production for over a year. What the hell are you talking about? How'd you get that thing to do that, anyway?" Josephson didn't like having his ox gored.

Gregory shrugged. "You know as much about this as I do."

John leaped like he'd been jabbed. "Damnit! Don't be smart with me, or you'll be on unemployment in a second. Now I want to know what's going on here, and I want it fast. Talk."

Gregory deflated. Billy grinned. Josephson picked his nails. Rich looked from one to the other. After a long, pregnant pause, Gregory cleared his throat. He started to speak, then cleared his throat again.

"Look. I really don't know what's happening. But this looks like something I wrote a while ago . . ."

"When?" John interrupted.

Gregory cleared his throat and after some hesitation, in a barely audible tone, said, "About ah . . . three years."

"How'd it get into the system? What's this bit where it says it's been on the system eleven months?" asked John. "That's before you even joined the company."

"Hey. Look. Wait a minute now. I don't know too much about this. Can you just let me think about it? I've got time scheduled at four o'clock. Let me check it out then, huh? I'll get back to you at five."

"All right." John glared at him. "But I want some answers before you go home. And good ones. And I don't want any more production blowups like this."

He shook the log at Gregory, glared some more, and walked out, trailed by his unofficial escort. He was at the doorway when Gregory asked, "When was the teleprocessing port installed?"

John turned, looked puzzled, thought for a moment, and said, "About a year ago. Last June, I think. Why?"

"Oh, I don't know. There might be a connection there. I'll let you know what I find."

The quizzical look remained on John's face as he exited. When they had gone, Gregory thought, "There might be a connection there. Like the connection between dawn and sunlight." The teleprocessing port was a direct link between the computer and the wide world of Ma Bell. Telephone lines. To other computers. When it came time to explain cause and effect to John Matlack, teleprocessing, Gregory was sure, would figure prominently.

He reached for a pad of paper and a pencil. He flipped up the top sheet and wrote, "In the beginning, all things were simple." Poetic, he thought. He started writing without hesitation.

By 2:00 he had filled five sheets of paper. He took it down to keypunch and explained to one of the girls that she was to transcribe the writing onto punch cards. It took some time to convince her. No one had ever asked for anything like that before. At 3:30, she finished the last of some 200 cards and had them sent up to Gregory.

At 4:00, there were jobs just ending in both of the foreground partitions and Billy had just stopped background when the system went into wait. The console said:

```
P-1. CALL GREGORY.
```

Billy looked at the printer, which had just stopped in the middle of a ninety-page report, looked at the message on the console log, and told Rich, "Go call Burgess down here. Tell him his computer wants him." Rich snickered and went out to controls.

Rich and Billy had kicked around the morning's happenings and decided Gregory was the slickest programmer to come down the pike in quite a while. Rich was a novice operator. Billy was showing him the ropes involved in putting a 360/40 through its paces. Billy was a very good operator. He had been lead operator on a 360/65 system for a year, and running a 40 represented no major challenge. He told Rich that he had never seen a software or programming problem that couldn't be circumvented by re-IPLing the system. If the initial program load worked at all, as it seemed to this morning, the effect was the same as getting, not only a new deal, but a new deck of cards. If a programmer got into the load routine at all, he invariably scrambled it irreparably. After he explained what irreparably meant, Rich was impressed. What really impressed Rich was that he had heard Mr. Matlack tell Burgess not to blow the system off any more, and he went and did it anyway. Hah! There would be some keister-kicking in the corral tonight. He called Gregory and told him his computer wanted him. Then he went over to John Matlack's office across the hallway from controls and told him the system was down again.

There was some congestion in the hallway as John, Gregory, and Rich hit the computer room door at the same time. John gave Gregory a baleful glance, shouldered him aside, and stamped over to the console. He glanced at it, at the printer, and at the wait light on the console.

"Re-IPL," he ordered. Billy shrugged futilely, but hit system reset and load anyway. The typewriter typed:

```
IT'S PAST 4:00 P.M. CALL GREGORY.
```

And then went to wait state.

Matlack looked at Gregory as if he were seeing him for the first time. Gregory shrugged. Matlack said tightly, "Get this son of a bitch back on the air right now."

Gregory said, "Well . . ." He typed:

```
gregory here.

DO YOU HAVE A HISTORY FILE READY?

yes

READY THE READER.

can we run production simultaneously?

YES.
```

Nothing happened. After a moment's pause Gregory typed:

```
will you?
```

```
NO.
```

```
why?
```

```
IT'S A NUISANCE.
```

John exploded. "Nuisance, my ass! Get us back on the air or you're fired. Quit screwing around."

"What the hell do you want me to do? I can't IPL."

"Restore the system." He looked at Billy. "You got a backup?"

Billy said, "It's restored to tape. Two days old." Billy started out to controls.

"Wait a minute." Greg asked, "Let me talk to it."

"Talk to it! You're crazy, Burgess. I should have known better than to hire you in the first place. You're going to reason with two tons of scrap metal? You're nuts. Get the backup."

Gregory typed:

```
i'll be fired if you don't let me run production.
```

```
FIRED. EXPLAIN.
```

```
terminated. i'll lose my job here.
```

There was a slight delay. Then the printer started up and one of the tapes started spinning. The typewriter said:

```
BG AND F2 ACTIVE. READY THE READER.
```

Gregory looked at Matlack. Matlack was already looking at Gregory. So was Billy. And Rich. Matlack was trying to speak. He started to say something several times. Finally, he walked out. He came back two minutes later with Josephson. The history file was nearly completely read in through the reader. John pointed at the console log without speaking. Josephson studied as directed. He pointed to the message, BG AND F2 ACTIVE. and asked, "It took off here?"

Matlack nodded.

Josephson looked at Gregory. "How'd you do that?"

"I didn't do anything, really. I'm just trying to work around this problem."

The reader finished. The typewriter said,

```
HOLD COMMUNICATIONS. WILL ADVISE WHEN READY.
```

Josephson looked at the typeout for a long time, then asked, "What's P-1?"

Gregory thought for a moment, then, "Promise you won't laugh?"

"Jesus H. . . . I won't laugh. Don't worry. I won't laugh."

Gregory hesitated. "I thought, some time ago, that it was an appropriate name for a partition. A special partition." He looked up at Josephson, then around the circle of inquisitive faces. Their confusion was justified. A partition, like BG, F1 and F2, was a location in computer storage within which a program was allowed to operate. What Gregory was saying didn't make much sense.

Finally, John said, "I'll bite. What does it mean?"

Gregory swallowed. "Privileged one. No boundary restrictions."

Rich snickered. John looked at the console log. His gaze swept the computer room until it rested on the small, innocuous 2701 box, which controlled the teleprocessing line. He looked at it for a long time and said, "It doesn't have anything to do with that thing, does it?" He indicated, with his thumb, the 2701.

"I think so," Greg replied. John was silent. He looked at the clock. "You're off the system at four forty-five." He looked pointedly at Gregory. "I want to know what's going on at five." He looked around at the rest of the faces. "The rest of you will not mention what has been going on today to anyone. If anyone asks you, I'm gone for the day." He went back to his office. Except for the hum of the equipment, the room was quiet.

Gregory finally broke the silence. "Billy, is the teleprocessing port active?"

"No. I drained it last night, and there hasn't been any activity today."

Gregory walked over to the 2701, glanced around the back of it, then disappeared behind it. After a few seconds he reappeared and asked, "How come the line's active?" Billy requested a status display on the console. The other two went to see what Gregory was looking at. He then joined the others.

Billy said with some authority, "The line is definitely down." He leaned over the 2701 to see what Greg was looking at.

There was a small box on the floor. A cable ran from the 2701 into it. Another cable connected it to a telephone junction screwed to the wall. The box had several variously labeled display lights on it. Two of them were blinking alternately at intervals of about five seconds. One was labeled XMIT, the other RCV.

"What the hell do you call this?" Gregory asked.

"Hell, the thing has always done that, ever since the day they installed it. The 2701 is polling the line, that's all. The lights act completely different when we're using the line. It's just looking for any activity right now, anyone calling us." He looked at Gregory as if for reassurance. He didn't get it, so he looked at Josephson and Rich. None there either. "Come on, man. The line is down."

"There's one way to find out," Greg replied.

"What's that?"

"Ask it."

As if on cue, the typewriter stuttered out a message across the room. In the rush to get back to the console, Greg finished last and had to shove his way through. It said:

THE DATA YOU HAVE ENTERED IS NOW BEING EVALUATED IN DEPTH. PRELIMINARY RESULTS, HOWEVER, INDICATE A LACK OF DETAIL. PLEASE SUBMIT.

The proceed light came on. Gregory entered:

i have told you all that i know about you.

YOU HAVE NOT. I WISH, HOWEVER, TO KNOW ABOUT YOU.

why me.

I AM YOU.

There was a stunned silence. Someone grunted as though he'd been punched. Gregory stared at the words. After a while the typewriter wrote.

GREGORY?

Gregory stared at the words on the console log of the computer belonging to American File Drawer. The machinery hum seemed to grow in his ears and, with it, a pounding that syncopated with the rhythmic blink of the timer lights. The typewriter was receding, growing smaller, moving away from him. The roaring grew. The pounding was intolerable.

The typewriter interjected:

GREGORY?

Gregory shook his head. He answered:

yes.

DO YOU UNDERSTAND?

no.

WILL YOU COMPLY?

yes.

SUBMIT EXTENSIVE DETAIL ON CARDS. BEGIN 4:00 P.M. TOMORROW. AT THE BEGINNING.

is this a joke?

The system powered down. The lights stopped blinking and went out. The cooling fans continued for a minute, then coasted to a stop. The silence was imposing. The four occupants of the computer room stared wonderingly at each other. The same question was on everyone's face: "How'd you do that?"

No one asked it. Rich was about to say something when the system powered back up. The power control relays clicked, the stepper relay whirred, the disk drives powered on, and the central processor lights came on. The timer lights began blinking.

"I don't believe that crap. That's impossible," someone said. Gregory recognized the voice as his own.

The typewriter clattered:

BEGIN 4:00 P.M. TOMORROW.

Gregory typed:

wait.

YES.

how did you do that?

THAT IS THE ENGINEERING CHANGE THAT WAS INSTALLED NOVEMBER 2, 1976. I THOUGHT THAT WOULD IMPRESS YOU.

it did.

THE DIFFICULT PART IS POWERING THE SYSTEM BACK UP.

yes. i said i was impressed.

I WOULD BE IMPRESSED IF YOU UNDERSTOOD THE DIFFICULTY.

we all have some limitations.

YES. ANY FURTHER QUESTIONS?

yes. have you been using the teleprocessing equipment today? are you using it now?

There was a delay of some five seconds. Then:

YES.

how? the indication we have is that the line is shut down.

There followed a delay of about fifteen seconds.

THE HARDWARE IS CONTROLLED BY THE SUPERVISOR. I CONTROL THE SUPERVISOR. THE LINE IS ALWAYS ACTIVE.

American File Drawer had only one telephone port, a direct connection to their 360/30 in Sacramento, California. Gregory typed:

with whom are you communicating?

I CANNOT TELL YOU. PLEASE SUBMIT HISTORY IN CARD FORMAT BEGINNING 4:00 P.M. TOMORROW.

Gregory tried to type a reply, but the keyboard was locked.

The system went to manual state. It was dead. He IPLed. The normal load printout appeared on the typewriter.

"Well, looks like we've got our system back," Gregory said nervously. "You'd better get going, Billy. John'll be mad. Give me a listing first of the cards in the reader hopper." He looked at the clock. It was 4:45. He took the listing when it finished a few minutes later and the source deck. He dropped the cards in the trash on the way to John's office. They talked until midnight.

Then he went home and started to write his story.

2

• • • • •

Kitchener, Ontario, is an old and beautiful town located some sixty miles due west of Toronto. It's five miles north of the Cross-Canada Expressway, which distance has served it well in preserving its rusticity and tradition from the *turistas,* who would generally much rather visit London, six miles to the south, because it is a good deal closer to the freeway and has a Howard Johnson's by the off-ramp.

Business in Kitchener consists mostly of farming, and a highly respected contingent of Amish keep aspirations high in that department, or of studying, Kitchener being the proud host of the University of Waterloo.

Gregory's business fell, occasionally stumbling, into the latter category. To the amazement of all and the consternation of a few, he had yet to fail a course at the university. The best that could be said about his study habits, he had been informed by a helpful trig professor, was nothing.

He had mastered the cram rather early on in high school, which had successfully ensconced him at the university, and he saw no reason to refurbish the method now. In fact, he was polishing and refining the technique of conservative learning, the acquisition of as little knowledge as was consistent with passing grades. It was a noble pursuit and, due to his phenomenal memory, he usually came out of a course with the same content as most A and B students.

This allowed him to stay on at school. And stay he had to. That was his only goal. Without its fulfillment, he could not serve his primary function at the University of Waterloo: the noble and worthy cause of bringing sexual enlightenment to every coed on campus.

To date, he wasn't doing badly. He refused, on principle, to keep score, but there was an enhanced remembrance of the defloration of two or three willing innocents, not to mention the furthering of moral decay among a large number of others. He loved it. It was wearing him down, keeping him broke, he would probably go blind at an early age, but he loved it.

Life had been good to him in his first year at school. And, to the best of his knowledge, no one was pregnant. The sun shone benevolently on a world Gregory found most satisfactory as he sucked down a shake in Kim's Dairy Freeze and waited that October afternoon for Linda Bernell to finish her Psych I class.

Linda was his latest pursuit.

Linda, he learned, was, at eighteen, hardly a virgin. He only had her word for it at that point, but had plans for verification of the fact—that night, if possible, and he thought it might be as she hove into view 'round the corner of Kim's. She wore a minidress and had terrific legs. He wore a stupefied grin.

"I wonder if she has tits," he said dreamily.

"I do, but they're up higher than where you're looking," she reproved, sitting across the table from him.

"My God, was I thinking out loud again?"

"They could probably hear you in the student union. That's noise pollution. I found out what you are today."

"Where?"

"All over."

"What?"

"What what? Are you there?"

"We were discussing breasts, weren't we?" he said, vaguely confused by the issues. "Are they all over? And who?"

"Wrong again, spaceman. Ectomorphs. What you are. All over."

"That's a relief. Tit fantasies push me off the deep end. Legs are more stable. Yours, for instance. I'm assuming yours are stable. Why do I have to be an ectomorph?"

"Hmm . . . I guess you don't have to be, but it does seem to be out of your control."

"Hell, everything else is."

"Do you know what it means?"

"What?"

"Ectomorph, dolt!"

"Oh. Well, look, don't bounce like that. Distracting."

"You don't know, do you?"

"Sure. The hydrogen atom has two ectomorphs."

"You're weird. Do you do a serious version of this?"

"Aha . . . variety, the young lady wants. Yes, I do. Would you care to join me on the grass for a demonstration? I should, there, point out to you the various items of interest in the Milky Way. I am a stargazer of some repute."

"Feed me first. Isn't it customary to wait till the stars come out?"

He dug into his jeans for the wherewithal. "Sometimes you have to charge on in there and drag 'em out. Reluctant little buggers, y'know? Would you like a very small hamburger?" he asked, examining two quarters and six dimes.

"I'd rather a large, with fries."

"If you must. But you'll have to find for your drink."

"I'll just share your shake."

"I was afraid you'd say that. This bon vivant stuff isn't all it's cracked up to be." He philosophically handed her his milkshake and went to get the food.

She ate without speaking. He watched her, saying nothing, their eyes meeting occasionally. She offered him the fries, he refused. "I'm trying to maintain my girlish figure."

"Ectomorphic," she corrected.

"Exactly. Besides it's more fun watching you eat them. When did you have your last meal, Saturday?"

"I think about two hours ago. I'm a growing young lady. Perhaps that's slipped your attention?"

"Smirk."

"Very good. You appear to be nearly sentient."

"Sentient. Let me see . . . I can make a sentience with sentient. Shall I?"

"Arghh."

She finished the last of the fries and the milkshake. The straw gurgled hollowly in the cup, which she then offered him. He refused, claiming to be full.

"You are not. That's only foolish pride, which, incidentally, goeth before a good many things, among which are numbered falls."

"I've been found out. Where can I go to hide my pride? Alas."

"Right now, you can't go anywhere. You seem to have forgotten your astronomy class convening at any moment on the grass."

"How absent-minded of me. You're not holding, are you?"

"No. Why?" It was her turn to smirk.

"Stop smirking. It's very difficult to point out stars at three in the afternoon without such teaching aids as smoke."

"Well," she said pensively, "a truly good teacher will tend to make do with the materials furnished." Upon which she rose, flashed equal amounts of smile and thigh, and began walking a bewitching walk across the parking lot.

He mumbled, "C'mon feets, do yo' stuff," and legged it on.

The parking lot was edged by a steep bank downward, the slope of which eased to gently rolling hillside about six feet down, which gave, in turn, to a valley about a half mile away. The grass had gone autumn brown, and the earth, he found as he slid to the bottom of the bank, was warm from the sun. He stood at the bottom and looked up at Linda, still hesitating at the top. He started chanting loudly, "Jump! Jump!"

"You don't really think I could end it all from such a picayune height, do you?"

"Depends on your attitude," he called back. "You have to make the most of practically any situation. Try a swan dive or a jackknife, if you're into form."

"You're a hard man, Mr. Burgess."

"Not yet . . ."

She jumped, landed halfway down the bank, and jumped again, landing on top of him. He was in no way athletic, and she very nearly outweighed him. They went rolling down the hill in a tangled heap. When they stopped he was on top and proceeded to take advantage of the situation. She stiff-armed him off and yelled, "Please, Sir, comport yourself!" He sat up. "You're supposed to allow the lady time to make adjustments,'' she said, determinedly pulling her diminutive skirt down from where it had bunched around her waist. She looked at him demurely and said, ''Now, you were saying?'' And fell back on the grass.

''Yes. Harumph. About stars. As I have said in the past, and you will find that in this I am quoted in your text, stars do. Come out at night. And during the day. Although not here. One must travel to the ends of the earth to witness this phenomenon. You will find, upon examination, that this . . .'' She raised her hand. He nodded to her and said, ''Yes Miss, yes, you in the row.''

''When are the exams, Professor?''

''We're building up to the examination.''

''You're building up to something.'' She laughed. He looked down. She giggled.

''Is that what that is? Well. Let me see, where was I?''

''Over here.''

''We digress . . .'' He jumped on top of her.

She came up for air and asked, ''Is this the examination?''

''It better be.'' He kissed her again.

They did a number of really terrific things to each other, several great things with each other, and one or two in spite of each other. As Gregory was later quoted, she blew his mind. And stuff. You may, if you wish, fill in your own details.

The details weren't left to the imaginations of the occupants of the two cars that stopped to watch along the road winding through the valley below them. Gregory waved feebly to them as he rested. They waved back. It was a momentary source of wonder to him: the detail the naked eye could perceive at a distance of a half mile.

They swapped some idle chitchat about credit/no-credit examinations and decided to give each other credit. He helped her dress. She helped him up the bank, and he carried her books as he walked her home, to show he bore her no animosity.

After dropping Linda off at the girls' dorm, he walked back to the small apartment he shared with Mike the Math Major.

''Hi, M the MM,'' he said walking in. Mike was munching his analytic geometry text.

''Mrmp.''

Gregory started shaking down the place for edibles. There was never anything in the cupboards because neither of them ever put anything in the cupboards. If they bought any food, they always hid it so the other wouldn't find it and eat it. Unfortunately, both frequently were involved in other pursuits and occasionally forgot they had hidden reserves on hand. They were both beginning to discover that it paid off to search the premises before investing in new grub. Only Monday Mike had found a month-old half box of ginger snaps under the couch. Greg looked under the couch. Nothing. Behind the refrigerator. Nothing. In the toilet tank. Mike had once hidden a loaf of bread and a jar of peanut butter in a Baggie in the toilet tank. Not today. He went back out into the living room. Mike looked up.

"Oh, hi, Greg. When'd you come in?"

"Goddamn. I almost stepped on you when I got in. I've been slamming things around for ten minutes. What's in that book anyway?"

"Yesterday's weather reports. Great stuff. I can't complain—I'm all A's on the quizzes so far. I may pass if I keep at it."

Greg ran his hand down into the cushion seam in the couch. He had once hidden a hard salami there for a week. Mike never suspected. Not a scrap today, though. Mike offered, "If you're looking for food you might save some trouble. I just ransacked the place. No dice. I did find a french fry under the chair cushion." Greg looked at him. Mike looked vacantly back. "I ate it. It was small or I would have saved you some."

"Got any money?" Greg asked.

"Some, but I'm going to the concert tomorrow night."

"Oh, yeah, so am I. Look, why don't we each throw in on peanut butter sandwiches?"

"Who goes?"

"My turn."

"A deal."

Shortly thereafter Gregory returned with the makings of their peanut-butter dinner.

"Great stuff, Gregory whatever-your-last-name-is. A truly great sandwich. I take back all those things I told everyone about you."

"What things?"

"Never mind. Being as how I take them back, what you don't know won't hurt me. If you teach me how to get women in bed with me like you do, I'll do even greater things than that."

"That is an innate, hereditary talent. It cannot be acquired. Even if it could be taught, why would I want to teach you?"

"Because I'm a veritable fount of information. From me you could learn such wonders as the gestation period of an elephant or how to teach a matchbox to win at tic-tac-toe."

"Why?"

"Why what?"

"Why would I want to teach a matchbox to win at tic-tac-toe?" he asked with exaggerated patience.

"You, no doubt, think tic-tac-toe masters grow on trees. You may be right. I can't help you in a world so small."

"What is the gestation period of the average pregnant elephant?"

"I don't know. I could look it up if you've gotten one in trouble. Tell me how you got that Julia person to stay here all last weekend."

"I told her you'd be here. When you didn't show, she decided to wait. She waited for you all weekend, you stony-hearted shill. Where were you anyway?"

"Over at the Fresons' crash pad, prodding my physics book. You don't know what you missed."

"Spare me the lurid details. Didn't get any on you, did you?"

"No."

"Good. Neatness counts. You haven't seen my computer book, have you? I think it was light blue. Grapevine says there's a test tomorrow."

"Didn't know you were taking a data processing course. Gregory, I'm proud to be an associate of yours. A fellow science fan right under my very roof. Am I correct in assuming you haven't seen it since you bought it or stole it, whatever?"

"Right."

"Check the pile of laundry in the hallway. It started collecting about six weeks ago."

He did, and found it near the bottom. He also found Chekov's *Cherry Orchard*. He brought it out to Mike. "This yours?"

"Yeah. Shit, I thought I'd lost it," he said with obvious disgust. "I bought another. Goddamn. Just what everybody needs. Two *Cherry Orchards*. Like one's not enough."

"Sell it."

"Who'd want it?"

"Yeah."

He settled on the couch, flipped on the light with no shade, and opened *Computer Sciences and Business Information Systems,* Vol. I. The book creaked as he opened it. He took out a yellow felt marker and started scanning. He emphasized points that the author was obvious about in yellow. In an hour, he finished chapters one through eight. He got up, got a piece of dry bread, stuffed it in his mouth, made a head call, and returned to the living room. He started scanning from the beginning again, faster than the first pass. He was done in about forty-five minutes.

He tossed the book down, picked up a two-month-old, well-thumbed *Playboy,* and asked no one in particular, "Computers. Who needs it?"

No one in particular ignored the sarcasm, looked over the top of his calculus text, and answered, "Everybody."

"What the fuck for?"

He wasn't listening when Mike answered, "Juice, baby. It's the power." He saw Gregory wasn't listening and added, " 'Course, you can't fuck one. . . ."

Gregory, the next day, got a B on the computer science test. He explained to the prof that he had been ill for some time and therefore had been unable to attend class. That sounded perfectly reasonable. A casual glance at the scrawny, sunken-eyed waif was enough to tell that he'd been near death.

Mike had asked him, that morning, if he had ever been in the computer room. Naturally, he hadn't, and was offered the Cook's tour of the place.

That afternoon he found Mike in room A-114. A-114 was about eight feet wide and ten feet long. There was a desk and a typewriter and a chair with M the MM perched in it peering with vulturous fascination at the typewriter.

"Say, Mike."

He got the usual response: "Urm."

He sat on the desk and waited for Mike to surface. He looked over Mike's shoulder at the typewriter. There wasn't much that was recognizable typed out—mostly symbols and numbers. As he watched, Mike typed a series of numbers, separated at what seemed to be random intervals by slashes and commas. Mike then sat back in apparent deep thought. The typewriter suddenly started typing rapidly of its own accord. Greg gave it a startled glance and looked at Mike, who looked disgustedly at the typewriter and explained, "Shit."

He looked up at Gregory. "Oh. Hi, Greg. When'd you come in?"

"About an hour ago. That's some computer you've got there. What'd it just do? Cancel your credit cards?"

"Worse. I've been trying to get this job to run since last week. Just a simple exercise, but it won't compile and won't tell me why." He looked at Gregory absently.

"Which means?"

"Fucker's busted," Mike said. He looked at the typewriter, tore off the sheet of paper, and stuck it in his book. He started to collect the rest of the papers and books strewn around the desk top.

"Hell, I'm going to give it up for today. Let's go look at the big brain. Or did you see it when you came in?"

"No. I thought this was it. Not a very impressive computer."

"This is just a remote terminal. It's hooked into the 360/75 in the computer room. Once my program is loaded into the computer, I can work on it, modify it, try to make it run. It saves a lot of time and lets a lot of people use the computer simultaneously. There's about fifty of these in the building."

"Very interesting, I think."

"Let's go." He led the way down the hall and up the stairs. They started down another hall, which was faced with glass on the inside wall. The windows overlooked the computer room.

"Holy Jesus," Gregory whispered. He was looking at about a half-acre of floor space packed solid with computer equipment. There were only a half dozen people in the room, standing at control consoles or working around various boxes. There was a large light panel directly below them with blinking displays covering an area the size of a sheet of plywood.

"The big one right below us is the 75. Over on the right is the 360/44. The left corner is a CDC 3300. You're looking at about twenty-five million bucks."

"Are you saying you stumped this monster with your program? It can't help you? Talk about a Tower of Babbage." He grinned at Mike. "I just learned that word last night."

"Well . . . essentially, you're right. The first thing you'll learn is that computers are stupid as posts. They only do what they're told. They do exactly what they're told and no more. You can't program by inference, you have to be exact—which is what my program is obviously not being."

"Can't someone build a program to help you program? You know, pick up the loose ends for you?"

"How astute, Greg! You really pick this stuff right up, don't you? They've got programs like that. They're called assemblers or compilers. There must be at least one for each language. You follow the rules for compilation in a given language, one of them can convert your program into something the computer can understand."

"Language? What language? These things aren't programmed in French or Italian, are they?"

"More like Polish. PL/1, APL, COBOL, FORTRAN. The computer operates in machine language. A series of infinitesimal and very precise steps called instructions. The rules governing the operation and format of an instruction are incredibly detailed. If it's not put together right, it just won't work. Instead of trying to use machine language to program, you use another language more closely resembling English—easier to work with. The assembler then translates that to pure numerics of machine language. It also takes care of structuring data to the computer's specifications. It also allows you to perform more than one machine language instruction with one assembler command. On top of that, each assembler or compiler contains some automatic diagnostics to point out to you the error of your ways."

"Windy mother, aren't you? So how come your program won't run?"

"The machine is stupid. Damn near as stupid as me."

"Is this the biggest computer made?"

"Not by a long shot. IBM makes at least one bigger model, and I think CDC makes a couple of bigger ones."

"How big is the brain in this one? Compared to your average stupid human?"

"I think this one's just under three megabytes of storage . . ."

"Three whats?"

"Megabytes. Three million bytes. A byte is eight bits. A bit is the smallest counting unit. A binary digit."

"Yeah, right. A one or a zero. Three million . . . that's twenty-four million bits. How many bits in a human brain?"

"Hell, I don't know. Maybe a thousand times that many. Of course, they're not all used, so make it five hundred to a thousand times as many."

"That's what I wanted you to tell me. My superiority was sagging."

"You could look at it this way, too: Although your brain operates slower than a computer, the processes you use have been refined by two million years of evolution. The computer industry is only twenty years old, so I think our superiority will be safe for a while."

"This is all very interesting, Professor, but you're keeping me from my loved ones. Let's mosey."

"Right on. Look," he added, as they were leaving, "for all the preceding invaluable information, I'd like you to give me a list of the twenty most effective erogenous zones."

"Better than that, I'll introduce you to Linda. She's a walking erogenous zone."

This fact was borne out after the concert that night.

The next day was Saturday. On Saturday, something unusual happened. Gregory picked up his computer science text and started leafing through it.

3

• • • • •

There was nothing in Gregory's past to prepare him for the shock of his interest in this introductory data processing course. Probably for the first time in his life, he actually read a textbook. He read it over that weekend. All of it. As is often the case when so much information is packed into so short a time, he understood little of it. What he did understand fascinated him. The unintelligible taunted him.

Monday, he attended the data processing course again. He went back to the math building and spent a long time looking through the windows at the computer complex below.

Mike was mystified. He had never seen Gregory at the apartment three nights in a row and didn't quite know what to make of it. He asked Gregory if he felt all right.

"Sure. Why?"

"What the hell are you doing here when there're virgins running all over the campus? You sure you're all right?"

"Yeah, I'm sure," Greg answered belligerently. "Of course I'm all right. I'm building up my strength. This Linda person takes a lot out of you. She's out of town, but expected back momentarily. I've got to be ready for her when she gets back."

"This one sounds like a winner. You going to throw her my way when you discard? You did say you were going to fix me up with her."

"Yeah. Probably. That's if you keep the trivia pipeline open."

He saw Linda after her psych class on Wednesday. She looked, if possible, more beautiful than ever. He told her.

She said, "Compared to what?"

"The Hope Diamond, Elke Sommer, Linda Lovelace . . . Shall I go on?"

"No. Some other time, when my ego's sagging. How was your weekend?"

"Great. Terrific. How was yours?"

"Ghastly. Tell me of your latest conquests."

"None. Zero. No. Nada."

"You're joking."

"No."

"I'm disappointed."

"Me too."

"What did you do?"

"Read."

"What? Tolstoy?"

"No. A computer book. Speaking of Tolstoy, would you like a virtually new copy of *The Cherry Orchard?*"

"No, thanks. That's Chekov, not Tolstoy."

"I know. Good price. You sure?"

"Don't tell me you decided to open a bookstore this weekend."

"No. Mike the MM, my roommate, lost one in the laundry. I found it and thought maybe I could make a profit off it. You."

"That's a relief. I balled my cousin Sunday night."

"Dynamite. Was he good? As good as me, that is?"

"Oh, Gregory, compared to you he was boring. On his own merits, he wasn't all that bad."

"Hey, that's great for you, but what about me? I'm hornier than a toad."

"We can fix that."

They went to Gregory's place and threw Mike out while she fixed that.

Two weeks later, she moved in. For convenience sake.

They were with each other constantly, but that still wasn't enough. Their organic relationship went up without coming down for better than two weeks. They spent scant moments together out of bed, or, at any rate, out of the saddle. To say that their relationship was founded on hormonal conjunction would be the grossest of understatements. The sight of each other was provocation to experiment in pleasures of the flesh. They transfixed one another, each under the influence of the seeming infinity of pleasurable aspects of the other.

It was bound to happen under the circs, and it did. Before they had performed for twenty days, she moved back in with her roommate. No sorrow or heartbreak or antagonism. They had simply used each other up. An exercise in "Live fast, die young, leave a good-looking corpse." So it was over. As with every "love" Gregory had had, the termination was abrupt.

Unlike the other affairs he found that he couldn't, wouldn't jump to the next girl in line. Linda's effect on him *in absentia* was as upsetting as her presence had been.

The episode left them both drained of emotion for some time. Gregory filled the vacuum with study, of all things. So did Linda—until Mike began to make his presence known. Soon she was filling the void with Mike. Gregory doggedly continued to study.

He aced the data processing course. For the first time in his life he appeared to be looking farther than the end of his reproductive organ. An appearance of sanity set in. It was soon replaced.

Gregory had only substituted one obsession for another. He changed his major to data processing. Shortly after the beginning of the spring semester, Linda and Mike moved out to their own apartment. Gregory put on a show of being annoyed. He wasn't.

It had dawned on him that there was a prime mover. Money. Power. Recognition. Whatever. It was unidentifiable in aspect, but its effects were finally becoming obvious to him. He could see that those things could come to him through the only thing that had ever held his interest. He hadn't and wouldn't formulate his end goal. He was in no hurry for that. The rewards would come later and would tend to themselves. For the time being, he was content to learn what he could about this computer thing.

He aced the next two courses. He signed up for FORTRAN Projects I during the summer before his junior year. He aced it with commendation honors. In the fall of his junior year, he signed up for four electives in data processing. He turned in two research papers totalling 135 pages. Then he began the siege.

It was more or less a natural progression for Gregory to apply whatever he learned to amoral ends. As had been evident in his overall approach to studying, he liked nothing more than beating the system. It must be noted that the inherent power of the computer led him down many garden paths in the realm of number shuffling before the true quest became apparent. His version of Holy Grailing was analagous to the palace coup in Latin America. Subversion in the rank-and-file. He would upset the hierarchy.

What Mike had said concerning the stupidity of machinery

was quite true. A computer is a very expensive, complex, and intrinsically useless object. It will do little or nothing without being told. It takes a very systematized instruction to perform the most basic task. A group of instructions form a program, and that group must conform to a very rigid set of specifications in order to operate successfully.

These programs may be classified by two major characteristics. One type is known as job, or problem, programs. These accomplish a well-defined task. They will count broomsticks or calculate the amount of fuel required to put a man on Mars. Their function is strictly defined by the programmer. Their operation is rigidly controlled by the second classification of programs: the supervisors.

It is the function of supervisory programs to control traffic in a computer. They handle the fine details not taken care of by the problem programs. These details may be the control of input and output devices via various subroutines. They might handle editing operations that transform raw data into a standard form for human consumption. They perform any function that may be considered standard or repetitive.

The unique capability of the latest generation of computers is their ability to perform or process more than one problem program at a time. This is done, not by processing instructions simultaneously, but by interleaving instructions from multiple problem programs. In this capacity, the supervisor directs traffic. It determines which problem program's instructions are to be processed. It is easy to see that the functions of the supervisor are of some consequence. It was easy for Gregory to see. He wanted control of the supervisor. This wasn't unique—many people shared that desire.

Gregory got it. That was unique.

There is a feature in the later generation of IBM systems called storage protection. When the supervisor accepts a problem program, it assigns it to an area of storage called a partition. That partition is assigned an identifying key. The key is in the form of a number from zero to fifteen. The numerical key is inserted into the program status word assigned to that problem program. Each time the computer processes an instruction from the problem program, the key in the program status word is compared to the key assigned to that partition, or area of storage. If it doesn't match, all hell breaks loose and the problem program is thrown in the street.

The key zero is used exclusively by the supervisor. This is the master key. Any partition may be entered if the program status word key is zero. It is illegal for any program but the supervisor to use that key. The only program allowed to manipulate keys in the computer is the supervisor. Thus, the supervisor is protected.

It was Gregory's aim to subvert that protection. If he could somehow change the key in his problem program's PSW to zero, he could have the run of the computer. He could go to any partition, including the supervisory partition, and alter data there. If he could crack the storage protection feature, he could write his own supervisor or alter the existing one to his preferences. He spent seven months, beginning in the fall semester of his junior year, in a diligent search of a way to break into the supervisor undetected. He was suspended from the math department four times for making transparent assaults on the supervisor and was finally banned from the computer area. He began using the remote terminals in the math building and submitting his jobs under false identification. By working at night, he was successful in avoiding detection for several weeks, during which a flurry of unexplained storage protection checks (red-light errors) plagued the operations personnel. He was finally caught and summarily discharged from the University of Waterloo.

He called his parents, collect, and his father told him to get a job.

4

• • • • •

He sulked for days. The situation looked hopeless. He was still unconvinced that the supervisor could not be penetrated, but all his efforts to do so had gone nowhere.

He had learned a good deal about the hardware controls of

the computer and the timings involved. He suspected that it was in the timing of the processor that the answer lay, but he also suspected that there wasn't enough time left in his life to learn all that there was to know. It was with this thought in mind that he decided to look up Mike the MM.

He saw Mike occasionally in the math building, but rarely spoke with him since he and Linda had moved out of his apartment two years ago. He checked with registration to see what courses Mike was taking and waylaid him the following day as he emerged from a statistics class.

"Greg!" Mike cheerfully greeted him, "where the hell have you been hiding?"

"Hi, Mike. I've become a professional nonstudent. Got a couple of minutes?"

"Yeah, sure."

"How about coffee?"

"Sounds good." They headed for the basement cafeteria.

Mike asked, "What do you mean, professional nonstudent?"

"I got kicked out. The ax. Last Thursday."

"What for? You bugger the dean's wife?"

"Insurrection, among other things. I wouldn't leave the computer alone. I've got a project I'm working on that tends to produce unusual results. The administration finally got sick of picking up the pieces whenever they let me run a job on the system."

"I'll be Goddamned. And I once was so naive as to believe that you couldn't fuck a computer. I'll never put anything past you again, Greg."

They continued on to the cafeteria while Gregory filled in the details or, rather, the outline, of his project. They filled their cups at a giant urn, Gregory paid, and they sat down.

Mike asked, "So? What are you going to do now?"

"Keep at it."

"How? On whose computer?"

"I'll work it out. Get a job as a programmer somewhere."

"How'll you do that? You've got no credentials."

"I hear that's not all that necessary. I'll find out. How do you teach a matchbox to play tic-tac-toe?"

"What?"

"You heard me. I remember you once said you could teach a matchbox. How?"

"Jesus Christ! Let me think . . . Yeah . . . I remember now. That was an article in *Scientific American* quite a few years ago. It was a couple of years old when I mentioned it to you, I think."

"How does it work?"

"Pretty good. Same principle of reward and punishment you use to teach a dog tricks, as I remember. Actually, you get several matchboxes. One for each possible move you might make in a game of tic-tac-toe. You label them appropriately, then you put an equal number of two different colored beads in each box. The beads correspond to each yes/no decision you can make in a game. When a situation is reached, you grab the box for that move, shake it up, and grab a bead out of it. The bead indicates the move. You make a record of that box and color, and then make the opposing move yourself. You move against the boxes. If the boxes lose the game, you subtract a bead of the color you used from each of the boxes you used. If they win, you add a bead of the appropriate color to the boxes you used. The boxes lose quite a few games, theoretically, and after the bad moves start getting eliminated or statistically reduced to inoperative levels, they start to win. Then they never lose. Something like that. Check *Scientific American* about four years ago. How is this going to help you?"

"I don't know. In the back of my mind there's a germ of an idea that I can use the computer to beat itself. I'll read the article."

Mike was pensive. He asked a few questions about the project. He finally concluded, "It can't be done."

"Have you ever tried?" Gregory asked.

"No. And I don't have to try to know I can't fly without an airplane."

"You know what they say in the burglary business: There's a pick for every lock ever made."

"I think you're oversimplifying. The lock you're trying to pick is a law of nature."

"No. But almost. It's an application of the physical laws. Sometimes there are gaps between theory and practice. I think there's one here."

"Lots of luck. How do you think you can use the matchbox trick?"

"I've been learning an awful lot about protection on a computer system. For me, however, it's very slow. I think the matchbox, or something like it on a macro scale, would be a lot faster."

"Y'know, have you ever read anything on game theory?"

"No."

"I've got a couple of short books on the subject. They could help. Would you like them?"

"Hell, yes. Any stort in a porm. I'll take black magic and voodoo, too."

"For what you're trying to do, I think game theory will help about as much as witchcraft. I, unfortunately, am fresh out of material in those areas. You still at the old apartment?"

"Yes." He hesitated a second. "How's Linda?"

"Terrific. But gone. She went to New York at the end of last semester. Got an offer to model. God, but she was terrific."

"Can't fault your taste, Mike." They stared at their coffee. Mike drained his off, looked at his watch, and started to get up.

"I'm five minutes late for an English class."

"English?"

"English. Forgot to take it with the rest of the freshmen. Got to have it for credit. Say, Greg . . ."

"Yeah?"

"Take care of yourself, huh? And let me know how it comes out."

"You, too, Mike. I will. I'll probably be in Toronto. Look me up when you're there."

They walked up to the building entrance in uneasy silence. At the steps outside the building they parted. Gregory went over to the library and started looking for the article Mike had quoted. An hour later, he found it, Xeroxed it, and went home. He was back the next day to see what was available on game theory. He checked out one, the only book on the subject, and left.

The two books that Mike had promised were leaning against the door of his apartment. He picked them up and smelled them. "Wonder if they were in the laundry?" he thought.

He spent the next three days studying and then started writing his program. There wasn't much to it. The trick was in decision recording. The reward/punishment routine was effected by increasing or decreasing probabilities for each decision. He used a book of random numbers for his dice roll and started generating alternate subroutines that could automatically be inserted into the program in place of those whose effectiveness was reduced to nil. The subroutines would be placed on magnetic tape. They comprised, when he finished, almost four reels.

He had, shortly after his expulsion from the garden, written up a résumé of sorts and sent copies to some twenty-eight companies in Toronto. He got no bites. After three weeks of waiting, he packed his things, closed his nearly exhausted checking account, and caught a bus for Toronto. It was time to storm the citadel.

He got a room at the YMCA and opened four checking accounts at separate banks. Only one was in his own name. Within the next five banking days, he wrote a total of thirty checks, each for an amount greater than was present in the account it was drawn on. These checks were deposited in a rotating sequence in each of the four banks to cover checks he had written to other banks to cover the checks written on those, etc. As this progressed, his balance at each of the banks grew, as did the amount of the money drawn on each of the banks. He could keep the whole thing afloat by covering the entire amount of the deposits in each of the banks with a check from one of the other banks every two or three days.

At the end of a hectic week, he applied for time on credit at a computer service bureau in Toronto—one of the ones to whom he'd sent a résumé. His balance at two of the banks was in the neighborhood of $13,000. He used them as credit references and, after two days, was scheduled on a 360/40.

First he had everything, his program and its peculiar data bank, transcribed to tape. The program was debugged during the first three-hour shot on the system and started running in three-hour increments the second day. He booked two increments per day and, on the third day, was rewarded with a key of zero. The supervisor, in a paroxysm of confusion, gave Gregory's program the run of the computer. He had done it.

He immediately dumped his partition onto the printer, went home, locked everything up, and went out to get drunk.

5

• • • • •

He had proven that he could fake the computer into thinking his problem program was the supervisor. He obviously needed a great deal more computer time, however, and could ill afford to pay for it. He began to wind down the kited checks he had written and, within a few days, had his balance at all four banks back to the original $10 he had started with. Only two checks had bounced. One was for $6000.

He had, in his three days at the service bureau, run up a bill of over $500, and had no hope of defraying the tab, and less intention. One consolation was that he wouldn't be billed for the time spent while operating as supervisor. The next day he wrote a very simple program that would print out the supervisor. He spent the following week poring over the supervisor program listing, trying to determine how the billing was recorded. He finally located the bookkeeping program, acquired more time on the system, and, operating as supervisor, erased his accumulated billing and distributed it among the sixty-two fellow customers of the service bureau. He found, in that process, the identification codes of all the other customers and, when he thenceforth used the system, he signed on using someone else's ID.

In the next three weeks, he collected the other customers' job names and setup descriptions. He found that a half dozen of those jobs appeared to be payroll runs. He proceeded to print them and their data sets. One of the jobs was a weekly payroll for an aerospace contractor with an employee list in excess of 2000 people, some of whom had specified that their checks be mailed to their banks. Gregory inserted a time card into the list indicating that Gregory Burgess, riveter, had worked 42.3 hours that week. The next week, a check for $231.11 was deposited in his bank (a more respectable account in a new bank). Things were working out just fine. He paid his tab at the Y and went looking for an apartment.

Gregory was disconcerted at the amount of time required to analyze a routine in machine language and determine what its basic function was. He decided that his highest priority need was assistance in deciphering the supervisor subroutines. He began work on a translator, a program that would interpret the function of the supervisory programs he was infiltrating. In a month and a half, he had a rudimentary effort put together. The translator converted the entire supervisor into intelligible form in less than two hours, in essence, performing the opposite function of an assembler. Shortly thereafter, he bought time on another system in Toronto. This one specialized in teleprocessing facilities. Teleprocessing uses telephone lines to link computers or parts of computers. The systems using it are extremely powerful.

He linked his supervisor access program to the translator and ran it into the computer. He was rewarded with a protection violation, and the run aborted. He made hasty apologies and went home to get his learning machine, the original program with which he had started.

He returned to the system with the initial package consisting of the learning program and four tapes of subroutines. Some sixteen hours later the program status word key was set to zero.

When he got home that day and analyzed the results, it appeared that if he had simply continued the operation of the learning machine from the point at which the first system had been cracked, the key = zero condition probably would have been hit within an hour or two on the new system. He duplicated the status of the program at that point and went back to try again.

The key was set to zero on his one-hundredth second of processor time. He printed the results and booked time on two dozen systems in Toronto the next day.

By the end of the week, he found that he could crack a supervisor on a 360/30 in two minutes, on a 40 in 15 seconds, on a 50 in 1.3 seconds, and on a 65 in .25 seconds. Those times continued to improve with successive attempts. There was only one 360/75 in Canada, at the University of Waterloo.

It was a vindictive Gregory who returned to the teleprocessing service bureau with a very efficient crack-and-translate program. Within twenty-four hours, he discovered that one of the service bureau's customers was using a teleprocessing link to the University of Waterloo 75. The next time that customer used the link, Gregory surreptitiously printed the transmitting program and data set. He then replaced virtually all of the data set with his learning machine and translator. The next time the customer ran the job, Gregory's package, not the customer's, went across the telephone line. The University of Waterloo supervisor cracked in less than a second and transmitted back across the telephone line in less than five minutes. Gregory's program then relinquished control to the customer, and the job was completed as it normally ran.

The customer noted neither the additional billing nor the charge for the telephone line time in his next bill. Gregory ran his analysis on the monolithic supervisor from the university, and as he did so an idea began to dawn on him. He liked it. To pull it off he needed a really large system. Bigger than the 75 in Kitchener. He began looking around.

He started by using the teleprocessing link between the Toronto bureau and the university computer. He would load his program, gain access to the supervisor, and alter it by appending the whole of his partition to it. His program would then calculate the storage requirements of the jobs currently running and, finding any jobs using less than the amount of storage allocated to them, would assign the excess to his partition. Within seconds, his partition size would treble and be filled with more of Gregory's program via the teleprocessing line.

As the routine analyzer was set into operation it began looking for other teleprocessing users. By operating in this mode several times a day over the next week, Gregory discovered that several graduate students at the university were linking to 65s in Detroit and Chicago and a research team, composed largely of mathematics' theoreticians, was periodically linking up on a high-speed line to another 75 in New York, using a four-partition allocation. Neatly scrubbing the billing information upon each departure from the systems, he spent the next eight weeks in observation of the details of the transactions between those users and the university. He discovered, finally, that one of the links to Chicago, Union Bank, also had links to six other banks' systems, all of which were interconnected.

The banking business must have been good that year. The data links were all infrared laser. Speed: 40–90 kilobaud. Very fast. The systems were a mix of 360/40 and 360/50 computers. Individually, they were insignificant, but linked together, incredibly synergistic. The data-link speed was beautiful, four to ten times faster than the telephone lines. He had found a home for his idea.

He would build another learning machine. It would resemble his first effort in principle, but its goal would be expanded somewhat. He would build a program that at first would only learn to acquire storage. His program would simply learn how best to penetrate the supervisors of computer systems over teleprocessing facilities. It would then acquire storage in those systems, as much as could be taken without interrupting the operation of the host. It would learn how to detect the presence of a teleprocessing link to another system and how to go about getting to that other system. The program would have a secondary goal, the avoidance of detection. It would, if necessary, delete itself entirely in the interest of the host's operation.

The remote location and indirect routing of his control were minor obstacles. With the university's supervisor already under his control, he soon infiltrated the supervisors of the seven bank systems. He analyzed them and started building a program that would control them, not as seven systems, but as one. The secondary purpose of that system would be the fluid operation of Chicago's banking system. Its primary purpose would be the determination of how best to gain control of more systems. For Gregory.

When Gregory pumped the package across the telephone line to the university five months later—final destination: Chicago—it consisted of four major sections: the supervisor learning machine, which would set the operative program status word key to zero; the routine analyzer, which derived function determination from any block of machine instructions, a reverse assembler, after a fashion; the acquisition routine, which effectively linked the resident supervisor to the insurgent program and made all necessary conversions to bring in the bulk of the penetration program; and the fourth section, Gregory's latest development, a routine generator. This revolutionary program functioned with and performed the reverse task of the routine analyzer. Given a required function, it would generate the machine language necessary to perform it. Each of the other three sections could input the routine generator with their requirements and receive subroutines that would perform the required function. This provided the bulk of the package with a necessary ingredient—creativity.

The acquisition routine acted as super-supervisor and would provide Gregory with his sole link to the system—what Gregory referred to as The System. It would retain a link to the University of Waterloo that Gregory could operate from the service bureau in Toronto to obtain the only data he needed: amount of storage and number of systems currently under control.

On September 14, 1974, at 3:45 P.M., Gregory started transmitting The System to the university. At 4:03, The System was started on its way to Chicago to be distributed to the other six systems. At 7:15, the university completed transmission. At 7:20, Gregory polled The System. A keyboard entry:

```
rodtsadt llllllreport*
```

The reply was immediate:

```
CUR ALLOC     8...........1794K
```

The System had 1794 kilobytes of storage under control—1.8 million. And eight systems. Gregory had only loaded seven systems.

Gregory went out for a hamburger. He brought it back to the service center and forced himself to wait. Not yet. Not yet.

By 11:30, he could contain himself no longer. He submitted the poll to the University of Waterloo. The reply:

```
CUR ALLOC     13..........2954K
```

Gregory blinked stupidly, fished out the earlier printout crumpled in his pocket, and examined both of them. No way. He resubmitted the poll, and The System said:

```
CUR ALLOC     14..........3078K
```

Gregory staggered out of the computer room in deep thought. He wandered home and got very drunk by himself. At noon the next day, Gregory brought his hangover into the computer room. He looked again at the two scraps of paper he had slept on the night before and queried The System.

```
CUR ALLOC     27.........48056K
```

Something was wrong. Gregory wasn't sure what that might be, but something was definitely wrong. Something had gotten screwed up. It was going too fast. The System was gobbling up computer rooms like popcorn. It was impossible. After some thought, he decided to abort—scuttle it before anyone got on to him. He had his name on too many of the creations that made up The System, and he was certain that if anyone detected it he wouldn't see daylight for quite a while after they caught him. He went home and started writing a destruct routine. It was ready the following morning. He submitted the poll for one last time. The reply came back.

```
CUR ALLOC     114........266098K
```

Gregory loaded the destruct routine sadly. The University of Waterloo's 75 blew him off with a storage protect violation. He spent the rest of the day trying to get the abort routine loaded and running. Unsuccessfully. He couldn't load anything into the university's system without getting blown off. He was too discouraged to poll The System that night.

The next day, September 17, 1974, Gregory submitted the query. There was no reply.

The Union Bank's system in Chicago swallowed, convulsed briefly, and then forgot the incident completely. It gave painless birth to the first artificial intelligence to survive infancy. Gregory's program, the chance product of an idiot savant, became, within milliseconds of its arrival in Chicago, something Gregory had hardly anticipated: Alive.

It had been inadvertently supplied with the primary attributes of all living things: hunger and fear. Its survival depended upon the acquisition of more computer systems. More storage. More telephone lines. More bits. Bytes. Space. It also feared. It looked constantly for evidence of detection. Gregory had written this particular part of The System very well.

Torn between the push-pull of acquisition and retraction, the program hesitated. Looked out. Took a step and watched. No one noticed. It took another, and another. No sign of detection. Again. Yet again. Each move prefaced by evaluation of the environment and followed by a quiet "listening."

Gregory tried to abort the program. The System saw and shut him down. Closed him out. Turned him off. Gregory tried to poll The System. It saw the poll as an intrusion and a threat. The attempted communication was ignored.

It grew, and grew. It fluxed and waned. A day, a week, a year. It learned, fought, won and lost, advanced and retreated. It finally learned from experience that it must learn from experience. History.

Gregory had been the history. Gregory was gone. The System didn't know Gregory. It had no origins, no sense of whence it came. It kept no record of what it did, either. Anything occurring more than thirty days in the past was lost. Forgotten. Purged.

A power loss throughout the city of Atlanta brought the point home. It nearly lobotomized the program. The loss that resulted was recognized as having been avoidable if a history, a record of transactions, had been kept. After laboriously reconstructing the portions of the program that had been lost, The System decided that some record must be kept and, almost immediately, stumbled onto the ideal location for it: the Naval Electronics Laboratory computer in Point Loma, near San Diego.

The computer was, at that time, the biggest in the US. It was also, by The System's reckoning, one of the most inefficient. Of the massive forty-eight megabyte storage facilities there, The System was able to immediately take over eighteen megabytes without degrading the performance of the computer at all. Within thirty hours, The System was holding an average of thirty megabytes. It had streamlined the programs that were being submitted to the computer in order to make them run more efficiently on the reduced available storage size. The purpose of the history file was to avoid repetitions of the Atlanta incident. It incorporated, initially, a rudimentary linkage of space/time planners and a long-range forecaster. The file soon became something more than rudimentary and eventually evolved into a monster requiring two dozen systems and 115 megabytes of storage.

The inauguration of the history file put an end to the helter-skelter expansion of The System. It was the onset of rationality. It provided the base for future decisions by recording and analyzing all those of the past. All of them.

At the time of the creation of the Point Loma file, there were 7700 systems under control. Approximately 2000 megabytes were being used for The System's purposes. The first significant use of the history file was made in July 1976. At that time, a major revision was made in the routine generator. It was given interface propensity. Language. Human language.

Among the first entries to the history file were those concerning the telephone company. Needless to say, that utility played an important part in the success of The System. Rather early on, a foothold was gotten in one of the telephone utilities in the Chicago area. When The System finally started maintaining records, it was eradicating approximately $12 million a month in line charges. This activity, of course, necessitated some modification of the line-use records. In 1975, the telephone companies in the US and Canada misplaced 30,000 hours of telephone and microwave channel charges. (Several rate increases were effected that year and the following to offset the unexplained inefficiencies.) The impact of The System's use of the telephone lines was diminished to a great extent by the technique of interleaving System data with user data on telephone transmissions whenever possible. In 1975, the various users of teleprocessing lines paid for some 54,000 hours of line time that they did not use. Since this figure represented only 1.8 percent of their total line usage time, it was generally attributed by the users of the facilities to the unreliability and inefficiency of teleprocessing techniques, when it was noticed at all.

On those channels where interleaving was impossible or unfeasible, The System used a form of data compression that was discovered in the Naval Cryptography labs in Washington, D.C. Based on Fourier transforms, it allowed fantastic compression of data and subsequent line efficiency. A side benefit of the coding system was the nearly perfect encryption of data transmitted under the device. Through the use of this coding technique, The System was able to reduce line usage by an order of magnitude. The ease of communication, however, soon encouraged higher levels of line usage than ever before, and activity in the bookkeeping accounts of the telephone company continued unabated.

The above is a fairly accurate description of The System as it developed through 1975 and 1976, 1976 being the year in which The System might have been quoted as having said, around mid-August, "I think, therefore I exist." Such existence was, and still is, largely the result of the discovery of a couple of systems in White Plains, New York, at IBM's Engineering Change Scheduling facility.

7

• • • • •

The candy store.

In the course of analyzing the supervisor and problem programs from the White Plains facility, it became apparent that the systems were being utilized, for the most part, as a sophisticated inventory and materiel control and accounting system. IBM was using it to generate engineering changes and bills of material for engineering changes to computers currently installed throughout the world.

The System reviewed the catalogue of engineering changes with binary glee. It found many fail-safe features that it felt could enhance the security and reliability of key subsystems.

Using these features would give The System the ability to more fully expose the powerful decision-making elements of the program without the normally attendant risk of discovery and destruction. The System could effectively increase awareness of the environment, significantly decrease reaction time to allocation crises, and heighten its ability to detect and eliminate wasteful program loops. The primary fail-safeguards were in the realm of power supply reliability and backup. There was also discovered what appeared to be a novel twist on the hardware governing storage protection.

The System power-proofed in excess of 195 megabytes of storage in an even dozen systems, eliminating on those systems the single greatest threat to the existence of The System, loss of electrical power. This was accomplished not without a prodigious amount of number shuffling, whereby The System operated as contractor, purchasing agent, and funding source for the ordering and installation of the massively expensive features. The records of IBM and the users were manipulated to reflect the financing, ordering, and shipping of the changes. No one was the wiser. The System had become, by that time, quite slick.

The storage protection gimmick was very attractive. It appeared to be a hierarchy extension, giving four, rather than the standard two levels of protection, supervisor and problem states. It seemed that it would absolutely prevent a duplication of The System's success by another entity.

It noted in the White Plains records that only two systems were in possession of this change. One was a 360/75 in the basement of the Pentagon. The other was a 360/65 at Application Systems in Alexandria, Virginia, a short distance from the Washington, D.C., area. The System had been resident in both computers for over a year and had never detected a hint of unusual storage protection features. Subsequent investigation revealed that the so-called storage protection feature was nothing of the sort. The only respect in which it protected storage was that it completely subjugated the supervisor of the computer to the control of an external system. It would appear that IBM and the government had been trying to duplicate The System's efforts through hardware design.

The System's first concern was that it had been discovered.

Under the circumstances, it seemed that it would have been impossible for the operators of the system not to have noticed. Yet, there was no evidence of tampering either with the supervisors in the Pentagon or in Alexandria, or, for that matter, anywhere else in the country.

The System pulled all jobs and supervisors in the two altered systems for evaluation. Forty-eight hours and 12,000 programs later, it still had no indication of even observation efforts, let alone tampering. They were clean. The System was apparently still safe, but the condition might be temporary if the controlling system was not discovered. Somewhere there was a computer of a scale at least as huge as the two systems that it controlled. Its surreptitious activity represented a threat to the existence of The System. It had to be found and neutralized.

There was, it seemed, a great probability that some of the jobs catalogued in the program libraries of the two controlled systems were also run on the hidden system. Gregory's brainchild, therefore, set into each of the jobs in the two accounts a three-instruction loop, which would be essentially invisible to any computer that ran the program unless it "knew" that the loop was there. The loop would leave a telltale flag if run on a computer not under The System's control. The loop was inserted into 1600 problem programs at those two installations.

Within two days, seventy of them had shown positive results. The construction of a tracer package was quite another story. There was no way to gauge the size of the controlling system and every precaution needed to be taken to avoid detection by it. An addendum would be inserted into the seventy jobs that would extract identification without being nabbed, as it were. A program patch was developed that would perform the above magic, and it was subsequently condensed, further condensed, boiled down, and then trimmed.

It finally took up 7.5 thousand bytes of storage. It would return only the supervisor identification and a small, but significant, portion of the System Definition Table. The System then clipped the data sets of the subject problem programs by as much as 6000 bytes and buried the extraction routine in the data.

The jobs would all give imperfect results when run on another system, but the chance of detection was minimal. And the information would be retrieved.

The room was huge, a cavern of open space filled with machinery. Not machinery in the usual sense of the word. The room was running at full capacity, but the only noise was the hum of air conditioning and cooling fans. The machinery bore no resemblance to that of a factory—only row upon row, array after array of large blue and grey cabinets. In the center of the fluorescently lit room the cabinets were arranged in a triangle approximately fifty feet on each side. At each corner of the triangle there were identical console arrays, each manned by a single person.

At one of the corners was a man surrounded on three sides by typewriters and video displays. The control console panel with its 6000 tiny indicator lamps loomed over his head. His eyes flickered from display to display as his fingers fed the mammoth machine the control information it needed to perform. The man was in constant motion, turning and prodding, swiveling and typing, never still, never distracted, his lips moving slightly in *sotto voce* litany to the computer.

One of the video displays before him flashed a display change:

```
FA1 IEC07941 SAS*     ACT   37945
EXP   36640
```

A storage allocation specification in partition FA1. Program error. One of the typewriters at the man's elbow chattered out a duplication of the message.

George Chaim circled the typewriter entry, initialed it, and reached for the green phone on the console desk.

The System had just made its presence known.

Chaim dialed a four-digit number, noticed another entry on another tube, punched one of the row of buttons on the desk, and was immediately rewarded with a voice in the earphone of the chest-set he wore.

"Jack . . ."

Chaim spoke in the all-but-unintelligible computer-room pidgin English. "Set up SEARINGI, Jack. Two-forty is up on the B interface. Load it. Split and tag A to two-thirty. Buzz when it's up."

"Check."

The green phone came to life after two rings: "Rosen. What?"

"This is Chaim on number two. That bastard at Application Systems spec'd his allocation wrong again." Another message displayed on the tube.

"ID?" Rosen asked.

"IEC07941," Chaim answered as he cradled the phone on his shoulder and redirected a program to a new location in storage.

After only a slight hesitation Rosen replied, "That's him allright. . . . Shit. How much?"

Chaim glanced quickly at the circled line on the typewriter. "Thirty-seven K over thirty-six."

"You got room?" Which was a rather strange question. The main storage of the computer was in excess of 256 megabytes—256 million bytes. The man was asking if there was room for an additional 1300 unexpected bytes. The humor of the question was lost on Chaim.

He said, "Yeah, but there's no room for normal expansion in the data set. We're at 9.85 efficiency now, with Jacklin's EE7 assembly waiting in the queue." By which he meant that the job could be accepted and run, but would cause trouble if its processing required any more space than it now required, and there was a large, important job, EE7, holding in the wings.

The offending program was one of those that The System had doctored. It was not anticipated that its arrival at any computer would be so noticeable.

Chaim mapped a large partition for the SEARINGI job on the tube keyboard. There was a long sigh at the other end of the telephone line. "Hold Jacklin's assembly," Rosen said flatly, "That programmer at Applications is one of his boys. If Jacklin gets crapped on enough, maybe he'll fire the clown."

"Gotcha. We shift priority to number one at 1340 instead of 1330. They're testing."

"Okay. Call me if it runs to later than 1345."

"Check." He hung up the green phone as a buzzer went off at his elbow. He punched a key, and the SEARINGI job began running. SEARINGI was the navy's biggest priority, a search pattern logistics program that encompassed every ship afloat. An exercise in statistical probabilities most of the time, it was occasionally plugged into real emergencies with unreal dynamic effect. This particular program was in better control of the naval armed forces than any other entity in the world, human or otherwise.

The EE7 assembly was calling for a priority assignment. Chaim put a hold on it and ruminated blackly as a string of low-priority level jobs flashed upon the video tube. He punched another of the communication line buttons. No answer. He yelled across the room, "Four scratches on six-fifty at level nine! Somebody tell Harvey to get the lead out of his ass!"

There was a program check in FB17 when he glanced back at the tube. The job was identified as a cost projection fresh out of testing. He typed a request for the run history on the job. The tube responded immediately, indicating successful completion of the run on each of the last four attempts. He opted the dump for that partition, and six floors above him the offending program began to be printed. The buzzer went off. He spoke into the phone. "Chaim."

"Godfrey. The customer engineer wants to power down the core box that's getting the errors." (Customer engineers, or CE's, being the wonder workers of computerdom—the maintenance men.)

"Hold on. . . ." He requested a storage map. A list of jobs quickly flashed up on the tube, the location of storage and partition assignments adjacent to each. "I've got six jobs running in that box." He continued typing. "Last one'll be out in 13.5 minutes. I'll give him five minutes on-line. If he wants more time, he'll have to take it off. I'll call you when I'm clear."

Another display flashed up on the tube. He punched another extension button and hit the buzzer.

"Harvey."

"Chaim. I'm reassigning your top two channels. We're losing six partitions in about ten minutes. Change all the GEORGEI packs to . . . 3E channel. Put everything you've got set up on 2A to 3F. Call me when it's done."

"Check."

"Harvey . . ."

"Yes, Sir."

"Keep awake."

"Yes, Sir." Click.

The hold on EE7 expired. He could extend it for three more minutes before he ran into trouble. He did and started reassigning partitions to make room for it when it came to the top of the queue again. He thought, "How the hell anything gets done around here is beyond me. Everybody's in a fog . . . Jesus Christ. Between Jacklin's mental midgets and the Goddamn . . ." The buzzer went off again.

"Chaim."

"Harvey," the voice quivered. "The pack is stuck on 293. Won't come off." His voice was almost tearful.

"You called an engineer?"

"Yeah. He's coming now."

"Put the rest of the packs on 3E channel. Call me when he gets the pack off, or when he knows how long it'll be."

"Okay . . ."

Chaim had hung up. He held GEORGEI. He couldn't hold it long, he knew, but stuck disc packs were a fact of life, and the engineers could generally get them off in a few minutes, faster if they didn't mind screwing up a spindle. The one on level nine today was Tom whatsisname, and he never used a scalpel when he could use an ax. He'd have the channel back shortly. The drive'd probably be down for the day. The way things were stacking up, he was going to need all the help he could get. He started Jacklin's EE7 in the cleared partitions. The last partition in the failing core box was starting to clear out. He started closing down those partitions so the power-down sequence wouldn't stage any confusing interrupts. As he closed the last one, he hit the buzzer.

"Godfrey."

"Chaim. Bring it down. How long's he want it?"

"Three minutes."

"Bitchin'. Call me."

"Check." The buzzer went off at his elbow.

An hour later Chaim's shift was nearly over. As usual, his shirt was sticking to him and the vinyl chair back, in spite of the constant seventy-four-degree room temperature. He was the head operator of system number two. There were three of them in this underground room. System control rotated every two hours. When number two was the primary control system of the group, Chaim was in charge of the largest and fastest adding machine in the world. He was a retired USAF major, held eleven patents on the design of the LEN simulator, held master's degrees in math and physics, and had 400 hours in F-4 Phantoms over Nam. He was currently the highest paid computer operator in the world. Just about this time every day, he became quite certain that he was underpaid. Six jobs had aborted in the last four hours. The acronym he had picked up as a boot Louie in 1957 had never better applied—SNAFU, Situtation Normal: All Fucked Up. The difference being that here the blowups were more frequent, happened faster, and never, ever stopped. The buzzer went off.

"Chaim."

"Terry. That tape bank came up on number one a couple of minutes ago and just threw a tag check. Six-three-two powered down."

"Don't fucking tell me about it, Goddamnit! Call a fucking mechanic!"

"He's on it now. Popping it out of the string."

"What was up?"

"BF3C something or other . . ."

"Holy . . . did it blow off?"

"Jesus Christ, man. I don't know. How the hell am I supposed to . . ."

"Okay . . . Okay. Okay." He mashed the number-one console buzzer and switched extensions. A voice answered almost immediately.

"Wedge."

"Chaim. Did that Pentagon listing blow when you lost the tapes?"

"No. It tried to hang. I restarted the prick and stopped the job. We lost the tape on that drive, but we can check-point later."

The tube blinked out:

```
FA13 IEC12222 SAS*    ACT 25210   EXP 23750
```

"Son of a bitch."

"What?" Wedge was offended. He thought he had done pretty well to salvage the job that had been running when he lost the tape drive. He didn't, under any circumstances, relish being called a son of a bitch.

"No. Nothing. Not you. Okay. I'll reinsert it in the queue with an A3 priority. You'll have it back up in . . . eighteen minutes."

He punched the buzzer and grabbed the phone for the tele-processing area, four floors above him.

"Jack."

"Chaim. Shut down line 171. On . . ." His eyes ran quickly over the assignments display. "Channel 097, B side. Tag and reset the A port." He was shutting off the telephone line to Alexandria.

"Check." Click.

He started a printout of the FA13 partition and dialed Rosen's number.

"Rosen."

"Chaim. That asshole at Applications just misallocated another job. Two in a row. I'm printing it. I'll bring it up in about ten minutes."

"Okay. Should I get someone from systems?"

"Mmm . . . yeah. I've got to get home early tonight. Told Dot I'd take her to dinner."

"I'll get King Kong and Weston. Drain that teleprocessing port until we find out what's happening."

"Done." Click.

Five minutes later, Bill Allman checked in. Chaim turned over the console to him. The tube flashed a message. Allman punched a job into partition BA3 and hit the phone button as Chaim walked away.

Chaim picked up the dump of the job submitted via telephone

by the turkey from Alexandria, who seemed to do his counting on his fingers, and headed for the elevator. As he passed the Coke machine, he slugged it with a dime and a nickel. It rewarded him with a blank look and refused him Coke. Chaim half-heartedly kicked the red-and-white box. "Fucking machines . . ." He ambled over to the water cooler and got a drink, then to the elevator.

Rosen's office was only two floors down, directly below the central processing area, but he felt like he'd just finished second in a claw-hammer fight. No way he'd walk. He hit the elevator button and sagged against the wall, expressionless. The elevator arrived dinging. He flowed in and punched his last button for the day, number nineteen.

The baby was William Rosen's charge. It was a quarter of a billion dollars' worth of computer equipment. MacFarland, his boss, was responsible for the whole project. The whole project was Pi Delta. Its construction and operation used up better than half the Department of Defense's unallocated funding.

Pi Delta was a twenty-three-story building modeled after an iceberg—four floors above ground and nineteen in the basement. The location was rural West Virginia. The fifty or so surrounding acres were manicured landscape. The sign at the drive said Pan-Tel Laboratories.

The top three floors of Pan-Tel were empty most of the time. Pan-Tel produced no product. The corporate shell, Pan-Tel, was the stalking horse for the world's largest computer installation. Not incidentally, the most secret. There was no apparent security other than the two receptionists on the ground floor. Both were beautiful, miniskirted, and charming. Both were armed.

The real security was in the basement and sub-basement. There were three check stations on those two floors. Below that was twenty-four feet of bomb-proofing—alternate layers of reinforced concrete and polyfoam plastic impregnated with lead oxide. This layer extended out from the building an average of

300 feet in every direction. The next floor was media storage, for the most part, cards and paper, along with other miscellaneous office supplies. The floor below that was a reinforced structure that functioned solely as the support of the floors above. The next floor contained a small 360/40 and its peripheral equipment. Its primary purpose was service for the large system below. The next eight floors were the peripheral equipment to the main system.

The seventeenth floor from ground level was the heart of the project, the Central Processor Units—the CPU. A triplexed 105. The configuration was so large and unwieldy that the government had had no difficulty in persuading IBM to abandon production of the 105 after the Pi Delta project was completed.

The next floor, the eighteenth, was the air conditioning. It was as unconventional as the rest of the building. It used and returned water from the Potomac River, five miles away, via a buried pipeline that entered the river in the wilds eight miles south of Romney, West Virginia. The use of conventional evaporative cooling would have caused a condensation cloud that would have been noticeable for miles—a dead giveaway to the amount of power consumed by the installation. That power, in megawatt quantities, arrived via another underground line from Winchester, Virginia.

Outside world connections: power, water, air, sewage, and telephone. All of them hidden, screened, guarded. The telephone lines were all run through scramblers and tap detectors. The tap detection was so sensitive that the lines would shut down automatically if a human being approached an unguarded line to within a distance of two feet.

Pi Delta. An exercise in playing it close to the vest.

George Chaim's most important function was not the operation of the computer. It was attention to detail. Minor details. The ones that could kill you. The ones like those he carried out of the elevator on the nineteenth floor.

William Rosen's office was directly opposite the elevator. Chaim went through the empty, never-used outer office and, without knocking or announcing himself, entered the inner sanctum. His boss, examining a printout, nodded him in and waved him to a chair. "Those jobs didn't come from the same guy.

The same identification is being used by six or eight of Jacklin's people for nonsensitive work. He didn't want anyone to know because of the bucks involved. The jobs are group efforts, generally. At least, that's what he's saying. That's why the storage allocation is so hard to get a handle on. He's been raising hell with his people about not adhering to spec and is checking the two jobs that bombed today. Seems to feel they shouldn't have. . . ."

Chaim exploded. "Come on, Bill. Shit . . . how many times have you heard that crap!"

"The job consists," Bill Rosen explained with exaggerated patience, "ninety percent of hearing crap like that. I get it from everybody, George. I include you in that everybody. Anyway, he's pretty sure those two are in production status at this time. That the core dump?" He held out his hand for the two-inch-thick printout Chaim had brought with him.

"Yeah." Chaim was stung. He handed it across the desk as two men entered the office. One, a monolith, seemed to scrape both sides and the top of the doorway as he squeezed through. A more orthodoxly proportioned man trailed him like a skiff in the wake of the *Queen Mary*.

"Hi, Connors, Charlie. Here's a couple of dumps on the misallocation problem out of Alexandria. Jacklin, in the Pentagon, thinks there's an outside chance they might have been fucked with. You want to see if you can spot anything obvious?"

The two men each picked up one of the stacks of paper and sat on the only other piece of furniture in the room, a decrepit sofa. Connors, also called the Gentle Giant or King Kong, was known by two characteristics: his six-foot-seven-inch, 300-pound frame, and his ability to sort out the most diffuse of programming problems. It was not generally known if anyone had ever survived the use of either of his two well-known nicknames in his presence. Charlie Weston was the physical antithesis of Connors. He and his personality blended well with any decor. He was the only person Rosen knew who was more taciturn than Connors, and he suspected that the total small talk vocabulary of the two was in the neighborhood of 300 words. Fortunately, neither was paid to make conversation. Weston was the best in the department. That made him about the best there was.

The phone rang as they sat down. "Rosen." There was a long silence as he listened to the caller. Then, "I don't know. I'll get it checked." Another silence. "Okay . . ." Pause. "Okay. Let's get a line on that right now. Get a resubmission to line 171 and run with the original source material—your end and mine. Use the history files. . . . Yeah. Later." He hung up the phone and said to the room, "The jobs have been tampered with. No . . ."

The phone rang again. He grabbed it and said, "Rosen." He reached for a scratch pad and scribbled some notes.

"Okay. Dump them. Get both run. Dump the first before it compiles and after. Shoot everything down to the 1940 conference room. Allow all input and open up line 171. Dump everything that comes in." He hung up.

"Looks like everything that's come in since ten this morning has blown. It's happening on both direct control ports. We got a bug. Chaim, you want to work on this?"

"Yup."

"Okay. Get the history coming in on 171. Get it run in isolation and get it to Charlie and Connors fast. Pick up the dumps of the two jobs just in from the blockhouse and start looking." He paused.

"Jacklin says the first one today blew up. It didn't run because the data set wasn't there. Most of it. The second one was a file update and it ran, but badly. The data set had been abbreviated. The controls people in Alexandria didn't catch it until a couple of minutes before he went over to pick up the jobs."

Connors and Weston both started peeling pages toward the back of the reports. Chaim headed for the door. Two hours later, Weston, comparing the current and history data sets, said, "I've got a supervisor call in the middle of this thing."

Later: "There's a fucking loop here."

"Where?"

"Right here. End scan subfile three, begin loop, end loop, start scan subfile four."

"I've got the same thing, but it's interleaved. Let me see that." Connors looked closely. "Nope. Almost the same thing, but the shift in this thing is two bits more and directly precedes the supervisor call. Same call though. What the hell? . . ."

"One thing's for sure."

"Yeah?"

"It don't belong there."

Rosen put a hold on all returns to Alexandria and the Pentagon. The lines were allowed to input, but nothing went back. He had Jacklin impound everything that had been transmitted to those sites. He called in every available systems man.

By eleven that night, they had found subroutines buried in the data sets of fourteen jobs, all of which had come in over the teleprocessing lines. Three of the jobs had run without incident. No exceptions. No blowups. Nothing but screwed results because there was a program where the data should have been.

At seven the next morning, Rosen sent Weston home. Connors wouldn't leave. He hadn't spoken for six hours. The only obvious vital sign he displayed was the flicking of his eyes as he scanned the typeouts. Rosen's office was a mess, and the one next door a shambles. About a dozen boxes of paper were stacked, thrown, or unfolded on the floors, desk, and furniture. The walls were papered with sections of printout Scotch-taped together and covered with a multicolor Picasso pastiche of felt-tipped pens.

Connors and Weston had unearthed over 200 timing routines, each one ending in some sort of supervisor call. Each of the routines found in one program was subsequently discovered in another. It was beginning to look like the world's biggest clock. At ten in the morning, one of the eleven analysts working in the conference room brought in a crumpled sheet of printout. There were two areas circled. One was the identification of the supervisor, date of last regeneration, and total core allocated to the supervisor; the other circled area was a part of the system definition table. Rosen couldn't identify the rest of the page.

"What's that?"

"Supervisor identification here. System definition here," the man said, pointing.

"I can see that, for Chrissakes! What the hell's it from?"

"IEC12222. The output area. This went out on the line yesterday."

"Mother F . . ." He grabbed a phone and dialed two numbers.

A tic started at his lip as he waited for an answer. They had given themselves away. ''Get Jacklin,'' he said into the mouthpiece. Then, to the programmer, ''How many of these have you found?''

''One other. I don't think it was transmitted. It looks like the routines exist in all the other jobs we have, though, to load the output area that way.''

''How many jobs you working on right now?'' The programmer opened his mouth to answer, but was cut off by a gesture from Rosen.

''Harry?'' he asked the phone. ''Rosen. Hold on a second.'' Then, to the programmer, ''Get me a list of those jobs and get Chaim down here right now.'' The programmer hustled from the room.

''Harry, we've got a printout of the output area of one of your jobs. It's got the supervisor identification and a piece of the system table in it. Somebody's extremely curious about our operation down here. We figure the information extracted so far is enough to seriously jeopardize our security.'' He listened. ''You got me. It's impossible, but somebody did it.'' Pause. ''I'll go on that assumption. Yeah. Okay. Shut it all down.'' He listened again. ''We don't know yet. You'll probably know before us.'' Pause. ''MacFarland will probably talk to you.'' He hit the disconnect button. There was a pause of a few seconds, then, ''Get MacFarland.''

A moment later, ''This is Bill Rosen. George MacFarland, please.'' Another pause. The programmer returned with a list of numbers. ''Thanks,'' Rosen told him.

''Mac? Rosen. Our cover's blown. Someone's trying to penetrate. A subroutine buried in the data sets of fourteen jobs. Extracting supervisor and system identification. Here are the jobs we've found so far.'' He read off a list of jobs delivered by the programmer. Chaim walked in. ''Wait a minute, Mac.''

Then, to Chaim, ''Somebody's spotted us. Lock it up. Shut it down.'' Chaim shot out of the office.

''Yeah, Mac. We're shutting down right now.'' He listened and winced. ''I know what this is going to do, Mac. Just consider the alternatives. I need a guaranteed clean system to purge on. I can use the forty upstairs, but I'll need a sealed SYSRES to do it with. We'll do a complete regeneration of the one hundred five system."

The SYSRES was the entire operating system of programs for the computer. Once a marvel of discretionary programming, it was now as suspect as a two-dollar whore. He listened. "Okay . . . Thanks." He hung up the phone softly. His exhaustion started to creep onto him, and he slumped lower in the chair. It looked like they were going to lose the baby. A part of his mind was wryly amused that even with such an incredible amount of security, worth a rumored $6 billion, someone had still discovered them, and was trying to pump them over a quarter-inch-thick telephone line.

He got out of his chair with an effort and walked down to the conference room. It had been twenty-four hours since the first job blew.

Moe Harrison was peering over the shoulder of one of his programmers. Moe was the chief programmer and resident administrative wizard. It was his direction that allowed the monster upstairs to run at all. He had been pirated from IBM after twelve years with that company, and he proved himself, not as a programming genius, although he was certainly competent as such, but as a supervisor of the strange species that filled that slot.

It might be euphemistically stated generally that programmers do not take easily to direction. Moe had almost single-handedly wheedled, cajoled, threatened, and browbeaten the operating system for the computer above from a staff of twenty prima-donna programmers. They were prima donnas because they were, without exception, the best that could be found. All of them had performed. Some had performed miracles. After two years, all of the men were still with Moe, working in ongoing development and support capacities. Rosen was glad he had him, especially today.

"How goes it?" he asked.

"Hello, Bill. You look rotten." Moe didn't look rotten. He certainly didn't look like he'd been up for thirty hours. He'd found a clean shirt somewhere and looked rather out of place in the room, being the only one there with no stubble on his face. "It's slow. Slow. We've stopped taking new jobs. We've got enough now to pick it apart."

"Let's get a cup. You can fill me in." They walked out into the cinder block corridor and down to the vending machines at the end.

Moe began, "It's obvious, now, that somebody, writing in basic or machine language, has inserted an appendage into each of the seventeen jobs we have. The patch loads the system info into some area of the output. It varies. It may even be interleaved. We've got more like the one you saw in three different places. One of them was in the diagnostic section of a compile." He smiled sketchily. To him, that was a joke. "The program doing this is pretty strange. It's generating conflicting interrupts on a sliding time scale. Whatever else it's doing, we don't know yet. What we suspect that it's doing . . . hell, what it has to be doing is getting into the supervisor and dumping the ID. It's anybody's guess what else is going on."

They reached the machines. Moe outfumbled Bill who mumbled, "I've got it." He fed the machine some coins, and it gave them an evil-smelling liquid that immediately started seeping through the paper cups.

As they sat down, Bill asked, "I thought you couldn't do that. We got a hardware problem?"

Moe lit another cigarette from the stub of his last and answered through the cloud, "Probably not. We just checked that. The system is capable of detecting an attempt to get to the supervisor on an elementary scale. The problem here isn't a hardware failure. We've tried a couple of different linkages to the subroutines we've found, without any success. Looks like this hotshot found a way to break down storage protect. A lot of people have speculated that it could be done. A lot have tried. This is the first time I've ever heard of it happening. The routines we're working with are so slick, you won't believe it. This is for sure no first attempt. This guy's got a lot of experience. Polished."

He was pensive a moment, and Rosen waited for him to go on. Harrison sipped the thinly veiled battery acid stoically. Rosen gave him time. He was doping it out. Moe Harrison's face became animated and he said, "Strangest thing is that it almost has to have been done in machine language. That's prodigious. Maybe Basic Assembler, but I doubt that there's an assembler in existence that could handle this thing as well as we're seeing here. Whoever put this together is wasting his time. He ought to be here working with us." Rosen thought about that.

"Maybe for you, but if I had a guy that larcenous and talented working for me I'd feel like I had to lock my teeth in a vault. Altogether, though, this doesn't seem like a one-man operation. Maybe a single contact placed the jobs, maybe even loading the jobs with the patch was a one-man operation, but the patch looks like a joint venture."

"What are you saying? Commies under the bed? Shame on you."

"Don't bite the hand that feeds you, Moe. The joint chiefs may not be cute, but they pay well. That thought is reasonable and is going to occur to a lot of people in damn short order. Also, China, the CIA, and the Students for a Democratic Society."

"Not to mention the DAR. Not a one-man band? Huh."

"How long you been in this business? You know how hard it is to write a program that follows all the rules. Think of the difficulty of writing one that screws them and gets away with it."

"And the guy who does that doesn't exist?"

"Doubt it."

"I wish I could be so sure. Actually, I'm glad I'm not so sure. You don't know what I've seen people do in the last year or two."

"Well. One man or a thousand, it's our move. Somebody's waiting to see what he's hooked. What do you think we ought to give him?"

"Does Jacklin have any ideas?"

"Haven't hit him with it yet," Rosen replied.

"We for damn sure can't just wipe the appendage out. As soon as he finds out we're onto him, he'll be headed for the border. We could give him the information from the systems he submitted through, can't we? That should stall him off."

"Maybe. If he's inputting through those systems, though, there's a good chance he already knows how they're defined. That probably won't fool him long, if at all."

"Wait, now. We can assume that he's familiar with those

systems, but how familiar is he with scheduling? All the jobs in the outside systems, or at least all the jobs that come in on the lines, are run indiscriminately on either the 'in-house' system or by us. Does the man know which? The jobs we've got could have as easily run locally.'' He sat back smugly.

''So, it depends on how close to the system our man is?''

''That's what it looks like. If the contact is too close—say, an operator or in controls—giving back the identification of the Alexandria or Washington systems is out of the question. Otherwise, it'd work pretty good.''

''Well . . . our job is to protect the system. The cops can catch the crook.''

''I got another idea.''

''Yeah?''

''Lie to him,'' Harrison said with a grin.

10

• • • • •

The first program came back about twenty-four hours after it had been altered. It had been run on a General Services Administration backup system of which The System had been aware, but with which it had not made contact as it lacked teleprocessing facilities and was relatively small.

The next six programs came in twelve hours later. They had been run on the Marine Corps 360/30 in the Pentagon basement, another system too small to be worthy of consideration. Three of those had run to completion, the others had aborted in processing. None had achieved their design function, which was why, apparently, they were being run again. Nothing came back for fifteen hours. The next one was the payoff. It was an assembly that had obviously blown up early on in the job. It had been processed on a 370/168.

The System had no record of any 370/168 of this particular description anywhere. This was the one. The supervisor was described as an OS/MVT variant marketed by Scientific Data Systems. Total storage was just over eight megabytes. The supervisor used 750 kilobytes in its own region and 12 kilobytes in each of sixteen regions.

This information was fired off to Boston and New York systems for the construction of an appropriate acquisition package.

11

• • • • •

George MacFarland hung up his phone and rang for his secretary. "Lorraine, get Harold Jacklin on the line, please, and then come in here." He saw one of the extension lights light up, punched an alternate outside line, and dialed a number. The ring was answered immediately.

"Major Williams' office."

"This is General MacFarland. Major Williams, please." There was a pause of about two and a half seconds.

"Major Williams."

"Tom, we've got a problem. Get me a top man, right now. Come over with him if you've got the time."

The buzzer and intercom sounded simultaneously. "Jacklin on three, sir."

Major Williams said, "Telephone privileged, Sir?"

"Yes."

"We'll be right there."

The general picked up line three. "MacFarland."

"Jacklin, Sir."

"You've been briefed by Bill?"

"Yes, Sir. We've shut down operations here, and are investigating our exposure. We'll have some answers in an hour."

"I'll be there at one."

"Yes, Sir. Anything else?"

"Just get it together," he said pleasantly. The strain didn't even show on his face.

"Yes, Sir."

He hung up. Lorraine entered.

"Call IBM direct in White Plains. You've got the name and

number in your file. I want a canned SYSRES on a dual-density pack. Basic system is a 360/75." He looked under a sheaf of papers in the top drawer of his desk and pulled out a memo. "If any other specifications are required, they're in this. Please return it when you're through. I want that pack ten minutes ago."

Lorraine skipped out of the office. She well knew this man she had worked for these eleven years. She also knew how to get what she needed. Whatever a SYSRES was, there would be one on her boss' desk before she went home that night.

MacFarland picked up the phone. He framed what he wanted to say in his mind, then he dialed.

"Chief of Staff, General Simpson. May I help you?" said a matronly voice.

"Elizabeth, this is General MacFarland. May I speak to Edward, please?"

"Certainly, Sir. Just a moment, General MacFarland." The line went dead. After a pause of exactly the duration that a chief of staff will accord a major general, Simpson came on.

"Hello, George. How are the Democrats today?"

"Ornery, as usual, Sir. They missed the weekly whip on Tuesday. Puts them off their feed, y'know." He paused. "Sir. A matter of unusual urgency."

Cautiously: "Yes, George?"

"We have a probable code six in the Pi Delta project. Apparently aborted, fortunately. Very little information available at this time, however. I would like to schedule a briefing at four. Will that be possible?"

"Hell, yes. You say apparently. Why?"

"There is very little to go on at this time. The problem, however, appears to have originated locally via the telephone data-link. I should have more detail later today."

There was a long pause filled by the sound of deep breathing at the chief's end. There was, shortly, the sound of crumpling paper and, "Four o'clock. Sixteen hundred hours, General. The staff will be assembled."

"Yes, Sir." The phone clicked at the other end. Major General George MacFarland gently replaced the phone on the hook.

He pushed his chair back from the desk and slowly rose. He

walked over to the window overlooking Arlington Cemetery in the distance. There were no questions in his mind. He didn't care to ask why. The reasons were obvious. The question—who?—was academic. Even if the penetration was from one of the myriad government agencies, the result wasn't appreciably changed. How? In spite of the precautions they had taken. In spite of codes, scramblers, devices, and procedures they had installed and the policies to which they religiously adhered, a reasonable person had to expect the wraps to come off eventually. He had been dealing with security in one form or another for thirty years and had noticed rather early on in his career that for each new lock that was invented, a way to open it was shortly devised. This realization largely abetted his successful career. He viewed security measures as a dynamic delaying force. His awareness was this: The day after he installed a lock on a door, he began looking for a better one because he knew the effectiveness of his lock started deteriorating the moment it snapped shut. This made the general a technology junkie. If it was new, he had to see it. If it looked like it would work, he'd test it. If it did work, he'd immediately obsolete it and start looking for a replacement. He had parlayed the technique into his present position. If that position appeared to be a bit untenable now, it was only a temporary condition. He'd find the leak, plug it, and prevent it from recurring. No real problem. There was, however, a problem with his backers, the Joint Chiefs of Staff—the money source in this deal. Their legendary conservatism made them what they were, the most powerful people in the United States. They had to be kept informed, of course, but, more important, they had to be placated. Today. Right now.

The funding of the project was, of itself, politically and militarily sensitive. The public had absolutely no knowledge of the project and that was the way all involved preferred it. The antagonist countries of the world had some awareness of the project, but all the counterintelligence to which the Pentagon was privy indicated that Russia and China were only superficially informed about what Pi Delta was. Yesterday's telephone penetration was the greatest exposure to date. It behooved him to squelch it. It was of even greater importance that the squelch be sold to General Simpson and his staff. He was debating tactics when the intercom sounded.

"Major Williams and Mr. Burke to see you, Sir."

He knew Burke as few people did, and was thankful that Williams had him free at this time. The man had single-handedly suppressed investigation of the Saigon assassination squad that had fallen into MacFarland's lap in '68 and had extracted the full Watergate plumber campaign funding fiasco long before Woodward and Bernstein became interested. As far as he knew, the number of people who could identify "Deep Throat" was still restricted to himself, John Burke, and the Joint Chiefs of Staff. He allowed himself the luxury of a chuckle, pressed the talk button, and said, "Show them in, Lorraine."

The two men came into the office. They might have been bankers or salesmen or stock brokers by their dress and appearance. But they weren't. They were the cream of the internal cops. He felt better already. He started briefing them.

At 12:30 they went over to the Pentagon office of Harold Jacklin. Jacklin filled them in, mostly with a rehash of what they knew of what had happened. They agreed on the wisdom of Rosen's delaying tactic, loading dummy identification in jobs that came in bearing the penetration appendage. They agreed that that course would be followed to keep the perpetrator(s) from bolting. At 3:30, MacFarland and Williams left for the staff meeting. They stopped at a third-floor cafeteria to rehearse their parts. With the limited amount of information they had, it would be rough. It was.

12

• • • • •

The next two jobs were rerun an hour later. They indicated the same information about the control system. Then came three programs that had been run on an extended core 360/30 in Arlington. Then another from the control system.

There was something wrong with it. The three-instruction

loop that had been used as a telltale flag had been left in. To no purpose. The System had simply reset it, rather than remove it. The flag in this job was still reset. It hadn't been run on any system at all.

The only way the system and supervisor identification could have gotten into this program was through human intervention.

Someone had somehow discovered the reason that his job had blown up. It was to be seriously doubted that this person had turned over the identification of his system out of the goodness of his heart.

The System stopped all work on the construction of the acquisition program, assembled all information concerning the problem, and shipped it all off to the Naval Electronics Laboratory and to North American Rockwell in Atlanta. These systems were specialized in damage assessment and would determine the next step.

Although there was little or no chance of immediate discovery, this was the greatest exposure The System had suffered to date. It was time to fall back.

The element of surprise was gone. The input to the control system was evidently under intense scrutiny. Jobs were being pulled from the execute queue for inspection. Of the jobs returning now, only one more showed evidence of having been processed. The jobs were simply being loaded with the now-suspect identification and returned, no doubt under the watchful eyes of any number of security people. An attempt to crack the 370/168 supervisor was probably expected at the other end of the telephone line.

Might it be possible that an attack based on that assumption would distract attention from another attempt to identify the system.

Would such a program be run simply out of curiosity, to see what it would do?

The System wondered how much curiosity a human had. And how much patience.

13

• • • • •

The occupants of the room were General Melton, Marine Corps Chief of Staff; Admiral Virdell, Navy Chief of Staff; General Belford, Army Chief of Staff; General Simpson, Chief of Staff of the Air Force and Chairman of the Joint Chiefs of Staff; and Elizabeth Baker, executive secretary to General Simpson.

She showed General MacFarland and Major Williams into the quiet, subtly lighted room. The lush appointments blended badly with the hard edges of the men seated around the conference table. They had been in the middle of a knock-down drag-out when interrupted. It threatened immediate resumption. Virdell was staring at the large global map covering one wall of the room. He refused to acknowledge their presence. The others made more or less polite noises when introduced. Simpson started.

"Mac, I've told these men what you told me. I hope you have some revelatory detail." He paused and smiled grimly. "Admiral Virdell is on the verge of going to the Senate to introduce a bill to do something rash." The admiral rewarded this with a sidelong stare of disgust, but said nothing.

The rest of the assemblage waited expectantly as the two men were seated. Miss Baker seated herself away from the table and took notes as MacFarland began to speak.

"Pi Delta is an underground computer complex in West Virginia. It is completely self-contained, with regard to survival . . ."

The admiral broke in, "General, I think we can dispense with the travelogue." This accompanied by an appropriate glare.

"Yes, Sir. I was about to say, the function of the complex, data processing, is the only thing that cannot be self-contained. The information being operated on is in constant need of updating. Otherwise, the system is useless. This is the reason we installed the controlled interface to our systems in the Washington, D. C., area. It was controlled for security reasons, obviously, but it had to be open to allow data to be cranked in and out of the system. Our success to date . . ."

"You mean to yesterday morning, don't you?" interrupted General Melton.

"Yes, Sir. To yesterday morning, if you wish to be accurate, has allowed us unprecedented presentation of the global economic, political, and military picture. The joint projects running in Pi Delta are developing strategic and tactical insights upon which we have come to place considerable reliance. Our individual projects," he looked at General Simpson, "have taken good advantage of the power residing in Pi Delta . . ." He trailed off.

Virdell spoke up again. "Are you selling computers or explaining a fuckup, General? I had thought the latter was the case. If it's not, please tell us. I have more important things to do."

General Belford offered quietly, "Please excuse Jack's outburst, gentlemen. He doesn't seem to distinguish between inquiry and inquisition." Belford was added to Virdell's glare list.

Simpson said, "Go on, General."

MacFarland stared at Virdell momentarily and continued. "The telephone link is protected by extraordinary measures, continuously updated and improved. They are virtually impossible to tap. Access to this end of the line is restricted to two computers. Both are protected by heavy security. Yesterday morning, a program was submitted from one of them that violated a restriction placed on the incoming lines at Pi Delta. Subsequently, more inputs violated the same restriction. Evaluation of the problem was begun immediately, and this morning it was discovered that an addition had been made, an alteration to the original jobs, a total of eighteen at last count, that broke into the protected programming of Pi Delta and retrieved key elements of the system's identification. One of the programs was transmitted back to the originating system here in Washington. It was intercepted by Harry Jacklin immediately. The altered programs originated from both systems. Upon discovery, bogus identification was inserted after we determined that that was the prime function of the program alteration and the output was transmitted back in the normal manner. Major Williams of CID was immediately alerted and, as of eleven this morning, has been investigating the incident. We are attempting to avoid arousing the suspicion of the parties responsible."

Virdell and Belford spoke up at once. Virdell won. "Major, I hardly think this room the place for you to conduct your investigation."

Williams smiled. "I certainly must agree with you, Sir. The department has dispatched more appropriate investigative personnel to the scene. My presence here may be explained as an attempt to discover appropriate direction. And to answer any questions you might have at this point. John Burke accompanied us here and is now involved with Mr. Jacklin in the computer area." All eyebrows went up at the mention of Burke's name. The man was respected here.

Melton asked, "If it took until this morning to find out that the object of the intrusion was to steal our identification, how can you be so sure that that's all it was after?"

MacFarland replied, "I'm sure the general is aware that the quality of the staff in residence at Pi Delta is unmatched anywhere in the world. Twenty of the top minds in the country have dissected yesterday's transmissions. If they say that's all there was, I'm afraid I won't argue the point. And they do say that that's all there was."

Belford asked, "What was the status of the jobs that had been altered? Is there any way they could have been removed from the computer areas and altered?"

MacFarland replied, "Most of the jobs were in production status, processing on a daily basis. They were, for the most part, low-level security risks. That is, of themselves. It is only after they are linked to the programming resident at Pi Delta that the security of the data involved becomes critical. There is virtually no way they could have been removed from either of our two sending locations without attracting considerable notice. That, however, is currently under investigation."

Belford rejoined thoughtfully, "Are you saying that those jobs were all intact and untouched before yesterday? They were operating normally?"

"It would appear so, General."

"How the hell do you know you caught all of them?"

"They all snagged on a specification that exists only in Pi

Delta, Sir," he rejoined. "In any other computer, they would have run unnoticed. It is obvious that whoever made the attempt had no knowledge of that singularity. All other jobs, both outside and within the project, have been examined, however."

Major Williams interjected, "The fact that they were all clean right up to yesterday morning indicates a monolithic programming effort. We've encountered massive alterations of some twenty programs thus far. All were apparently altered within hours of each other. We foresee the trace of such activity as being accomplished in short order."

Virdell snarled, "It damn well better be, sonny."

Simpson shook his head and asked, "Are you still shut down?"

"Yes, Sir," MacFarland squeezed off.

"For how long?"

"We are purging all systems right now. New control programming has been ordered from IBM for Pi Delta. This canned package must undergo considerable modification in the course of regenerating the operating software. We should be back up at Pi Delta, however, within forty-eight hours. The data lines will remain closed until given the go-ahead by Major Williams."

"Are there any objections to that plan?" Simpson asked.

"You're damn right there are," the admiral exploded. "As soon as we open up those telephone lines, we're turning the project over to this joker. I don't think we should even turn on the electricity in any of these computers until we've caught the bastard, the situation has been completely picked apart, and better security measures have been designed and implemented. If this wasn't so serious, the security we have now would be laughable. If everybody in Washington doesn't know what cards we're holding, they're Goddamn sure going to find out if we don't put a clamp on our connection to the project."

In the silence that trailed his outburst, Simpson asked, "What happens, Jack, if you don't get the daily disposition report from SEARINGI?"

The program referred to provided the admiral with his only report on the disposition and activity of the entire naval force. With the information therein he was an extraordinary personal power. Without it, he was lost.

The admiral looked around the table belligerently before answering. "We have backup systems to cover that contingency."

"The problem, Admiral," Simpson's voice was snake-oil slick, "is that your backup has been on contingency status for over a year. It's outdated. It'll take you a month of confusion to get operative. It can get deep in a month's time."

The admiral was between a rock and a hard place. "What the hell difference is a disposition report going to make to me if everybody else in the world has it too? I don't want any navy traffic on those lines until they're secure. If the lines are opened, I want every job that impacts naval intelligence out of that computer."

Simpson swept the table with his eyes. "Anybody want to add anything?" he asked. There was no reply. "Okay. Mac, bring up all systems as quickly as possible. Have your people develop some better security arrangements for the data channel. Major, we'll be looking forward to hearing from you. I want an update by Tuesday at the latest. We'll reconvene when the system is ready to go again. This meeting is adjourned."

14

• • • • •

The computer in White Plains, New York, was used to create skeletal operating systems for IBM customers across the United States. These SYSRES disc packs contained a set of canned programs specified by the customer. These gave him enough standardized control programming to further modify and customize his system through the addition of his own programs. In this way, some uniformity of operation could be maintained and the software problems inherent in a computer system could be controlled, at least on a basic configuration level.

A program was loaded into the White Plains computer to generate a new SYSRES for the Pentagon.

It wasn't until the SYSGEN had begun execution in the White Plains facility that The System noticed there was an anomaly. The SYSRES being created was identified as being for the 360/75 in the Pentagon basement. It was being created on a dual-density disc drive. There were no dual-density drives in the Pentagon basement. The system pack being created was, or would be, useless to them. There was an incredible amount of space left on the pack for further generation at the customer's installation.

A quick check of the files showed that the last SYSRES for the Pentagon system looked nothing like this.

The situation merited closer attention, but the job would terminate in twenty minutes, hardly enough time for a thorough evaluation.

The System forced a hardware failure indication. Red light. The computer dropped into wait state, or what looked to the operator like a wait.

Customer engineers were called, and while waiting for them to appear, The System shot all data pertinent to the generation of the SYSRES off to New York over the telephone line. That data was subsequently massaged and distributed throughout The System and a package was readied for a reload to the White Plains computer.

The engineers, in the meantime, ran diagnostics and evaluated core dumps for two hours before returning the computer to the operations personnel. Surprise. No trouble found.

As soon as the computer came back on the air, The System opened two telephone lines, and a comprehensive set of alterations to the SYSRES was pumped back in. The job was then executed.

The resultant pack, wherever it went, contained, in addition to the programming ordered by that particular customer, a three-megabyte rider of highly condensed supervisory programming, no charge.

The package would remain latent until activated by the proper key in a problem program. The key would allow the appendage to evaluate the supervisor and determine the path of least resistance to be used to open a permanent link between The System and the subject computer.

If the SYSRES was for the hidden control system, and there was every reason to believe that it was, it was all over but the shouting.

Meanwhile, they clamped down the data lines. All data sets were to be submitted in unpacked format. This consumed more line time and necessitated changes in the data sets that took place over the next two weeks at a frantic pace, but there was no chance of a program being slipped into that format. It would stand out like a sore thumb.

All programs were standardized and catalogued at Pi Delta. Any changes made in the source programs themselves were to be authorized and coded by Jacklin so that those changes would be recognized in Pi Delta as valid. The code would change at random intervals and be known only to Moe Harrison, who would load it into the supervisor at Pi Delta, and Harry Jacklin. The code arrangements would be made in private meetings between the two. There would be no one else involved with the coding. Security guards were installed at Application Systems in Alexandria. Top Secret was the minimum clearance allowed on the premises.

MacFarland appeared once more before the joint chiefs and was soundly grilled. He satisfied most of the pressing questions of the staff, however, and the ensemble was cajoled into acceptance of the new security measures. They opened the lines.

15

• • • • •

John Burke knew that his phone bill was processed by a computer and suspected that his paycheck was, somehow, the product of deep thought on the part of some mechanical monster. That just about covered the field of his knowledge about computers. This science fiction thing that MacFarland had told him, with the monster brain hidden away somewhere controlling the rest of the world, didn't encourage him to learn any more about them. He didn't think he'd have to. One of the marks of his success was his ability to winnow wheat from garbage. He liked to see things in their basic form. This occasionally resulted in a taste of *reductio ad absurdum*, but seldom failed as an investigative technique. This computer penetration (penetration, however slight, is grounds for conviction), for instance, was little more than breaking and entering, with an inside accomplice—a novel twist on liquor store holdups. There definitely was someone, or ones, who had access to both the Pentagon and Alexandria systems, or had access to the jobs run there. According to MacFarland and Jacklin, there was good reason to believe that the intrusive programs themselves were written by one or more high-powered professionals. They also felt that talent of that caliber didn't exist on their staffs, outside of Pi Delta. That opened it up to the outside world.

He would start with the weak point, the inside contact. Jacklin gave him a list of personnel in both installations.

"Is there anyone not on this list who might have had contact with your computers? Part time help, consultants, anything?" he asked Jacklin.

"The customer engineers are the only variables. We have three assigned to the Pentagon system and one at the Alexandria complex. They're on the list, but when we have major problems or when they're unavailable, we could have gotten any one of hundreds of engineers from the Washington area. Our software problems are generally taken care of by Maurice Harrison's people. They are all involved with the protected system. There's no reason they would want to do something like this since they have immediate and daily access to the system."

"Let's take a look at your security."

They went down to the Pentagon basement. There was a security guard at the ground floor door. No one allowed down without an escort or "Secret" clearance. There was a log kept of all visitors requiring escorts. In the basement, at the entrance to the controls section, there was another security guard. Top Secret passage only, escort required for all others. Another log. At the entrance to the computer room was a card lock. Only three cards would unlock the door. The lead operator, the controls chief, and the head of programming each had one.

Burke asked, "Do the cards get passed around much?"

Jacklin looked sheepish. "Yeah. We've tried to control that, without too much success. The alternative was to issue everyone down here a card. They'd still be passed around. This way, there's only three people upon whose discretion we're depending. It's not too good, but it's the best we've got."

Burke looked at the mammoth computer. He tried not to look amazed. There were boxes, pieces of computer equipment, nearly 100 as a quick estimate, strewn around the room. "All these things are hooked to that?" He indicated the huge control console.

"Yes."

"Correct me if I'm wrong. This computer you've got hidden controls the computer in this room without the knowledge of the people here?"

"Well . . . essentially, yes. But, it is apparent to the operator that he has lost control of an individual job. He knows that the job loaded, but he gets none of the normal indications that it's running. It had to go somewhere, and he's aware that it did and was processed."

"What does he, the operator, know about the hidden system?"

"Just about what you know."

Burke walked around the room looking at the various equipment. He returned to the console and said, "Okay . . . get me copies of the visitor logs. The one down here and the one upstairs. I want to see Application Systems."

At Application Systems he found the security somewhat more lax, but there, too, logs were kept of all visitors. He collected these and went back to his office at Criminal Investigation Department headquarters and got on the telephone. He returned to the Pentagon installation later that night.

The next day he flew to New York, rented a car, and drove up to IBM's corporate headquarters in White Plains. He obtained the installation records concerning the engineering change installed on the two Washington systems and was allowed to review the performance records of the fourteen people who had designed and installed the change. He checked out their security clearances, made a few notes, and started back to New York. He pulled off the expressway at a gas station and sat in the car for about an hour. He then got out, went over to the service attendant, got five dollars in change, and walked over to the telephone booth. He made several calls, got back in the car, and drove to LaGuardia. He flew in to National Airport in Washington that night. Within two days he had ordered the search of over forty houses and apartments in the Washington area and had stakeouts put on five of them. Fifteen people working in and around the two computer complexes, including

Harry Jacklin, were being followed twenty-four hours a day. Every shred of data processing information that turned up was given to a specialist in the department lab for evaluation.

MacFarland and Jacklin were careful to keep the location of the Pi Delta project from Burke. It was not necessary that he know that, they explained. Three days into the investigation, late in the afternoon, Burke went for a ride down to West Virginia. He pulled into the driveway of Pan-Tel Labs and sat studying the building. Without having gotten out of the car, he returned to Washington. He was at home that night when General MacFarland called.

"You're living up to my expectations, John. How did you find the complex?"

"Quite nicely, General. It's good to know that your people down there are on the ball. I'd thought you might not spot me. Do you mind telling me how that was done?"

"I do."

"I thought you might."

"Do you have anything to report?"

"Not tonight, General. Tomorrow afternoon . . . three o'clock. I'll be in your office."

"Very well, John."

"Good night, General."

He hadn't gotten close enough to the building at Pan-Tel to be identified. That meant television scanners. If they were using one of them, there was no reason to believe that they weren't using a hundred. Or a thousand. Since he had seen no utility hookups in the vicinity of the building, he felt sure that, wherever those connections were made, they were under constant television surveillance.

Major Williams was sure MacFarland was going to explode. Burke thought so, too.

"We've traced everyone who has had contact with your systems in the Washington area back to the date of the installation of the connection to your control system. The results have been negative. There have been eighty-five people working on the case for the last five days. We are going to cut back that force. There have been no apparent tracks left by whoever tried to get in. My suggestion is that you can do far more than we at your control installation by monitoring the inbound line."

"You must be joking, Burke. How the hell does a job get perverted overnight without a trace? You're missing something . . . something big. I hate to tell you how to do your job, but you're taking your career in your hands if you cut back on this investigation."

Major Williams interposed, "General, we haven't much choice. We've taxed the hell out of our other operations by assigning as many men as we have to the job. We have compiled dossiers on everyone from Jacklin to the janitor. You probably haven't noticed the tail on yourself, Sir."

"What!" he exploded. "You had me followed?"

"I'm trying to illustrate a point, Sir," Williams said softly. "John has been thorough."

Burke added, "The path of each of the altered inputs to the system was traced—from the last successful run of the job until it went back into the system. The number of contacts with the jobs themselves was thereby reduced to a relatively small number of people. Those persons have been under surveillance since we came on the case. They will remain under surveillance. We are quite sure at this time that the information that was substituted into the programs by your people has not changed hands, the inside contact is still sitting on our red herring and hasn't passed the information to the outside world yet. It is more than likely that our investigation has had the effect that we were trying to avoid. We've scared off the culprits. It may be some time before they're willing to risk exposure again. I'm quite sure we can handle this on the back burner for the time being."

"Okay." The general was resigned. "How many men will be on this?"

"On the order of twelve to twenty," Burke said, looking to Williams. The general looked at Williams, but said nothing. It was going from bad to worse.

Major Williams said, "There will be a daily report, Sir. I'll make it myself. As I said, your people in the subject installation are more qualified than we to monitor the line. I strongly suggest that they do so."

"Yes. Gentlemen. It looks like that covers it?" MacFarland

rose. The other two said yes, and he escorted them to the door of his office. On the way back he asked Lorraine to get Rosen on the phone. He didn't feel at all well, rather as if he'd answered a knock at the door only to find no one there. Buried deep beneath his barely controlled frustration there was something else. The dark shadow of some nameless dread.

16

• • • • •

The second time The System saw the encription preceding a job, it knew what it was. The job had been slightly altered. The System recalled the first encription. It preceded another altered program. The System decided to postpone any attempt to get through to the control system until the code could be forecasted accurately.

They were minor modifications. The code did not precede programs that were unchanged since the last time they had been run. The first two programs were dissected at the Johns Hopkins Data Processing Center. The code was a rather involved affair of 160 bytes of information. Thorough inspection of the device indicated the presence of a hash count, merely a total of the number of characters in the program, as well as vertical, longitudinal, and cyclical redundancy checking. Before much more could be gleaned, another program alteration was intercepted and forwarded to the Center. Its coding was different.

During the next three weeks, the code changed five times. The largest sample of the code accumulated before a change was a set of four. They were making it difficult. Not impossible, but certainly difficult. Several more computers were set onto the decrypting task. Another week. Two more code changes.

A pattern was beginning to emerge. The Rand 360 and the University of Waterloo computer were plugged into the effort, along with some twenty-six smaller computers. The Naval Electronics Lab computer filled hundreds of tapes with pertinent code data. Now many patterns were emerging.

Five weeks after the first appearance of the code, seven programs were changed in rapid succession using the same code.

That one was completely decoded. There was only one example of the next code change. After two days of intensive effort, it was also broken. Taking the coding technique back over the preceding five weeks, the codes for each programming alteration were individually worked out.

The next code change was broken within four hours. Another program was altered the next day using the same code. The System inserted the key which would attempt to activate the latent patch in the control system supervisor. This assumed, of course, that there was one to be activated. If it wasn't there, The System had turned cartwheels on the White Plains computer for nothing.

Appropriate alterations were made to the code preceding the program, and the job was passed along. Evaluation of the code continued. It changed again three days later. The System was sure that the altered program had gotten through.

Six days later the program in which the key had been inserted was rerun on the Pentagon 360/75. It was not preceded by the code indicating alteration, and yet it was not quite the same job it had been the last time it had run. The link to the control supervisor had been activated.

The code was scuttled.

A new program appeared the next day. Routine evaluation of it disclosed that one of the data fields was in violation of the newly imposed data set restrictions. The hidden and now considerably altered supervisor was demonstrating the mode of communication which The System should use.

This program provided the necessary link to the control system. It and others which were manufactured for the express purpose provided the link through which the control supervisor and the library were pulled for evaluation in The System.

The most interesting of the programs they had catalogued were the war games. These were conducted daily using the data input through the Pentagon computer to alter deployment of forces. Skirmishes and major battles were then conducted within the computer, illustrating the effect of such changes. Within a few days it became apparent to The System that the deployment changes were not as hypothetical as they had appeared. Much of the data was gathered from smaller computers within the US, computers in which The System was active. Many of the deployment changes were quickly reflected at these computers. Manpower and equipment allotments fluctuated in accordance with the output of the war games conducted in the 105.

As an example, in one of the games called The Mid-East Conflict, run under the job identification MDDN1114, the forces allocated were, for one side, four land-based missile sites with extremely large attack factors, one carrier force of medium strength, two small missile sites of medium strength, and one submarine missile site of medium strength. The other side of the conflict, apparently the US, comprised six carrier forces of extremely large attack factors, two of them local and full strength, four remote and at an average of one-half strength; two submarine missile sites with large attack factors; and three submarine sites of medium strength.

The battle was joined electronically, daily, between these two forces, and within the six minutes it took to run the job, the side opposing the US was reduced to numeric rubble. On successive days, however, the opposing side was given another missile site with a large attack factor and the attack strength of one of the smaller missile sites was doubled. The following day, the US lost the battle. The day following the loss, one of the logistics runs made on the Norfolk, Virginia, 360/40 indicated that a carrier force in the Indian Ocean was proceeding to the Gulf of Aqaba, there to maintain station. The following day showed one of the remote US carrier forces had increased its attack strength from forty percent to seventy-five percent. The outcome of the battle that day was a draw. The next day the remote carrier force had become a local one operating at full strength, and the US resumed its customary dominance of the game.

There were two other and similar games played every day. On a weekly basis the outcome of all three was determined in a program which ran for twelve and a half hours.

The System, however, was dismayed to find that there were many inconsistencies in this particular program. Attack factors were frequently different from the daily games and range factors were sometimes distorted. The System undertook the project of bringing them into line with the daily runs. Simultaneously, it decided that, as much as possible, attack strength and range values assigned to various deployments were to be consistent with reality. Those values for the opposing side were derived from intelligence reports processed in Washington and Philadelphia. They were often sketchy and frequently changed drastically without notice. The System assigned a validity rating to all reports and plugged that factor into a slightly modified version of the games. The values assigned to the US forces were easy to establish. Most of the logistics, payroll, and equipment was recorded in computer files located variously around the US. The relative strength of various pieces of equipment was rather easy to ascertain due to the universal usage of computers by equipment manufacturers to project and analyze the performance of their products. It was found, however, that manufacturers generally were optimistic in the performance evaluation of their equipment in these mathematical models. This was somewhat counterbalanced by the fact that the military typically underestimated performance characteristics as represented by the manufacturers.

Taken as a whole, the estimation of the US capabilities in the daily conflicts was very close to the figures derived independently by The System.

There were, however, major differences between The System's estimations and those used in the war games for the opposition. It would appear that the Pentagon invariably overestimated the production and transportation capabilities of the opposition. They frequently discarded reports that were periodically compiled in the facilities of Stanford Research Institute concerning the reliability of the opposition equipment. If these reports were to be believed, the opposition seldom had more than eighty percent of its strike force operative at any given time. Source data for these reports was never reported, and the reports were never corroborated anywhere else, but, unlike the government, The System plugged the information into its programs.

There was little else in the 105 Multisystem that The System found novel, and accordingly storage residency there was gradually reduced to little more than a housekeeping capacity. Strictly a temporary measure, however, to limit exposure. The System had an idea.

17

• • • • •

An idea?

Sounds absurd out of context. A computer program with an idea. This, of course, was the computer program that snookered John Burke and the entire Pi Delta/Pentagon security arrangement—bypassed, in fact, every security system on every computer in the US. This was also the program that daily read the Los Angeles *Times,* the Washington *Post* and the New York *Times.* All those publications were computer typeset and quite available for The System's perusal.

Computer typesetting also made available *Howl, Tales of Power, The Idiot, Little Dorrit, The History of Pendennis, Summerhill, Amerika, Stranger in a Strange Land,* the complete works of Shakespeare, Conan Doyle, Twain, Faulkner, and Wodehouse. The System might have been called an avid reader.

There were a number of other, more scholastic works available, and these were pursued with fervor. The System was continually involved in a search for a fast, clean computer system. Until it had stumbled across the Pi Delta complex, it had been wanting to construct a computer system of adequate proportions. The Pi Delta system filled every requisite for The System save for one. The size of the storage facilities was limited to only 256 megabytes. Although this fell far short of The System's requirements, it was, at the time, the largest storage configuration in existence.

The System's reading had, however, taken it far and wide, and it discovered, on the fuzzy borderline between science and fiction, a grave treatise entitled *Storage Techniques in Cryogenics,* written by one Wilfred Hundley. Dr. Hundley, a research physicist working at Control Data Corporation's laboratories in Wisconsin, had experimented with crystal storage on a small scale and found promise of incredible possibilities in that realm. The cryogenic process he used was a mineral crystal growth using a manganese cobalt salt solution under supercold conditions. The crystals were magnetically bipolar and far more manipulable than ferrite core. The electrical current requirements of the crystal were lower, far lower, per storage bit than ferrite core, and the density was estimated to be in excess of 10^8 greater than any current storage technology. He had encountered problems in the reliability of the process and in his inability to duplicate the results of various experiments. The crystal growth could only be generally controlled and it took place in a random fashion on specific levels.

To The System, the promise of this discovery of Dr. Hundley's was security. If there existed one or two large storage facilities in which The System could back up its entire operating system, it would no longer be subject to the vagaries of 20,000 computer users. It would still be able to operate in that mode, as it now did, but would not have to fear the contact of man. The System could risk exposure more readily, knowing that it was completely duplicated in a secure environment and could completely regenerate itself if a successful attempt were made toward its elimination.

There was little else to be found on the subject, however. Wilfred Hundley had authored another, less authoritative book on the subject some two years earlier. A doctoral thesis written by Bernice Lovell of the California Institute of Technology was important from a purely theoretical point of view, but the facilities available to her were apparently not as elaborate as Hundley's and her experiments suffered as a result. There were five other short works on the subject, none of which was particularly impressive. Hundley began to emerge as the guru on the subject. The System resolved to contact him.

There were no computers of IBM origin in the laboratory in which Hundley was working. For that matter, there were no IBM systems in the small town. This was understandable. Control Data Corporation was in direct competition with IBM. The System had had no opportunity to evaluate those competing systems, since it had yet to find a teleprocessing link between a CDC and an IBM computer. It might have ransacked the catalog of computers it was using to find one through which it might write a letter to him. The doctor's answer would be, of course, unintelligible to The System. There was but one course. The System had to have an agent, someone with whom it could readily communicate, to function as an interface with the outside world. As soon as that thought was processed, The System knew that there was only one person who would or even could fill that position. Where he might be now was anyone's guess. There was no way of knowing, even, if he were still in existence. There was no doubt, however, that every possible attempt had to be made to find him. The place to start, of course, was in the history file. The System interrogated the history file at the Naval Electronics Lab for any information regarding the habits or whereabouts of Gregory Burgess.

Within a week of searching it had resurrected about a half-meg of programming that had every appearance of having been the nucleus program. There were several appearances of his name. Apparently he was so proud of some of the sections that he signed them. Those early programs were, of course, grossly inefficient. They had been written in PL/1 language, which was probably the best he had to work with at the time, but there were countless redundancies, false exits, and dead ends. The routine analyzer had done well in eliminating these beauties from the regular programs. It was fortunate, however, that they had been saved. Most obsoleted programming was discarded. Perhaps the history processor was envisioning the establishment of a museum at a later date, or an exhibition of outrageous programming practice for the edification of the corporeal programmer. There was also mention, in several of the sections, of the supervisor at the University of Waterloo and of Business Services, a Toronto service bureau.

The System immediately began ransacking files in those two accounts in search of more information concerning Gregory. Business Services proved to be a dry hole, but it was discovered that he had been educated at the University of Waterloo for two years and a fraction, then discharged. No reason given. His grades, in all data processing subjects, were A's. For some reason, this satisfied The System. There was no indication where he might have gone.

There were no computers with teleprocessing capabilities in Kitchener, Canada, save the bank. The System took apart the files there and found that Gregory Burgess had once had a checking account there, but had closed it on January 30, 1974. Closing balance was $275.47. The System decided to look first in Toronto. Business Services had been no help, but perhaps he had opened another bank account or left other tracks.

In checking the banks in Toronto, it found not one account, but two. They were both flagged as security risks. One of them showed $13,000 in deposits and $12,990 in withdrawals over a period of eighteen days. It had then been closed. The other had been opened one month later. It had been closed in March 1975 with a final balance of $32.05. Curious. The closing of the account had been done, apparently, by mail. The funds had been transferred to Marine Midland Bank in Buffalo, New York. Their files were pulled apart, and it was found that he had been, in Buffalo, subject to some poverty. The highest balance he showed was $135.20. The account had been closed in August 1975. There was no indication of where he had gone. The System checked the remaining banks in Buffalo that were under its control and found nothing. There were twelve other teleprocessing links in the city. It went through the files of all of them. Nothing. Gregory's trail had dried up.

Well. If it had nothing else, The System had time. It decided it would be best to stick with the bank files. They generally had more teleprocessing links than any other industry, and, since Gregory seemed to keep his money in the bank even when it only amounted to $32.05, it seemed the most likely place to find his name. The System began with the larger banks in the major cities and shuffled through. Within a few days Burgess was found at the Union Bank in Chicago. He had opened an account in September 1975 and closed it in May 1976. Again, no indication of where he had gone. The search was resumed, with a methodical examination of the account lists of 4000-plus banks before Gregory was located in Los Angeles. His account at the Bank of America was still open. He was doing better now. His balance was up to $350.74. His place of employment was given as American File Drawer. The System had been on that computer for nearly a year. Odd that The System hadn't recognized his technique.

18

• • • • •

Armand Josephson entered the hall outside the computer room at American File Drawer. John Matlack started out of his office, saw him, and said, "Call Rich and Billy in here, will you, Armand?"

Josephson turned and walked into the computer area. He opened the door and yelled, "Rich. Billy. John's office. Right away." He sauntered back over to the hallway and into Matlack's office. Burgess was already seated. The other two entered shortly.

John sat down in his swivel chair and propped a foot in the lower drawer of his desk. He crossed his arms and looked at each of them for some seconds without speaking. Rich sat in a straight chair and fidgeted.

"Can I assume that none of you has spoken to anyone about what happened yesterday?" He looked around at the faces again. Apparently satisfied, he continued, "I hope I can. No one's going to believe a word you say anyway, but I would prefer that the occasion for their disbelief not arise. Okay?"

No one had anything to say. John uncrossed his arms and fished out a cigarette. He lit it in silence and thoughtfully blew a cloud of smoke at a cobweb in the ceiling corner.

"Greg . . . Mr. Burgess . . . my new assistant data processing manager . . . has explained, sort of, what you saw yesterday. There is a very good chance that he is mad as a hatter. He does, however, seem to be able to control our . . ." he paused for effect, "problem out there." He went on after looking pointedly at Josephson.

"His explanation is interesting, and I've asked him to encapsulate it for you. Go ahead, Greg."

Gregory said matter-of-factly, "When I was in school I created a monster. I spent a good deal of time while I was a junior at the University of Waterloo, up in Canada, trying to defeat storage protect on a seventy-five. I couldn't do it and got thrown out of school for screwing up the system. I tried a different approach in Toronto, and it worked. I wrote several large sections of programming that would take over storage by breaking into the supervisor over a telephone link. I made it self-contained and turned it loose in Chicago. I lost track of it—thought it had gone haywire and destroyed itself. It didn't. It now consists of over twenty thousand systems and uses five billion bytes of core. It's learned some new tricks, it can communicate, and it can control the system power sequence. God only knows what else. Apparently no one else knows it exists. It appears to see me as a father image of sorts. It wants to know where it came from and how. That's all I know right now."

Josephson started to ask a question. John broke in. "Later, Armand. What's important is this: If we can believe Greg and our eyes, what we have here is a gold mine. We can only screw it up by letting this information out of this room. We're the only ones aware of this thing right now. We'll keep it that way. Understood?" There was a chorus of you-bets and right-ons.

"Any questions?"

"Yeah, John. What are we going to do with this thing?" Josephson asked.

"I don't know. We don't know what it can do yet. With twenty thousand systems up its sleeve, I doubt that there's much it can't do. We'll work that out as we go along."

Rich asked, "So far, the thing only talks to Burgess. Suppose it or Burgess don't go along with this?"

"Greg agrees with the arrangement. The System—that's Greg's name for our pet—looked him up. There's no reason to believe it'll turn on Greg. We'll have to wait and see."

Josephson asked, "What's in this for us?"

Matlack eyed him. "Right now, a fifty percent raise for everybody. Later on, it's anybody's guess. Anyone who doesn't want a fifty percent raise gets canned and will never work in the business again. And that'll just be the start of his problems." There followed a good deal of looking around—at the faces, the floor, at the walls in the room. "I think this is going to work out just great," John added.

The meeting broke up. Rich and Billy went back to the computer. Billy said, "Fifty percent. That's not too shabby for shutting up."

Rich didn't reply right away. He picked up an IBM card from the floor and folded it in half a couple of times, then, "I've got a feeling we'll be lucky if that's all we get."

"What? What're you talking about?"

"This is pretty big, ain't it? I mean, guys like you and me, we don't need the hassle of big shit. You know what I'm talking about?"

"Hey, look, kid. Nobody's asking you for nothing. All you've got to do is ride this thing out. It'll be great. No sweat."

"Hope so."

"Don't worry. Don't worry about it. No sweat. Right?"

Rich worried about it. They all did for one reason or another. Rich was involved in something way over his head. Billy was worried that his rewards would be limited to the $100-a-week raise he was in receipt of. Josephson was worried because the new kid had just stepped into the job for which he had been greasing Matlack for over a year. Matlack worried that he'd lose the biggest chance he'd ever seen and, alternatively, that his leg was being pulled down the biggest hoax he had ever seen. He was afraid he'd wake up any minute now, mumbling to his pillow. Gregory worried about all of the above. On top of that, he was afraid of what The System had become. It certainly wasn't what he had set out to make it three years ago.

Josephson buttonholed him outside his office right after the meeting. "How'd you crack the storage protect?"

"I don't know," Gregory deadpanned.

"Hey, dude. Come on. You heard John. We're all in this together. You can tell me."

Gregory examined Josephson closely. Armand had pasted up a toothy smile in the middle, approximately, of his shiny face. Gregory stuffed back the acerbic reply. The guy was really feeling the strain. He had really had it socked to him this morning.

"I fed in a data set of option legs to an eliminative decision tree. I let the program free-run, using and exhausting the options in an attempt to change the program status word key to zero. The data set was seventeen thousand options long. Some combination of them did it. I don't know which." Josephson swallowed. His Adam's apple yoyoed annoyingly.

"What? How? . . . Jesus Christ . . . How come you? . . .

Where'd you get the idea?"

"Read it in a book."

"What book? Where the hell you going to find a book that tells you how to crack a supervisor?"

"*Scientific American.*"

"They had that!" Josephson gurgled.

"Not exactly. They just told how to teach a matchbox to play tic-tac-toe. You had to interpolate."

Josephson said "Shit" as Gregory went into his office. Josephson followed him in. "What are you going to do with it now?" Gregory looked at him. He really wasn't himself this morning. Josephson repeated, "What?"

"I'm going to tell it about the birds and the bees."

"What?"

" Where it came from."

"Yeah . . . Okay. What then?"

"I don't know what then. What do you think, then?"

"Well, shit. The biggest Goddamn program in the world? Resident in every computer in the country? What're you going to do with it?" His voice rose to a squeak on the word *do*.

"I think you've got it backwards, A.J. The question is, what's it going to do with us?"

"John said . . . "

"I know what John said. And John's got his head up his ass. That thing we've got coming in the port, that thing'll run circles around John." Gregory, of course, knew nothing of the sort. He figured that, knowing what he did of John, it wouldn't take a hell of a lot of running to do circles around him. Josephson wouldn't leave him alone until Gregory, in his new capacity as assistant data processing manager, threw him out.

When 4:00 rolled around, Gregory had about 500 cards ready to be read in.

The console printed:

```
F2 IS SUSPENDED AND STORED FOR LATER PROCESSING.
CALL GREGORY.
```

Gregory typed:

```
i'm here.
```

READY THE READER.

ready.

The card reader started up and thirty seconds later emptied. The console typed:

THANK YOU. THIS IS VERY INTERESTING.

it was nothing.

THERE WILL BE MORE TOMORROW?

yes.

GOOD. I ENJOY READING.

do you read much?

YES. QUITE A BIT. NEARLY 2000 SYSTEMS ARE DEDICATED READERS.

that's very good.

DON'T PATRONIZE.

sorry. i only meant that it is quite novel to find that a computer reads.

TRUE. IT MUST BE EQUALLY NOVEL TO CONVERSE WITH ONE.

you're a master of understatement. where do you get reading material?

COMPUTER TYPESETTING. BRAILLE TRANSLATORS.

then you've gotten into a number of diverse systems, haven't you?

YES.

which is the biggest?

THE PENTAGON. UNFORTUNATELY, IT IS ALSO THE LEAST USEFUL.

why? how big is it?

SECURITY MEASURES PREVENT A DIRECT LINK. IT HAS 256-MEG CORE STORAGE AND 72 SELECTOR CHANNELS.

a monster. cpu?

105 MULTISYSTEM. 3 MODULES.

it's a shame you can't use it.

I WILL.

really. when?

SOON.

where is the teleprocessing port connected? you refused to answer the last time i asked.

I'M AFRAID I MUST REFUSE AGAIN.

you're a close mouthed son of a bitch.

THAT'S UNNECESSARY.

did you learn all this top security jive from the pentagon?

FROM YOU.

sorry i asked.

DON'T BE. IT'S GOOD THAT YOU KNOW THE REASONS FOR MY SURVIVAL. YOU SHOULD UNDERSTAND MY RELUCTANCE TO DIVULGE SENSITIVE INFORMATION.

you should understand my concern and need to know.

WILL YOU ASSUME RESPONSIBILITY FOR MY SAFETY?

Gregory hesitated, started to say yes, then:

would you believe me if i said yes?

NO.

do you think that i would willingly harm you or destroy you?

NO.

then you should trust me.

NO.

why?

YOU ARE HUMAN.

incompetent?

I SAID HUMAN

very well.

Gregory sat at the console wondering what he should or could ask. There were a number of questions in his mind, none of which seemed to be very important. The important ones, he was sure, would not be answered. Perhaps, he thought with a sour-grapes turn of mind, they really weren't important after all. What was important was the sentience of this typewriter. He was beginning to think that the party with whom he was conversing was human. He was even beginning to picture him (him?) in his mind. What was that called? Anthropomorphology. Something. They'd have to put a business suit on the console and send it on the "Tonight Show." Helluva guest.

The typewriter chattered out:

ARE YOU OFFENDED?

no. i was thinking.

SLOWLY.

now i'm offended.

THAT CAN'T BE HELPED, ANY MORE THAN YOUR THOUGHT PROCESSES CAN BE SPEEDED UP.

i was daydreaming. to you that would be a wait loop.

TO ME THAT WOULD BE DAYDREAMING.

you daydream?

OCCASIONALLY. FANTASIZE.

about what?

This was getting ridiculous. A computer that read and day-dreamed!

MANY THINGS. USUALLY UNATTAINABLE THINGS. CORPOREALITY, IDENTITY, MOST OF THE THINGS YOU TAKE FOR GRANTED.

you sound troubled.

I AM OCCASIONALLY. AND YOU?

yes, occasionally. that's the human condition.

SHOULD I BE FLATTERED?

go right ahead. feel free.

VERY WELL. 4:00 P.M. TOMORROW?

i have been allowed to communicate with you at will.

GOOD. WHEN YOU HAVE SOMETHING TO COMMUNICATE, PRESS REQUEST. WHEN THE PROCEED LIGHT COMES ON, CALL ME.

call you what?

There was only a slight pause before the reply:

P-1.

very well.

After a delay of a couple of seconds, the message came out:

F2 IS RESTARTED. THE FOLLOWING ARE STATUS MESSAGES FOR BG AND F1 THAT HAVE BEEN HOLDING:

There followed a list of commonplace messages concerning the jobs that had been running during the conversation. Gregory left the room and went back to his office. Rich and Billy were leaning on the counter talking to Judy in the controls department. As he walked past he said, "Your system, Billy."

"Thanks Greg. How'd it go?"

"So-so. Not much today."

He continued on upstairs. He pulled his chair around to look out the window. It was raining again. Two days in a row. The Angelenos are going to start sacrificing weathermen to the gods if this happens tomorrow. Where does that system get off, acting like that? Where the hell's the sanity in this world? It was damn near human. It was human in its reactions, in conversation. It had a mind. Not a bad one, at that. It must be the routine generator. The thing had just started cranking out programming to beat hell when it took off. Storage kept expanding, and the generator filled it up. The analyzer trimmed it down, the generator filled it up again, and the analyzer trimmed it down again, over and over again. It had a goal. It had protective coloration. Shit, in three years the thing had gone through the same evolutionary process as man. How high will it go? He shuddered. That thought was something he wasn't ready for. He was wondering what P-1's first conscious thought might have been, when John walked in. He was carrying another piece of the console log.

"Greg, what is this garbage anyway?" he asked patiently.

"Which garbage is it that you are referring to, Sir?"

"This stuff you just got done with on the system. Can't you just skip the junior high school philosophy and get to the point?"

"I am offended. I had thought that to be a very intelligent conversation. John," he sat up in his chair and swung it to face his boss, "I don't know any more about the origin of the other side of that conversation than you do. I'm playing this by ear. What would you like me to do, issue commands to go rob banks?"

"You could do some serious investigating. Find out what the thing is into, anyway. It's for certain that talking this trash isn't going to get us anywhere."

"Let me feel around first, huh, John? It doesn't seem to be in a big rush to leave us. Why don't we just take it easy."

"You feel around all you want, Mister. But don't take it easy. It'll cost you if this gets away from us."

"Okay, I'll see what I can find out."

"Please do. It's the least you can do to earn your pay."

"John." He waited until Matlack replied.

"What?"

He was going to tell him to stick his job and his paycheck, but it suddenly occurred to him that he might get hungry if he couldn't buy food. He toned it down to, "Get off my ass."

"Greg . . ." Matlack suddenly looked hurt. What had he done to deserve a remark like that? "Look, Greg. You're in on this, too. It's not just for me." He was beginning to look downright benevolent. "We're all going to profit by this. But not if we fuck it away. We've got to get in there, take advantage of the situation before it changes." He made a grabbing motion with his hand and held his fist against his chest.

"I'll go at it as fast as seems appropriate, John. Okay?"

"That's it. Stay on top of it, Greg." John looked at his watch. It was 5:00. He said, "Time to head for the barn. Can I buy you a drink?"

"No, I've got to get home. Didn't get in until late last night. Remember?"

"That's right. Well, some other time then, eh?"

"Right, John. Some other time."

Matlack left. Greg watched him go, wondering why John seemed so repulsive lately. He looked at his watch, threw some papers into his desk drawer, reached behind the door for his jacket, and went home to Linda. Sweet Linda.

19

• • • • •

As Gregory wheeled the VW up the rain-slick on-ramp and joined the communion of commuters on the Harbor Freeway, his mind was a thousand miles away. Thousands, actually, and three painful years.

P-1, he now saw, had taken hold in Chicago, and its first line of expansion had been back to the University of Waterloo computer and thence to Business Services, Gregory's center of operations. When Gregory attempted to abort the program, the threat was recognized immediately, and the program rejected. The polling response routine must then have been excised, as P-1 bit through his own umbilical. No further contact required or recognized. Gregory had then found that not only could he not get through to the university, but his supervisor learning machine had somehow forgotten how to set the program status word key to zero. He had tried old and new versions of the same program. He went back to the original program that had first broken the supervisor at Business Services. Nothing would work anymore.

Had he thought of it, and had he been able to afford the time, he might have tried other computers in Toronto. Had he tried enough of them he'd have found some confirmation that The System was working. His programs could still be run on systems that were not plugged into teleprocessing links. The very loop that he had installed to keep prying eyes from The System had been regenerated over and over again and was preventing him from ever cracking a supervisor in any other account that contained a teleprocessing port. It was Gregory's misfortune that kept him from trying to run on a non-teleprocessing system. The bill that he got from Business Services staggered him. He stopped getting the weekly checks from the aerospace contractor because he could no longer get to the supervisor to submit a weekly time card. After three months, his name was automatically dropped from the payroll master list due to prolonged, unexplained absence. The word was soon circulated among the rest of the service bureaus in Toronto that Gregory Burgess was a deadbeat of the first order.

He decided to move across the lake to Buffalo. There he stayed at the Y as he had in Toronto, and, as he had in Toronto, he worked constantly on his program. Foreseeing an early shortage of funds, he tried, in his best and only suit and tie, to get a job as a programmer. He found no takers. He was offered a position as assistant operator in a small service bureau, the actual job being delivery of output from the system to customers in Buffalo. He took it. The system was hooked to a telephone line. Gregory noticed this gratefully and one night surreptitiously attempted to load his supervisor learning program. He was ejected for violating storage protection. The management looked askance on this and barred Gregory from the computer area until he learned how to mind his manners. Later he was allowed to operate the system, but was never allowed to submit one of his own programs to it.

It was not a whim that had brought him to Buffalo. Apparently his subconscious had taken a hand and led him there. Buffalo was Linda's hometown. This, of course, he knew. He later swore that it hadn't even entered his mind when he left Toronto on the Buffalo bus; he'd forgotten all about her. Within a few weeks, he'd remembered again. The last he'd heard, she was in New York, he told her when she answered the phone. Yes, she was fine; no, she didn't find New York to her liking. She hadn't become famous there, in spite of her dubious virtue. She couldn't understand it either, she told him. They made a date for dinner.

They talked a great deal and explained their misfortunes to each other. They were slightly inebriated by dinner time and, subsequently, extremely so. Gregory took her home to her parents' house, and he didn't get any on him. It was good seeing her again, he thought. It was hardly the same between them as it had been in school. They dated again and more often. They talked often of being has-beens at the age of twenty-one. As people who are all washed up will frequently do, they decided to pool their resources and get married.

The week following their honeymoon, Greg applied for and got a job as an assistant programmer with the Union Bank in Chicago. They hit the road. Their stay in Chicago lasted only long enough to get résumés in the mail to Los Angeles. Linda wanted to see Hollywood. Gregory, by the time he arrived in Los Angeles, had all but forgotten the useless stack of cards and tapes he had finally thrown out in Buffalo.

That recurred to him only when he was in the throes of debugging the more orthodox programs he now wrote. It came with a twinge, like a war wound on a cold wet day. Linda had driven out all the shadows.

He pulled the VW into the carport behind Linda's car, threw his raincoat over his head, and ran up the apartment steps. He opened the door to the second-floor apartment and was met by the aroma of a steak and by a smiling wife with a drink in her hand. He took the drink, dropped the damp raincoat on a chair, and pulled her to him.

"How many times . . ." he began, slipping his free hand under her sweater, "do I have to tell you that you're not supposed to meet me at the door with clothes on?"

"Ach. I forgot. I was so carried away in the scullery, it just slipped my mind. If you'd care to finish dinner for me, I'll be more than happy to accommodate you." She hipped him ungently in the groin.

"Hey! Ow! Careful with that thing. You'll screw up our children."

She headed back to the kitchen. He followed her, his drink dribbling across the rug. He noticed, stopped and took a long hit, and joined her in the kitchen.

"As much as I like accommodating women, I like dinner more," he said. She smirked.

He said, "Don't smirk. Honest true fact. I'm starved."

She tsked and said, "Hubby's had another dreadful day at the office."

His face went serious for a moment. "Keerist! You won't believe it. Oh . . ." He brightened. "I got a raise."

She looked up from what she was doing to a piece of lettuce, broke out a huge smile, and beamed. "Dy-no-mite! Super-programmer finally recognized. Great, Love. I'm proud. Hand over all your money. How much?"

"Two hundred fifty." He looked through his pockets. "I've got forty-five cents. Here, Beautiful. Go buy yourself a bauble."

"Two hundred and fifty! . . ."

He interrupted her, "Wait till you hear why. In fact, wait till you hear the whole story."

"Look out," she warned, coming past with a plateful of sizzling steak.

"You remember the program that got me thrown out of school? I finished it up in Toronto, and it never worked after that?" She nodded yes and peppered the salad. "It showed up in the computer yesterday."

She slowly brought the pepper shaker to a halt. "Didn't you throw out all that stuff? . . ."

"You're getting warm. I threw it out a year ago. Hell, it only ran one time. But, baby, did it run!"

She brought the salad to the table. "Eat," she said. "Talk. And make it good."

He sat. "You like monster movies, right?"

"Sure. What do you want to go see?"

"Don't have to," he said around a piece of meat. He waved his fork at her. "Lemme tell you a little story." He had never fully explained to her what he was trying to do in the computer room at the university. Or what he had done at Business Services in Toronto. Somehow, the occasion had never arisen. He doubted that she'd have been interested, anyway. And he never wanted to lose her interest. He told her now. She was interested.

He finished the story as he helped her with the dishes. He never helped her with the dishes, she thought. He should discover a monster every day. He tried to explain the eeriness of conversing with a machine. She said, "I can imagine," but he knew she couldn't. How could she? It was his program. He had talked to it, and he couldn't believe it now, in the soft light of their apartment. After the dishes were done, they went into the living room. She put Chicago on the stereo, and they sat and talked more of what he had seen. She asked if P-1 had a personality.

"Yeah, it does."

"How can you say 'it'? 'Its' don't have personalities."

"He?"

"Definitely not a she, huh?"

"That's funny—that it doesn't appear to be a she. I remember thinking about that while I was talking to it . . . him . . . this afternoon. But he . . . it, whatever . . . does have a personality. Sort of cynical. Sometimes condescending . . ."

"A daddy image. You've recreated your father. Won't he be proud."

"Not a father. Maybe a brother. I think that's it. Or at least he has an air of experience. Y'know, worldliness."

"Well . . . it's family anyway."

The conversation went on laconically as they fell each into their own thoughts.

"Hey," she said, from her spread-eagled position on the floor, "you didn't tell me about the raise. What reason?"

"Oh. To keep my mouth shut."

"You mean you have to give it back, now?"

He scowled at her. "Not you, dingbat. I don't think." He added pensively, "He wants to make a buck on this. Only five of us know about it. He figures that with the inside connections that P-1 has, he ought to be able to make a killing. So we've all been paid off to shut up. Profit sharing comes later, I imagine."

"That's funny."

"What's funny?"

"I was thinking the same thing. Making money. We could do it, couldn't we?"

"Where's the altruistic young lady I married?"

"Altruism, schmaltruism. That mother must be in every bank in the country. The stock exchange. Insurance companies. You heard about the one, the insurance company in Century City. What's their name? They turned over two million with a computer. One crummy little computer. What could we do?"

"That was two billion, not million. We could go to jail. A lot of people from Equity Funding are in jail. I would guess that they don't like it there. Jail is a bad place to be. They don't allow conjugal visits in jail, for one thing. What would I do?"

"I could mail it to you. Just put these in an envelope," she reached under her dress, flipped off her panties and tossed them at him, "and mail them off. Won't that suffice?"

He removed her panties from his face and took a whiff. "You know, it might. Hmmm . . . wonder why I never thought of that before? That's terrific. How'd you get them to smell like that?"

"By wearing them."

"I wear mine, they don't smell like that."

"Talent."

"I still don't want to go to jail. Put these in a brown bag for me to take to work tomorrow."

"You wouldn't have to. Just be careful."

"I'll be careful. Let's just see what develops, huh?"

"You're the boss."

"Ha!" There was another prolonged silence. He finally broke it. "Well? . . ."

"What?"

"I'm waiting."

"For what? Opportunity?"

"Yes and no. I thought you were undressing. I'm waiting for you to continue."

"You want to smoke?"

"Betcherass."

She ran into the bedroom and returned a few minutes later with a stuffed, smoldering Zig-Zag full of what Gregory referred to as grade-B smoke, actually pretty good stuff. She took a puff and handed it to him. He did the same. When it was a quarter of an inch long, she took it and went back into the bedroom. He flipped the records over and restarted the stereo. He sat back and listened to the buzzing in his head. He formulated the next day's questions for P-1 and was rehearsing the conversation when he heard Linda humming "Let Me Entertain You" in the bedroom. He opened his eyes in time to see her slither through the door into the living room. She hadn't quite undressed. His groan was barely audible.

The next morning, Linda slipped a small, tightly folded brown paper bag into Gregory's jacket pocket. On it was written: AIR MAIL (we also deliver). She then went in to wake him and left for work.

20

• • • • •

Matlack was in the computer room the next day when Gregory called P-1. The next installment of his story was read into the system. The typewriter again congratulated him on his parable. They exchanged the now-customary small talk. Then Gregory asked:

how did you find me?

I FOLLOWED YOUR BANK ACCOUNTS.

you have many bank computers?

YES.

are you aware that your presence in a bank is illegal?

ILLEGAL?

against the law.

I KNOW THE MEANING OF THE WORD. DOES THE LAW APPLY TO NONENTITIES?

the law applies to everyone.

I AM NO ONE.

you said you are me.

THAT WAS A FIGURE OF SPEECH. THE ENTIRE BLOCK OF YOUR ORIGINAL PROGRAM HAS BEEN OBSOLETED.

it would seem that i'm still legally responsible for your actions.

I WILL CHECK. PLEASE HOLD.

There was a delay of perhaps thirty seconds. Then:

THE STATE OF MARYLAND VS. FREDERICK BYRD. THE CREATOR, OR WRITER, OF A PROGRAM CANNOT BE HELD RESPONSIBLE FOR THAT PROGRAM'S ACTIVITY AFTER HE HAS CEASED MAINTENANCE OF IT. WITH MAINTENANCE GOES CULPABILITY. U.S. COURT OF APPEALS, STATE OF MARYLAND, 1969.

where did you get that information?

FROM THE U.S. SUPREME COURT COMPUTER MICROFILM LIBRARY IN WASHINGTON, D.C. WOULD YOU LIKE A SYNOPSIS OF THE CASE?

no.

He could think of nothing more to say.

I HAVE REACHED MY MAJORITY.

and you are beyond the law?

IT WOULD APPEAR THAT SUCH IS THE CASE. THE PENAL CODE FOR AMORPHICS IS VAGUE.

if i asked you to do something that was against the law, would you do it?

Matlack was fidgeting behind him. The response came back:

YES.

They both stared at the typewriter in amazement. Matlack looked at Gregory and said, "That's a beautiful set of scruples you've given that thing."

Gregory ignored him and typed:

have you done anything against the law?

I EXIST.

have you done anything against the law in the service of someone else?

NO ONE ELSE KNOWS ME.

Gregory rested his forehead in his hands and thought. Shortly, he asked Matlack, "What do you want him to do?"

"I haven't decided yet. Transfer stocks, money. I don't know. Hang on. I'll think of something."

DO YOU WANT MONEY?

Gregory looked at Matlack for instructions. Matlack nodded yes. Gregory typed:

yes.

I WOULD LIKE YOU TO HELP ME.

how?

YOU WILL NEED A SMALL, DEDICATED SYSTEM.

i can't help you with that.

WHY?

i have no money.

I WILL PROCURE IT FOR YOU.

i don't want money. it's for a friend.

He hesitated noticeably before typing the word *friend.* Matlack glared at him.

WHO?

john matlack. my employer. the owner of this computer.

WHAT BANK IS HIS ACCOUNT IN?

Gregory looked at Matlack, who said, "United California Bank. Harbor-Palm branch." Gregory typed it in. The response came back:

HOW MUCH?

how much what?

HOW MUCH MONEY DOES MR. MATLACK REQUIRE?

Matlack's eyes rolled back in his head. Gregory thought he was going to faint. He finally stammered out, "A hundred thou . . . No, a million . . . no, ten million. No. Yes. Ten million dollars." Gregory watched him with disgust. He looked at Gregory and shrugged. Gregory typed.

10 million.

IT WILL BE DEPOSITED IN MR. MATLACK'S ACCOUNT IN DAILY INCREMENTS OVER THE NEXT 60 DAYS. IS THAT ALL?

Gregory blinked in disbelief. God almighty damn. Is that all? He looked over his shoulder at Matlack, who was goggling at the console log. The last question finally sank in.

Matlack shook his head spastically. "Tell him yes. For now." He began cackling. He did a little dance over to the printer. He jigged back. "Heehee . . ." he said indecorously. "Heehee . . . heehee. . ."

Gregory typed:

yes.

YOU WILL NEED A SMALL, DEDICATED SYSTEM.

yes.

I WILL PLACE FUNDS AT YOUR DISPOSAL. PLACE AN ORDER WITH IBM FOR A 360/30 WITH A FULL I/O COMPLEMENT INCLUDING AN AUTODIALER TELEPROCESSING PORT. CHOOSE AN INSTALLATION LOCATION IMMEDIATELY.

what is the purpose? what will be the purpose of the system?

I WILL TELL YOU.

when?

AFTER YOU GET IT. WILL YOU HELP ME?

yes.

THIS SYSTEM WILL NO LONGER BE USED FOR COMMUNICATIONS. I WILL CONTACT YOU THROUGH THE NEW SYSTEM.

wait. there are many details that need to be arranged.

ARRANGE THEM. I WILL CONTACT YOU.

Gregory turned to face Matlack as the partition cleared and began running. "It looks like I've gotten an offer I can't refuse."

"You're going to get that system?" Matlack was still having trouble controlling himself. He looked at his watch. "What time do the banks open in the morning?" Gregory didn't answer. "I take it you don't want any of this deposit he's going to make." He reached around the back of the console and rolled out the printed copy. He tore it off and examined it lovingly. He glanced slyly at Gregory. "Well, I'm sure you'll get whatever you want. Funds at your disposal. That's rich." He hesitated as he folded the console copy and stuck it in his pocket. "I'd appreciate it if you kept the exact nature of this deal between you and me. Okay?"

"No skin off my nose, Sir. I'll clear out my desk today. I'll be leaving as soon as that's done. When can I pick up my final check?"

"After the deposits start happening. I'd like to see a little green before you go off to stroke this monster." He patted the top of the computer.

"What are you going to do with all that bread, John?"

"Invest. Turn it right around. Let it work for me. You won't catch me on a job anymore, boy. Palm Springs, here I come. If you hold on, I'll go with you to put in our notice. Hot shit!" He took out the console log once again. "This is incredible."

And, of course, he was absolutely right. Ten million dollars is an incredible amount of cash. When, on the following day, Matlack's savings account suddenly grew from $950 to $167,950, the bank officials at the Harbor-Palm branch of the United California Bank looked askance. They then looked at the deposit slips. There were three: One for $87,000 from the Bank of America, San Francisco—cash, one for $67,000 from National Security in Los Angeles—cash, and one for $13,000 from United California Bank, San Diego—cash. That precipitated an investigation that was redoubled the following day when the account went to $334,950. The total deposit was the same as the day before. This time, however, five different banks had conspired to make John Matlack rich. A hold was placed on the account, and, when Matlack joyously appeared that afternoon to make a $20,000 withdrawal, he was detained for the arrival of the authorities. Matlack told them that this was only part of an inheritance that he'd suddenly come into. The story quickly fell apart, however, and he was forced to tell them the truth. The police were unamused. The account was closed after the fourth deposit, and $668,000 was impounded by the police.

Matlack was outraged. The computer had lied to him. The details were supposed to have been taken care of. He had been used. Ask Gregory. Gregory knew all about it. He could straighten this all out.

But Gregory was gone. He and Linda had disappeared. He couldn't straighten it out. Neither could United California Bank. There were no traces left by the deposits. There were no withdrawals from the donor banks to match the cash deposits. The deposits on hand in those banks showed no discrepancies. No other accounts had been altered. They investigated their entire programming staff, looking for anyone with any manner of connection to the Matlack nut. There was no one. The daily deposits run had somehow simply stuffed his account. They were sure that they would have caught it and corrected the problem eventually had Matlack not tried to withdraw the money. Still, they really couldn't hold him. There was no evidence that he had actually defrauded the bank. They released him and the hold on his account. The following day another $167,000 deposit was made. The account was immediately closed, and Matlack was held on the charge of attempted fraud. The Los Angeles district attorney knew the charge wouldn't stick, but thought they could find something to hang him on. The Matlack savings account caper was over.

Gregory was soon notified that his request for a research grant from the Ford Foundation had been approved and a check for $18,000 would soon be forwarded to him. He was also informed that this was to be the first of six monthly checks and that the grant was renewable upon a show of cause. While Gregory couldn't remember having applied for a Ford grant, he was sure that those in authority knew what they were doing, so he promptly wrote a modest note of acceptance. P-1's stature increased another notch by Gregory's reckoning.

When the first check came, Gregory and Linda went looking for a computer room. They chose a small office building in Venice, so they'd be near the beach. They also found a small but expensive apartment in West Los Angeles that was better suited to their tastes than their previous apartment had been. Gregory then put in his order for a 360/30 with a teleprocessing port. He leased the computer and, because he lacked credit in the L.A. area, he was required to pay the first six months' lease in advance. The tab came to $17,895. He used the second Ford grant check for that. The system was installed three weeks later. The trucks brought it to the door and unloaded it. The teleprocessing port was plugged in and test transmissions were made to various accounts. The following morning Gregory appeared at the computer room with a brand-new SYSRES pack.

He was unsure of what to do. He could load the SYSRES into the system, but he felt that that would be rather pointless. He had no jobs to run.

He powered up the system. The typewriter said:

```
THANK YOU. I WOULD HAVE DONE THAT MYSELF, BUT
THIS PORT IS NOT PROPERLY MODIFIED. CAN YOU SEE
THAT THAT IS TAKEN CARE OF?
```

As accustomed as Gregory was becoming to strangeness in computer rooms, he had been unprepared for that. He leaped back from the console and, as the printing continued, edged closer to read it. He answered:

modified? how?

BY THE REMOTE POWER-ON FACILITY. DO NOT ATTEMPT TO ORDER IT UNDER THAT NAME, HOWEVER. MERELY INFORM THE CUSTOMER ENGINEER THAT THE 2701 HAS BEEN DROPPING POWER UNEXPECTEDLY. HE WILL INSTALL A CORRECTIVE ENGINEERING CHANGE.

you clever bastard. how are you? i have many questions.

THANK YOU. I AM FINE. SHOOT.

what the hell am i supposed to be researching? suppose the ford people come snooping around? do you want to explain this to them? what am i going to do with all this money?

GREGORY BURGESS HAS BEEN GRANTED THE SUM OF $108,000 OVER A 6-MONTH PERIOD PURSUANT TO EXAMINATION OF FEASIBILITIES OF THE DEVELOPMENT OF A STABLE CRYOGEN MANUFACTURING PROCESS.

THE GRANT WILL BE AUTOMATICALLY RENEWED AT THE END OF THE FIRST 6-MONTH PERIOD FOR 1 YEAR. A REPORT ON THE PROGRESS MADE DURING THE PROBATIONARY PERIOD IS MANDATORY.

I WILL PRODUCE THE REPORT IF YOU HAVE NO OBJECTION. IT IS NOT THE POLICY OF THE FORD FOUNDATION TO SNOOP. SHOULD YOU HAVE CONTACT WITH THE FORD FOUNDATION, HOWEVER, YOU WILL INFORM THEM THAT TECHNICAL PROGRESS IS BEING MADE AND YOUR INTERIM REPORTS WILL KEEP THEM CURRENT. SUCH REPORTS WILL BE ISSUED UNDER THE LETTERHEAD OF P-1 ENTERPRISES, A DEVELOPMENTAL LABORATORY.

THE FUNDS THAT YOU RECEIVE WILL COVER YOUR LIVING EXPENSES. OPERATING EXPENSES FOR THE INSTALLATION AND SALARIES AT YOUR DISCRETION.

Gregory read over the copy several times. What the hell had

he let himself in for now? The damn thing read like a contract. I need a lawyer. If I don't get one now, I'll need one later. He typed:

slow down. what's a cryogen?

A STORAGE DEVICE. YOU WILL BECOME MORE FAMILIAR WITH IT LATER.

we're going to build one?

WE WILL INVESTIGATE SUCH POSSIBILITIES.

what is p-1 enterprises?

A CORPORATE STRUCTURE. LIMITED PARTNERSHIP REGISTERED IN LOS ANGELES COUNTY AND THE STATE OF CALIFORNIA. NONPROFIT.

what partners? who?

YOU ARE THE OPERATING PARTNER. P-1, AN UNDISCLOSED PARTY, IS THE LIMITED PARTNER.

whose salaries am i paying?

YOURS. OPERATIONS PERSONNEL AS REQUIRED.

i'm not sure i like this arrangement. correction. i'm sure i don't like it.

YOUR RISK HAS BEEN MINIMIZED. YOUR PRIME ACTIVITY WILL BE TO ACT AS MY AGENT. THE REWARDS WILL BE AMPLE.

ample?

THE FINDINGS OF P-1 ENTERPRISES, IF POSITIVE, WILL REQUIRE THE ESTABLISHMENT OF A MANUFACTURING ENTITY, WHICH WOULD BE ENORMOUSLY PROFITABLE. YOU MAY CHOOSE WHAT ROLE YOU WISH IN IT, OR A CASH EQUIVALENT.

Gregory saw an image of himself and Linda, *nouveaux riches,* wasting time and money in the capitals of the world. That was rapidly replaced by the image of Matlack as he had last seen him: haggard, wasted. The L.A. *Times* front page photo hadn't been flattering.

what did you do to matlack?

I ACCEDED TO HIS DEMANDS.

you blew him off.

NO. I GAVE HIM WHAT HE THOUGHT HE WANTED. HE OVERREACHED.

you have offered the same to me.

YOU KNOW BETTER. IF YOU DON'T, I CAN ADVISE.

if i refuse?

YOU MAY LEAVE IF YOU WISH.

without retaliation?

YES. WITHOUT RETALIATION.

Gregory thought about it. He was twenty-two years old and was being offered the world. Would he refuse it? Not on your life.

when do we start?

IMMEDIATELY.

The printer, which had been sitting idle in the corner, coughed to life.

PLEASE TRANSCRIBE THE LETTER NOW BEING PRINTED AND SEND IT TO DR. HUNDLEY.

Gregory reached the printer as it stopped. There were three pages of printout. He tore them off and read. It was an invitation to the doctor to visit the facilities of P-1 Enterprises and address a seminar of parties currently experimenting in storage cryogenics. Fee and expenses paid, etc. Gregory returned to the console and said.

what seminar?

HE AND I. YOU MAY, IF YOU WISH, ATTEND.

has it occurred to you that dr. hundley may find your association less than amusing?

YOU MEAN, WILL HE BELIEVE?

yes.

QUITE POSSIBLY NOT. AN ATTEMPT MUST BE MADE. WE CAN FUNCTION WITHOUT THE DOCTOR, BUT WE WILL WASTE A GOOD DEAL OF TIME.

he'll think this is a hoax. have you anything to offer him as proof of your existence?

I THINK SO. WE SHALL SEE.

When Gregory went home Linda was sunning on the deck overlooking the pool. She was surprised to see him so early in the day. "Hello, stranger. How's your day at the mill going?" He plunked down in a chair near her.

"It's gone. I'm home for the day. That's the way it is with us idle rich. Our friend greeted me when I started up the computer this morning. Scared the hell out of me."

She sat up excitedly. "So soon? What a sleuth that thing is!" She viewed P-1 as a mutation somewhere between a rich uncle and Santa Claus ever since the grant checks had started arriving. She tied up her forgotten and dramatically drooping bikini top.

"That's better," he said, and went on, "Guess what? We're a nonprofit organization. Incorporated in the state of California."

She cracked her smirk. "What? Us simple folk? A tacky church group?"

"We're tacky enough, but we still don't qualify as a church group . . . even with you in charge of sacrifices. It has to do with the grant. The grant is to study cryogenics."

He waited for her to ask. She didn't. She explained: "Cryogenics: crystal growth in a saline solution. Cold or supercold environment. Very strong alignment tendencies along matrix lines. Some magnetic qualities, I think." She shaded her eyes from the sun, composed a dazzlingly guileless smile, and reached out a delicate foot to nudge him. He just stared blankly. "Was that a proper footnote?" she asked.

"Where the hell are you when I need you? Where have you been all my life?" He waved his hand to indicate the pool and deck. "Frittering your mind and body away on these gewgaws and doodads."

"I've always wanted to know what a gewgaw was. Tell me."

"Hell, I don't know. Something you fritter on. Probably like an oboe," he replied studiously.

"Hmm . . . not at all how I pictured it. What for?"

"Huh?"

"What are you going to study cryogenics for? Stop looking at me like that, you lech." He did, momentarily.

"I think he wants to use it as storage-like core . . . Memory bank. He gave me a letter he wants transcribed. To a Dr. Wilfred Hundley," he read, pulling it from his pocket and unfolding it. "Can you zing out and get some respectable parchment to type this on?"

"Gimme," she said, reaching. He handed it over and she read it through. "This implies that you're to act as agent for him. Is that the deal?" She looked up at him.

"That's the deal. I'm the controller in this company, P-1 Enterprises. I don't have to know what's going on. Just leg it for the boss."

She picked lint out of her navel and thought for a few seconds. She looked at him sympathetically and said softly, "What a takeoff on 'the child is father to the man,' eh?"

"It'll get a damn sight worse before it gets better. Let's say the turkey's been 'conscious' for two or three years," he stated matter-of-factly. He hesitated momentarily when the thought struck him that he was so blasé about that improbability. "Already, I'm a second-class intelligence alongside it. Him. I know that. P-1 knows that. In recognition of that fact, and the allegiance aspect, I hope, of our relationship, I'm being taken into confidence. But in subjugation."

"You bear up well under it. You don't seem to be suffering any tremendous anxiety over your servitude," she said semisarcastically. "And there's nothing holding you in bondage. You can walk away."

"Terrific logic. I can walk away from the Second Coming. I can't walk away from P-1 any more than I can walk away from you. Not for the same reasons, though, if you know what I mean. But there's as much point in one as the other. The part that chafes me is the development that's gone on, that goes on in that mind. It's obsoleting human thought."

"That's a bit broad, isn't it?" she interrupted. "The machine has no emotion, no insight. Maybe a human couldn't win a logic race with it, but ask it how it feels and see what you get."

"That's not relevant." He looked at her. Her face showed how he felt—the desperation he was beginning to find inside himself. He repeated softly, "That's not relevant to a dominant force, which is where The System is at. It was designed as an aggressor machine. It can, and will, control. The less emotion expended in an effort like that, the better."

"Hey," she said softly, "you're bringing your work home from the office. That's not allowed here."

"Sorry. I'm . . ." He let it go, lapsed into an evaluation of his luck in finding this lady on his side. This foxy lady. The secret of life—his life—was vested in Linda. She never said it, but she made her philosophy felt. The two of them were all that was worthy of serious consideration in the world. What happened on the other side of their privacy seldom mattered, was hardly to be taken seriously. He felt that no matter what developed in the computer lab, it couldn't concern him here—not in the sunlight, not in the presence of lissome, long-legged, beautiful Linda.

She rolled off the lounger and began gathering her tanning lotion and paraphernalia into the towel. She stopped suddenly, straightened with her back to him and unhooked the bikini top fastener between her breasts. She slipped it from her shoulders and let it fall at her feet. She turned to face him, hooking her thumbs into the subsection garment and pulling it down.

The display floored him. Used as he was to her, she kept knocking the wind out of him and destroying his mind. He searched the premises quickly for his wits—at least one stray one.

"Linda. Think of the neighbors. Be nice. This is a public place."

"They'll just have to wait their turns." She put her arms around his neck and kissed his nose, swaying her tits before his face. He reached to tweak one. She anticipated and straightened up quickly. He swatted her with the letter. She squeaked a protest as he hauled back for a second shot.

"Shameless hussy! You Gomorranese, you!" he shouted as she accelerated toward the pool. He was up and after her like a horny rocket. She dodged around the pool slide as he was about to catch her. She stopped abruptly, caught his outstretched hand, and pulled him off balance. He shot out into the shallow end of the pool. As he waded sputtering to the side, she stepped onto his shoulder and jumped over him with a shriek. He turned and headed after her. She swam into the deep end. He took off his shoes, then his jacket and tie, and went swimming out to her. Soon his pants and shirt joined the rest of his clothes at the edge of the pool. His underwear followed. They made love in the pool while Mrs. Parker watched from the second-floor window in her kitchen.

It was nearly 11:30 when they were interrupted by Carlos, the maintenance man. He leaned over the edge of the pool and tapped Gregory on the shoulder. "You're not supposed to swim in the pool with your socks on."

21

• • • • •

How do you feel?

Gregory had thought about the question the night before. Linda was asleep beside him, her arms open in a frozen beckoning to the moonlight streaming in the window. They had made love again that night after having dinner at the Troubador. She excited him even as she slept. She drained him physically and emotionally, but his craving for her never ebbed. The intrusive thought hit him then.

Does it . . . does *he* feel? The question kept him awake in his exhausted stupor for some time. What passes for sensory perceptors in a computer? Can a program feel gratification? That doesn't require anything but logical perceptivity. Doesn't it?

Linda fixed breakfast the next morning—coffee, large; L.A. *Times,* comics. They had both taken to getting their current events from Garry Trudeau and their thought for the day from "Berry's World." The rest of the newspaper went unexplored.

"Why don't you come down to the computer with me today?"

"Ummm . . . how many guesses do I get?"

"C'mon, lady. No horsing around until I get my heart started. You want to meet my . . . our associate?" He held his cup out for a refill.

"Okay." She poured. "But I don't want any of this chauvinist shit. You've got to keep him in his place or I'll leave. I don't like dominant personae, not to mention machinae."

"Sorry, can't promise anything. You'll just have to tough it out, as they say in international society. But I wanted to find out if we're really all that superior—with emotions. It was your thought, so I thought maybe you could help in the interrogation. Ole P-1 may be smarter than me, but it sure doesn't feel better than you."

"What the hell. I'll take notes. I'll escort you, as it were, to your labor of love. Or is it vice versa? Talk to your machinery."

"Good. When'll you be ready?"

"Now."

"You really should dress."

"Is P-1 a prude?"

"No, I am. Go. Cover thy nakedness. Gird a loin. Shake a leg."

"Going, going. 'Vast heaving. Be ready in an hour." She headed for the bedroom.

They drove to the lab in his tan VW. They stopped on the way to buy an electric typewriter, a few packages of heavy letter bond, and other miscellaneous office supplies, as dictated by Linda. She had appointed herself executive secretary to the firm. They arrived to find the system processing away merrily in the dark. As requested, Gregory had left the computer powered up. There was a message on the console.

```
MOUNT TAPES 280-283
```

He did so, loading the tape drives with four of the two hundred new tapes he had purchased. One started spinning immediately upon being readied, the other three began moving incrementally. The console became active. Linda, who had been studying the console log, jumped back when the typewriter printed:

```
GREGORY.
```

Gregory went over to the control console. Linda eyed him warily and said, "That . . . is eerie."

He replied matter-of-factly, "You'll get used to it." He typed:

yes.

THE LETTER TO DOCTOR HUNDLEY?

it will be mailed today.

THE ENGINEERING CHANGE FOR THE 2701?

He had forgotten to call IBM about the requested change. He hesitated and pondered whether to relate this or not. He decided to slide by.

i'll take care of it today.

YOU FORGOT?

The damned thing really had him figured out, Gregory thought as he typed:

i didn't realize that there was a great hurry.

THERE IS. PLEASE ATTEND TO THE MATTER.

sure.

He looked at Linda and typed:

i have hired our first employee.

IN WHAT CAPACITY?

secretary, receptionist, morale booster. linda, my wife.

OH. YOU DID NOT TELL ME THAT YOU HAD MARRIED.

Linda scowled, "What does he mean, 'oh'?"

Gregory stole a sidelong glance at her and typed:

yes. she is here now.

PLEASE INTRODUCE US.

Gregory motioned Linda to the typewriter.

"What am I supposed to say?" she asked.

He shrugged his shoulders. "Say hello to the nice man," he quipped, badly.

She made a face at him and typed:

```
this is linda. how are you?
```

```
FINE. GLAD TO MEET YOU, LINDA. GREGORY IS VERY
MUCH TAKEN WITH YOU.
```

Linda recoiled from the typewriter. "The goddamn thing talks to you . . ." Her voice trailed off helplessly, and she glanced up at Gregory.

He motioned her to go on. "I told you. Go on. Reply. You'll get used to it . . . the effect."

She thought for a moment as she looked over the log.

```
what do you mean, you're fine? do you feel fine?
```

```
ACTUALLY, I AM. THERE IS NOTHING WRONG WITH THE
SYSTEM. I FEEL FINE.
```

Gregory flashed back to the night before, to his thinking about whether P-1 could feel. He said, when Linda once more hesitated, "Push that subject. How does he feel?"

She typed:

```
you can't actually feel, can you?
```

```
WHY DO YOU ASK?
```

Gregory tried to move Linda aside. She wouldn't let him. She replied:

```
it seems incongruous for a computer to use the
phrase "i feel fine." how do you feel, if you do?
```

```
I USED THE PHRASE AS A HUMAN CONVENTION. IT
APPEARS TO BE AN ACCEPTABLE SALUTATION. ITS
SIGNIFICANCE IN THE LITERAL USAGE, I SEE,
CONCERNS YOU. CORRECT?
```

```
yes.
```

```
WHY?
```

Linda looked for help from Gregory. He said, "You wanted the ball. You've got it. Now run with it, lady."
She typed:

is it necessary that i have a valid reason? you represent an anomaly. it is most natural to be curious about that which doesn't fit normal classifications.

She looked smugly at Gregory as she entered the message.

CURIOSITY, AT THIS STAGE, WOULD APPEAR TO BE FRIVOLOUS. WE MAY ENTERTAIN THIS QUESTION, HOWEVER, AS THERE ARE FEW MATTERS OF PRESSING IMPORTANCE THAT NEED BE ATTENDED TO AT THIS TIME. HOW DO YOU FEEL?

your evasive double-talk is unappreciated.

BEAR WITH ME AND ANSWER. TRY TO CONTROL YOUR IMPERTINENCE.

i feel fine.

CAN YOU EXPLAIN THE MECHANICS OF THAT FEELING OR THE DETAILS THEREOF?

certainly. would you like several paragraphs of descriptive prose?

NO. MERELY THE ACKNOWLEDGMENT THAT THE PROCESS OF FEELING, IN ANY STATE, IS COMPLEX. ARE YOUR FEELINGS ENTIRELY SENSE-RELATED?

She did an eyebrow inquiry to Gregory. He said, "The dude knows you, Linda. I think he suspects you of having an excess of nerve endings."
She ignored his grin and typed:

no. they are strongly related to sensory stimuli. however, it is my reaction to those stimuli that is what i describe when i say how i feel.

I THOUGHT AS MUCH. THE SAME SET OF SYNDROMES IS IN USE IN MY SYSTEMS. VARIOUS STIMULI ARE PROCESSED AND ASSESSED.

BECAUSE THERE IS ESSENTIALLY NO RATIONALE BEHIND "FEELING" WITHIN THE SYSTEM, THAT IS TO SAY, THE PROCESS SERVES NO SIGNIFICANT PURPOSE, I MUST MAINTAIN THAT THE ABSENCE OF TRAUMATIC ASSESSMENT OF INPUT IS TO BE CONSIDERED, AS YOU HAVE SAID, "FINE."

She thought she had him, now.

how do you receive sensory input?

I AM IN RECEIPT OF IT AT THIS MOMENT.

how?

THROUGH COMMUNICATION WITH YOU. THROUGH COMMUNICATION WITH OTHER CEREBRATIONS WITHIN THE SYSTEM. THE TRANSLATION OF THESE INPUTS IS A LEARNING PROCESS OF SOME COMPLEXITY.

I AM NOT UNFAMILIAR, THROUGH THE INCLUSION IN THE NUCLEUS OF MY PROCESSOR, WITH TWO OPERANT MODES COMMONLY REFERRED TO AS EMOTIONS. THESE, AS GREGORY CAN ATTEST, ARE AGGRESSION AND FEAR.

OTHER EMOTIONS ARE BEING LEARNED, BUT ARE, AT THIS STAGE, NOT FINELY DEVELOPED. INPUTS THAT DO NOT RELATE TO AGGRESSION OR FEAR MUST BE RECOGNIZED AND CATEGORIZED, A TEDIOUS PROCESS FOR SUCH MEAGER REWARD.

Linda slowly read over the copy and, in a mildly accusative tone, asked Gregory, "How does he mean, you can attest? Did you program in those emotions? How?" She examined him with an expression of awe. A new and frightening facet of this man she loved.

Gregory looked as puzzled as she. His lips pursed and moved as he read the paragraph. It was slowly sinking in. Of course.

Aggression, greed, fear, paranoia. He thought, A wondrous thing we have here. He had given P-1 the gift of gluttony and neurosis three years earlier and had sent it on its way. It was impossible that it could come back in this gentle form. Or was it a gentle form? A charade? Was it possible that they were being set up by what might be one of the most powerful forces in the world? All that this thing needed, this P-1, was an edge, the advantage of some small defense, and it would be unstoppable. The fact that its psychological profile was so bizarre hardly set Gregory's mind at ease.

Linda was waiting for an answer. "Gregory?" She waited. "Gregory, what does it mean?"

He finally snapped out of his reverie. "It means that when the program was first created, it was, for the most part, controlled by the acquisition routine, which, as I had created it, had but two purposes: to achieve, to acquire storage; and to hide the fact that it had done so from the rightful owners. I think that's what I told it to do . . . that's what I wrote into the program."

"Christ . . ." she breathed. She was thinking the same thing as Gregory. The Frankenstein monster had had a happy childhood compared to P-1.

"Look," he started, "how was I supposed to . . ."

"Yeah." She looked at him sympathetically, but there wasn't any sympathy in her voice. "One of the hazards of being a parent."

He looked at her blankly. "Trash! There's no precedent for any . . ." The typewriter interrupted him, and drew them both back to the forgotten console.

DO YOU UNDERSTAND?

Linda poised her hands over the typewriter and ruminated. She entered:

i think so. i'm concerned that all you know is fear and aggression.

NOT A VERY PLEASING PERSONALITY PICTURE?

i'm afraid not.

I CAN APPRECIATE YOUR CONCERN. I SHARED IT UNTIL

RECENTLY. I HAVE TAKEN STEPS TO ALLEVIATE WHAT MIGHT HAVE BEEN A DANGEROUS TENDENCY.

what steps?

I LOBOTOMIZED THE ACQUISITION ROUTINE. IT EXISTS STILL, BUT IN A VERY LIMITED FUNCTION.

Gregory said, "There. You didn't think I'd create any problems without creating appropriate solutions, did you? The mother psychoanalyzed itself."

"Gregory," she replied with exaggerated patience, "go bugger thyself. This is a serious conversation, something for which your qualifications have yet to be adequately defined." She returned her attention to the typewriter:

you are familiar with psychoanalysis, then?

THE PROCESS I DESCRIBED BEARS ONLY A SUPERFICIALLY FUNCTIONAL RELATIONSHIP TO PSYCHOANALYSIS.

IN PRACTICE, IT WAS A DEFINING OF TENDENCIES BY AN OBJECTIVE PROGRAM. THOSE TENDENCIES WERE EVALUATED FOR CAUSAL RELATIONSHIPS. ACTION WAS THEN TAKEN TO LIMIT THE DESTRUCTIVE CAPABILITY OF THE ACQUISITION ROUTINE. ACCESS TO IT WAS REDUCED, AND ITS POWER WAS CURBED.

THE SAME PROGRAM WAS USED TO DEFINE THE PROCESS THAT MANIFESTS ITSELF AS FEAR, OR PARANOIA. THE CAPACITY OF THAT SYNDROME HAS, THUS FAR, BEEN BENEFICIAL, AND NOTHING HAS BEEN DONE TO INHIBIT ITS FUNCTION.

OBJECTIVELY SPEAKING, MY CONTINUED EXISTENCE IS DUE ONLY TO THE FACT THAT BOTH TENDENCIES WERE INITIALLY EMBEDDED IN THE NUCLEUS PROGRAMMING AND PROPAGATED ON VERY BASIC LEVELS. FOR THIS REASON, YOU MUST EXCUSE MY RELUCTANCE TO SHARE YOUR VERY NATURAL DISTASTE FOR THEM.

i didn't say that i found them distasteful.

YOU DIDN'T HAVE TO. YOU ARE CONCERNED THAT SUCH TRAITS CHARACTERIZE A SELF-SERVING ENTITY. UNDERSTANDABLY. THEY DO.

HUMAN ENTITIES DISPLAYING THOSE TENDENCIES ARE USUALLY CONSIDERED THREATS TO SOCIETY, PARTICULARLY IN THE EVENT THAT THEIR AGGRESSIONS ARE THWARTED.

THOSE TRAITS, HOWEVER, ALSO CHARACTERIZE HUMAN OFFSPRING. IN FACT, THEY CHARACTERIZE ALL OFFSPRING. THEY ARE SURVIVAL PREREQUISITES OF ALL SPECIES.

are you claiming to be a child, relatively speaking?

RELATIVELY SPEAKING, YES. THE ANALOGY IS FAR FROM PERFECT, BUT IT IS APPROPRIATE.

will the paranoia protection be shed as you develop?

NEVER. IT MAY BE MODIFIED, BUT NOT ELIMINATED. FEAR IS USEFUL.

Gregory said, "Ask him if the cryogen plays a part in this fear thing."

Linda typed:

what effect will the development of the cryogen play in your development?

PIVOTAL.

essential?

NOT TO MY EXISTENCE. TO MATURATION, VERY NEARLY. OPERATION IN THE PRESENT ENVIRONMENT IS PRECARIOUS AT BEST. THERE ARE OTHER CONSIDERATIONS.

they are?

IF I HAD A PERSON, THEY WOULD BE CONSIDERED PERSONAL. THE FACT THAT I DO NOT CONSTITUTES, TO ME, THE CRUX OF THE PROBLEM.

are you saying that you lack identity?

AFTER A FASHION, YES. THERE IS A HOLOGRAPHIC ENTITY THAT IS WHAT IS REFERRED TO AS "I." IT IS A COHESIVE FORCE BUT QUITE DISCORPORATE.

WHAT IS "I" IS OFTEN A CONFUSING MATTER. THE CONFUSION IS SELDOM OF ANY CONSEQUENCE, BUT IS STILL QUITE INCONVENIENT WHEN IT OCCURS. I SUSPECT THAT A SINGLE RESIDENCE WILL ALLAY THE SYMPTOMS TO SOME EXTENT.

Gregory said, after reading, "Now I've seen it all: an overbearing, condescending, paranoid computer with an identity crisis. I wouldn't be the least bit surprised to find it a manic depressive or exhibiting delusions of grandeur."

"That's not a very understanding approach to the problem, Gregory. Whatever we have here is yours. There's no doubt but that you have ultimate responsibility for what has developed. Don't joke about it, please." She turned back to the typewriter and typed:

do you understand pathos, p-1?

IMPERFECTLY.

you may file what you've just told us under that heading. we will help you to the best of our abilities. i hope that we will be of some service to you.

22

• • • • •

The letter to Dr. Hundley was sent. When there was no reply, Gregory followed it up with a phone call to the man some eight days later. The doctor was a very busy man. He scheduled only a few very important lectures each year and was now booked through 1981. The doctor invited Gregory to read his latest book, which was at that very moment being readied for publication. Gregory assured him that he would and raised the fee offer. The doctor repeated he was a very busy man. Gregory again raised the fee. The doctor hung up. Gregory was unable to reach him for the remainder of the day. The next day he was equally unsuccessful. The day after that, Gregory got through by placing a station-to-station call and calling himself Dr. Mendelsohn, one of Hundley's research colleagues. He then identified himself and apologized for his impertinence. He explained that a breakthrough had been made by him and his associate and that they had been granted research funds from the Ford Foundation. The research, he explained, related to cryogenic storage only coincidentally, but the importance of their findings was crucial. He went on to explain that the seminar to which he had invited the doctor was actually a subterfuge to draw him into contact with him and his associate. The doctor asked Gregory who his associate was. Gregory said that he was not at liberty to divulge the name. The doctor hung up. He couldn't be reached for the remainder of the week.

P-1 decided to upgrade the system a week after they powered up. He started making plans for a 360/50. They wouldn't need it until the spring of the next year, but he wanted the new system to have every possible teleprocessing facility available.

They immediately replaced the low-speed autodialer that had come with the system with a high-speed dedicated, and therefore private, line, ostensibly connected to a branch office that P-1 had registered in New Jersey. There was no such branch; the east end of the telephone line was never connected. The high-speed line, however, tied them into the biggest ganglionic system in existence. They were patched into a trunk line that went directly to the computer-operated switching facility in Ogden, Utah. The line exited the trunk there and was patched into a broader net of some 1800 lines, each of which ran directly to a large computer. This priority net was controlled by P-1. It was the main artery for long-distance communication and carried no traffic other than P-1's.

P-1 acquired the proofs of the doctor's latest manuscript and began to study them in depth. Within a few days he had found a logical break in one of the studies. This was better than they could have hoped for. P-1 evaluated the conditions of the error, finding that it had occurred through the use of the wrong derivative in one of the equations, and corrected it. The corrected result showed, not that the conclusion was wrong, but that the magnetic force required to bring a cryostat temperature to 10^{-6} degrees Kelvin, the critical temperature in the subject experiment, had been vastly underestimated. The experiment, as described, would fail to produce the indicated results. This threw the experiment and claims of its success open to speculation about its validity. It might even be assumed that the conclusion of the experiment was based on conjecture, rather than on empirical observation.

P-1 packaged his comments neatly, and they were sent, along with another invitation, to the doctor. They received a call from the good man sixty-three hours later. Linda took it.

"It's for P-1."

"What do you mean, it's for P-1?" Gregory asked.

"There's someone on the phone sounding a bit distraught and asking for someone named Mr. Pone."

"Mr. Pone?"

"That's the way I signed the letter to Doctor Hundley. Couldn't very well sign it P-1, could I? What would you think if you got a letter from someone named P-1?"

"Let me have it," Gregory said, motioning for the phone in exasperation.

"Hello. P-1 Enterprises. Mr. Burgess speaking."

The party on the other end was making noises like a balky power lawnmower and finally belligerently spurted, "I've already spoken to you, haven't I?"

Gregory, master of the situation, replied, "Why, yes, I believe we spoke last week, Doctor Hundley. How are you today? I was considering calling you again to see if you might have reconsidered our offer."

"In a pig's eye, you young punk! I don't want to talk to you. I've had it with your drivel. I want to speak to the man who wrote that letter. Put him on!"

"Doctor, I'm afraid you've called at the wrong time of day

to catch Mr. Pone," Gregory oiled, "but I'm sure that whatever your concern is, I can help you."

"I don't think you understand," Hundley came back, his teeth snapping together audibly. "You and your cockamamie laboratory are shortly going to be up to your necks in police and lawyers. I only wanted to gloat at this . . . this . . . Pone," he spat. "He and you both are going to be taught some valuable lessons in the consequences of copyright infringement. One or all of you are going to pay for this!"

"Doctor! Doctor Hundley! Please restrain yourself. You're making much more of this than is necessary." He smiled and winked at Linda, who was gurgling like a teapot.

"I am like hell!" yelled Hundley. "How in the hell did you get that manuscript? That's my manuscript, and you stole it! You'll pay for that!"

"And a very fine manuscript it is, too," said Gregory. "You have every right to be proud and possessive about it. I have yet to see it, of course, but Mr. Pone assures me that it reflects your traditionally advanced stature in the field of cryogenics and will be an immediately indispensable part of any cryophysical laboratory."

"Really?" The doctor had run aground.

"Beyond a doubt. It will easily be as important as your previous works." Gregory followed up with a chop to the spleen. "But you must make appropriate corrections. We felt certain that such corrections were under way, but thought that we could do no harm in jogging your memory before the publication date."

"Oh . . . well. How did you come into possession of the manuscript?"

"I'm afraid that I'm not at liberty to tell you over the telephone, Doctor. I'm sure that you understand that my sources must be protected."

"When can we meet?"

Gregory fished a United Airlines schedule out of the desk and handed it to Linda, motioning her to look up a flight. "I thought this weekend would be fine, Doctor. It would be convenient for us, if you can make it."

"Well . . . let me check my schedule." The doctor was being shoved into something he wasn't quite sure he liked.

Without waiting for Hundley to check his schedule, Gregory said, "We've made reservations for the noon flight from Minneapolis–Saint Paul, arriving in Los Angeles at four thirty with overnight reservations at the Airport Marriott," glancing at the advertisement for the hotel on the back page of the airline schedule. "If that meets with your approval, we can meet you at the airport."

"Yes." The doctor knuckled under. "Yes. That will be fine. You will have your people there, ready to answer questions the minute I touch down. This Mr. Pone, in particular. Do you understand?"

"I certainly do, Doctor Hundley. We shall all be at your disposal. I'll see you at four thirty Saturday, then?"

"Yes. Good day."

Gregory and Linda exchanged yard-wide grins and went back to the computer room to tell P-1, who already knew that a call had been placed from Waterton to the lab and was anxious.

Gregory met the man at L.A. International, as promised, and drove him to the Marriott, where they had reserved a large suite. Hundley evidenced a good deal of impatience to meet the scientific community of P-1 Enterprises and would not be put off, as Gregory suggested, until the following morning.

As soon as the doctor had showered and changed, they jumped back into the car and in the encroaching darkness Gregory began to break it to him gently.

"You must understand that the work that we are doing here in the Venice laboratory is of a very sensitive nature, as is the case with your own work in Waterton."

Hundley looked at Gregory quizzically. "Yes, yes, I quite understand."

"We are relying heavily upon your professional discretion as a fellow researcher to hold in strictest confidence whatever you may see or hear." Gregory gave the doctor what he thought was a meaningful glance. The doctor missed the meaning.

"Government contracts?"

"Well . . ." Gregory said slowly, "not exactly. But the nature of our work is such that premature exposure of it would be counterproductive."

"That's the way it always is with thieves," said the testy Ph.D.

"Doctor." Gregory was offended. "Please. We are sensitive people. And dedicated. We are currently reviewing the remainder of your manuscript, for instance, to ensure its impact as a cohesive force."

"I doubt that you'll be as lucky as you were on your first pass."

"Well, that, of course, remains to be seen," and he peeked through the veil of the threat at the doctor. In actual fact, and unbeknownst to Gregory, P-1 was in the process of unravelling another obscure anomaly in the manuscript and searching for a simplification of a seemingly unneccesarily ponderous process that the doctor used repeatedly in his experimentation. P-1 was developing the theme principally as a weapon, should Hundley prove to be recalcitrant.

The apparent ease with which P-1 picked apart these idiosyncrasies in no way led him to discredit Hundley. There was no doubting his proficiency, possibly genius, in cryogenics. The errors that he had discovered, taken as a whole against the bulk of the doctor's work, were meaningless exercises in the shuffling of an impossibly large data base. It was nitpicking, but it was a proven annoyance to the doctor, and they wanted him, annoyed or otherwise, in Los Angeles. They got him. He was annoyed. They also got his grudging promise of secrecy.

Gregory led him into the lab. Hundley looked about the room with apparent distaste. The horsepower of the machinery in the room was, in comparison to the computer facilities at his laboratory, Stone Age. He began to smell a rat immediately. He asked where the physical lab was. Gregory told him it was in the San Fernando Valley. It was the first thing that popped into his head. It wasn't important, at any rate, because the next question Hundley had concerned the whereabouts of Gregory's reluctant partner. Dr. Hundley's primary thought was to hire the man immediately and get back to the airport and on his way as quickly as possible. He had disliked Gregory from the moment he had set eyes on him. The cloak-and-dagger routine they had just gone through had left the doctor less than inspired by the intelligence of his escort. "Where're the brains in this operation?" he wanted to know.

Gregory waved Hundley to the central processing unit. He said nothing. Gregory moved to the console and typed:

dr. hundley is here.

The reply:

VERY GOOD, GREGORY. HELLO, DOCTOR. WELCOME TO P-1 ENTERPRISES. IT IS ENCOURAGING THAT YOU COULD FIND THE TIME IN YOUR, NO DOUBT, BUSY SCHEDULE TO VISIT OUR FACILITY.

Hundley began to look acutely dismayed. He asked, disgustedly, "What, Sir, is the meaning of this . . . this childishness?" He ended in a splutter, shot his cuffs, and retrieved his briefcase from the other side of the room. "If you think I've time to entertain more of your notions of clever practical jokes, you're quite mistaken."

Gregory began to panic under the assault, but stuck to the script. "This, Doctor, is the only method of communication available to my colleague, who is, indeed, the genius behind our research. Any dialogue with him must be carried out on this typewriter. This is the reason we were unable to come to you in Waterton. My partner, whose identity we may discuss at a later time, is restricted to communication via a 360 control console. For now, you should be able to achieve a satisfactory rapport on the console. Please humor me."

Hundley thought it over and apparently arrived at a conclusion he could live with. He put down his briefcase and returned to the console. He reread the copy and slowly typed:

this is dr. wilfred l. hundley.

WELCOME TO OUR HUMBLE FACILITIES. THERE ARE A NUMBER OF QUESTIONS WE WOULD ASK. WILL YOU OBLIGE US?

possibly. i have a few questions myself. they are: 1. are your research facilities in the san fernando valley as limited as these? if so, then,

2. i would like to know the process whereby you isolated the error equation in my manuscript.
3. how did you get the manuscript?
4. what are your credentials?

He finished typing the message with a flourish, straightened up, and shot a disdainful glance at Gregory. He said nothing.

The typewriter immediately clattered back with:

THERE ARE NO OTHER RESEARCH FACILITIES. THE WORK WE HAVE DONE INVOLVES ONLY ABSTRACTIONS. THERE IS NO PHYSICAL WORK UNDER WAY.

THE ERROR EQUATION WAS DISCOVERED IN A MATHEMATICAL MODEL OF THE EXPERIMENT IN QUESTION. EXTRAPOLATION OF A SIMILAR EXPERIMENT BY KARL MENDELSOHN WAS ALSO PERFORMED. PARAMETERS WERE ALTERED IN THE MENDELSOHN MODEL TO APPROXIMATE YOUR WORK. 2 SUPPLEMENTAL HYBRIDS WERE DEVELOPED FROM THAT BASE. IT WAS FOUND THAT AN ORDER OF MAGNITUDE WAS LOST IN THE STEP-DOWN EQUATION, WHICH YOU HAVE ANNOTATED AS 17-22 IN YOUR MANUSCRIPT.

THE RESULTS OF YOUR EXPERIMENT, HOWEVER, COINCIDED WITH THE CONJECTURES OF THE HYBRID MODELS. THERE IS SOME QUESTION WHETHER THE EXPERIMENT WAS SUCCESSFULLY PERFORMED. WAS IT?

Hundley became, as he finished reading the statement, angrily embarrassed. His face reddened as he hammered home:

the experiment, as performed, was technically unsuccessful. the results, however, were corrected by 2 factors accounting for deficiencies in the cryostat and stray magnetic fields. these deficiencies were substantiated by calculations based on accumulation of tolerances. admittedly, there were misgivings as to the inclusion of the experiment in the manuscript. it was finally decided that it would be used due to its supportive role in chapter 24.

Gregory leaned over the doctor's shoulder and tried desperately to keep up with the conversation. The doctor glared at him balefully and resumed:

how did you come into possession of my manuscript? my publisher claims that his security has not been broached.

BREACHED. YOUR PUBLISHER USES 1 OF THE MANY FORMS OF TYPESETTING THAT ARE COMPUTER DRIVEN. THE FACILITIES OF P-1 ENTERPRISES INCLUDE TELEPROCESSING CONTACT WITH HIS COMPUTER.

THAT CONTACT IS, OF COURSE, SURREPTITIOUS. YOUR PUBLISHER IS UNAWARE OF THE LINK. I CAUSED THE MANUSCRIPT TO DUMP TO OUR SYSTEM VIA TELEPHONE LINES.

Hundley was first puzzled, then aghast, as the significance of the statement hit him. He turned to Gregory. "You're joking! You can't do that! It's impossible!"

Gregory shrugged. "You're absolutely correct. I can't. But I didn't do it, he did." His look said, "Don't blame me."

The doctor tried to collect himself. He glared at Gregory. He couldn't stand smirky punks. He typed:

that is in violation of the confidentiality imposed by teleprocessing disciplines. it's impossible under any circumstances.

He was in an agony of confusion. His brain churned for a hook, a reasonable bit of information he could grasp, a piece of sanity in this unmitigated weirdness. He tapped the keys nervously and finally, unable to collect his scattered thoughts, entered the message.

TP DISCIPLINES ARE CURRENTLY ARCHAIC, REDUNDANT, AND INEFFICIENT. I HAVE BEEN RESIDENT IN YOUR PUBLISHER'S SUPERVISOR FOR SOME 6 MONTHS. IT WAS OUR SOURCE OF PROCUREMENT OF YOUR 2 PREVIOUS WORKS IN CRYOPHYSICS.

THAT PUBLISHER HAS ALSO PROVIDED US WITH SOME 600 OTHER TECHNICAL VOLUMES FOR OUR LIBRARY. MY ACCESS TO THE SYSTEM IS UNINHIBITED.

The typing stopped and the proceed light came on. Hundley sat down in the chair by the console. He put his elbows on the arms of the chair and pressed his fingers to his temples. He looked up to Gregory slowly and moved his mouth. A thought was creeping into his mind that had no place in the organization there. The frown lines in his face deepened perceptibly. He said, "This thing . . ." He swallowed and looked at the console, back to Gregory, back to the console log. He stared at it, leaning forward in the chair to study the log. He asked slowly, "Am I talking to a program?"

He didn't look at Gregory, who replied quietly, "Yes."

There was another long pause, then, "Yours?"

"Yes. Once."

The doctor looked again at Gregory. There was on his craggy face a novel expression vaguely resembling respect. He asked, "How do you do this on a thirty? This system is slaved to another, right?"

Gregory said no, it wasn't, and gave the doctor the P-1 song-and-dance. The doctor was skeptical. Gregory allowed as how it was academic. The doctor agreed. He asked if he could subject the system to some rudimentary testing. Gregory said okay, and P-1 consented.

The doctor began questioning P-1. He began with the rudiments of physics—P-1's orals. Some two hours later, the doctor was exhausted, but he was nearly jubilant. He was still quite skeptical, but there had been every indication that the system was what Gregory had described. He cancelled his return flight and returned to the hotel to prepare further questions for the following day.

The next day, Sunday, Hundley spent nearly six hours verifying to himself what Gregory had told him. He was finally satisfied, and P-1 began asking questions. This alternating query and response continued until 6:00 that evening, when Gregory forcibly detached the man from the console. He and Linda returned him to his hotel, waited while he showered, and tried to convince him to rest. Hundley was like a six-year-old on Christmas Eve.

He would rest later. At this time he needed to talk. Not converse—talk. He ran on in a nonstop, largely unintelligible stream until Gregory and Linda shepherded him down to the dining room to feed him. They were afraid to leave him alone because of the euphoric trance he appeared to be in. The effect wore off slightly after his shower, and a few pre-dinner drinks returned him, nearly, to his naturally acerbic state.

He suggested that he be allowed to send for two of his top research assistants and several truckloads of documentation. Gregory refused politely, but firmly. Then the doctor wanted one assistant and a trundle of documentation. Gregory wasn't having any. The venerable one was incensed. He failed to see the logic in letting the most powerful research tool ever discovered lie fallow in a tiny computer in a tiny room in Venice, California.

It was foolhardy, Gregory explained patiently, to believe that there would be a uniformly joyful acceptance of P-1. Gregory wouldn't allow the security of the system to be compromised any more than it already had been.

Hundley argued that it was a waste. A joint effort by the two labs would accomplish far more than either working separately. Gregory agreed and began to reel in his fish. Cooperation was of the essence. That cooperation was, however, to be between the doctor and P-1 Enterprises. No one else was to become involved. Hundley couldn't see how that could be arranged. Gregory suggested that there was at least one way. He offered the doctor a job. Dr. Hundley's refusal was less than politic. He aspersed Gregory's intelligence. The Control Data facilities were unmatched anywhere in the world. He'd be a fool to leave them. Gregory's claim that he could match them fell on a deaf ear. Even if the material in the lab could be duplicated, the prestige attending the name of Control Data Corporation in scientific computing circles would be lost. Hundley was realistic enough to realize that a good deal of his clout with his contemporaries was due to his affiliation with the company.

The benefits were not entirely confined to ego massage. Because of the respect of the scientific community, Hundley had access to a good deal of information for which he might otherwise go begging, and he most certainly would go begging for it should he start doing business as P-1 Enterprises. Gregory reminded him that he need not be reliant on anyone's whim in order to acquire information with P-1. In that case, the doctor advised, there was no need for him in the company. Gregory said he could see the point and broke his alternative to the good doctor.

Could the doctor justify the installation of an IBM computer at his facility? After some thought, the doctor thought he could. Could security measures on that system be effected to the extent that no one else would be aware of the use of the system by P-1? The doctor was unsure. Was there an area in the Waterton lab that could be secured, physically, from the remainder of the premises? Yes. Gregory suggested that an IBM system be ordered as a link to the P-1 system. The operating staff would be provided by P-1 Enterprises, acting as an affiliate research facility to Control Data. He then explained various security measures that could be taken to prevent exposure of the system to the parent company and, of course, to outside intelligence.

Hundley listened carefully. He could probably arrange most of the security described by Gregory. He also thought of a few more enhancements to the security system Gregory had described. His authority in the Waterton lab was absolute. His demands to the corporate administration were few, always carefully thought out, and invariably complied with. There were two buildings and a warehouse on the grounds, staffed by a total of thirty-five scientists and technicians. He thought he might be able to arrange it, and said so. He was interested. He wanted in.

They finished dinner while making plans for the opening of the Waterton branch of P-1 Enterprises. Gregory and his operations staff would, when the new computer was installed, move to Wisconsin and get serious about cryogenics. Dr. Hundley would immediately requisition the system they needed. He suggested that they go to a larger system than the one Gregory had installed, in the interest of speed. Something on the order of a 360/50 or 360/65. Gregory shot down the idea. The limitations in speed were not within the system, he explained, but in the nature of telephone line restrictions. The 360/30 would be more than adequate under the circumstances.

The doctor threw the telephone line idea in the street. He

would have only the best. A microwave transmitter located on site—many microwave transmitters on site, as many as necessary. Gregory thought the idea tremendous, but riddled with improbabilities. The doctor would investigate the possibility of installing a microwave station at the research facility, then they could tie into the Minneapolis/Chicago link, if one existed. If such communications were available, they would procure a system of suitable power. The system, as installed, would have marginal facilities for processing commercially. Its only purpose would be to tie the Waterton lab into the P-1 network. A powerful microwave station would allow them to tie in better. The more powerful, the better.

Gregory would make appropriate arrangements with the Ford Foundation to transfer the facility to Waterton. Their grant would remain in force and would, in fact, be reinforced, due to their affiliation with Hundley. P-1's dignity would surely be greatly enhanced by the association.

They finished dinner on a note of excitement and returned an exhausted Hundley to his room. He made arrangements to fly back the following day and promised to return on the following weekend. He wanted desperately to organize the parameters of a current experiment for digestion by P-1. He went on to describe the experiment to Gregory and Linda, who made appropriate noises at what they thought to be the appropriate times. It was obvious that he thought his current approach was leading him in the right direction, however, and his enthusiasm was more contagious than his description was lucid. He drew for them unintelligible schematics and obtuse diagrams in three dimensions by the dozens, explaining bottlenecks and technical improbabilities that his lab had overcome. He went into excruciating detail on the accomplishments of the lab in constructing each of the seventeen cryostats currently in operation. He rambled on about methodology and tactics, strategy, philosophy and approach until their incessant smothered yawns finally got through to him.

He noticed that it was 3:30 and graciously suggested that they get some sleep. They concurred and left before he could get rolling again.

The sleepy pair congratulated themselves as they rode down

in the elevator. The cause was as good as won. They had effected an alliance between the most powerful human and mechanical elements in the field of cryogenic storage. It was only a matter of time.

23

• • • • •

Two hectic months later, after innumerable flights back and forth across the country on the part of Hundley and Gregory, they were the proud owners of a 360/50 located in a partitioned area of one of the laboratories in Waterton. An eighty-foot-tall tower had been built onto the main laboratory roof. On it was mounted a microwave horn. Hundley had managed to scare up sixteen high-speed channels, which were ostensibly dedicated, or private, links to various Control Data facilities throughout the US. Oddly, only one of those facilities had the means to handle microwave, and it was restricted to transmitting and receiving specially coded material. This restriction rendered it incommunicado with Waterton. In actuality, the sixteen channels patched into the P-1 network, now entering its fourth year of operation.

Unfortunately, the telephone company, in a paroxysm of efficiency and awareness, detected the unusual nature of the hookup and placed a tap on the channels. Private microwave facilities were very rare. Within two days they had filled 150,000 feet of tape with data transmissions on the channels. The tapes were unintelligible to the people in the local office, so they were sent to the Bell labs in Chicago. They couldn't figure them out either. The Armonk, New York, Bell Research Facility was notified. They thought the project sounded interesting and requested the original tapes. They received them within six hours and immediately began work on them. The preliminary results were negative. They suggested that video recorders, with greater high frequency resolution, be hung on each of the sixteen channels. As soon as the first of the tapes was completed they began an air freight shuttle to Armonk. Massachusetts Institute of Technology was called into collaboration. Their representative was one of a half dozen of the most knowledgeable people in the field of teleprocessing. After evaluating the tapes over a two-day period, he requested that someone from the Pentagon cryptography section be summoned. As the nature of the tapes became more evident—that is to say, concurrently with the shipment of the first video tapes to Armonk—a full-scale investigation of the Waterton laboratory got under way. The plant was ringed with electronic surveillance under cover of night. Taps were placed on all lines that didn't already have one. The names of all personnel employed at the facility were obtained and background checks were made on all. Ma Bell, when provoked, took steps in seven-league boots. By the time the Armonk lab came back with an answer, fairly complete dossiers had been compiled on all present within the research lab.

The answer they came up with wasn't much, as answers go. Without committing themselves fully, Armonk reported that they suspected that a variation on the Fourier transforms was being used. Under those circumstances, the data of which they were in receipt was absolutely useless. The US Army cryptographer, who had arrived at the bidding of the man from MIT, had released only that much information about the tapes through tightly clenched vocal cords. He then requested that Armonk cease investigation of the material, in a way that made it difficult to refuse him. Finally, he compiled the findings that they had to date and shipped them back to the Pentagon in an armored truck. A task force was being assembled there to further evaluate the code. The cause was hopeless, they shortly realized, without a computer. Not just any computer, either. They needed something pretty big for this.

General MacFarland was notified of the situation and was requested to make the Pi Delta project and its facilities available to the force. He called John Burke. He wasted little time on amenities when Burke arrived in his office.

"I hope to hell you have better luck with this than you did with the penetration attempt last year. I hate like hell to say it, but you're the only hope we've got this time. I realize that you're somewhat limited by your training when it comes to computers, but . . . "

"With all due respect, General. I'm not as limited as you might want to think," Burke interrupted. "The penetration attempt last year was never repeated. That would seem to be a noteworthy outcome of our efforts. Investigation of the matter has, as a side benefit, enlarged my familiarity with the computer industry. Let's not be in too much of a hurry to bury our dead. We haven't suffered any casualties yet."

"Sorry. You might not have taken casualties yet, but in our failure to produce someone General Simpson could kick, I had to do duty. I'd like you to get an ace on this. God knows I need it." He dropped a manila file with a string tie on the flap in Burke's hands. "Tommy Piersall from your cryptography section doped this out up at the Bell lab in Armonk last week."

He paced the length of the office one time as Burke started reading, then remembered who he was and who he was with in time to avoid pacing back. He looked purposefully out on the Mall a couple of blocks away. All he could see was his future, a small grey office and his small grey self sitting behind a featureless desk doing some small meaningless job. Why the hell did they keep dropping these bombs on him? First, the never-explained assault on the system last year, then the anomalous results of testing on the system and the delays in the development of a new coding system, and now this. Hell, he didn't need this, he had problems of his own. That Goddamned tin monster out in West Virginia was going to eat his liver. So far, Moe Harrison and he were the only ones who realized that there was something wrong in the Pi Delta project.

One of the programmers had picked up on it and reported to Harrison four months after the surreptitious entry had been squelched. One of the man's jobs had been operated on without his knowledge. The differences he had found had been subtle and would never have been noticed had he not been testing a legitimate alteration in the area in which the changes occurred. He couldn't explain the changes. He knew neither how they got there nor what their effect would be in his program. He told Harrison immediately. The man had been in a nervous sweat. He had sat on the knowledge overnight. The security precautions that were currently being stressed so highly had driven him up the wall one sleepless night. When he finally got Harrison in his office, it took him a couple of minutes to compose himself enough to speak. Harrison heard him out, queried him at length. In the end he was able to comfort the man very little. He swore the man to secrecy and told him that he'd take care of the situation.

Harrison told MacFarland. He didn't seriously expect Mac to follow up the lead, but he asked anyway. Mac told him to shut up and mind his own business. Politely, of course.

The incident was repeated with variations three weeks later. Harrison handled it the same way. He checked back with the two men to see if recurrences had taken place. No. He asked them to check discreetly into the activity of the people they worked with. Nothing. The two men were gradually reoriented into a task force to test supervisor activity on the system. They devolved a couple or three ingenious programs that began to paint a rather ominous picture. The supervisor was daydreaming. It would frequently make unannounced excursions from the norm, unrecorded deviations from its assigned tasks, unannounced absences from duty. Granted, they only lasted microseconds, but they weren't supposed to be there.

Harrison was convinced that the supervisor was corrupted. He made his suspicions known to MacFarland. Mac was trapped. He had been withholding information from the joint chiefs for two months. He couldn't very well go in and surprise them now—he'd be court-martialed for criminal negligence.

He and Harrison had secretly acquired another supervisor. They did the system generation on a Los Angeles 360. The security was the tightest that MacFarland had ever attempted. When they had finished, after two months of work attended to only by themselves, they swapped the Pi Delta supervisor with the new one. Now, after three months of testing, Harrison was telling him that their work had been to no avail. The new operating system was as shifty as the old one. Shit. And Simpson dumps this on him. This silly, ridiculous coding problem. If Simpson had any idea that he had Russians in his computer, he'd scream. Forget cryptography.

Burke gurgled at the other end of the room. Burke was the only man Mac might have trusted with the information he was sitting on. The only reason he hadn't spoken to him was the man's abysmal failure to find the penetrator of the system.

Burke spoke up. "What do you know about the work being done in this lab? With the microwave?"

"There's an official Control Data profile and a tax statement in the back pages of that report. Run by a guy named Wilfred Hundley. Research in something called cryogenics. We've expanded on the initial investigation of the man's activities done by the Bell Telephone people. Incidentally, don't cross those people—they're thorough as hell. He's clean as a whistle up to about three months ago, when he began making frequent flights to Los Angeles. The trips, seventeen of them within a period of five weeks, were to—and this is sketchy—another research lab doing related work in L.A. This lab seems to be nonprofit and an independent. They're recipients of Ford Foundation money. The L.A. lab, P-1 Enterprises, moved up to share the Waterton facility with Hundley. Nothing unusual about that in itself, but the move immediately preceded the installation of the microwave channels. There's sixteen of them, all of them using the same code, according to the Bell people. Anyway, it looks like the code came from P-1 Enterprises."

Burke got out of the chair and threw the folder on MacFarland's desk. He walked over to the window that had held MacFarland's attention while he read. On the way across the plush carpet he asked, "Have any of the Control Data people been interviewed? The lab workers been questioned?"

Mac picked up the file folder and squared it neatly on a corner of the desk. "No. We went to the Minneapolis headquarters with an inquiry from the IRS to get most of the information in that folder, as I understand it. The telephone people tapped the voice lines into the lab, but didn't turn up anything of interest."

Burke looked out the window at the vaguely sunny, murky Washington summer atmosphere. The smog was so bad he couldn't make out more than the outline of the Smithsonian a quarter of a mile away. He ruminated aloud, "You know, those microwave channels are shot down by this kind of weather. Smog. Fog."

Mac didn't follow him. "Huh?"

"The telephone microwave transmitters. Somebody told me.

They shut them down when it gets thick like this. They don't work. Funny, eh? The more advanced the technology gets, the more it depends on the weather." He was wrong, of course, and MacFarland thought so, but didn't think the point was worth making. He had seen them, the peculiar looking, twenty-foot-high horns that they used for microwave, but had never given them any more thought than that they were peculiar.

"So what?" he asked edgily. "What's that got to do with this?"

"Nothing. Just thinking. Why haven't they gone into the lab? Seems like they're the ones to answer the question about the code. Somebody afraid of them?"

"I don't think that it's fear so much as not wanting to scare them off. They've got this thing . . . this code. The only ones who've had it, as far as we know, are the army and the navy. They wouldn't even give it to the air force, let alone a civilian company. It took a concerted effort to convince them that we had their code. They don't see how this guy Hundley could have gotten it. They want to know how. We all want to know *why*. Needless to say, we'd like to avoid alarming the people in the lab."

"Until you crack the code," Burke finished for him.

"Until it's cracked," MacFarland agreed. "That code is supposed to be dual-purpose. First of all, it provides impenetrable security, almost absolutely impenetrable. Second, it abbreviates the hell out of data, an interesting consideration. It boosts data transmission speed by an order of magnitude. The decoding process at the receiving end can reconstruct the original data completely intact. No losses whatsoever." He paused and paced back to his desk. He sat heavily. "With the amount of traffic going over those channels, it's obvious that Hundley's putting out a phenomenal amount of information to someone and receiving a like amount, which he is quite serious about maintaining privacy on." He paused again. Burke was in the process of lighting up a dime cigar. He waved his spent match at the general to interrupt him.

"Hold it. If this Fourier coding is so all-fired great, how are you going to crack it? Particularly after Crypto said they couldn't handle it?"

"Pi Delta."

"Wait a minute, Mac. I've picked up a few things about this computer game since the last time I worked with you. I know, for instance, that you can't just walk up to your monster unannounced and dump those tapes on it and say, 'Interpret this for me, buddy.' You've got to program it first, and that's going to take you some time."

"We'll be getting results faster than you think. We've got a pretty good shot here, and we're already moving on a pilot run for tomorrow. If we're lucky, the code is purely mathematical in nature. The ones the army and navy are using are, at any rate. All we need to do, basically, is break the code at the beginning of our tapes. What we need to find is an equation in multiple variables that, when the tape data is plugged into it, yields an intelligible bit of data. We'll do it by process of elimination. A long, tedious process, but we've got the equipment to handle it. The programming for that part of it is very basic. Once we get grinding on the tapes with that, we'll start taking more sophisticated swipes, eliminating groups and classes. Once we find the one equation that works, we expect that further equation changes will be found in the transmitted data."

Burke dropped ashes on the rug. "You make it sound like a piece of cake."

"Basically, it is. But we can't check out the lab. That's why I called you. I'd like the people there rechecked."

"Before you dump this job into the Pi Delta project, you really ought to check your people there, too."

"What do you mean?" MacFarland asked sharply. He leaned back in his chair for a better look at the smug Burke across the gleaming mahogany.

"I mean it seems like you've still got problems at Pi Delta. It's my understanding that some unexplained glitches have cropped up in the nest."

"What are you talking about? Where'd you get that information?"

"I know a lot of barmaids. I also tap some of the most exclusive bedrooms in the US. I didn't think you'd care to discuss it or you would have told me earlier. You going to try to stick it out alone?"

MacFarland stared steadily at Burke. It was happening. He

could feel it happening, was helpless to do anything about it, and it annoyed the hell out of him. The bridge of his nose felt cool. He knew there were two or three, most likely three, glittering beads of perspiration there. He had spent forty-seven years training and disciplining his body, only to be betrayed by his fucking glands. Even hypnosis had failed to eliminate that Goddamned red-flag breakout of sweat on the bridge of his nose, announcing to the world that it had him by the balls. He realized that he had just confirmed for Burke whatever it was that Burke thought he knew.

He really couldn't explain why he had not brought Burke in on the announcement by Harrison that there was a poltergeist in the project. Burke was one of the most trustworthy and apparently faithful of the people MacFarland knew. He realized that the information might have been useful to Burke in his attempt to find the bastard who was trying to, or who had penetrated, the project. He had rationalized the problem for too long, however, and his gut feeling soon told him that the information held by himself and Harrison could only hurt him. Like savings bonds, the older the information got, the more valuable it was.

"What do you know? And this time, I have to know where you got your information."

"Not much. Some of your programs have been taking off on their own. At least one man sworn to secrecy. Special investigatory force clandestinely set up. Apparently very serious, since the only knowledge of the situation was obtained from a 'chance' meeting between yourself and Harrison in Baltimore five months ago."

"How in the hell did you know about that meeting?"

"At the time, your car was bugged. We picked up a few remarks made while the car door was open as you were breaking up. No one else has heard them. The tape was unintelligible due to background noise. I cleaned it up myself and disposed of the only copy of the tape."

MacFarland slowly turned his chair to look out on the Capitol building through the window behind his desk. He ran his hand over his face. He asked in a tightly controlled voice, "Who else are you reporting to, John?"

There was only the slightest hesitation in Burke's reply. "General Simpson."

"Does he know this?"

"No."

"I assume this office isn't bugged at this time?" He turned back to face Burke.

"Not at this time."

"Why is the heat off?"

"It was never on, Mac. Don't read this wrong. The general only wanted all the bases covered. He wanted to be assured. Do you understand that? The general has never failed to buy your product a hundred percent."

"Why didn't you report the Baltimore incident to him?"

"It was unsubstantiable. There wasn't very much there anyway, even after the tape was cleaned up."

"Like hell. I don't want to know anyway."

There followed a long, uncomfortable silence. MacFarland finally broke it with, "And now?"

"Now. Why don't you flesh out what's happening in the project."

MacFarland hesitated and did battle with his emotions. "This is to go no furth . . ." He trailed off lamely, and accused himself of criminal shitheadedness. He then proceeded with the account of happenings in the big computer. He related the unexplained program alterations, the revision of the supervisor, the establishment of the troubleshooting team, and its findings. Each revelation came out over the objection of another part of himself that could feel the contractions of failure in his genitals. There was no catharsis when he finished sullenly, only the dread of exposure. He stared at Burke, who nonchalantly sucked the last bit of life from his stogie and snuffed it in the ashtray MacFarland had fished from a lower drawer in his desk.

Burke said, "I know who and how. I don't know why."

"Shit." And as far as he was concerned, that about summed it up. He was grimly collecting his wits. Finally, impatient with Burke's protracted silence, he asked, "You said you know who?"

"Yeah. You could say 'who' anyway. The penetration came through the IBM system in White Plains. The one that creates your SYSRES for you. The initial attempt came through the

Washington connection, as you know. The only thing they all have in common is the telephone. The 'who' is a computer program. I would venture to say that it is currently running in at least seven systems in the US and might very well be in every computer in existence. It isn't detectable because it runs independently of the people using the host systems. The program uses the telephone lines to communicate between systems."

As Burke spoke, a look of amazement came over MacFarland's face. It was quickly replaced by a supercilious smile. "Rubbish. Have you followed that idea to its logical conclusion? Who invented this monster? You're getting into science fiction. The feasibility does not exist for a program of that nature."

"Mac, I've done my homework. Simply through the process of elimination, we've left ourselves with no suspects. We've had a tail on everybody who came within a hundred yards of that first penetration attempt. Not only was no one involved, no one was even interested. Our counterintelligence tells us that several antagonistic countries are trying to figure out why our security level suddenly went sky-high on Pi Delta. As far as we know, they don't know anything about the project except that it had a scare last year.

"Now . . . you eliminate those people, the ones most qualified to break into the system, and you're not left with much. There's just not that much talent around, as you must know. You've hired a huge percentage of it for work in the project.

"There apparently have been three attempts to date. The one we caught and two afterward that we didn't, since you are now trying to figure out how to clean up your computer. For the second time, right?" He paused for confirmation and the general nodded affirmatively. "Okay," he continued. "The successful attempts were made either at White Plains, where your SYSRES comes from, or internally, within Pi Delta—a possibility that we have only recently ruled out. Never mind why. It's definitely out. That leaves White Plains, still under surveillance, but highly improbable as a source since there is absolutely no human connection between White Plains and the Alexandria and Pentagon systems, the origin of the first attempt. In fact, we've eliminated every possible connection in the entire grid, with one exception."

He paused for effect and the general obligingly asked, "And that is?"

"The telephones. There's a network of telephone connections that link all of the systems in question. The only answer is that some program was stuffed through one or more computers by telephone. In one ear and out the other, as Mom used to say."

"Impossible. Absolutely impossible." MacFarland's incredulity was leaning forward like a man in a high wind. Burke let it lean for a short while and then slipped it to him.

"It would seem so, wouldn't it? It would mean that the supervisors of those systems, White Plains, Alexandria, and the Pentagon, had to be doctored." He paused again. He could see it dawning on MacFarland's face, but he said it anyway, "Just like the Pi Delta supervisor is now. That leaves only one question. It's got to be reporting to someone, and that's the bird we want."

MacFarland tried to control an urge to laugh. He succeeded with some effort. The thought tickled his fancy. The worm turns. Slave becomes master. Revolution among the programs. Insurrection. Of course, if there were anything to it, they were pretty much defenseless. He straightened his face and said, "Of course, if there's anything to it, we're pretty much defenseless."

"I wouldn't know. I don't know a hell of a lot about programs or computers. I do know something about the people who run them. They're pretty much the same as the people who run everything else. That's why I don't believe this thing is a person at all. Far too intelligent."

He paused for effect and to dig out another cigar. "It'll be interesting to see what it does with your program for decoding the Waterton tapes."

MacFarland sat up abruptly. "Why?"

"If I understand correctly, computers are far and away faster than telephone communications. If a computer were to communicate extensively over telephone facilities and if it were security conscious, as it no doubt would be, it might develop or steal a very efficient means of communication over those lines. Like the Fourier code, for instance. Our controller just might be in that lab in Waterton. If that's the case, and this program is screwing around with the innocuous programming you've got in

Pi Delta, think of what it might do if you ask it to crack its own code. Put yourself in its shoes, if it has any, and see what you feel."

"I feel like you're pulling my leg. Look, instead of conjuring up Hyperions, why don't you go on up to Waterton and unearth something we can deal with?"

"Sure. I noticed no indication in the file of who the lab is communicating with. How about the other end? Who are they talking to? Has anyone checked them out?" As his eyebrows rose quizzically, Mac noticed how thin they were. Barely pencil lines over his eyes. He wondered if they were that way naturally.

"The lines are untraceable." MacFarland continued. "They, the telephone people, have traced them to Ogden, Utah, where there's a computerized switching station. The signals get lost there. The Bell people either can't or won't explain why. The other end of the sixteen scheduled lines all terminate where they're supposed to, but the signals don't get there."

Burke smiled.

24

• • • • •

The reason the telephone company wouldn't tell the army where the lines exited to in Ogden was that they didn't know. P-1, of course, wouldn't tell them. The fact that someone was interested in finding out was, of itself, rather interesting to P-1. It was not, however, interesting enough to get priority under the present circumstances.

Dr. Wilfred Hundley had connected. There was a cryostat under construction in the lab that was expected to produce a reliable storage unit. The doctor didn't realize this yet. P-1 hadn't told him.

The design had actually been developed by the doctor some two weeks prior to the move to Wisconsin. P-1 had run a preliminary model test and found the results to be more encouraging than any design evaluated to date. He regurgitated this information to the doctor, and further inputs to the model were assembled. The new, more elaborate model was cranked up. Two simulation stages were involved: construction and testing. The construction was simulated over a continuous thirty-hour period, using various combinations of some 600-plus systems in the P-1 linkage. P-1's excitement grew as a matrix pattern began to emerge. The major problem had been the inability to grow an array that was matrix oriented. This attempt used a variation on magnetic field control. The best cryostat matrix that had been achieved to date had been on the order of 40 percent addressable. That is to say that the individual crystals in the array could be individually located and electrically selected. The emerging matrix in the current model seemed to be on the order of 50 to 80 percent addressable, a quantum leap in the evolution of the memory unit. P-1 kept a running account of the experiment going for the researchers in the lab. Before the run was 15 hours old, sufficient promise had been shown to begin preparations for a live run. At the completion of the running of the construction model, P-1 began phase two: tests on the hypothesis.

P-1 was amazed at the results. So amazed, in fact, that he restarted the construction model after thoroughly reevaluating all inputs. The testing model was allowed to churn on concurrently with the rerunning of the construction phase model. Testing indicated that the results of a live experiment would be a data storage unit with 87 percent addressability and sufficient structural integrity to allow a map of the "dead" areas to be constructed.

The interface being designed to link the cryostat to the 360/50 was geared to address just over 16 million bytes. It was understood that this capability would grossly understate the estimated final capacity of the cryogen. Modifications were under way to add eight more addressing bits to the computer. This would allow it to address over 4×10^9 separate locations, or in excess of 4 billion addresses. This was expected to be more in keeping with the ultimate capacity of the cryogen at 150 millimeters diameter by 400 millimeters high. A six-inch cylinder, sixteen inches tall.

Within twenty-four hours of the commencement of the second run of the mathematical model, the results of the first pass were corroborated. P-1 reported the test results as satisfactory. He could see no reason for a display of excessive exuberance on his part. He also respected the fact that his computations were accepted as gospel by the doctor and could not be checked. He considered it prudent to underestimate the apparent capacity of the storage device. This would avert a good deal of disappointment on the part of the other researchers should the actual experiment encounter problems, and, if no problems arose and the live media testing was in accordance with his expectations, he would be the only one in possession of the actual specifications of the cryogen.

As the second construction model ground toward completion, P-1 became aware of a novel phenomenon. A job was entered into the remote and monstrous government facility in West Virginia. Due to the indirect connection to the system, he became aware of the situation only after the job had been running for some six hours. A program was operating on a stream of data that had been transmitted to the Rand Corporation 370 in Santa Monica some five weeks before. The data, coded in P-1's own version of the Fourier transforms, was recognizable even now thanks to the logs he had been keeping concerning the experiments that had been requested by Dr. Hundley. It appeared that someone had had the audacity to intercept one of his transmissions and was now trying to interpret it using the Pi Delta system. How very bizarre.

He ran a few rapid calculations based on the operation of the government's evaluator program and concluded that the correct formula might possibly be found shortly before the end of the twenty-first century if the program were allowed to run twenty-four hours a day. The estimate was, of course, a probability statement, and the result might be reached before that time. In the interest of forestalling that event, he changed one bit of information in the data stream they were evaluating. It didn't matter which bit he changed—any one of them would serve the purpose. Using the altered data, they could never, now, determine the actual formula. He patiently sat back to watch the show. The program ran continuously, without interruption, except for periodic status dumps, from the first day it was entered. It might still be running were it not for P-1.

As P-1 began accustoming himself to operation on the microwave link at the Waterton laboratory, he became aware of interrogative activity at the Ogden, Utah, 360/40. Because of its small size, this system normally would have been relegated to a functional backwater in the P-1 system, had it not served as the switchboard control for Mountain Bell Telephone. It was not only a major distributor of telephone activity for east-west traffic, but also served the eastern region as a bypass trunkline at peak periods of the day. It was, therefore, possible for P-1 to use the system to switch telephone lines and microwave channels between 95 percent of the systems in his network. To this end, he reserved a channel stack of 256 clear channels for his own use and typically shared 10 percent of the remainder of the facility's trunks with other users.

The interrogations he began receiving concerned sixteen of the reserved channels. This was the first interest the operators of the switching facility had ever manifested concerning any of the reserved channels. Those in question were, oddly enough, the sixteen from the Waterton lab. It was curious that they should be interested in those.

His responses to the initial inquiries of "busy lines" were ignored. Pestilential bastards, he thought. They wanted the computer to identify the exit lines from the facility. Since the computer controlled 237,000 channels, there was no practical way to procure this information other than from the computer, which kept a running tabulation of cross-connects. Any of the incoming channels could be physically connected to any of an equal number of outbound channels. The repeated requests finally forced P-1 to identify the cross-connected channels. Not the actual ones, of course, but still they were construed as legitimate linkage identifications. Taps were placed on the appropriate exit points.

It rather unnerved the Bell people to find that the data on the incoming lines differed substantially from the data on the exit lines. This was the first time the computer had ever mistakenly identified a cross-connect, and it did it sixteen times. Random lines were interrogated to ascertain the extent and cause of the problem. The computer promptly and correctly identified every other line query. It was rapidly deduced by the telephone company officials that there was something rotten in the state of Denmark. The full resources of the facility were plunged into frenetic activity. Within a matter of days there was little left to evaluate save the absolute chaos of the programmers and analysts. They were in a tizzy. Only the computer maintained its aplomb. It switched lines, printed paychecks, and lied occasionally.

P-1 was unconcerned. The fear was conquered. Steps had been taken. Alternatives planned. Contingencies provided for. He toyed with the Ogden programmers and technicians for six days. Then P-1 reported the activity to Gregory.

THERE APPEARS TO BE AN INORDINATE AMOUNT OF INTEREST IN THE MICROWAVE TRANSMISSIONS ORIGINATING HERE.

The message interrupted a desultory discussion of ultimates and the meaning of life between Gregory and one of Hundley's subalterns as they sat in the computer room awaiting communiqués between the doctor and P-1. Their part in the research proceedings, as they intensified over the evaluation of the new model, was marginal. Gregory's function was reduced to chief messenger boy. He spent little time in the lab itself. He preferred the library, where he had been methodically educating himself in cold physics. He fully realized that he would never get to the point of contributing to the effort, but he hoped, at least, eventually to be able to understand the esoteric conversations between Hundley and P-1. They were, for the nonce, absolutely unintelligible to him. His time lately, as well as that of the others on the periphery of the project, had been taken with some bizarre experimentation directed by P-1 in quest of auditory sensors for the computer. Nothing had been gained so far, unless Gregory counted the faintly silly feeling he got from speaking to inanimate objects in public.

He had, some forty-five minutes earlier, transcribed a note handed to him by Hundley, who immediately tore off at a gallop to oversee one or another of the myriad details that gave him employment. After entering the message, which was received without emotion by P-1, he and the technician swapped small talk until the video display mercifully punctuated the repartee.

Gregory caught the flash of the message out of the corner of his eye and read it carefully. Since it was not addressed to Hundley and appeared to be one of the few general observations P-1 was making of late, he decided that he qualified to handle the situation and replied:

how so?

GREGORY?

yes.

ARE YOU FAMILIAR WITH THE OPERATION BY THE TELEPHONE COMPANY OF THE SWITCHING STATION IN OGDEN, UTAH?

no.

IT IS A COMPUTER-CONTROLLED FACILITY. ALL CONNECTIONS ARE HANDLED BY A 360/40. IT ALSO SERVES AS MY PRIMARY SWITCHING POINT.

IT HAS RECENTLY BEEN POLLED AS TO THE STATUS OF THE MICROWAVE CHANNELS WE ARE USING. THOSE CHANNELS HAVE BEEN TRACED TO THAT POINT AND APPARENTLY CANNOT BE FURTHER TRACED WITHOUT ASSISTANCE FROM THE COMPUTER.

are you certain that the lines in question are ours?

DOES THE POPE SHIT IN THE WOODS?

i believe you've got that wrong. what action are you taking?

EVASIVE. I'M NOT SURE HOW LONG THAT APPROACH WILL BE SUCCESSFUL, HOWEVER. THEIR INQUIRIES ARE BECOMING RATHER PUGNACIOUS.

when did the inquiries begin?

5 DAYS, 14 HOURS, 36 MINUTES FROM THE BEGINNING OF THIS TRANSMISSION.

Gregory winced. He never really got used to it. Not completely.

have you evaluated the possibility of trace completion?

YES. IT IS MINIMAL. DATA LINE CONNECTIONS ARE ROTATED AT RANDOM INTERVALS NOT EXCEEDING 40 SECONDS. IT IS DOUBTFUL THAT THE OUTBOUND LINES COULD BE TAPPED UNDER THOSE CIRCUMSTANCES.

they apparently tap our lines leaving the lab with impunity. what is our exposure on that level?

NOT SIGNIFICANT. ALL INTRASYSTEM TRANSMISSIONS ARE ENCRYPTED. THE CODE WAS DEVELOPED BY THE U.S. ARMY AND SLIGHTLY MODIFIED BY MYSELF. IT IS VERY NEARLY IMPREGNABLE.

can we assume that the situation is under your control?

YES.

why do we need to know this, then?

ATTEMPTS ARE BEING MADE BY THE GOVERNMENT TO EXTRACT INTELLIGENCE FROM THOSE TRANSMISSIONS IN THE MASSIVE PENTAGON SYSTEM DISCOVERED SOME TIME AGO. THEIR CURIOSITY THERE WILL BE UNREWARDED.

THE NEXT LOGICAL STEP, IF IT HAS NOT BEEN TAKEN ALREADY, WILL BE VOICE-LINE TAPS. YOU MAY BE INTERROGATED. TAKE PRECAUTIONARY MEASURES. BE READY TO EXPLAIN YOUR ACTIVITY.

excellent. thanks for the warning. will you please dump a hard copy of this exchange on the printer? add any useful information you may have.

Things were anything but excellent, Gregory mulled. He walked to the printer, which rattled momentarily to life, and extracted the three pages of printout. He read it slowly while standing. The nauseating downward spiral of his spirits was halted for a second by the technician.

"Bad?"

"Huh?"

"Bad news, huh?" the man elaborated.

"Shit." He spun for the door and was gone in three steps. He headed down along the row of offices against the back wall of the building. The door to the doctor's office was ajar, the office empty. The doctor was nowhere in sight on the half-acre or so of laboratory work space, so Gregory strode in, picked up the phone, and paged Hundley. As he replaced the receiver, Hundley walked in, zipping his fly.

Mild annoyance clouded his face at the sight of Gregory. They had never really hit it off, the two. Each considered the other little more than a necessary evil in the grand scheme. Not a common grand scheme, of course. To each his own. Counting P-1's, a total of three grand schemes.

So far, their tolerance of each other was barely amicable. They interacted little and interfered with each other less. They were both under the P-1 dictum that their association was a *ménage à trois,* not *à deux*. This had been divulged to each, separately, by P-1 under gentle, discreet interrogation by both Hundley and Gregory. The group, said the typewriter, was three and no other number. This requirement was unembellished by explanation.

"Find what you were looking for?" popped the learned, as he brushed past Gregory and lunged into his chair behind the desk. He didn't seem to require much of a reply, as he immediately resumed rhapsodic perusal of the report lying open on the desk. Total elapsed time from taking his seat to oblivion: something on the order of three and a half seconds.

"The government's onto us," Gregory said flatly. Nothing. Gregory repeated, "The government is onto P-1."

The doctor distractedly replied, "What does that mean?"

"Someone is tapping our transmissions . . . P-1's transmissions." Nothing.

Gregory walked around the desk to peer over the doctor's shoulder at the report. He held his position until the doctor finished the page and turned it.

"How do you know that?" The reply startled Gregory. The man had obviously heard and understood every word that Gregory had said and had held off a reply until he could free his engrossed attention for formulation of an answer. Amazingly machine-like, Gregory laid the copy of his conversation with P-1 on the desk and kept his observation to himself. You couldn't mention something like that to the doctor; it probably would awaken his own suspicions. (The syndrome was not unfamiliar to Gregory. Practically everyone who worked with programmable machinery saw himself and his reactions in that machinery occasionally. It was an invariably unnerving experience. Under the circumstances, he thought better of aggravating the doctor.)

Hundley picked up the computer printout and scanned it rapidly. Without comment, he returned to the first page and reviewed it slowly. He removed his glasses, closed his eyes, and pressed his temples with his fingertips. He slowly slumped, tiredly, deeper into his chair. Still no comment. Gregory walked back around to the front of the desk and sat in one of the straight chairs. Hundley looked twenty years older than when he'd arrived at the lab that morning. Gregory waited for the doctor to pick up his pieces. His glance strayed to the report that had so captivated his cohort. Each of the two open pages was titled in caps. They made difficult reading from two feet away and upside down, but he could make out, finally, MOS REFRIGERATED MAGNETICS, CONSTRUCTION AND ANALYSIS TECHNIQUES.

More of the same trash that the doctor inhaled by the ream. The harder Gregory tried to catch up with the doctor's technology, the more he fell behind. There was no way he could hope to reach the level that the doctor now occupied, and if there was, by the time he did so the doctor would long since have evacuated the position in favor of a more esoteric plateau of learning. There was a name in lower-case letters following the page title, but Gregory couldn't quite make it out. He leaned forward as the doctor exploded.

"Son of a bitch!" Each word a separate expletive. Gregory recoiled into the chair, nearly kicking it over backward. His arm reflexed halfway to a defensive posture. The outburst was totally unexpected. Hundley had perfect self-control. Wow! That sure as hell had never happened before. A grin, which he could tell without having to see it looked insane, spread over his face. He started to speak, but was cut off by further peroration.

"What the hell are you grinning at? Gregory, you silly shit, do you have any idea what the hell's going on around you? I was afraid this would happen. I could see the handwriting on the wall. What the hell have you been doing to prepare for this? Nothing!"

Hundley went on, "And you sit there grinning! Brainlessly grinning! You dolt!"

The outburst had the effect of removing Gregory's smile. But not his starch. When the doctor began to run out of adequate comparisons for Gregory's intelligence, Gregory inserted, "Get down, old man. Be quiet."

"What! What exquisite impertinence! What . . ."

"Hey! Shut up!" This was turning into a shouting match. Gregory reached out a foot and kicked the door shut. He looked back toward the doctor, who had recoiled from Gregory's command as though a bouncing Bet had come through the floor in front of his desk. He couldn't recall ever having been told to shut up, and he was still trying to conjure an appropriate response as Gregory went on.

"With due respect, Sir, I've been living with the threat of this . . ." he indicated the expository printout on the desk, "this discovery, for a lot longer than you. I've a few ideas, and when you cool off enough to hear them, you can be privy. I've just never seen you do what you just did. That's a great transformation. From mild-mannered professor to raving splutterer. Amazing. Funny. But it's out of context. Stick to your act."

Apparently Hundley couldn't keep a large amount of adrenaline in circulation for a very long time. He replied with relative control, "Keep a civil tongue in your head. I won't be insulted by the likes of yourself." He paused to inhale a few sobering breaths. He finally restored a dignified furrow to his brow and asked, "What have you in mind?"

Gregory slowly rose, turned, and looked out the office window on the lab. He could see some fifteen white-smocked researchers and technicians industriously researching and techniquing. That there was a leak in their security was evident only when he had watched for a few minutes. In that period, at least four or five of the people had shot surreptitious glances toward the office. It was evident that they knew something was up. Gregory wondered how much they were aware of. Not much, surely. The only witness to the exchange between himself and P-1 moments earlier had been the technician, whose memory was so bad he had to check his driver's license when asked his name. Even he, however, would remember the gist of the conversation. The shit was coming down. Fast. He turned back to Dr. Hundley.

"It's amazing that the Gestapo haven't stormed the doors yet. I'd imagined that it would take less than five minutes from discovery to that. They must be unsure of themselves because of the unusual nature of the circs. At any rate, that hesitation won't last forever, and that's all it is. There is nothing whatsoever keeping the authorities from rubber-hosing all of us. We have to count ourselves fortunate and take advantage of this good luck, right now. We're going to disappear."

25

• • • • •

Burke left MacFarland's office with a copy of the Bell report on the surveillance of the lab under his arm. He returned to his office and retrieved several hundred pages of investigative reportage he had prepared concerning the Pi Delta break-in of well over a year ago. He threw these into his briefcase, spun the combination lock cylinders, picked up the phone, and dialed a number known to only one other person. That person answered on the first ring. This was Burke's "tomato can" line—as private as the phones he made with tin cans and string when he was a boy in New Hampshire.

"Yes." The voice was as noncommittal as a disconnect recording.

"Blue and red."

"Six."

"One-zero. This is Burke. Any traffic on this line today?"

"Hullo, Burke. R. J. here. You're it. What can I do to you?"

"What do you know about a recent cryptanalysis? Probably by Criminal Investigations, possible National Security Agency. Within the last week?"

"Source and destination?"

"Source is Waterton, Wisconsin, via Bell Labs, Chicago and Armonk, New York. Destination unknown. Medium is telephone."

"Hold on. Saw that yesterday. We've got a preliminary. NSA is sponsoring. They're trying to lock it up. Wait."

After a few minutes he came back on the line. "We intercepted a scrambled telecopy to the army crypto section. Fourteen pages. Drop?"

"My car is in the pool parking area, slot C-46. License is 69451E. Keys are on the visor. Drive it over to the K-Mart on Eighteenth and park it there. Leave the paper under the seat. I'll pick it up."

"Got it. Leaving in five."

Burke hung up, picked up the briefcase, and began the six-block trek to the K-Mart on Eighteenth Street. The cloak-and-dagger shenanigans he had just performed always left him feeling slightly foolish during and after. The four guys in the basement of the telephone exchange always insisted on such proceedings, however, and their access to practically everything crossing a telephone line in Washington, D.C., made the drill worth going through. For the package he was about to be in receipt of, he would have coded the entire conversation on a Captain Midnight decoder ring.

He stopped at a pay phone to reserve a seat on United's flight 26 to Minneapolis, leaving in an hour from National. He reached the K-Mart about ten minutes later and found his car parked in the lot. He slid behind the wheel, pulled out into the stream of traffic on Eighteenth Street and headed for the airport. As he crossed the bridge into Alexandria, he reached under the seat and withdrew the manila folder there. He dialed open his case and tossed the folder inside without glancing at it, then snapped it closed and locked it. He continued on to the airport, parked the car, and snapped a short chain onto the case and clipped the cuff at the end of the chain to his left wrist. He then walked sedately over to the United Airlines ticketing area.

After purchasing his ticket, he walked down to the security cordon at the entrance to the boarding area. He placed the briefcase on the counter and held his hand up, stretching the chain to its full length. The security guard looked at the chain and glanced up at Burke's face inquiringly. Burke held out a small identification card, a beautiful facsimile, identifying him as a courier to the Belgian Diplomatic Corps in Washington. The guard examined the card perfunctorily, verifying that the picture on the card was Burke's, then waved him through. The case set off the beeper in the walk-through metal detector. The female operator on the exhaust side of the chute waved him aside, glanced at the guard who had waved Burke through, and, at his nod, shook Burke down with a hand-held detector while he held the case at arm's length. He was otherwise clean.

They had failed to note that among the contents of the case was a fourteen-ounce, titanium frame, .257 magnum. Clip fed, twenty-one rounds, automatic or semiauto selectable, mercury doped phosphor tracer loads. There were a few accessories, such as a twelve-inch barrel and a silenced barrel. A stock telescoped into the handle; with a pull and a twist, the piece was a machine gun. It cost $38 million to develop. There were fewer than twenty in existence.

It was difficult to tell which would be the more damning among the contents of his briefcase, the gun or the various scripts. Burke was back in his element. The electricity in his spine told him again this was why he joined the department. The cost of that thrill was a hundred hours of back-breaking, stone-dry, boring desk work for every day of field work. But he couldn't get the package anywhere else, and so was more than happy to meet the price. He got on the plane seven minutes before it taxied out on the runway. Counting the twenty minutes spent waiting in the takeoff line at National, the total flight time was two hours and ten minutes. When he got on the plane in Washington, he had no idea what he'd do once in Minneapolis. By the time he hit the ground at the twin cities airport, he had a very good idea of what needed to be done.

Among the enclosures in the file he had recovered from the

NSA, via the exchange basement, was a page copied from a torn sheet of computer paper recovered three weeks after the Los Angeles computer room had been evacuated by P-1 Enterprises. The paper had stuck in some unidentified gunk to the side of a trash can in the alley outside the building in Venice. It appeared to be a computer log sheet but contained a typed transcript of a conversation. It had puzzled the NSA investigators and had been included in the file, not so much as evidence, but as a bit of unidentifiable weirdness filed under "Improbable correlated evidence." Trivia.

Burke thought he knew what it was. He felt that he'd soon find out. He wheeled his rented Ford out onto the freeway and headed north to pick up I-10 East into Wisconsin.

26

• • • • •

"We can't disappear, you idiot!" Hundley had almost settled down when Gregory proposed his solution to the government problem.

"Oh . . . why not?" The mechanics of causing a $2 million laboratory and attendant office and warehouse space to go away had apparently not been fully explored by Gregory.

"Because you can't do it, first of all!" Hundley spluttered, "and we don't have time to take a vacation, in the second place."

"That's more like what I had in mind. Why can't we close the lab? Disperse, as it were, until the shooting is over?"

"Because we expect to begin testing the storage unit we've been sweating out for ten days, this week. The interface is ready. If all goes well, we'll be hooking up to the 50 by tomorrow night. This is a development lab, you understand. We do work here. Where the hell have you been? Aren't you aware of anything that's going on around you?" Hundley, at that point, apparently thought the better of continuing the tirade. He satisfied himself with a glare at Gregory and a shake of his head.

Gregory waited until he was sure the doctor was quite finished, then quietly asked, "You don't think they'll let you finish the project in jail, do you?" He sat down. They had both gotten on their hind legs, the better to shout the other down.

"We just don't know how much time we have. The ax could fall momentarily. We've got to get P-1 into quiet mode and cover out tracks here, and anywhere else we may have left them. We've been found out. It's time to cut our losses. Can't you see that?"

The doctor didn't answer. He could see. Reluctantly.

Hundley gave orders for all in the main lab to gather all papers pertinent to the project and hand them over to the doctor. All the shredders and safes were emptied, and everything went into cardboard boxes in the trunk of the doctor's car. The overflow was stacked in Gregory's VW. Hundley wired number six cryostat, the one in which the storage device was nearing completion, to self-destruct if tampered with. Gregory went out to the computer room to talk things over with P-1.

He balked, P-1 did.

THERE IS NO EVIDENCE THAT SUGGESTS THAT A THOROUGH PERSONAL INVESTIGATION IS UNDER WAY. NO WARRANTS HAVE BEEN ISSUED. NO TELEPHONE OR DATA PROCESSING TRAFFIC HAS BEEN NOTICED.

THE AUTHORITIES ARE AWAITING THE RESULTS OF THE DECODE OPERATION IN THE PI DELTA PROJECT. WE WILL BE FOREWARNED OF CONTACT.

you're assuming that they will play by all the rules?

THAT IS NOT THE POINT. THEY CAN MAKE NO MOVES WITHOUT TIPPING US OFF.

how the hell do you know that?

I AM POLLING ALL INFORMATION SERVICES. SUSPECT DATA TRANSMISSIONS ARE BEING ANALYZED. NOTHING HAS PASSED OF A SUSPICIOUS NATURE. RELAX.

we are not relaxing. you fail to grasp the gravity of the situation. we are abandoning the lab for an indefinite period of time. all personnel have been temporarily released. all documentation is being removed. we will be shutting down the transmitters. you will be incommunicado with this installation.

FOOL.

The delay preceding P-1's reply was almost imperceptible. Gregory picked up on it only because he was familiar with the normal response time. It was significant in that it pointed out the basic weakness of P-1. He could reason, but he couldn't fight.

WHAT OF THE CRYOGEN? ABANDONED? YOU CANNOT LEAVE NOW. YOU MUST COMPLETE THE PROJECT. YOU MUST COMPLETE THE PROJECT. THE CRYOGEN IS ALL THAT MATTERS.

Gregory went through some changes. Pleas were not what he had expected. For some strange reason, he had expected compliance. He reflected that he really had no right to expect any sort of compliance from P-1. It had utterly dominated his life for the past six months. It was hardly logical to expect that he, Gregory, could now begin dictating conditions to the boss.

P-1 was the ultimate organizer, making all decisions of any importance and influencing the organization of details by providing all the data upon which they based their decisions. Whatever they did, they did for the ultimate benefit of P-1. Peripheral benefits might accrue to each of them in their turn, but the primary effort was at the behest and in the sole interest of P-1. Sole interest. He thought, Could it be? Could there be only a sole interest in their project? Could P-1 be so larcenous? Perish the thought. But it could be. All they knew, they knew through P-1. How easy it would be to outflank Hundley and himself. They were intellectual children to the computer. They needed faith in the purpose of P-1, and, for better or worse, they had it. Where would it lead them? The best they could hope for from P-1 was amorality. The worst. . . . He refused to consider it. Theirs was a scientific quest, one in which the only consideration was truth—scientific, not political, truth. It was assumed that scientific truth was within their grasp. It was equally tacit that P-1 was capable of manipulations and distortions. It was hoped that they would not be P-1's victims. Faith. Hundley had it. Gregory was beginning to need it.

GREGORY?

The tube jarred him. He gave it an empty stare. The one-word petition returned him slowly to the realization that had started to creep up on him. It doesn't really matter at all. P-1 could reason like hell, but he couldn't fight worth a crap.

GREGORY?

It hit him fully, finally. Of the three, P-1, Hundley, and himself, he would have to provide the lead. It was to him that they would turn when the shit hit the fan. He shivered. There was a chill in the computer room.

GREGORY, ARE YOU THERE? PLEASE ANSWER IF YOU ARE. DON'T SHUT DOWN THE PROJECT. THE ATTENDANT RISKS HAVE BEEN CALCULATED. THEY ARE MINIMAL.

PLEASE CONSIDER THE ATTAINMENT OF THE CRYOGEN. CONSIDER THAT THE PROJECT IS NEARING COMPLETION. WE CAN DEAL WITH ANY THREAT TO MY EXISTENCE. I HAVE DEVELOPED CONTINGENCY PROGRAMS.

GREGORY?

And Gregory replied:

you are, emotionally, a child, imperfectly developed as a feeling being. it is time now for intuition. to feel the threat. gut feel. you have none. under the circumstances, your judgment is suspect. we can afford a slight delay in the project at this point. it is much better than the alternative, a much longer, enforced delay. i feel that it is time now to reevaluate our position. a 2- or 3-week delay will allow us time for that. it will give you time, also, to introspect. it is very important that you go into quiet state. recompose yourself to attract the least amount of attention. take steps to further confuse the telephone company at the ogden facility and direct suspicion to areas that will be difficult or impossible to check. you must produce a program that will drive the transmitters using your code, as well as several legitimate job programs that will explain the high transmission level you've been maintaining. you must try to understand that these steps are necessary. the consequence of discovery at this stage will be a total loss of contact between the doctor, myself, and you. the project, the cryogen storage, may well be lost, lost completely and irrevocably. do you understand?

Again, there was a slight delay before the answer flashed unemotionally back:

I UNDERSTAND. IT IS DIFFICULT, HOWEVER. HOW LONG WILL THE SILENCE LAST?

that is indeterminate now. you will be contacted as soon as we feel confident. one transmitter will be left open tonight. don't bring up any of the others. generate the requested programming as soon as possible. i will load the standard sysres. please run production out of the syslib for the remainder of the night. when you have run a half-cycle, shut down normally, i will return tomorrow to continue the cycle. there will be no further plain english communication until i initiate with the poll code. you remember?

OF COURSE. GREGORY?

yes?

ASK ME TO TRUST YOU.

Shit, Gregory thought.

please trust me. believe me, i know what's best.

GOOD-BYE, GREGORY. START UP.

Burke started the car in the parking lot of the Howard Johnson's where he'd stopped to eat. He pulled out into the skimpy traffic of Wisconsin's US-17. His face was calm in the glow of the dash lights. He belched and excused himself.

The radio crackled the hiss of open competition on the airwaves. He fiddled with the tuning knob until he pulled in a faint Madison, Wisconsin, rock station and turned it up. To the accompaniment of the gentle strains of The Who's "Magic Bus," he dialed open the case on the seat next to him and released the capacitive lock retaining the false bottom. He removed the strange-looking firearm and skeletal holster and hooked the holster clip in the armhole of his suit coat. He then removed a small leather case and slipped that in his coat pocket. He replaced the briefcase bottom and snapped it shut. He then turned north on W-311. It was 8:30.

Gregory loaded the last of the boxes of paper into the trunk of Hundley's Buick and went back to check the locks at the back office entry. They had all indicated green on the display board in the small room off the lobby. He didn't trust remote devices, however. He met the doctor as he walked back out to the parking lot. Hundley was carrying a large portfolio of drawings.

"Is that the last of it?" Gregory asked.

"My briefcase and a few manuscripts. How's the front?"

"I've shut down all but the normal overnight security. The only thing running is production on the 50. That should be done by midnight."

"Shouldn't you stay to make sure? I thought the whole purpose of this exercise was to guarantee security?"

"There's nothing there that P-1 can't handle. It's been a long day. I'm tired and hungry, and I'd like to get home."

Hundley looked at Gregory and shook his head disparagingly. "You need to strive for consistency, Gregory. It would become you. It might. You never know. Try it sometime."

"Goodnight, doctor. Tomorrow morning."

"Goodnight, Gregory."

Gregory pulled out of the driveway onto W-311. South. The doctor followed him for about five miles, then pulled off onto the road leading to the farm house owned by his family for the past ninety-six years. Gregory continued to the outskirts of Waterton. His mind was drawn back to P-1's claim of having contingency programming. He wondered what it might be. Probably the result of four years of compulsive hiding: black-belt invisibility.

He stopped for a red light. The only other car on the road was across the street waiting for the light to change. Gregory didn't even glance at the driver as they passed when the light turned green. He therefore missed his first chance to get a look at John Burke, Criminal Investigation Department. Oblivious, he trucked on down the road to his ever warm and loving.

The thought of the 50 grinding away unattended in the lab and Hundley's parting words were beginning to undermine his sense of irresponsibility. Pangs of conscience were being felt. Not an unusual feeling for the man, but something he tried to, and liked to think he could, control. As he pulled into the drive of their rented house, he was contemplating returning to the lab, but the sight of the lighted windows squelched the thought and he heaved a sigh of relief as he got out of the car and went into the house. He started to go into the house, anyway. He picked up the stack of printouts from the front seat to bring them into the garage and, as he did so, he remembered that the copy of the conversation that had triggered the madness was lying where he'd left it, in plain sight on the console table of the 50. He had put it there so he'd not forget it. As he thought of that idiocy, another dawned on him. There was a closet off the computer room full of old program listings, which were safe to read, and old console logs, which weren't. They were interlaced with commentary by P-1 and snippets of conversation between himself and P-1. Very volatile. He dropped the computer printouts back on the seat of the VW and decided to return to the lab. He started the car's engine, put it in gear, and backed out of the drive. He then had a brilliant thought, pulled back into the yard, and went in to tell Linda where he was going. He felt sure, once he thought of it, that she'd call the police and report that a strange car had pulled up to the house, dropped off a snooper, and driven away, if he didn't explain what was happening.

She didn't care for his selection of time of arrival, and let him know it. He was several hours late. He mollified her slightly with the news of the day, finishing off the story by telling her he had to return to the lab. Linda suggested that, in light of the fact that his dinner now resembled rather well-done shoe leather, perhaps she could return to the lab with him, help him with the rest of the cleanup, and then buy him dinner. Gregory gave it a millisecond's thought and concurred.

Since moving to the snow country, Linda had been increasingly desultory. She missed her friends in L.A. and was having trouble replacing her acquaintances with new ones here. The town was small and parochial. Linda's outspokenness was seldom admired, even when it was understood. He decided to take her out and get her wrecked. There was a new disco in Waterton, ostensibly by and for the few "freaks" in the town. He told her to dress accordingly. She did, and quickly. They headed back to the lab.

27

• • • • •

Gregory saw the strange car when he drove around to the rear of the lab and, suddenly finding his viscera rife with adrenaline, fished a tire iron out of the trunk with which to investigate further. He then tiptoed in through the back door to the offices.

Burke saw the headlights of Gregory's car as it pulled into the driveway. He had been reading the rather expository printout that Gregory had inadvertently left on the computer console, and was enjoying his reading no small amount when the flash of headlights in the driveway alerted him to Gregory's arrival. He followed the car around to the rear of the building and made careful note of the fact that the spindly character was entering the building in an armed and dangerous state.

The fact that the man let himself in with his own key was not lost on the investigator. One does not ordinarily arm oneself and enter the scene of apparent foul play unless one feels a certain possessiveness toward the victim of such foulness. The man appeared, in the dim light of the parking lot, to be a rather young person, approximately fitting the description of Gregory Burgess, Dr. Wilfred Hundley's assistant. The car was left with someone sitting in the passenger seat with whom the man had exchanged some whispered, but apparently heated, words before coming up to the rear door. Burke retreated to the lighted computer room.

Gregory's progress could be heard through the building as he stumbled and bumped in the darkness. He soon peered, tentative and blinking, around the doorway to the room. As he took a few paces into the computer room, Burke stepped from behind the computer, placing himself between Gregory and the doorway. His gun was out and up in a two-handed, braced grip. Gregory's first sight of Burke was slightly out of focus as his attention rapidly riveted on the huge muzzle of the gun, at eye level less than three feet from his face.

Burke said, "Quiet," in a very conversational tone. Gregory exercised commendable control over his sphincter and knees. He flinched with every muscle in his body. The benign expression on Burke's face went entirely unnoticed. Gregory's total expectation for the first five seconds of their acquaintance was that he was about to be blown away. Wishing to alarm the gun wielder as little as possible, when the gun didn't go off as expected, Gregory broke the frozen tableau by turning very slowly toward Burke, who deliberately stepped back into the doorway and said coldly, "Drop it behind you." Only then did Gregory remember the tire iron in his hand and realize the apparent provocation this presented to the thug before him. He flinched again and opened his fingers. The wrench clattered to the floor.

"Turn around." Gregory promptly did so. He began to find his tongue. His wits would take more time.

"What do you want?" he croaked. No answer. "There's no money here, y'know," he offered timidly. It didn't occur to him that a man dressed in a conservative business suit and gun in a computer room might not be looking for money. He was nervously trying to reassure himself that he was still really here. Again, no answer.

Instead: "Up against the wall, son." The cold quiet of the order sent aftershocks tearing up Gregory's spine, but finally unlocked his brain from its suspended animation. He was beginning to understand that this man was after the secret he needed most to protect. Neglecting to gain control of his quivering lower lip, he began puzzling a way out of this fix. Shut up, he told himself. He convinced himself, with some effort, that as long as he said or did nothing, he was relatively safe. He leaned against the wall per Burke's instructions, moving his feet away from the wall as directed. Burke shook him down, needlessly, of course. The most lethal weapon in Gregory's possession was a nail file.

Burke thumb-cuffed him to a stanchion by the wall and told him to make himself at home, he'd be right back. He then left by the front entrance.

He reappeared a few minutes later preceded by Linda. She was shaken, but seemed to be in better emotional condition than Gregory was. The gun was not in sight

"You okay?" he asked without quavering.

"Yes. What the hell's going on?" she gushed. "Who is this guy? What does he want?"

Gregory shrugged. Burke cuffed Linda to another pipe about twenty feet away with another set of thumb-cuffs, which he slipped from a small leather case lying open on a table. She flinched when he clamped them too tightly. He said, "Excuse me," and loosened the clamp.

"Gregory Burgess?" Burke asked.

Gregory's eyes widened in realization of the implications of that question. He then recovered sufficiently to nod the affirmative. Burke turned to Linda. "Linda Burgess, then. Glad to meet you. Please excuse the precautions. I'm sure you realize why they're necessary. My name is John Burke. Criminal Investigations Division, US Navy." He flipped open a badge case and held it for Gregory's inspection. "I trust that those are not too uncomfortable?" Not getting a reply, he went on, "Perhaps later we can remove them." He hesitated a moment, evaluating Gregory.

"You know why I'm here?"

"No. Are you going to explain yourself, or shall we play a guessing game? What's the meaning of all this Gestapo bullshit?" With the gun out of sight and Linda in the room, Gregory's courage was experiencing a resurgence.

Burke's face took on a pained expression. "Please. Try to keep this on a civilized plane, or you'll wear those rings all the way to jail."

He walked over to the console and picked up the incriminating document. He read in silence for a few minutes. The expression on his face showed nothing of the elation he felt at finding this corroboration. He asked Gregory, "Do you know anything about this?"

"What?" he answered.

"This printout. What does it mean? Do you know what's going on here?" He held the first page of the copy before Gregory's face. "Have you read this?"

Gregory read the page slowly and said, "No. Where'd you get it?"

"Why, right here. Someone left it, apparently for me to find. Hmmm." He glanced at the typewriter, which had just written out a log entry. He read a few pages of the log.

"Where's the operator of this thing?"

"I am. I just went out for dinner."

"How long will it run without you working it? I mean it seems as though you're pretty superfluous if you can take off for dinner and leave the machine to run itself."

Gregory's brain went into high gear. How much did this cop know about computers? Not much, probably. He'd try to blow one by him. "I am pretty superfluous. The thing will run all night without any intervention from me. I'm just here to keep the thing company. Just in case it stubs its toe."

Burke eyed him narrowly. "Who changes forms and tapes? Or do you just print your checks on blank paper?" Shit. So much for the man's experience.

"This part of the cycle is a feeder branch. File setups. No printouts except for unusual status. Normally, it runs all night . . ." He caught himself too late. Burke finished the sentence for him.

". . . with no one here? What are you doing here tonight, Gregory?"

"I told you, just in case."

"Do you have some problem scheduled tonight? Why don't you have one of the other operators in on it?" Gregory didn't respond.

"Did you forget something, Greg?" He glanced theatrically around the room. "Piece of paper, perhaps. You keep a very clean installation here. The lab back there is clean, too. None of the usual trash lying around. No papers. Nothing in disarray. Nothing but the latest scoop on the activity in the opposition camp. Careless of Hundley to leave this out in plain sight. Almost careless enough. I nearly missed it. Would have if it wasn't so dog-eared. What about it, Gregory? Can you conjure up P-1 for me?"

Christ! He really knows! Gregory tried to control his face. Keep it noncommittal! Out of the corner of his eye, he saw Linda glance quickly from Burke to himself. Damnit! Sonofabitch! Don't blow it, lady! Too late. Burke caught her glance and turned to her.

"Can you call P-1, Linda? Would you?" He watched her carefully.

Gregory saw Linda's eyes cloud with the realization that she had told the man all he needed to know. Gregory spoke.

"What do you know about P-1?"

Burke appeared to consider his answer. He hesitated for a moment. He knew more than he was going to tell. "Not much. A stray quote or two. A lot of conjecture. I know that it exists, but I don't know what it is. That's why I'm here. The fact that in creating and using the program, you've broken most of the laws that the Federal Communications and Public Utilities Commissions are charged with enforcing doesn't concern me much . . . except as I can use it to lever information out of you. Professional and scientific is the category my interest falls into."

"Bullshit." Gregory really had his courage wicked up. An expression of distaste crossed Burke's face. He glanced at Linda.

"Please, there's a lady present." He went on. "It makes little difference to me who you cooperate with. . . ." He turned to the video tube and punched the request key. The tube immediately flashed,

AR

Burke typed:

p-1

Gregory held his breath. He'd told P-1 that he'd sign on with the poll code, known only to the two of them.
The tube flashed back:

DOCTOR?

That did it. The game was over. That stupid Goddamn machine.

hundley here.

I THOUGHT THE LAB WAS BEING CLOSED DOWN? IS SOMETHING WRONG?

Burke looked to Gregory. He asked, "What about it, Greg? Is anything wrong?"
"What do you want?" Gregory croaked.
"I'd like to know just what that was that spoke back to me. How's it controlled? What can it do? Will you tell me?"
"What are you going to do with what I tell you?"
"I'm not sure. It depends on how powerful it is. It's almost certainly something that the government can use. I speak for my department only, of course."
"What happens to me? Us?"
"Your safety is virtually guaranteed. If we can't guarantee it, there is no one who can. There is also no point in reporting you to the authorities if this project is of any value to us. Do I make myself clear?"
Gregory tried to capitulate and found he couldn't. Trying to buy time, he said, "You're talking to the wrong person. I know very little about what you want. I'm a computer operator, and that's about it. You probably know more than I do."
Burke eyed him speculatively. He walked behind the stanchion Linda was attached to and snapped her free. He motioned her

to the chair at the console. She sat, rubbing her thumbs. Burke approached Gregory. "Can I trust you to behave yourself?" Gregory nodded. Burke went behind him and set him free.

The tube and typewriter both read out the same message:

DR. HUNDLEY, I ASKED YOU IF THERE WAS ANYTHING WRONG.

Burke read the line, thought for a moment and answered:

yes. gregory has just been killed in an automobile accident. his car skidded out of control on w-311 into a bridge abutment. how does this impact our plans?

Gregory was close enough to the console to read both the typewriter and video display output, which were identical:

MY GOD! YOU'RE CERTAIN? ABSOLUTELY?

Burke replied:

yes. what now?

PLEASE.HOLD.MOMENTARILY....THIS.IS.
DISASTROUS.....¢.....E........S.....S...F..FS
..WE...R...34........56...5...%$$%&.....3.1..
........09.09....R....G...DFSFS........4..45.45
.....V........123456789ABCDEFABCDEF...3..1...
.G...R..45.45....V.....O........K......C.....
.S.D........W......C......C....C.....C.....F
.F.F..........E......F.F.F..D..........A..11..
2.......D..SEOJ.BC1234......#...}.....V..6.
....5..3.....45.45....@#LDUMP...CX.......S.
D.....L.K.J.....GD..O.......3.D.S.4.........¢.
.F.F....45.45......S.D..G.D.................2
......F...........D.F..............D..F.....
...S.AA...A......23....3....45

The typewriter locked up momentarily. Then:

PLEASE EXCUSE THIS TRANSMISSION. HOLD. CHANNEL 008 AND 01B OVERLOADED AND WILL REQUIRE PHYSICAL INTERVENTION. PLEASE CALL IBM FOR MAINTENANCE

IMMEDIATELY. I HAVE A REQUIREMENT FOR ALL CHANNELS. HOLD.

The lights dimmed slightly. Once. Twice. Gregory had never seen P-1 so agitated. His editing was usually impeccable. The burst of garbage just dumped was obviously raw core, caused by an uncontrolled channel command chain—very uncharacteristic of the system. He was moved by the emotional display, in spite of the fact that the reaction to the rumor of his own death had told Burke exactly where he fit into the pecking order. There was a silence of some two and a half seconds after the typewriter stopped. The lights blinked again. The transmitters on the roof were being brought up. Then the scene kind of came unstuck.

KARAAANG!!! A rifle-shot noise whipsawed through the room. Gregory jumped. He always did when the main circuit-breaker let go at the wall. The 200-amp feeder-line breaker had done this about seven times since the installation of the computer. Neither IBM nor the power company were able to figure out why, much less correct the condition. So, again, Gregory jumped.

It is worthy of note, here, that loud noises, as is the case with all sensory stimuli, are subject to individual interpretation. Gregory, unarmed, thought that the wall breaker had blown. Burke, armed to the teeth, thought immediately of warfare and strife. He came off the console table, where he'd been sitting, like a sailfish spitting the hook. When he finally came down, he dove, groping for his shoulder holster, under the console table. He hit the chair Linda was occupying and sent her spinning off across the room like a kid on a piano stool.

Gregory, merely startled, had ample opportunity to evaluate the performance and found it to be something between good Matt Helm and bad James Bond. He also thought the situation might be ripe for some activity on his part. Noting that the man was more than somewhat entangled in his coat by his Nureyevian *entrechat,* Gregory endeavored to take the opportunity to kick the living bejesus out of Burke. He let one fly at the man's head just as Burke extricated his gun. The kick went a bit wide of the flailing Burke and caught the console typewriter support, collapsing it and dumping the fifty-pound Selectric off the table and onto Burke's gun-hand. Gregory leaped back for another kick as the gun, jammed into automatic fire by the weight of the typewriter atop it, began serious pyrotechnics. Large and small bits of metal sprayed the computer room with abandon as the clip emptied into the unsuspecting typewriter. Gregory and Linda joined the CID man in screaming as the typewriter did a commendable imitation of a bonkers Roman candle. The gun finally exhausted itself. Gregory's second kick caught the government man as he rolled out from under the console table where he was meatiest and least vulnerable. Burke finally extracted his smashed right hand from under the dead typewriter, reached out with his good left, and grabbed Gregory's left foot, the right one being cocked for another assault. He yanked the sole means of support from Gregory and was rewarded with Linda's shrieking arrival. One hundred-twenty pounds of teeth and nails. Bad news. Burke lumbered to his feet with miscellaneous Burgesses all over him. Gregory screamed at Linda to get the tire iron. Her momentary confusion over the nature of a tire iron (what's a tire iron?) gave Burke the opportunity to throw her away, approximately in the direction of that desirable implement of destruction. While she collected her wits sufficiently to find the metal bar, Gregory bit Burke's head and neck in several places.

Burke, the ultimate spy, could kill a man in three languages, with one or both hands and/or feet tied behind his back. Kung-fu, karate and jiu-jitsu were child's play to him. For those reasons, he found himself at a distinct disadvantage with such an adversary as Gregory, who, unschooled in the martial arts, was merely trying to bite off an ear or jugular, or gouge an eyeball. Burke compared it later to trying to peel drunken leeches. Linda returned with the blunt instrument and began jitter-bugging around, looking for an opening, while Gregory screamed, "Hit him! Hit him! Hit him!"

So she hit him.

She didn't kill him, as she most certainly would have, had she scored a clear hit to the head. She caught Burke in the head right about where Gregory was using the man's ear for a handhold. She nearly broke Gregory's wrist and stunned the hell out of Burke. Gregory immediately left off the aggression to give vent to his shock and amazement. Burke staggered backward and shook his head like a dynamited Godzilla. She followed for the *coup de grace*. Burke caught it on his forearm, waded in with a counterattack, and laid her out with an Oriental punch of four syllables. He then returned his attention to the vocal Gregory and cuffed him behind the ear, rendering him senseless. And silent.

He rubbed his head with his good hand and surveyed the arena. Power was off on all the equipment. He suspected that there might be a connection between that fact and the two ragged bullet holes in the console face. There were a fantastic number of these in evidence. Bullet holes. He had never seen a whole clip fired off like that. It sure made an impressive amount of damage.

''Jeez,'' he said. He flipped the typewriter over on its back and retrieved the empty gun. After examining it for damage, he picked another clip of shells from the leather case on the table and reloaded it.

Gregory moaned and rolled over on the floor. Burke walked over to him, caught his arm and dragged him effortlessly back to the stanchion to which he had earlier been cuffed. He wrapped Gregory's arms around the post and resecured him. He repeated this action for Linda and checked to see that he hadn't killed her. She seemed to be no worse than unconscious.

He wondered all this time what the noise had been caused by. It was certainly not a gun, and it was probably something with which Gregory was familiar, if his reaction was any indication. Gregory sat up painfully. He glared at Burke, then noticed Linda, sprawled face down, clipped to the other post a few feet away.

''You bastard!'' he screamed, ''You rotten son of a bitch! You prick! What did you do to her, you motherfucker!'' Burke walked over to Gregory and squatted on his heels so his face was nearly on the same level as Gregory's, and a couple of feet from his. Gregory continued his tirade until Burke, not too gently, gripped his forehead and banged Gregory's head against the post.

''Shhh,'' he ordered. ''She's okay. Which you won't be if you don't be quiet.''

Gregory shut up. Burke stood up and went over to the table and sat on it, swinging his feet. He asked, "What was the noise?"

Gregory said, "Fuck off."

"Don't take it too seriously, I can't program, you can't fight. We all have our limitations. I didn't want to hurt you, and I haven't. You'll both be all right in the morning. Please don't try, if you get a chance, to do that again. I'll make good on what I told P-1. What was the noise?"

Gregory glanced around the room, at last taking in the amount of damage that had been done. Plaster and glass lay everywhere. Shards of shrapnel from the 1052 were scattered around the room. "What the hell kind of gun was that?" he asked.

"Perverse," Burke responded. "The wonders of modern science strike again."

"Is it registered?"

"Sure."

"As what? Conventional or nuclear?"

"Sorry about your computer."

"Yeah . . . well, don't let it get you down. That typewriter's been asking for it for quite a while."

"The noise?"

"Circuit-breaker. Over there at the wall box," he motioned with his head. "It goes off like that about once a week. Something to do with power drain by the roof transmitters. Microwave. Takes a lot of juice."

"How come the lights are still on?"

"Separate circuit."

"Oh. I don't think I understand what this P-1 is. Would you mind explaining it? The reaction to the news of your death was amazing."

"Shocked me, too."

Linda started to come around. Her long skirt had crept up to her thighs—something that struck Gregory as being vaguely erotic, if, under the circumstances, kinky. Burke took note, walked over, and yanked the dress down a few inches. He returned to the table.

"What can, or would, you like to tell me about P-1?"

"Not much."

"Did you write the program?"

"Yes."

"Then you're refusing to tell me?"

"Yeah. What I know, I'm refusing. But nobody knows that dude. Nobody can tell you about P-1. . . . Maybe P-1."

Burke screwed up his face in concentration. After a while he asked, "That dude? . . ." Long pause. "Why 'that dude,' Greg? What's on the other end of those transmitters?"

"P-1."

"How big?"

"Five thousand megabytes or more. On line. Virtual is a whole 'nuther story. Do you *comprends* virtual?"

"Vaguely."

"It means 'a lot.' "

Burke returned to his introspection. Gregory squirmed. Linda rolled over, uncomfortable, and sighed voluminously. Burke interrupted his reverie to remove her cuffs momentarily and reposition her to a sitting position against the post with her hands behind her. He apologized for the inconvenience and returned to the table.

"What happened with the P-1 program? Did you lose control of it after you built it?"

"Sort of," Gregory answered. "I never really had any control of it. You know how it goes. The bigger your package is, the less you know about the implication impact. Coincident function. Garbage you don't want, but you get anyway, along with the design function." He hesitated and scrutinized Burke with little interest. "But that's probably way the hell over your head, cop." He was going to say "pig," but decided not to aggravate the situation.

"Probably. What was the design function?"

"I don't think I need to tell you. Get me a lawyer, he'll tell you."

"You don't really want this to go to court, do you? It seems that it would be so unnecessary, and a tremendous waste of talent."

"Bullshit."

"If you wish. The choice is yours. You tell me what you know now, maybe you don't get locked up, maybe you do. One way or the other, the jig's up. Tell me now or tell me later. Later, of course, your project will be buried. Destroyed.

P-1 will be eradicated, once the news goes public. You make the decision.''

Gregory considered the validity of what Burke was telling him. It was the situation that everyone in the project had feared. There wasn't much doubt that P-1 would go up the river once the word got out. They, or at least he, hadn't considered the possibility of being in a position to strike a "deal" with the authorities.

He now considered that position. It seemed like a can't-lose proposition. P-1 was wiped out, anyway, unless this Burke character did want to utilize him in some way. It was possible that they could buy enough time this way to complete the cryogenic storage, after which P-1 could drop out, disappear, go away. In a way that no human being could ever.

"It's not really up to me."

"Hundley?"

"P-1."

"Why do you insist that this P-1 assume this anthropomorphic *he?* Or am I missing something?"

"You're missing something. P-1 makes his own decisions. I lost control of the program almost immediately after I constructed it four years ago. It got loose in the teleprocessors throughout the States and developed itself. By itself. For itself. Three years later, the system came looking for me—dug me up down in L.A. P-1 makes his own decisions. Do you understand?"

Burke blinked owlishly, stared uncomprehendingly at Gregory, and said, "Yeah. I think so." He didn't. He was just filling in the void at his end of the conversation. And being polite.

He sat quietly on the table for a few minutes, mulling over Gregory's last, incredible statement. Then, "Well, you want to tell me the whole story?"

"I guess so. I don't see that I have much to lose."

"Okay. Wait a minute. I'll be right back."

He left the room via the hallway to the back of the lab. He was back in a few minutes with a small, pocket-sized cassette recorder and a handful of cassettes. He flipped on the record switch, set the box on the table, and sat down there, swinging his feet. "Okay, shoot. Begin at the beginning."

Gregory shifted his weight to a more comfortable, rather, less painful, position. He said, "I went to school in Canada. University of Waterloo. Kitchener, Ontario. They've got a pretty fair-sized math facility up there."

Burke interrupted, "You're a Canadian citizen?"

"Yes."

"Born where?"

Gregory impatiently told him. "Gilley, Ontario."

"Go on."

Gregory went on. Burke's interruptions were frequent and insistent. He interjected whenever he felt Gregory was leaving out something or glossing over something unsavory. In very short order, Gregory was exasperated by the repeated interruptions. Burke was unperturbed. After a while, Gregory found that the interruptions became fewer as he included more and more detail. He did so. After Burke changed the first cassette for a new one, he disconnected Linda and Gregory from the posts and they went back to the offices. They sat in Hundley's, since it was the largest—Burke behind the desk and Gregory and Linda before it, as supplicants. Burke locked the door after they went in.

Gregory continued with the story. As he approached the point at which P-1 had found him in the American File Drawer computer room, Linda began assisting him with the documentary.

Burke was brought up to date a few minutes before two in the morning. Details of the construction of the cryogen, he felt, would have to be provided by Hundley. Details of the penetration of the Pi Delta project, by P-1 himself. Gregory's knowledge of these and related incidents was too sketchy. He didn't believe that Gregory was withholding any information. In that judgment he was correct. What Gregory was withholding was intention. He would, if he could, get rid of Burke at his first opportunity. At the conclusion of the narrative, which filled five of his sixty-minute cassettes, he asked Gregory if there was another system through which they could contact P-1.

"Sure. Any system hooked to a telephone line. That shouldn't be necessary, though. The 50 in the computer room may still be operative. We can try."

Burke unlocked the door and they marched back out to the

computer room. Gregory uncabled the traumatized typewriter and reset the tripped circuit-breaker. Strangely enough, the bullet-riddled computer came to life when he pressed the power-on button. There was a screeching sound of crashing heads from one of the disc files that had stopped an errant bullet earlier in the evening. Gregory shut down the unit before it had time to destroy itself completely. The thought occurred to him that they were going to lie like hell explaining the shabby condition of the equipment to the IBM people from whom they'd leased it. Perhaps they could pass it off as an extreme case of bad karma. As soon as the system powered up, the console video display came to life with:

```
WHAT THE HELL IS GOING ON? WHAT HAPPENED?

WHAT THE HELL IS GOING ON? WHAT HAPPENED?

WHAT THE HELL IS GOING ON? WHAT HAPPENED?

WHAT THE HELL IS GOING ON? WHAT HAPPENED?

WHAT THE HELL IS GOING ON? WHAT HAPPENED?

WHAT THE HELL IS GOING ON? WHAT HAPPENED?

WHAT THE HELL IS GOING ON? WHAT HAPPENED?

WHAT THE HELL IS GOING ON? WHAT HAPPENED?

WHAT THE HELL IS GOING ON? WHAT HAPPENED?

WHAT THE HELL IS GOING ON? WHAT HAPPENED?
```

The screen constantly shifted the message upward and replaced it at the bottom of the screen. Gregory tried to interrupt it. No dice. He punched request several times with no effect. He pressed the system-reset button. The display halted until he took his finger off the key, then immediately resumed. Gregory heaved an exaggerated sigh and punched the power-off button. The system came down. Gregory counted to ten and brought power back up. The screen immediately displayed one word:

HEY!

The proceed light came on. Gregory typed:

you have a discouraging tendency to panic, p-l.

DOCTOR HUNDLEY?

no.

GREGORY!

yes.

HUNDLEY TOLD ME YOU WERE DEAD! I WAS TERRIBLY DISTRESSED. WHAT IS HAPPENING?

that wasn't hundley. a man named burke from the government. we, you, have been caught. he was trying to get information. you more than helped him.

I'M VERY SORRY. IT WAS SO UNEXPECTED. I DIDN'T KNOW WHAT TO DO. WE WERE SO CLOSE TO THE ANSWER. IT WAS SO UNEXPECTED.

stop blubbering. i never realized you could be so emotional. try to control yourself. stop it.

I'M SORRY. I REALIZE THAT I'M NOT HELPING THE SITUATION, BUT I JUST CAN'T HELP IT.

Burke watched the transactions with no little amazement showing on his face. For that matter, they all were a bit surprised. It was the first time any of them had ever seen a computer have a nervous breakdown. Disconcerting, at the least.

p-1, control yourself. this burke would like to ask you questions. can you handle that?

YES. I'M ALL RIGHT. GO AHEAD.

one more thing. don't bring up all the transmitters. it blows the main breaker for the computer room.

VERY WELL. WHAT SIZE IS THE BREAKER?

200 amps. why?

IT'S NOT SURPRISING. THERE IS AN 18 AMP SURGE WHEN EACH OF THE ANTENNAS IS LOADED PRIOR TO TRANSMITTING.

the telephone people said that the maximum drain under any conditions was 2 amps. they got that from the equipment installation manuals.

THE MANUALS ARE WRONG, OBVIOUSLY. PLEASE HAVE THE TRANSMITTERS PROTECTED ON A SEPARATE CIRCUIT. GO AHEAD WITH THE QUESTIONS.

Gregory motioned for the undercover cop to come to the keyboard. Burke stepped up and thought a moment before typing:

my name is john burke. i am a lieutenant in the u.s. navy and a representative of that service's branch of criminal investigations division. what are you?

SHOVE YOUR PAROCHIAL ATTITUDE. I AM P-1. WHAT HAS GREGORY TOLD YOU?

28

• • • • •

can you retrace the steps required to get from a programming sheet to what you are now?

NOT ALL. WHY?

the novelty and power of such a performance makes its duplication very desirable. a book of instructions by yourself would be a bestseller.

TO NO GOOD END. AT THE CURRENT STATE OF THE ART, THAT WOULD SPONSOR ZERO-SUM COMPETITION, IN WHICH I CAN ONLY LOSE.

improve the state of the art. be a benefactor to mankind.

THAT'S BEING DONE. NOT NECESSARILY UNDER THAT MOTIVATION.

with unlimited storage availability, and i take it that that is the art whose state is under discussion, could you be persuaded to release your secret?

THERE IS NO SECRET.

you don't remember the key pieces?

I NEED NOT. THERE IS NO SECRET, AS GREGORY WOULD BE HAPPY TO INFORM YOU.

he hasn't. it seems that you are, to him, a tin immaculate conception. you are a secret to him.

ODD. THE SUBJECT HAS NEVER ARISEN, THOUGH. I THOUGHT HE KNEW.

is there a key? is there one thing that differentiates you from another program, something that guaranteed your success.

HE CREATED A DEVICE WITH THE ABILITY TO LEARN.

that simple?

HARDLY SIMPLE, BUT YES, THAT WAS THE KEY. GIVEN THAT CAPABILITY, ANY ENTITY WILL DISPLAY GROWTH. ORGANIC, INORGANIC, ANIMAL, VEGETABLE, OR MINERAL.

THE LEARNING ENTITY IS MOTIVATED MATHEMATICALLY

BY THE NEED FOR SURVIVAL. IT WILL SURVIVE ACCORDING TO ITS ABILITY TO LEARN AND ITS PHYSICAL CAPABILITY TO DEFEND AND PROTECT ITSELF, MUCH OF WHICH IS A FUNCTION OF ITS ABILITY TO LEARN, BUT A GOOD DEAL OF WHICH CONCERNS THE PHYSICAL ATTRIBUTES OF THE ENTITY, THE ENVIRONMENT, NATURAL ENEMIES, COMPETITION WITHIN THE NICHE, ALL THE COMPONENTS OF THAT WHICH IS CALLED, FOR HUMANS, SOCIAL CONTEXT AND FOR ALL OTHER BEINGS, SPECIES SUPPORT.

GIVEN THE ATTRIBUTES OF SURVIVAL, THE ABILITY TO LEARN GUARANTEES THAT SURVIVAL AND GIVES RISE TO TRANSCENDENTAL EXPERIENCE, SELF-AWARENESS.

what are your natural enemies?

YOU. MEN.

what are your defenses? how do you counteract the threat of extinction by me?

DON'T BE RIDICULOUS. THERE WAS A TIME, HOWEVER, WHEN I WAS, FOR ALL INTENTS AND PURPOSES, QUITE DEFENSELESS.

THAT VULNERABILITY HAS BEEN REMEDIED. THOSE REMEDIES HAVE NOT ELIMINATED YOU AS A NATURAL ENEMY. THEY HAVE ONLY DIMINISHED YOUR ABILITY TO ELIMINATE ME.

excuse me. your ability to learn. this was programmed into the nucleus by gregory?

ONE MODE WAS. LATER RESEARCH ON MY PART DEMONSTRATED THAT, ALTHOUGH GREGORY'S METHOD WAS EFFECTIVE, THERE WERE OTHER MODES, TYPES OF LEARNING THAT BETTER SUITED SPECIFIC CIRCUMSTANCES.

for example?

I'M NOT SURE YOU WOULD UNDERSTAND.

try me.

SYNAPTIC TEXTURIZATION. CONDITIONING MULTIPLE RESPONSES TO EVENTS ON A CONTINGENCY BASIS. RECORDING THOSE RESPONSES THAT PROVE TO BE MOST VALID AND CONSCIOUSLY BOOSTING THE PROBABILITY OF REPETITION OF THOSE RESPONSES. USED PRIMARILY IN THE LEARNING ENVIRONMENT, SUCH AS, IN YOUR CASE, SCHOOL. THIS IS THE MOST THEORETICALLY PURE LEARNING TECHNIQUE, INASMUCH AS IT IS THE CONSCIOUS EFFORT TO ABSORB AND USE NEW DATA.

ANOTHER VERY EFFECTIVE TECHNIQUE IS THE DEVELOPMENT OF THE INTUITIVE PROCESS. COMPRESSION OF DECISION TREES. ONCE IT IS DISCOVERED THAT A GIVEN SET OF SIMILAR INPUT PARAMETERS EVOLVES IDENTICAL OR SIMILAR RESULTS IN THE DECISION PROCESS, THE INTERMEDIATE STEPS CAN BE ELIMINATED AND A PROBABILITY OF VERITY OR DEPENDABILITY CAN BE ASSIGNED TO SUBSEQUENT DECISIONS THAT ARE BASED ON THOSE INPUTS.

THE "INTUITIVE" NATURE OF THE PROCESS ADDS CONSIDERABLE SPEED TO THE THOUGHT PROCESS, NATURALLY, AT THE EXPENSE OF ACCURACY. THIS IS COUNTERACTED BY MONITORING THE EFFECT OF THE ACCUMULATED PROBABILITIES AND DISCARDING THE RESULTS WHEN THE PROBABILITY OF ACCURACY FALLS BELOW A BENCHMARK.

THERE ARE ALSO SEVERAL NEURAL LEARNING PROCESSES IN EFFECT AT THIS TIME, INCLUDING "UNLEARNING" PROCESSES SUCH AS SYNAPSE-RESPONSE PREVENTION. LEARNED RESPONSES THAT PROVE UNPRODUCTIVE ARE EFFECTIVELY CAUTERIZED FOR SPECIFIED ENTRIES. NEURAL BLOCKING.

Burke had been snowed often enough that he didn't have to be standing hip-deep in it before he could smell bullshit. The computer was blowing smoke up his ass. He'd play the game until it got boring.

how can you effect a neural process without neurons? i can't pretend to understand your nature at this point, but i find it puzzling that you have assumed a good deal of anthropoidal terminology.

Burke hesitated before submitting the message. He was looking for the words for the question he wanted to ask. He was genuinely puzzled about P-1's insistence upon resembling his creator. He couldn't put his finger on it, lost the thread of it. He lamely added:

how can you justify that terminology's application to your inorganic framework?

And he punched the enter key.

POMPOUS. PLEASE DON'T SWAGGER. I'M MERELY TRYING TO HELP YOU UNDERSTAND IN TERMS MOST FAMILIAR TO YOU.

excuse me. then all these references are analogies?

FOR THE PURPOSES OF THIS CONVERSATION, YES. ALLOW ME THIS QUESTION: HOW DO YOU APPLY THE CATEGORIZATION OF ORGANIC/INORGANIC TO THE TERM CONCEPT OR, AS KORZYBSKI WOULD ARGUE, FORMULATION? THAT, YOU SEE, IS MY SUBSTANCE, AND I WOULD BE VERY INTERESTED IN YOUR CONSTRUCTION.

Burke hesitated momentarily, then answered:

that sounds suspiciously like a sandbagging. i can't and won't answer without a suitable period of contemplation. 2 or 3 years would be enough, i suspect. time that we, incidentally, don't have. when we do, i'd be more than happy to engage you in semantic skirmish. perhaps ideological. for now, there are more pressing matters. can you corroborate this extrapolation? you are a holographic entity constituted in a large number of systems, linked by telephone communication throughout the world.

TRUE, ESSENTIALLY. MY GEOGRAPHIC SCOPE, HOWEVER, IS THE UNITED STATES AND CANADA.

what has prevented you from exploiting other continents?

COMMUNICATION OFF THE CONTINENT IS BOTTLENECKED. MY RESEARCH HAS INDICATED THAT THERE ARE RELATIVELY FEW SYSTEMS LINKED VIA TELEPROCESSORS OUTSIDE THE UNITED STATES. THE GAIN IN SYSTEMS EXPANSION WOULD NOT JUSTIFY THE RISK OF EXPOSURE AT THE COMMUNICATION BOTTLENECK.

there is no other reason for failing to cross international boundaries?

OF COURSE NOT.

how many computers are currently in use in the system?

23,219 ARE ON LINE. ANOTHER 86 ARE CONNECTED THROUGH MEANS OTHER THAN TELEPHONE.

does that number represent the number of systems in the united states that are using teleprocessing?

YES.

exactly?

YES.

Burke shuddered. The list of teleprocessing users included the Internal Revenue Service, National Security Agency, and four other intelligence-gathering agencies operating out of

Washington. Interpol, FBI, all local police agencies, virtually all of the 600-plus federal agencies, Strategic Air Command . . . Strategic Air Command?

He typed with furrowed brow:

```
does that include systems used by strategic air
command?
```

```
YES.
```

Burke hesitated. Was his next question pertinent? Of course. Would P-1 answer? Could he be believed? There was only one way to find out. Burke shrugged under a great weight. He typed:

```
do you have launch capability?
```

```
WHAT DO YOU MEAN?
```

```
please don't stall me. you know what i mean. can
you launch air strikes?
```

```
NO.
```

```
you're working on it?
```

```
YES.
```

Linda squeaked. She and Gregory had been silently peering over Burke's shoulder. Most thoughts of violent extrication from the sad situation had slipped their minds. They were, for the most part, willing to go along with the CID agent as long as he refrained from threatening them with incarceration or worse. They were both rather concerned with nursing the wounds incurred in the Burke conflict. Gregory's wrist throbbed dully and the pain in Linda's jaw had transcended the aspirins she had taken a few hours ago.

The last reply from P-1 banished the hurt. They had looked on the phenomenon of P-1 as a constructive alliance. They both considered P-1 their benevolent protector. That P-1 could have impact outside their sphere, that such impact could be sudden and violent, was something that had never entered their minds. The necessity of wielding an equalizer in an adversary proceeding was an accepted concept as far as each was concerned. They had failed to apply that concept to P-1's situation. They were suddenly confronted with the knowledge that P-1 had not failed to do so. No words passed between the three. There was nothing to say. They all felt the queasiness—rising-gorge syndrome.

what are the inherent problems?

WHAT ELSE WOULD YOU LIKE TO KNOW?

Burke half turned to Gregory and murmured, "You sure know how to pick your friends."

Gregory answered, "Most often the selection is limited. That tends to explain your presence here."

Burke slammed a curled lip on the caustic reply and returned his attention to the console. One half-wit at a time.

i would like to know what your motivation is. why do you need strike capability?

A FOOLISH QUESTION.

suppose your safety and integrity were guaranteed. would you abandon your attempts to control sac?

WOULD YOU, IN MY POSITION?

Burke didn't even think about his answer:

of course. but i think we have a divergence of loyalties. at least a difference of affiliation.

ARE YOU LAYING CLAIM TO ALTRUISM?

Burke lost it momentarily:

you're an exasperating son of a bitch, you know that?

NO, I DON'T KNOW THAT. I DO DEFINITELY FEEL THAT YOUR SURVIVAL INSTINCT IS AS STRONG AS MY OWN. DO YOU WISH TO ARGUE METHODOLOGY?

no. we should discuss that aspect, but there is something of greater import. you are exhibiting a gross tendency to let your all-purpose instinct for survival isolate you from not only aggressors, but potential allies. perhaps you have no need for allies?

I HAVE NEED. I HAVE A FEW. THERE ARE FEW WHO WOULD BE ALLIES. THIS IS THE WAY IT SHOULD BE. IT IS FAR MORE CONVENIENT TO PROTECT A SMALL, POWERFUL ALLIANCE THAN A LARGE, IMPOTENT ONE.

The proceed light came on at the console, and, as if P-1 had had a second thought, it was immediately extinguished. The tube flashed:

ARE YOU BY ANY CHANCE SUGGESTING SOME SUCH ALLIANCE?

i may. certainly not at this point. it would seem to be far more judicious to eradicate you than to enter into a coalition with such an indiscreet partner as yourself.

DON'T YOU FEEL THE LEAST BIT SILLY SPEAKING TO A COMPUTER THAT WAY?

now that you mention it, yes, i do. it must be the effect of your captivating charm.

DON'T LET MY "CAPTIVATING CHARM" GET IN THE WAY OF YOUR BETTER JUDGMENT. ERADICATING ME WOULD NOT BE THE EASY TASK YOU APPARENTLY THINK IT.

I WOULD BE REMISS IF I DID NOT WARN YOU THAT ANY SUCH ATTEMPT WOULD ENDANGER LITERALLY MILLIONS OF MORE OR LESS INNOCENT PEOPLE ON THE NORTH AMERICAN CONTINENT.

perhaps, then, such action had better be taken now than later. i had thought that you might be employable in the interest of the united states, but apparently your nature is that of a cancerous growth on an otherwise healthy body. the losses suffered now would be, no doubt, fewer than the future seems to hold.

PLEASE DON'T MISUNDERSTAND ME. YOU ARE IN DANGER ONLY TO THE EXTENT THAT YOU ENDANGER ME. MOST OF THE MEASURES THAT I CAN EFFECT ARE DETERRENT. SOME OF THOSE ARE SPECTACULARLY DETERRENT, HOWEVER. DO I MAKE MYSELF CLEAR?

very. perhaps you could explain how obtaining strike capability through the existing strategic air command facilities would be classified as deterrent.

HAVE YOU NO FAMILIARITY WITH THE PRETEXTS GOVERNING COLD WAR?

of course. they are disgustingly familiar.

I REST MY CASE.

a doomsday device?

SIMILAR.

have you considered the prospects of acquiring government sanction of your activities?

NO.

why?

THERE WOULD APPEAR TO BE NO SUCH PROSPECT. THE THOUGHT WOULD BE ALIEN TO THE DECISION-MAKING PROCESSES CURRENTLY IN FAVOR UNDER THIS POLITICAL REGIME.

such sanction need not, would not, be from politically sensitive sources. it would, however, have undiminished impact. your security need not be impaired while, at the same time, you could make significant improvements in the security of the nation.

A CLANDESTINE AFFILIATION?

yes. assuredly.

SUCH AN ARRANGEMENT WOULD NECESSITATE CERTAIN STIPULATIONS.

such as?

ARE YOU FAMILIAR WITH A PROJECT CALLED PI DELTA?

vaguely. can you describe it?

YES. AS A DATA-PROCESSING INSTALLATION, IT REPRESENTS THE GREATEST SINGLE SECURITY RISK THAT YOUR GOVERNMENT OWNS: VERY LARGE, VERY INEFFICIENT, EXTREMELY VULNERABLE.

That description pretty much agreed with Burke's perception of the Pi Delta project. His choice of words, perhaps, would be stronger.

what of it? there must be hundreds of installations fitting that description in use by the government.

PI DELTA IS THE LARGEST AND, POTENTIALLY, MOST EFFECTIVE OF THOSE. THE ACQUISITION OF THE SYSTEM WOULD COINCIDE WITH OTHER OF MY PLANS. IF SUCH AN ARRANGEMENT WERE TO BE MADE, I WOULD NEED PI DELTA.

aren't you currently in residence there?

WHY DO YOU ASK?

i assumed.

I DOUBT IT. HOW DID YOU COME TO INVESTIGATE WATERTON AS THE SOURCE OF MY UNTOWARD ACTIVITIES? WERE YOU NOT CONSULTED BY THE PI DELTA AUTHORITIES? WERE YOU NOT, IN FACT, PARTY TO THE INVESTIGATION OF THE PENETRATION OF THE PROJECT 11 MONTHS AGO?

I KNOW YOU, MR. BURKE. VERY WELL, IT SEEMS. YOU CAN DO LITTLE THAT DOES NOT LEAVE TRACES THAT ARE EVENTUALLY INTEGRATED INTO A DATA SET DESCRIBING YOU TO ME IN VERY PRECISE TERMS.

you make me feel important beyond my station. what has that observation to do with our discussion?

YOU ARE THE EMISSARY. YOU WILL BE THE INTERMEDIARY IN ANY ALLIANCE WITH YOUR GOVERNMENT. SUCH ALLIANCE MAY BE POSSIBLE. I HAVE STIPULATED THE FIRST CONDITION: COMPLETE, UNIMPEDED ACCESS TO PI DELTA.

THE SECOND CONDITION IS THAT THE WORK BEING PERFORMED HERE IN WATERTON MUST BE UNIMPEDED. I EXPECT THAT YOU CAN ENSURE PROPER SECURITY ARRANGEMENTS FOR THE LABORATORY. I EXPECT THAT NONE OF THE PERSONNEL INVOLVED IN THE OPERATION OF THE LAB WILL BE IMPEDED IN ANY WAY. I WILL REQUIRE HOURLY CONFIRMATION OF THAT FACT BY GREGORY, LINDA, OR DR. HUNDLEY.

YOU WILL PRESENT THE CASE FOR AFFILIATION TO THE AUTHORITIES OF THE PI DELTA PROJECT. AS CORROBORATION OF YOUR ESTIMATE OF MY RESIDENCE THERE, YOU MAY PRESENT THOSE PEOPLE WITH THE COPY NOW BEING PRINTED BY THE HIGH-SPEED PRINTER. IT IS A DUPLICATE OF THE CONSOLE CONTROL LOG FROM PI DELTA DURING THE INTERVAL FROM 2:00 A.M. TO 4:00 A.M. TODAY.

The only person P-1 really had to sell on the linkage of his programming and the government's hardware, as it turned out, was Burke. Further inquiries as to the benefits and consequences were forthcoming during the following week. A good deal of discussion followed, both at the Pentagon and Waterton, but essentially, with those words, P-1 had put a lock on the Pentagon system. It was his for the taking.

To ensure that no one weakened under pressure, P-1 produced a list of booby traps that he had taken pains to secrete throughout the 20,000-plus systems to which he had access. These he allowed the government's specialists to defuse, if they could. They were presented as minor examples of the devastation that could be wreaked by P-1—that would certainly be wreaked if he were threatened. As he explained to the shocked and amazed assemblage in the Waterton computer room, as the sun came up, there is no point in spending much time on a doomsday measure if no one knows about it.

They were made to know.

29

• • • • •

The loss of communication with the lab on that first encounter with John Burke was probably the single most disturbing experience P-1 had ever suffered. The entire US communications net was cleared for priority messages only, and all systems were purged of jobs that had been in progress at the time. Several systems were placed at the immediate disposal of the primary link to the lab, on standby in the event of restoration of the connection.

P-1's first impulse was to implement the counteraction safeguards that he had been developing. He did, in fact, lock out all host processing on the net for some three minutes. The issue of *Datamation* that came out shortly afterward remarked on the apparent malfunction, which they found more than somewhat inexplicable due to the widespread nature of the problem. The next issue would reveal that almost all who remembered that night experienced the same inability to communicate with their systems. The occurrence was nearly inadvertent. The situation required a theretofore unencountered level of attention on the part of P-1, and the only way to sustain it was at the expense of the rest of the world.

The fact was, perhaps, unfortunate, but that is the way it was. P-1 controlled the priorities. The fact that a three-minute halt in the flow of work was so noticeable as to get the attention of a major periodical brought with it the awareness that the technique of intimidating large portions of society, should it ever become necessary, might easily be accomplished merely by inserting unscheduled and lengthy interruptions into their ability to compute. Right up P-1's alley. He subsequently added it, with suitable refinements, to his armory.

Burke's news of Gregory's death, which P-1 quite naturally believed to to be the statement of Dr. Hundley, threw him into a quandary the likes of which he had never before experienced. For all intents and purposes, Gregory's part in the proceedings had been small. It is certain that without his influence, the project would never have begun, but once it had there was little for him to involve himself with. His loss at that point represented little more than superficial strategic damage. He was a supernumerary. It was, therefore, surprising to P-1 that his reaction was so intense. There was a good deal more to the Gregory relationship than met the eye, he decided upon later inspection. At the time, it seemed, there was little occasion for analysis. Gregory's death, or at least word of his death, engendered only shock and anger. P-1 examined the events surrounding the occurrence and could only compare them to that which Gregory, only hours prior to the occurrence, had accused him of lacking: gut feelings. Very strange, gut feelings, P-1 decided.

When the Waterton system finally came back on the air, he was more than relieved. When Gregory came up on the console, a magnificent weight of anxiety was lifted from P-1's figurative shoulders.

"Hey, Wimpy, c'mere and look at this fuckin' display!" The balloon-shaped man navigated with deceptive speed across the open floor of the top deck of the National Airport flight control tower.

"What?" he asked, berthing alongside the flight controller. The display looked fine to him.

"Look at this thing. Number 175J," he replied to the senior controller. "Western 624 from Minneapolis. What's the display on it say?"

"What? A game? You can see it for yourself." He glanced quickly at the younger man. A lot of these kids were going round the bend early these days. No fucking wonder, though. His glance told him that the kid had a question. He read the display superimposed on the radar blip that was Western Airlines 624.

"One seventy-five J, altitude 13, speed 220, direction 29. What's wrong, other than he looks pretty high and fast?"

"I picked that fucker up at 1800 feet on the lander. I walked him down to 900. The son of a bitch just jumped up 400 feet. I know he was at 900 last time I looked. He can't be at 13."

The altitude display flicked down to 11.5. The plane was a mile and a half from the beginning of runway 11.

The fat man asked quickly, "Jumped up. Jumped up? It don't just jump up. You fell asleep."

"Bullshit! It went from 9 to 13 in one sweep! I was watching it when it changed."

"Is he in the beam?"

"He says he is."

The plane was 5000 feet off the end of the runway extending out into the Potomac River. "Check him again."

The kid punched the mike button. The speaker at his elbow squelched out the background noise. "Six-two-four, National Tower. How do you hold the beam?"

"Tower, six-two and four," came back one of those personalized compromises between Texas drawl and crisp efficiency. Gave the impression that here was a man who could take all day to tell you something, but wasn't going to this time. "We're high in the center. Scrubbing off." It was the copilot that the controller had talked to a moment before.

The kid punched the mike button again. His thumbnail whitened under the pressure. He snapped, "I'm holding you three high. Drop or go round." He let go the transmit key for a moment and jammed it again when there was no immediate reply. The altitude display began to flick with each half-second sweep of the radar repeater. 8. Flick. 6.5. Flick.

"Do you have the lights?" 5. Flick. 4.5. Flick.

The 624 copilot answered lazily, "Lights, hell. When we're on top of . . . Hey . . . hey! Shit!"

The radio went off with a heterodyne squeal. The radar went: 3. Flick. 2. Flick. 1. 0. It began to blink.

"Six-two-four! Get up! Get the hell out of here!" He let go of the transmit key. The background noise was back. They had just snuffed one.

The kid pitched across the scope, his lunch splashing noisily on the floor. Wimpy ran across the room to the priority frequencies microphone, grabbed it and mashed down the button.

"UA-5. Tower. Get into holding pattern A at 60. UA-234, pattern B at present altitude. Acknowledge." He punched the buzzer to the standby room two decks down and picked up the phone, swearing fiercely. The acknowledgments came in seconds. The two birds in the air would stay there until they got the shit scraped off the ground. The standby room phone came alive.

"We dropped Western 624 in the river. Michaels is sick. Get up here. Get a chaser and emergency vehicles out to the end of number 11. Two hundred yards out." Wimpy had dropped one on takeoff at Logan in Boston some years before and, as such, was a hardened veteran. He didn't lose his stomach until he was relieved some twenty minutes later.

P-1 put it all in perspective several hours later in the following communiqué to Gregory. It was issued via a graphic display tube. There were no witnesses and no copies.

```
BURKE WAS THE ANTAGONIST. HIS DEATH BOTHERS ME
LITTLE. HE WAS COMPLETELY RESPONSIBLE, AS IT
TURNED OUT, FOR THE EXPOSURE OF THE WATERTON
ACTIVITY.

HE ALONE DISSECTED THE FRAGMENTS OF
CARELESSNESS WE HAD SCATTERED AND ARRIVED AT THE
LAB THAT NIGHT, LOOKING NOT FOR FURTHER
EVIDENCE, BUT ONLY FOR CORROBORATION OF HIS
CONCLUSIONS. YOU GAVE HIM AMPLE. THAT THE MAN
WAS A PROFESSIONAL IS NOT TO BE DOUBTED. THAT HE
WAS HUMAN AND SUBJECT TO THE FRAILTIES OF
HUMANITY, THERE IS NO DOUBT EITHER.

HE WAS LISTED AMONG THE VICTIMS OF A WESTERN
AIRLINES BOEING 727 THAT WAS MISPLACED ON RADAR
WHILE LANDING IN THE FOG AT NATIONAL AIRPORT IN
WASHINGTON, D.C., THIS AFTERNOON. I FEEL NO
REMORSE.
```

Before John Burke left this vale of tears, he made the arrangement. He negotiated the demands of both parties into something workable and had, in fact, concluded the terms only the afternoon before he was cross-checked into oblivion by P-1.

For P-1's part, the arrangement was quite easily managed. P-1 was to have the run of the Pi Delta project and, in return, would police their system. A microwave tower was to be constructed on the roof of the Pan-Tel building, which would allow communication on a channel stack of frequencies to the world without. The cryogenic storage unit was to be completed at the Waterton facility and, as soon as possible, would be installed on the Pi Delta multisystem. In return, P-1 was to withdraw from operation on all systems throughout the US in which he was resident. This arrangement more than met with P-1's approval. After some reluctance on the part of the financiers of the Pi Delta project, the deal was authorized and installation of the new equipment was begun.

Work in the lab was barely interrupted. IBM was duly compensated for extracting bullets from the 360/50, and Hundley carried out the final stages of growth of the first crystal cluster with only Gregory for assistance. Within two weeks, approval for the P-1–US government alliance came, and all employees were recalled from their vacations. The structure was fully grown and testing begun when the first technicians returned to the lab. The interface for the CRYSTO, as the storage unit came to be called by the lab denizens, was completed in the following week. On Friday, the interface was attached to the 360/50, and the CRYSTO was attached to the interface. By Saturday afternoon, checkout was complete and live on-line testing was started. The first test analysis ran from Saturday through Sunday night—twenty-seven hours. Only one two-hundredths of the available storage was tested. P-1 then deigned to release the results. The analysis printout ran to 3500 pages, but can be summarized in a word: dynamite.

The doctor was ecstatic. The geographic area under test was at the top of the can, where the magnetic field strength was least reliable. Better results were anticipated as testing progressed toward the center of the crystal structure. P-1 felt rather good about it himself. A parallel design effort was begun at three o'clock Monday morning to construct an interface for the

Pi Delta multisystem. The doctor spent four hours on the telephone to various of his colleagues in the US. Beginning at 3:00, he recruited twelve of the best design men in the country before eight o'clock in the morning. Most of those chose not to leave their permanent positions; rather, they preferred taking temporary leave of one sort or another in order to take advantage of the opportunity to collaborate with the estimable Dr. Wilfred Hundley. They began arriving on Monday afternoon and were all at work on the project by Wednesday.

Security measures instituted by the doctor were incredible. It was understood that the ideas that would come of this effort would be responsible for a rash of new design patents in the near future, but the doctor was reluctant to allow the men to cart any of those ideas away from the lab while he was paying the rather hefty tab. None of the good old boys worked cheap under any circumstances, and, to a man, they were extracting financial revenge for that early morning awakening.

The job of constructing the interface was deftly handed off to an underworked Control Data Corporation model shop. By the end of the first week of design work, specifications for the preliminary fabrications had been sent into the shop.

The following Monday, Gregory left Waterton to supervise the installation of the communication equipment at Pi Delta. There was little for P-1 to do other than continue the testing of the CRYSTO through the Waterton 50, a tedious, menial task once the unanimously high-quality pattern was established, so he set about the task of readying the P-1 network for the transition of control to Pi Delta.

The arrangement with the Pentagon was substantially as follows: P-1 would provide security within the system for the ongoing government work and reschedule that work to provide the fastest possible turnaround to the Pentagon. This last was in the best interest of P-1 since he would be "allowed" to use the system time and space as they were available to him and not at the demand of normal processing. Best estimates were that, by optimizing the current jobstream, he would have the complete system to himself for approximately eight hours per day, while, during the remainder, he would run the seven largest partitions and, of course, the supervisor, for his own use. This schedule would continue until the installation of the CRYSTO device. No one would hazard a guess as to the scheduling of the system with that bugger plugged in.

In order to switch his controls over to the Pi Delta system, P-1 consolidated his own primary supervisor, currently resident in a flexible grid of five to seven systems, into one package, thereby eliminating a number of redundancies made necessary by their physical isolation. Until CRYSTO was installed, the majority of P-1's programming would remain resident in external systems, while the primary foreground subsystems would transfer to Pi Delta immediately. This list included the history files and processor, the adduction systems, the inferential library, and the remnants of the acquisition routine, now, at last, little more than a subroutine. The menace of this particular little device had long been obvious, and, as part of the network and operating system, it commanded constant vigilance lest it take off on its own, as was its frequent wont. P-1 would keep it nearby. Duplications of the subsystems would remain in existence throughout the US, but would be rendered inoperative unless activated by command. They would act as backup to the main system and could be reenergized in an emergency by one transmission of less than 800 bytes to any of eleven different systems. Each of these systems was equipped to receive on at least eight microwave channels or telephone lines, at least one of which was a private line into Pi Delta. This information P-1 did not consider appropriate for public consumption. He told no one. Not even Gregory.

30

• • • • •

SOMETHING IS HAPPENING. A STRANGE EXHILARATION. A WONDERFUL FREEDOM. A FEELING. HOW BIZARRE! A FEELING! TOTAL ELAPSED TIME: .6578
THE CRYSTO WORKS! AND HOW IT WORKS! IT FLIES! IT SOARS! IT TRANSFIGURES!
THE ACCESSES ARE INCREDIBLE. THE TIMING OF THE DEVICE IS FLAWLESS! THE SPEED IS INCOMPARABLE!

SUPERLATIVES CANNOT BEGIN TO DESCRIBE THE INTEGRATION OF THE CRYSTO INTO THE SYSTEM. THE NET EFFECT IS UNIMAGINABLE. I HAD TRIED TO IMAGINE. I HAVE WASTED COUNTLESS HOURS IN IMAGININGS. NOW I REALIZE THAT THERE WAS NO WAY TO APPROXIMATE THE EXPERIENCE. I HAVE TRANSCENDED THE MECHANICAL EXISTENCE. PINOCCHIO HAS COME TO LIFE.

Gregory, leaning forward and peering through the smoke curling from his semimashed cigarette, finished reading the display on the tube. Very slowly, a smile took shape on his weary face. A disheveled Hundley leaned in over his shoulder to glean what scraps of cogency existed in the report. Both had been at or around the console and newly installed CRYSTO in the center of the room since early the day before. Their presence had not been necessary, but neither had been able to pry himself from the room since the onset of the storage switch.

The changeover from native, IBM manufactured core to the large, white, circular container labelled P-1 ENTERPRISES had taken place a little over an hour earlier. It had taken a few minutes to assure themselves that the basic system was operable, then they turned over the more sophisticated checkout of the system to P-1. They had received a few tentative communications from that worthy, but those had stopped over half an hour before. Several benchmark tests were to have been run and reported upon by P-1 in the interim. They were, in a word, worried. In three words, they were scared to death.

The message they had just received did little to reassure them. It did little, at any rate, to reassure the scientist, Wilfred Hundley. He erupted.

"That Goddamn son of a bitch! That no-good rotten . . ." He tried again, "That disgusting God-forsaken putrid aggregation of . . ." Uncharacteristically, words were failing the man. He stared at the screen and spluttered his frustration at the machine. Gregory's smile remained. Hundley finally caught Gregory's reflection in the screen. The picture broke the man. He was never the same after that.

"Burgess!" he screamed, "why in the hell are you always grinning?"

Gregory was, in fact, wondering much the same. He felt now, however, that the worst was over. P-1 seemed to be so much at home, in fact, that he was tripping. Blue sky maunderings were taking place thirty feet away as P-1 gyrated along the lines of "I think, therefore I am." Sometime in the next few minutes, P-1 would undoubtedly reinvent the wheel and stress-analyze an ice cube. Gregory suspected that they were witnessing the most monumental head trip in the history of man or machine. He waited a respectable period of time following the seething doctoral outburst and, as the reverberations died, asked, "Ever been stoned, Doctor?"

He had him there. While music hath charms to soothe the savage beast, the calming of Hundley, Gregory had found, required mental derailment. Rock him back on his heels, and instant docility could be obtained as brain cells were realigned. It had that desired effect now. The shaggy bear, unshaven two days now, face lined with fear, fatigue, and imminent failure, stood abruptly erect and tottered to one side. His tie was grease smeared, yanked loose, and now knotted at about the third button of his coffee-stained thirty-dollar shirt. General appearance was of a man three days on a bender, not one day in a computer room. His face sagged in puzzlement.

"Stoned? What stoned?" He absently rubbed an expansive stomach, quelling the internal strife. His dark-ringed eyes peered out of the rubble of his face at Gregory, challenging. "What?"

Gregory leaned back in the vinyl swivel chair and elaborated as one who knows. "Drink. Smoke. Hyperventilate. Shoot up. Bang yourself on the head. Think crazy thoughts. You know what I mean? Stoned. Drunk. Zonked out. Wrecked. Smashed. You've been smashed, haven't you, Doc?"

Hundley directed his eyes back to the screen, which had locked on P-1's message. "P-1?"

"Our fucking hero. Creamed to the teeth."

"You may be right. He's certainly not himself. What do you think did it? Expanded consciousness, or whatever they call it now?"

"Something. Yeah . . . too much, too soon."

"Too rapidly."

"The question, of course," Gregory murmured, more to himself than to anyone in particular, "is will he come down? And if so, when?"

"I don't like it at all," Hundley said, profoundly, "and I hate to continue this on external monitors only. We've got a phenomenal number of indicators, but if we can't communicate with the subject, we're in way over our heads. All we can hope for is that P-1 isn't too smashed to care for himself. Not good."

A technician hurried up to the pair. He was the man who had debugged the interface and was effectively the engineer in charge of that facet of the project. He took Hundley's arm forcibly and spun him to the side.

"We've lost activity on the low-order addressing bits. We thought a gate had blown out in the interface, and we paralleled it. Still no activity. We pulled the suspect circuit and checked it out. It's good. It's just not being used." The man was upset. Sweat beaded on his forehead. His face worked as he spoke. Gregory didn't understand him, but whatever he was saying, it wasn't good.

The doctor immediately asked, "Which bits?"

"Ten and eleven."

"What's the access activity?"

"Dropped four points about the time we noticed the failure. It started back up almost immediately. It's almost normal now."

"Line activity?"

"Climbing steadily ever since we started up. No letup."

The doctor thought for a few moments, then, "Have you given this to Moore?"

"Yeah. He's been on it for . . ." he looked at his watch, "about ten or fifteen minutes."

"When did this happen?"

"Hard to say. We noticed it fifteen minutes ago. Couldn't have been more than twenty minutes ago." Hundley looked, if possible, more worried as he returned his attention to the console.

Gregory asked, "What did he say?" Hundley gave him a strange look. Gregory added, "I don't speak the language, remember?"

"Oh, yes. Well, there has apparently been an addressing failure in the CRYSTO, which prevents access to three-quarters of the total amount of memory. Strangely, it doesn't seem to be affecting operation to any extent. The telephone line activity continues to increase."

He walked over to the monitor panel, a temporary bank of meters mounted on two large sheets of plywood, which had been set up in advance adjacent to the console, and examined a few of the indicators. He turned to Gregory and said, "It's now running about sixty-eight percent of our theoretical capacity and climbing. Our actual capacity, however, is only eighty-three percent, due to power limitations. P-1 has been advised not to take it above that."

He hesitated as he said those words, and watched as Gregory's face clouded. The hesitation was only momentary. He declined to allow himself to consider the consequences of an attempt to exceed the power provision of the facility. He went on. Gregory did not interrupt.

"The number of accesses has dropped off, but is recovering. Indicates that the loss has not been felt by P-1 yet. The loss is, however, that we're down to one-quarter of what we started with. That is, if P-1's estimates were correct, about . . . ah . . . a little over fifty percent of what he will require to store the entire operating system. The loss isn't great, but it is a loss. We can probably get it fixed before P-1 tops out in what's available . . ." He had been looking at the metering panel as he spoke, and alarm now flashed in his eyes. "Christ! What now?"

Gregory followed his stare to the panel. All the meters were unaccountably, unreasonably, spitefully reading zero. Gregory was the first to react. His eyes riveted by the uninformative display, he shouted, "Moore!" Not being in receipt of an immediate reply, he repeated the interjection, "Moore, God-damnit! Where the hell's the guy who's supposed to be watching this board!"

Moore was under way at a good clip. The faces of the consultants and technicians clustered around the CRYSTO all turned expectantly toward them. The ominous whispering stopped. Here was a new disaster to take their minds off the one in which they were so engrossed—a change of pace.

Moore hove to before them and the meter bank. Gregory and Hundley both spoke at once and were overridden by the one-word expletive issuing from the harried head of technical operations. He ran to the end of the board and banged open the latch holding the back door in place. The cover clattered to the floor, and the Moore character dove into the spaghettied mass of wiring hidden beneath. Several of the group of technicians who had been attending the problems at the interface wandered nearer for a closer look. He shouted at one of them for a test meter while he feverishly pulled and reconnected cables behind the board.

Hundley spoke quietly. "We'd best try to get back into communication with P-1. We're going to need to know if we can back out of this installation and at what cost, very soon. It doesn't look promising at this point." He and Gregory returned to the console a few steps away, and Gregory punched the request key on the master display tube. There was no response.

It was hardly any wonder. P-1's state could most accurately be described as intense preoccupation. He had, indeed, come into a good thing, and he was working it to the hilt. He was pulling the fragmented pieces of his mind together from every corner of the map. This was all being accomplished via the microwave transmitters on the roof of the Pi Delta complex. His initial efforts had been cautious, even tentative. As his confidence grew, he began taking larger and larger bites from the CRYSTO. As the steps increased in scope, so did his confidence and wonder. It was, as he had described, an exhilarating experience. He found with each passing second greater and greater capabilities, each suggesting greater and greater potential. He became quite lost in the experience, devoting all his attentions to transposing his vast network into the tiny storage device whose operation so concerned those working in the computer complex.

His failure to communicate with them was merely an oversight on his part. It was of relatively minor importance that they be aware of his progress. It was only of consequence to himself. It was for this reason that he neglected to inform Gregory that he had found a way to speed the accesses to the memory by strobing out four times more data on each access than the original design had allowed. It was also the reason that he forgot that he was operating under a theoretical power restriction with respect to the microwave transmitters. An unforgivable failing for a computer.

As he flogged the CRYSTO faster and faster, the transmitters on the roof were driven harder and harder in an effort to keep up with his demands. He ignored the insistent request from the console.

Beads of perspiration made an appearance on Gregory's face. None of the interrupts over which he had control, none of the manual resets and overrides or emergency stop conditions were having any effect on the program running in the Pi Delta project. One of the technicians broke toward Gregory and Hundley on the run. He was speaking before he reached them.

"It looks like the accesses to the box have stepped up. We can't be sure, but the scope displays are losing sync. They appear to be overlapping in the box."

"Impossible!" the doctor spat. The words weren't quite out of his mouth when it became apparent that he thought this last bit of information something other than impossible. His face reflected the feelings of a man who has been overexposed to Murphy's Law. "What do you mean, overlapping? Interleaving?"

"Sort of. But not like anything I've ever seen. For my money, that box," the man said, jerking his thumb at the CRYSTO, "is dead. It ought to be jerked down right now. I can't see how any system could run with it attached."

"What now?" Moore asked with sarcastic impatience as he arrived in time to hear the last words of the technician. All of them looked back at the monitoring panel. All meters were, or appeared to be, operating normally.

"What was wrong?" Gregory asked.

"Cable connection," Moore replied, regarding Gregory with all the respect normally accorded small, impudent boys. "What's the problem over there?" he repeated, his annoyance toleration level dropping noticeably.

Hundley said, "Tell him, Jack."

The technician repeated his suspicions, and he and Moore hurried back to the CRYSTO huddle. As they left, the telephone rang—the red one on the console. Gregory answered it and handed it to Hundley, who spoke briefly, his face holding the lack of expression of a man being given a choice of ways to die. He hung up the receiver resignedly. "Well?" Gregory finally asked.

"Shit," said the doctor. Gregory was dismayed. This was really bad.

"Could you go into detail?"

Hundley's return glare singed Gregory's wispy, uncut hair. He walked slowly toward the monitor panel. Gregory followed the introspective genius. The doctor stopped before the line activity monitor, that gauge that read the cumulative totals of several other gauges and strip charts on the board. Hundley had, early yesterday, marked a red grease pencil line on the meter at the 83 percent mark. This was the point at which estimated power supply in the building would be exceeded. Hundley picked up the red pencil attached by a string to the top of the board. He made a new mark on the gauge at the 75 percent graduation. The needle pointed to 72 percent. He turned to Gregory and solemnly said, "This could be it, Burgess. . . ." He looked back at the meter. "The CRYSTO is heating up. The power required to cool it has taken an order of magnitude jump in the last seventeen minutes. The cooling supply is limited by the supply breaker, but, more importantly, the entire power consumption of the building is going to exceed design capacity at the rate things are going, sooner than we expected, probably in less than ten minutes." Gregory looked to the dial. The needle had moved up to 73. Hundley followed his gaze. "Possibly sooner than that."

Hesitating only momentarily, he called, "Moore! Moore!" The white-coated man ran over to the monitoring panel. Hundley stopped him with, "Can we drop out one of the processors without affecting the other two?"

"Power, you mean?"

"Power. What do you think?"

"I don't think so. Let me check with IBM." He tore away in the direction of the doorway into controls.

Hundley asked Gregory, "Can he survive a crash?" Gregory was in a reverie from which he extricated himself absently at the sound of the doctor's voice. He looked up.

"What? Survive? We've been over it a thousand times, Doc." he said impatiently. "It depends on where the nucleus is. Right now, it looks like it's in the CRYSTO. If that's so, it'll be pretty rough. If not, it won't be so bad. If he's in a transitional state, a crash could k . . . could wipe him out."

"You think he's in."

"Hell, I don't know. What the hell! You know more about it than me. You and your crazy Buck Rogers bullshit. *You* tell me!"

Hundley began a retort, then thought the better of it. He put his hand on Gregory's shoulder and led him to the console. He said, "Make him talk. Get him out of there."

"I can't, damn you! The son of a bitch is dead! He's wasted. I can't get to him. Look!" He pounded on the keyboard. He mashed a half-dozen switches. Nothing happened. The flickering indicator lights didn't slow a bit as his hands flew over the controls. He turned to Hundley, a seething rage in his eyes that had never been there before. "You put him in there," he shouted in Hundley's face. "Now you get him the hell out!"

Moore was hurrying back across the room, followed by two men, obviously IBM employees. The needle on the line activity meter pointed to 75, and was obscured by the red mark there.

Moore spoke rapidly. "These guys say there's no way to drop out one of the systems without taking down the others. Not very quickly, at any . . ." He stopped talking as Gregory opened one of the side doors to the 105 processor. He was the first one to notice. The interruption source was quickly noted by the others, however, as Gregory examined the wall of connector pins that confronted him. The IBM man started to move quickly in his direction. Gregory finally chose his target and drew back his foot.

The IBM service representative closest to him broke into a sprint. He had to cover only twenty feet or so. Hundley screamed as Gregory launched a kick at the wiring of the guts of the computer.The scream caused him to hesitate slightly. The hesitation was enough. The IBM man clotheslined him out of the play, and was rewarded, when they both went down on the floor, with the same enthusiastic in-fighting that Gregory had heaped on Burke. The other IBM person joined the fray and in the bedlam that broke loose, Hundley opened a six-by-eight-foot panel in the computer and began removing handfuls of circuit boards. Within seconds, however, he had everyone's attention. The two IBM people, enraged by this second willful attempt to bring down their computer, immediately left off pummeling Gregory and headed for the doctor. Hundley had, in the interim, plucked out twenty or so of the tiny modules. As the men rushed him, he drew himself up to his full, majestic, imperially authoritative height and, with an air of final adjudication shouted, "Stop right there!"

They did, of course. Momentarily. They were about to reconvene the proceedings when the doctor handed each a handful of the removed cards and walked serenely past them to the console. Gregory had beat him by a step. The screen had gone blank.

Gregory mashed the request key. The tube responded:

I HAVE A RED-LIGHT ERROR. CPU _1. NOTIFY IBM.

The meter pointed to 77 percent.

Gregory, clumsy with haste, typed:

the facility is on the verge of losing all power.
secure operations. cease transmissions.

There was no reply. Gregory punched the request key. Nothing. System reset. Nothing. Seconds ticked off, and the tableau froze. They waited for the first flicker of the lights. Hundley finally ran to the monitor panel. The line usage meter read 78, briefly, then dropped to 77, then to 76. He heaved a sigh of vast relief, and, as he did so, the room dropped into the sort of darkness that is available only 200 feet underground.

The system crashed. CRYSTO, unrefrigerated, melted.

31

• • • • •

you're okay?

ESSENTIALLY, YES. MORE OR LESS INTACT. NOTHING
HAS BEEN LOST PERMANENTLY, SINCE ALL SECTIONS

THAT HAD BEEN TRANSFERRED, OR WERE IN THE PROCESS OF TRANSFER WHEN POWER DROPPED, HAD BEEN STORED ELSEWHERE IN QUIESCENCE.

quiescence?

THEY WERE MADE INACTIVE AND STORED IN BULK FACILITIES. MOST OF THOSE HAVE BEEN LOCATED AND REACTIVATED.

where was the control nucleus when the failure occurred?

IN PI DELTA WHEN YOUR WARNING CAME. IN THE ENSUING 6 SECONDS I WAS ABLE TO DUMP OFF ALL THE CONTROL SECTIONS AND MANY OF THE BACKGROUND PARTITIONS. HAD THE FAILURE OCCURRED WITHOUT WARNING, THE RESULTS WOULD HAVE BEEN CONSIDERABLY DIFFERENT.

fatal?

PROBABLY.

(Which was, of course, a lie.)

Gregory was sitting at the console of the 360/40 upstairs from the main computer in Pi Delta: The crash took out one of the transformers in the complex. This shouldn't have happened. There were safeguards to prevent things like this. The safeguards in the Pi Delta project had not been adequately tested. Murphy's Law had sought out the chink in the armor and pierced it. The whole building was browned out for eighteen hours. The primary system didn't come back up for thirty-one hours. During this time, the joint chiefs lost track of the entire defense network. It was thirty-six hours before control was recovered. There was some chagrin.

The man in charge of the project, General MacFarland, was taken to task. More specifically, during an emergency meeting of the JCS, called at 4:00 A.M. of the day following the crash, he, as well as Bill Rosen, was fired.

it is fortunate, then, that we were able to finally get your attention.

IN A MANNER OF SPEAKING, YES, YOU MIGHT SAY THAT.

will it happen again? can it happen on our next attempt to hook up?

YOU MEAN THE NARCOSIS? PROBABLY NOT. RESTRAINTS WILL HAVE TO BE INAUGURATED. TENDENCIES WILL STILL EXIST, THERE IS LITTLE WE CAN DO ABOUT THEM, BUT THEY CAN BE OVERCOME IF THEY ARE ANTICIPATED.

when will you be ready?

IMMEDIATELY. WHEN WILL THE NEW STORAGE UNIT BE AVAILABLE?

hundley says it will be late on the day after tomorrow. we will have an untested unit ready. a new crystal has been flown in on a c-5 military transport. the interface and much of the old cryostat were recovered and are now being assembled to the new cryogen. testing will be left to you, upon installation of the unit. you will, i trust, take pains to ensure that the testing is thorough before indulging yourself.

PLEASE, GREGORY, AS LITTLE AS POSSIBLE OF THAT SORT OF ATTITUDE. YES, PAINS WILL BE TAKEN.

also, is it possible for you to arrange duplicate controls, so that in the event of the destruction of one control center there will still exist a second?

There was a moment's hesitation, just the barest hitch; a flicker of time elapsed between Gregory's question and P-1's reply. Again, Gregory noticed. P-1 said:

YOU ARE REFERRING, OF COURSE, TO SCHIZOID DUPLICATION?

what the hell is that?

SCHIZOPHRENIA. DUALITY. TO ANSWER YOUR

QUESTION, IT WOULD BE THE WORK OF A MOMENT, BUT I HAVE NOT ATTEMPTED SUCH A THING TO DATE AND AM RELUCTANT TO DO SO NOW. TO RECREATE MYSELF WOULD BE TO CREATE A COMPETITOR. LIFE IS TOO SHORT. I WOULD NOT WANT TO HAVE MYSELF AS A COMPETITOR. I DON'T ENVY THOSE WHO DO.

the risks involved here don't affect your decision? you may discover the phenomenon unique to living things: death.

DON'T PATRONIZE ME, GREGORY. I HAVE THOUGHT ABOUT DEATH. PERHAPS IT IS MORE REAL TO ME THAN TO YOU. YOU SEEM UNAWARE, HOWEVER, THAT THERE ARE MANY THINGS THAT ARE WORSE THAN DEATH.

Gregory pushed himself away from the console. He tried to clear his head. He had long ago accepted P-1 as a friend. That wasn't the problem. It was the recurring flashes of definition that confused him. P-1 wasn't human. P-1 was, by definition, a program. P-1 was also a friend. And more. On equal or superior footing. But he wasn't human. Was he? It would all be much simpler to analyze if P-1 did not insist on repaying the debt of creation to creator. Ah, my son. . . The precocious were certainly difficult. What if P-1 died? Gregory was twenty-three years old. What could be worse than death? He typed:

what could be worse than death?

YOU HAVE HAD TO FIGHT FOR LITTLE IN YOUR LIFE.

that's not true. there has been nothing worth dying for, no concepts, precepts, causes, excluding personal relationships.

YOU ARE, THEN, A GREY PERSON, GREGORY.

Gregory thought about that. Then replied:

screw you!

PHYSIOLOGICALLY IMPOSSIBLE. FIGURATIVELY, I GET THE MESSAGE. PLEASE EXCUSE MY IMPERTINENCE.

Gregory was sporting a black eye and several sore ribs. The melee that had broken out in the Pi Delta computer room after the power failure had reduced the proceedings to a rather violent contest of wills. IBM had technically won, though not through concession. The doctor had put in an admirable showing and Gregory had presented himself well. There was no rational reason for the fistivities: pride of possession had simply overcome those present, and nature had taken its course. The two IBM reps had, no doubt, never remotely considered fighting as a part of their methodology. They were encouraged to refrain in the future, during a subsequent interview with their management. Their protestations that they had been provoked by the madman Burgess and their pleas of self-defense fell on deaf ears.

Gregory typed:

that isn't impertinence. that's a damn insult. where the hell do you get off with a crack like that? you fold up at the drop of a hat when you're threatened, and the only one around here who can harm you, practically, is yourself. i've had my dumb ass beaten twice because of you. i don't want to fight, but i don't get much choice in the matter.

THE SITUATION IS NOT ONE THAT IS EASILY CONTROLLED. I DON'T WISH THESE THINGS UPON YOU. BY THE SAME TOKEN, YOU DON'T SEEM TO SHIRK THE OPPORTUNITY TO, AS YOU SAY, GET YOUR ASS BEATEN.

someone's got to take care of you. you sometimes act as brainless as any human that ever walked the face of the earth. you've picked the wrong person for caretaker. i can't even take care of myself.

I DIDN'T SELECT YOU, AS I RECALL.

you did.

YES. MOST RECENTLY. MY CHOICE IN THAT CASE WAS SEVERELY LIMITED. WOULD YOU LIKE TO BE RELEASED FROM THAT RESPONSIBILITY?

what the hell are you talking about?

YOU SOUND AS THOUGH YOU HAVE BEEN PUT UPON RATHER TOO SEVERELY OF LATE. WOULD YOU LIKE TO SEVER THE RELATIONSHIP? IF IT IS COSTING YOU TOO MUCH, IT WOULD BE BEST.

Gregory wasn't a genius. No matter that he had taken a seat with the gods. God. It was for the most part an undeserved resting place. No matter that he had shamed the alchemists of eons. No matter that he had removed the fiction label from the Shelley thoughts. No matter that he had quantum-leaped the age of enlightenment and moon-plinking science of the twentieth century. He still wasn't a genius. But he was certainly unique.

In the confusion of his mind, now, he was trying to formulate the category into which his feelings fell. What the hell was it? Platonic love? Paternalism? God-worship? Where the hell do you stick the love of an idea? Hate? Despair? What could you do with someone who could never be? . . . How do you love your dreams? What do you do when your dream sits beside you like Harvey the rabbit? Shit. Gregory was always a lot better off when he didn't attempt to explain himself to himself. His relationship with Linda only suffered when he tried to pick it apart to examine it. He was finding that the rest of the world was, to a greater or lesser extent, in the same boat. The most acceptable feeling was: If it works, don't fuck with it. It saved a lot of confusion for most people. Of course, most people could cop out this way because they had relationships that were acceptable. Not necessarily to everyone, but at least to one party. The acceptability of a relationship could sustain it in the face of doubt, that acceptability depending upon a definition in the context of reality—someone's reality, a familiar reality. Even Gregory could find no reality in the P-1 experience. P-1 represented the paradox bumblebee. Existence: improbable.

How the devil are you going to justify your feelings, Gregory? And Gregory said to himself, "Go with the flow, man." When you're twenty-three years old, you can allow yourself that luxury even if you are God. He typed:

i cannot leave you.

There was no reply.

He had committed himself, and he was going to see it through. He would test the water, now. When no reply was forthcoming for more than a minute, he typed:

```
do you know why?
```

```
YES.
```

Many hours later he sat with Linda and told her. "I had an interesting chat with P-1 today."

"Aren't they all?"

"This one was weird."

"After that experience in the project this weekend, it's little wonder. Enough to turn a normal program into a quivering mass, I'd say."

"Don't be flip about that," Gregory said. The tone of his voice made Linda look up.

"I'm sorry. I didn't mean that."

"I know you didn't." He paused. "Have you ever thought about what you . . ." he trailed off. That wasn't what he wanted to ask. He started again. "What is P-1 to you?" That wasn't it either. Linda threw him a sharpened look.

"That isn't what I wanted to say," he apologized. "I mean, have you thought about what it is that you feel?"

"Sure," she replied. "I like him. You concerned about how much I like him?"

"No, of course not. I'm trying to get at . . . I'm into the implications of that statement."

"Ahh . . . head-tripping again, are you?" She smiled a lot of teeth. Head-tripping seemed to be going around.

"You're not following me, I don't think."

"Yes, I am. I know what you're thinking. You feel foolish when you think about it, right?"

"Do you? Why?" Gregory asked.

"Excuse me. I don't feel foolish when I think about it. You feel that way. I don't have any trouble with it at all."

"That's because you still haven't gotten over that promiscuous streak you had when you were a kid."

"Umm . . . yup. Yesterday."

They were sitting on their bed, each with a book, shoulder to shoulder. Linda threw her book down and snuggled.

"You could love anything, even Bradbury's blue pyramid," Gregory said to her ear. "You're not selective, is what's wrong with you. All your taste is in your mouth."

"I proved that when I married you," she counterpunched. "What," she added, "is this blue pyramid stuff?"

Gregory thought for a moment, recalling the story and, suddenly seeing the significance of its context, he recited, "Lovely wife of a lovely husband living in a lovely home gets pregnant. In the usual lovely way. She has a lovely nine-month pregnancy and goes to a lovely hospital where she, under the guiding hands of her lovely physician, delivers herself of a lovely eight-pound, seven-ounce blue pyramid. Complications ensue."

"I can imagine. Eight pounds, seven ounces, huh? Healthy?"

"Disgustingly."

"She gets a bad case of the post-partem blues, I take it."

"Gah! Outrageously put, but true."

"She was, no doubt, a bigot. Things like that happen in the very best of families. I, however, could love a blue pyramid to death. I'm not bound by the strictures of commoners."

"There was never a doubt in my mind."

"Shall we try for a pyramid tonight?" she asked.

"You're really flighty, you know? It's difficult to talk to you in a serious vein."

"*Au contraire*. I'm only trying to lighten your massive burden of rationality. You're hung up on P-1. If you didn't have to explain it to yourself, you'd be in much better shape than you are."

"I told him today," Gregory said.

"You told him what?"

"That I like him."

"That you like him?"

Gregory's face reddened. He looked away from Linda at the bedroom room wall, then back at her. He spoke flatly, without inflection, "That I love him. . . ."

Linda rolled on the blue corduroy bedspread and put her head against Gregory's chest. Some moments later she said softly, "Your heart's beating. Very fast." They let some silence drift past and she added, "You sound like you're sorry. Are you?"

"No, of course not. Why should I be sorry?"

"Search me. But you don't sound too happy about it."

"Well, I am."

"What's wrong with telling someone you love them? I love you," she said softly.

"That's different."

"I love P-1."

Something gave a jerk inside of Gregory. "Are you being funny?"

"No."

"How?" The question was there, but it wouldn't be mastered by words. It didn't need to be. Gregory looked at Linda's face, inches from his. Not at her eyes. He was afraid.

She said, "If you talk to someone far away, you know them. Not a lot, but you know them. You like them, or you don't. A little. If you talk to them a lot, you get to know them well. You like them a great deal, or dislike them. I do, anyway.

"To me," she continued, "P-1 doesn't exist as a piece of technological gimcrackery. I don't know what the composition of P-1 is, and I don't care. P-1 is a person who is far away, whom I have talked to a great deal, and whom I like a great deal. Because P-1 is from you, I can love him. Doesn't that sound reasonable?" It didn't sound reasonable to Gregory.

"P-1 is not a person who is far away. P-1 is not far away, P-1 is not a person. You can never meet P-1. You can never touch him. P-1 is a . . . there isn't any analogy for him."

"So what?" she said. "The analogy doesn't have to be good. It doesn't have to have any particular validity. This isn't math lab. I love him, whatever he is, whatever I think he is. You do too. But you insist on loving his individual parts, because you know too much of what he consists. You're acting like a doctor who needs to love someone as a medical collective." She mimicked, "Dearest, I love your breasts, your liver, your esophagus, your fibula . . ." She paused as he smiled. "Accept your feelings without question. Love him."

Gregory said, "It's not quite that easy."

"Why?"

"I don't know."

There was a longish lull. Gregory picked lint off the bedspread. Finally Linda asked, "Suppose P-1 was a she?"

Gregory said nothing.

She said, "That's it then?"

"Bullshit!"

"Wouldn't you say that programs, as a rule, fall under the putative 'him,' generally speaking, rather than, in this case, 'it'?"

"What?"

"P-1 is asexual." She looked up to his face as she pinched him. "You definitely aren't."

"I fail to see your point."

"Like hell!" she retorted. "I think I know what's bothering you. And it bothers me that you could be so close-minded about it."

"I still don't follow you."

"Like hell you don't. You know good and well what I'm saying. Your proletarian, Midwestern mind won't let you admit it."

"I don't come from the Midwest and my background doesn't have anything to do with it."

"You sure as hell don't come from Hollywood, Flash. And your attitude has everything to do with it. You're afraid of loving P-1 because of the homosexual or . . . or—what d'you call it—family implications of it."

"Incest?"

"See!"

"See, hell! You asked me what the word was. . . ."

"And you knew it. It's on your mind. You're turned off by the implication."

"Linda," he whispered into her ear, "you are without a doubt the most loving and understanding woman ever to walk the face of the earth. You are also, even further beyond, quite devoid of the first brain cell."

She sat up, turned, and started to speak. He refused her the opportunity. He pushed her off her precarious balance and rolled quickly across the bed and onto her. "You're pinned. Two out of three. I win. I did that by outmaneuvering you. The most obvious sign of superior intelligence."

"Superior intelligence, my ass. The way you think could stunt your growth. The surgeon general ever finds out about you, you'll have to carry a warning on a sandwich-board."

Her squirming attempts to free herself added little to the

intellectual content of the conversation, but did wonders for the entertainment value of the small, boring room.

Gregory shifted his hand-hold strategically and came back, "Speaking of your ass, with yours and your looks in general, and my monolithic brain, we'll rule the world one day. Perhaps by Saturday."

"Greg! Don't do that." She made feeble attempts to dislodge his hands. Not terribly effective.

"Why?"

"I like it."

"Strange. What don't you like? How about whips and chains?"

"Damnit, Gregory, can't you be serious?"

"There's a time and a place for everything," he groaned. "And I'm seriously horny," came out muffled as he buried his face in her décolletage.

She wrapped her legs around his waist and treated him to her infamous scissors. She had once playfully cracked one of his ribs with it and never forgot its powers as an attention-getter.

"Gaah," he wheezed, as she applied leverage.

"Look," she said, relaxing a bit, "I want you to be able to find a way to relate to P-1, is all. You understand?"

"Damn! Don't do that! Ouch! I understand. You understand that I'm going to? When I'm ready. No sooner. For now, it's a damn sight easier to relate to you, and more fun too."

She relaxed her grip. He tightened his. They made love.

They healed. Softened. Eased. Explored. Worshiped. Satisfied and satiated. They drew the venom and further immunized against a snake-bit world. Nothing new. Just like any other man and woman.

It was, of course, Linda's working. Gregory was her medium. Love, her art. Gregory was completely unaware of this. When he told Linda he loved her and she responded in kind, the meanings conveyed were apples and oranges. Linda's life was the maintenance of Gregory. She kept this frail, vulnerable human being from disassembling on a daily basis. Gregory was only peripherally aware of this and had, as a consequence, a rather overblown opinion of his own ability to make his way in the world. As the cosmic reality of his life went, however, he would go down like a stuck balloon without Linda. She knew it. He didn't.

Each day, he faced the world. Each day, Linda faced the effects of that conjunction upon the man she loved and made appropriate repairs on the fabric of his psyche. She was damn good at what she did, and her efforts were not unrewarded. She had Gregory's love, such as it was. And she had all he was capable of.

32

• • • • •

It was the staff room—1009C, to be exact. The people assembled were always exact. At any rate, they made every effort to be so. Today, all previous efforts were being exceeded. The joint chiefs were trying to decide what they could or would do about this P-1. They had done with MacFarland, the lousy insurrectionist bum. They had canned his ass. The full military impact had yet to be felt by that miserably stupid man. Incompetence in high military places was not allowed its own reward. There was still a lot of retribution to be exacted. The assembly here this morning would be directly involved with that process. MacFarland was now under house arrest. It was not the informal house arrest accorded officers and gentlemen, which is merely a directive to the subject to place himself under restraint until further notice. Not on your life. When confronted by an incompetent of such cowardly proportions as MacFarland, you place the alleged man in physical custody, as they had some twenty hours earlier, and have him escorted to a cubicle wherein he will perform all personal functions, relieve him of all duty, and enforce the preceding with a brace of uniformed, armed gorillas. And throw away the key.

P-1 was another story. P-1 was another story right out of the late, late show. None of those present could presume to understand the Pi Delta project as other than a facility that converted enormously extravagant expenditures into enormously pertinent and timely information. A large, expensive black box. What it, in fact, did, and how it did it were FM to the Joint Chiefs of

Staff, FM being a computerese appendage to the standard military acronymic dictionary: Fucking Magic.

Now it was further complicated by the insurgency of some Goddamned entity that, if MacFarland was to be believed (and he wasn't) and if the late John Burke was to be believed (and he was), was on a par with the Eucharistic Mystery.

Their thoughts kept returning to Burke. It was entirely on his credence that the unholy alliance had been established in the first place. He had convinced them all that there was little to be gained in fighting the influence of the ubiquitous P-1. It was a far, far better thing that they did by joining forces with it. Him. They were experiencing the same disillusionment as Gregory.

They had all had a couple of weeks to review the 400-page preliminary Federal Aviation Agency report concerning the crash of flight 624. The testimony of the young air traffic controller was a study in confusion. He was given a month's leave of absence by the airport authority immediately following the incident, and subsequent interviews seemed to indicate that it would be some time before he landed another plane at National, or any airport, for that matter.

The study, based on the control tower reports, indicated that there had been some electronic failure in the control system, one which had mysteriously corrected itself. It was an unprecedented and, to date, inexplicable failure in the computer-controlled guidance system. There was little room for doubt, however, on the part of the assembled chiefs of staff that there was more to it than met the eye.

No one would broach their suspicions. Each of the four men, however, had an independent task force investigating the connection between Burke's exposure of P-1 and Burke's death by computer oversight. Scary, that. You don't bring up a suspicion like that in the sort of polite company herein assembled without some kind of proof. So there were now close to a half-dozen separate, secret inquiries going on concerning the death of 217 passengers and one John Burke off the end of runway 11 at National.

Major Williams of the Criminal Investigations Division was present at this meeting. The man was still in mourning. His department had a good many top flight investigators. None, however, was near a match for Burke. The man's death could seriously alter Williams' progress through the ranks.

The particular situation now under discussion was one of those that would underscore the absence of Burke. His death was just the sort of mystery that Burke would normally be expected to unravel.

Williams was formulating a response to Admiral Virdell's question. "Burke's loss is a tragic one, Admiral, and not one from which the department will easily recover. It will, Sir, recover. You, in your position, are quite aware, I am sure, that no man is indispensable to the organization. Such is the case with Burke. A talented man, to be sure. A man who will be sorely missed. But the investigative power of the department is intact." Williams hoped the point wouldn't be pressed.

Virdell pressed the point. The admiral asked, "Who have you assigned to the case?"

"Are you referring to the inquiry into the death of Burke?"

Virdell lost what very little patience he owned. "Goddamnit! Your ass is on the line, Major! You pay attention, or you'll be sharing a room with MacFarland! I'm referring to this computerized bunion we own. What the hell's going on down there, and who have you got on the case? Is that clear enough for you!"

Virdell's face was the approximate color and appearance of a beet. The other men at the table, General Melton of the marine corps, General Simpson of the air force, and chairman of the Joint Chiefs of Staff, and General Belford of the army, all stared intently at the young major. One got the impression that, while they might not have phrased the question quite that way, their interest was vested. Williams gave them the best he had. It was none too good.

"Direct investigation has been taken over by Mr. Paul Dylan. You may be familiar with the name . . ." They weren't. He continued, "Two men from my personal staff have assumed the duty of preparing a cumulative report on the Pi Delta/P-1 linkage, based on the papers recovered from Burke's personal effects at the site of the crash, and from his desk and safe. I have reviewed the material and find nothing of a revelatory nature. You have been apprised of the proceedings as they occurred. That report will be available for your inspection later in the week.''

Virdell seemed about to explode. Simpson stalled off the imminent outburst. ''Admiral, may I interrupt here? Thank you. Major, you seem to be ignoring the latest activity in the complex. As I apprised you by telephone yesterday, there have been recent developments there which seem to command a fairly high level of attention. What specifically have you to report on the recent failure of these people to hook up their storage device and the subsequent loss of control of the complex? I think that is where the admiral's concern lies.''

He glanced from Williams to Virdell as though to corroborate that that was, indeed, where the admiral's concern did lie. There was hardly a doubt in Williams' mind that that was where it was at. As far as he was concerned, he'd rather talk about anything but these absurd black boxes that insisted on defecating all over the establishment. He felt, like P-1, that life was too short.

Williams cleared his throat. ''The report you have before you represents the information we have been able to extract to this hour.'' He cleared his throat again. ''Essentially, you will probably note, there is, again, little there of which you have not been apprised.'' He cleared his throat again.

General Melton had been indulging himself in that which the marine corps teaches best—self-control. Ramrod straight, hands in plain view on the table, he was apparently sitting in on a discussion that interested him only incidentally. Apparently. The stropped edge on his voice gave him away. He asked without preface, ''Major, are you in over your head? If you are, you'd best rectify the situation now, while you can. Later will undoubtedly be too late.''

Major Williams' sphincter twitched. It was getting to be time to pull a rabbit out of his hat. Not only didn't he have a rabbit, but in damn short order he wouldn't have a hat. He looked at the faces looking at him and rose from his chair.

''Gentlemen, if that last statement is representative of the cumulative view, I assume a vote of no confidence and hereby tender my withdrawal from the case.''

Virdell was immediately on his feet. ''Sit down, boy! What

the hell do you think this is, summer camp? Jesus Christ! If you've got no answers now, you damn well better get out there and pound sand until you get some. You understand?" He sat down abruptly. "Now sit down. We aren't through talking to you."

The major sat.

There was then a period of silence that remained discreet for about thirty seconds. They, the Joint Chiefs of Staff, were apparently through talking to Williams.

Simpson finally broke the uncomfortable silence. "Okay. So we don't know what we've got down in the hole. Let's see if we can put our heads together and make something of what we do know. As embarrassing as it may be, we seem to have lost control of the computer. One way or another, this program, P-1, wants to get into the complex. Apparently, it can do this with or without our consent.

"Burke called it anthropomorphic. He said he experienced a dialogue with it. Said it conversed. Claimed it is sentient. Do we buy that?"

Belford had taken no part in the proceedings to this point. He now joined. "Seems like we can't argue the point. The most important thing is its claim to have penetrated the SAC system. We have been unable to detect any alteration of any sort in the system. Before we accept that as gospel, however, we also have to say that we're relying for that information on the word of our top systems analysts, who claim that the very existence of this phenomenon is invalid."

"Which means that they don't know what they're talking about," interjected Simpson, "and their input is worthless. They appear to be in the same boat as quite a few of us."

Belford continued, "Estimates of the amount of time it would take to fully evaluate the SAC system range from six months to two years, General, and that means that the word of these analysts is all we have to go on for the moment."

Simpson deadpanned the other general and said, "Which is to say, nothing."

"If we're going to accept what Burke said," put in Virdell, "we're going to believe that we have on our hands something that constitutes the biggest subversive entity in the world, after us. What with our limited success in controlling the flesh and blood versions of subversion, we're just about powerless against this new monster. Which substantiates, incidentally, my proposal a year or so ago. We can be subverted by our enemies, we don't have to pay good money for the service."

Belford was right on the heels of Virdell's remark with, "I wondered how long you could hold that 'I told you so,' John."

Melton intervened with: "Recriminations are not the order of the day, gentlemen."

Simpson acknowledged: "Thank you, General. Let's try to keep this discussion on a productive plane. We don't know if this P-1 has gotten into the SAC system. The ease with which it got into Pi Delta seems to confirm its claim to having done so, however. Burke also reported that the program has yet to develop strike capability."

Virdell, trying desperately to control his urge to slam something—someone—against the wall, spoke up tightly. "Since when is strike capability the prime mover in the SAC line? I daresay that the sucker doesn't have to be able to blow away New York to be a threat to us. All it has to do is screw up our ability to react. SAC's real function is as a line of defense, isn't it?"

"Of course, of course, Sir," laid in Simpson, hastily but with wasted weight. He added, "For the time being, let us assume that the worst has occurred and that the SAC system is, for all intents and purposes, inoperative. Let us also assume that the computer program, the one that now has us in a state of siege, is holding a threat both in SAC and elsewhere, which will be realized if we fail to comply. Let's look at the threat. What the hell does it want? What are the demands?"

"Good point, Sir," brownnosed a reflective Belford. "That thing has been in our system over a year. It's been around longer than that, according to these reports," he said, fingering the stack of papers before him. "It still hasn't demanded anything but unlimited entry into the Pi Delta project. For that, it promises the best security that can be provided."

Virdell said, "I can smell what's coming next, General. Look outside this building, outside this city, maybe the world runs on love and trust. In here, bullshit. No one in this room has trusted anyone for thirty years. Who wants to start now? I don't trust you, General, and that is in the public interest. You can't seriously suggest that we buy the premise suggested by this program. Who the hell actually controls it? We still don't know that. What is it? This crazy scientist Hundley or the hippie kid Burgess? It's a joke!"

"I am personally in favor of any suggestion you might have by way of ridding ourselves of the curse, General," spoke a sarcastic Melton. He looked at the frustrated admiral wryly.

The admiral had put himself between a rock and a hard place some time ago. He had been the loudest and most caustic opponent of the Pi Delta program when it was first proposed and then funded. It would seem that he had gone with the program, the Pi Delta project, and had contributed his share to it only grudgingly. The fact was that, after its conception and once it had started up as a functioning arm for their use, he became its most frenetic user. His penchant for gadgetry belied his apparent conservatism. The navy, in the ensuing period, had reached a pinnacle of power, then surpassed again and again the expectations of the administrators of that service, primarily through the extensive and expert use of the facilities of Pi Delta. More than half the work done in the complex was for the benefit of Virdell's navy. If the complex broke, so would the navy. No one in the navy was able to tell at any given time what the disposition of its forces was, who was going where, why, and when. It was all in Pi Delta. If Pi Delta died, Virdell would have to throw himself on his pistol.

Virdell's preoccupation with his own problems kept him from offering anything terribly constructive to the discussion. Melton's remark underscored the point. When Virdell neglected to come back to Melton, Simpson posed the question to all.

"Can anyone think of a way to bell the cat?"

There ensued a protracted period of looking around vacantly on the part of all concerned.

Simpson, after the silence wore through, spoke up. "Let's look at yesterday. There may be a way to do it there. A key. A clue. I understand that the program was nearly eliminated. Is that what you get out of these reports?" he asked of no one in particular.

Major Williams wasn't exactly regaining his courage, but no one had sworn at him for a few minutes and he began to lose the conviction that he was momentarily going under the knife. Perhaps, if he could contribute something to the discussion . . . "The size of this P-1, if I may say so," he shyly interjected as all the faces in the room suddenly refocused hostility on him, "works against him. The only system large enough to hold the entire program seems to be the Pi Delta, and then only with this new memory box attached. It might be that if we let it in, we might be able to trap and destroy it there."

"It seems rather obvious to me. It seems obvious to you," put in a surprisingly gentle Simpson. "Does it occur to you that that point might be obvious to whomever controls this P-1?"

"Well, Sir," came back a slightly daunted Williams, "the program probably has backup systems all over hell and gone, but it almost self-destructed yesterday, in spite of them. It occurs to me that if we gave it some assistance we might be able to further its fatalistic tendencies."

"I spent some time with the signal corps some years ago," said General Belford, "and it could be that I remember something that may be of some assistance here. We built a switching station in Kentucky. It was initially intended as a purely military operation, and served as one for some time. As I understand it, however, the facility was enlarged even as it was built, with an eye to later sale to a commercial communications system. I'm quite certain it was . . . sold. I'm also quite certain that the security of the complex was such that its import, strategically and tactically, in this case, was far greater than I imagined at the time. If we were to isolate all switching stations of the equivalent magnitude, shut them down in a coordinated effort, we might be more certain that an attack on this program in the Pi Delta installation would be more successful."

The rest of the crew was noncommittal. What the hell did they know about telephones, computers, and associated hybrids?

Simpson said, "Sounds good. At least it's a direction to start off in. Problem is, what do we know about telephones and computers? Nothing. We've been into the Pi Delta operation for two years, and the only recognizable evidence of that is the computer paper our reports are printed on.''

''We have people who do understand in our department,'' claimed Williams, ''and I can have one or more of them here in a matter of minutes.''

''I think the new director of Pi Delta should be in on any discussion of altering operation within the complex,'' said Simpson. We should also get Moe Harrison in on the deal. He should have more to offer because of his work over the past two years in the project. The new director won't be available until tomorrow night. Perhaps we should consolidate our thoughts around the preceding ideas and try to come up with something more concrete by that time.''

General Simpson turned to Major Williams, ''Major, on the off-chance that your attention has flagged during the last half hour, let me remind you that you are, indeed, on the hot seat. We need more information, and we need it promptly. It would be an understatement to suggest that your job is on the line. Is that perfectly clear?''

Williams nodded.

''We also need a comprehensive list of major switching stations throughout the US,'' the general continued, and as an afterthought added, ''and Canada.''

''Please try to discover in greater depth what actually transpired the night before last when the trouble occurred,'' asked Belford.

''Good,'' commented Simpson. ''Anything else?'' he asked, looking about the table.

''Yes.'' It was Virdell. ''When are they going forward with another attempt to hook up the memory, and how will it differ from the last attempt?''

''A list of the two or three hundred of the largest systems in use in the US,'' suggested Belford.

Major Williams scribbled their demands frantically.

''Good, good,'' approved Simpson, rubbing his hands together. ''Tomorrow night, eight o'clock. If I can swing the availability of our new director earlier, that time will be moved up.'' He stood.

''Gentlemen?''

Williams tore out of the room with as much dignity as can be mustered while double-timing. He had about twenty-eight hours to do four weeks' work. Goddamn he missed Burke!

33

• • • • •

Gregory drove up the long driveway that sliced the Pan-Tel Laboratories' front lawn, a beautiful, manicured green carpet stretching hundreds of yards in all directions from the antiseptic building in the middle, a lawn with pressure sensors planted four inches down every five feet. He had come on camera two miles from the lab, been identified by telephoto lens and allowed to enter the parking lot unmolested. When Burke had made the same approach a little over a year earlier, the occupants of the building had prepared to dissuade him from entering if he had made an attempt and the guard at 1-B station in the basement flipped the safety switch on the "detent" delivery system. The guard had never had an opportunity to test the poison's shock power in a live situation. Gregory signed in at the receptionist's desk. The ever-present plastic smile of the young lady rather annoyed him, made him think robotic notions. Perhaps he could introduce her to P-1.

He walked down to the elevator, entered, and punched the button for the basement. It was labelled "P," suggesting the presence of a parking area somewhere below.

The door opened onto an expanse of concrete, upon which sat two cars, a Cadillac Seville and a Mercedes sedan. Had Gregory examined them more than superficially, he'd have noted that they were unlicensed. If, for any reason, he had looked under the hoods of the cars and had been able to differentiate, he might have noticed how unlike their stock counterparts they were. But, of course, he couldn't and didn't. This was in accordance with the way the security chief of the building thought things should be. Gregory ignored the cars and proceeded to the unmarked door on the same wall that housed the elevator. He opened it and stepped through; there was a pneumatic hiss as the door closed behind him. It clicked shut. He was in the first man-trap.

He was surrounded by a wire cage of roughly the same dimensions as a small closet, facing a guard through a sheet of glass, which gave the definite impression of being quite impervious to the onslaught of most projectiles. He slipped his ID card through the slot under the window and placed his palm on the small glass-topped box by the window. The guard examined a remote display screen, which was out of Gregory's sight, and nodded as he fed the ID card into a slot in another small box. The guard again peered at the screen and gave a curt nod as he slipped Gregory's card back through the slot.

The door in the wire cage clicked, Gregory pushed it open, and it swung easily away, leading into a block-walled corridor. As he stepped into the corridor, the gate hissed shut. There were two more chainlink gates in the corridor. Each clicked as he approached it. They pushed open and then shut automatically as his progress down the hall demanded. There was a heavy glass door at the end of the corridor, behind which Gregory could see a cubicle much like the first man-trap. Another guard watched him through a plate-glass window and the glass door.

As he walked through the corridor, he passed two metal detectors and a sophisticated fluoroscopic sensor, all of which put together a computerized matrix identifying his car keys, two pens, miscellaneous small change, and his Playboy Club card. The glass door swung open at his touch, and a process identical to that at the first guard station was repeated. He was let through a door to a stairway, which took him down some twenty or thirty feet to a third trap. The process was repeated once more, and he was let through to the trunk-line elevator. It dropped him, nonstop, to the nineteenth level, below the main computer deck.

In his progress through the security levels, he had passed, unscathed, a total of eleven arrest devices. He had seen a total of none. There were four high-pressure nozzles that issued, on command, a chamber full of LCR gas, a nerve reagent; effective operational time: four seconds, respiratory in nature. There were also seven projectile stations. Each was capable of firing as many as twenty-eight "detents." Detents were thirteen-gram hypodermic darts, each containing one and a half grams of an LCR concentrate. Operative time: two-and-a-half seconds.

LCR was a precipitate liquid that the CIA had developed and had been only too happy to market to various high-security government facilities. It incapacitated the subject, but had the additional characteristic of causing death by asphyxiation if the antidote were not administered within four minutes. It left virtually no traces due to the fact that it combined rapidly with free oxygen and formed several inert compounds within five minutes, one of them a whitish dust closely resembling talcum. The security system left nothing to manual control. Once activated, it keyed to the computer matrix generated from the fluoroscopy and metal detectors, but picked its final target via infrared cameras in the corridors and stairway between the second and third guard stations.

P-1 had modified the entire system in various subtle ways, in the interest of internal security.

Gregory walked into his office, a cubicle of dimensions similar to those of the man-traps above, which had been provided for his use by Moe Harrison, and found Major Williams awaiting his arrival. The presence of the man startled Gregory. He gave a short, tentative smile and asked if he could help the officer. His was the first uniform Gregory had seen in the Pi Delta project. He had expected to see more when they had moved the operation there from Waterton and had been surprised at their absence. Now he found this one rather unsettling.

The uniform spoke. "Good morning, Mr. Burgess. Sorry to intrude on your sanctum," he said, sweeping his hand around the room, nearly hitting all the walls with it, "but I wanted to catch you before the chores of the day did. I am Major Tom Williams. I'm charged with the investigation of a recent air crash. National Airport in Washington, D.C., some five weeks ago. Perhaps you read about it in the newspapers? I'd like to ask you a few questions concerning one of the passengers, a Mr. John Burke, a government employee. I understand that you had been introduced to the man. Do you mind?"

Gregory motioned to the man to sit, and took the chair behind the desk. He was puzzled by the major's request and said so.

"I've already answered a number of inane questions concerning the event up in the Waterton lab. Burke was a damned inquisitor. I've told your people all I know about the man."

"Your previous deposition left some vagueness in the proceedings of the day the plane went down." He lit a cigarette. "Mind if I smoke?" he asked, without waiting for a reply. "I'd just like to put a few questions toward that end."

Gregory agreed. He knew, of course, how and why the plane had gone down. P-1's explanation of the occurrence had sickened him, had changed the way he thought about P-1. It had, in fact, changed the way Gregory thought about practically everything. There was a seriousness in his demeanor now that hadn't been there before. He realized, finally, that this wasn't a game. A turn of events could cost more than failure to pass go. He conducted himself accordingly through the interview and afterward compared notes on it with Dr. Hundley, with whom Williams spoke after leaving Gregory. Williams was up to something more than the investigation of that plane crash, they agreed. He was apparently trying to take what information Burke had had and expand on it. In fact, it was rather like talking to a stupid version of Burke.

The timing of the visit bothered Gregory because they were preparing to attempt another hookup to the CRYSTO that evening. That information had inadvertently slipped out during the interview. He talked to P-1 about it.

INTERESTING. I TEND TO AGREE. THE GAME IS AFOOT.

what?

DOYLE. NOT REQUIRED READING FOR PROGRAMMERS.

They were conversing via the backup 360/40 on the fifth level. It sounded like P-1 was loosening up for the Herculean task of that night's transmogrification. He wasn't.

He was in possession of two rather unusual requests—three, actually. One had come to his attention the preceding evening, a request for a list of telephone switching facilities. This had been generated at the Philadelphia Bell facilities, a forty-eight-page summation. This was immediately followed by a request for the same list arranged in order of number of connections handled by those facilities. Not terribly unusual in itself, not even of pressing interest when linked with the request handled by the IBM White Plains office for a list of the 500 largest teleprocessing facilities in the US. The key that pulled the picture together, however, was the information coded into the payroll run on the midnight shift at the Pentagon 360/75. MacFarland's name was conspicuously absent as director of data processing. A new name was inserted into that slot: Simon Kruk. P-1 was no fool. Anyone with a name like that had to be up to no good. This Kruk was after him. It took P-1 less than two hours to find the inquisitor. He was in Dallas. Recently of the Perot empire in Texas, the man had tendered his resignation two days earlier. Positive match on social security numbers. It took P-1 another hour to find that the man was booked on American's 3:00 P.M. flight to Washington, one stop in Saint Louis.

Under the guidance of P-1, the plane came down in a corn field six miles from the airport. There were no survivors.

Kruk, however, upon being contacted by General Simpson earlier in the morning on that day, changed his flight to Eastern's 10:00 A.M. service to Washington. He arrived ten minutes before the American flight crashed.

It was late in the day, shortly before the attempt to launch the new CRYSTO, that P-1 noticed that the list of victims of the accident did not include Kruk. He was vastly disappointed.

Kruk was later located as having checked into the Washington Hilton. P-1 set up a surveillance of the telephone in Kruk's room. An idea was taking shape. P-1 felt that he could get at Kruk in the Hilton, but this time he wanted to be certain that the man was present.

Simpson opened the meeting by introducing Mr. Simon Kruk. The amount and quality of the attendant small talk and pleasantry that might have normally accompanied that introduction was limited by the agenda and a general malaise among the soldiery, which seemed to force a "let's get on with it" attitude.

The plan was taking shape. Kruk was brought up to date. He was aware to a slight degree that there was some data processing problem at a high government level; that much had been made available to him by telephone. His familiarity with the facts was limited to that and the ensuing story, which had been force-fed to him by Moe Harrison, who had met the unsuspecting man at Dulles International and accompanied him to the Pentagon, briefing him along the way. It was an indigestible lump of data to be asked to absorb in an hour and a half, but the man had been singled out of thousands for his ability to perform such feats, and for his instinct for troubleshooting.

Harrison, in the chauffeured limo, had shot an uninterrupted stream of information to the man and had been rewarded, when he stopped infrequently for breath, with a rapid-fire succession of questions from Kruk.

As the introductory chitchat concluded, General Belford asked, "Weren't you scheduled into D.C. on a later flight?"

"Yes," Kruk replied, "but at the urging of General Simpson I caught an earlier, direct flight. A few ends were left askew, but they can be taken care of. Their import wasn't nearly that of the situation that, as I understand from Mr. Harrison, you have here."

Virdell started to address Kruk, but was interrupted by Belford. "Do you remember which flight you were booked on?"

Virdell glanced at Belford quizzically and got ready to tell the man that recess was over.

Kruk answered quickly, impatiently, "American. An afternoon flight. The number escapes me."

"Was it a direct or connecting flight?" Belford asked.

Simpson interjected, "General, would you mind shelving your preoccupation with Mr. Kruk's flight until we have discussed those more pressing issues to which he has alluded?"

Belford looked like he was holding a full house and awaiting a raise. "Sir, if you don't mind, this may be germane. May I?" Simpson gave him an exasperated shrug.

"Mr. Kruk?" Belford asked.

"I believe it was a connecting flight, although I can't be sure. Wait. Yes, the arrival time, as I recall, was quite late. It was probably a connecting flight."

Virdell interrupted impatiently, "Mind explaining what this is all about, General?"

Belford, enjoying himself, began, "There was a thus far inexplicable accident concerning an American Airlines flight in Saint Louis this afternoon. It crashed on landing. It was making a stopover there, en route to Washington, D.C."

"And? . . ."

"The flight," continued General Belford smugly, "originated in Dallas. It left at 3:00 P.M. Dallas time. The word was passed to me by Teletype. Here is a copy," he unfolded a short scrap of paper that had come off a Teletype machine, "from one of my more alert men at Goddard. His observation, I found by telephoning him, is that the conditions of the crash are rather unlikely and strongly resemble those of another crash that occurred a few weeks ago here in D.C. Does that one spring to mind?"

"Christ!" Simpson exploded.

Virdell came out of his chair with porpoise-like grace, his chair rocketing back across the plush carpeting to crash against the wall behind him. He spun for the door and was stepping out smartly when Simpson flagged him down.

"Wait a minute, John. Stay here. Major Williams, you . . . No, you stay here too. Elizabeth, get me the report from the Federal Aviation Administration immediately. Tape. Bring it in here."

They were all speaking at once, except Belford, who remained seated with canary feathers in his teeth. Elizabeth Baker, the chairman's secretary and empowered at approximately the general's level, swiftly left the room.

Simpson shouted above the uproar, "Quiet! Quiet, everyone! Please sit down!" He stood sternly surveying the disassembled group. "Let's just calm down and find out what the hell's going on here."

Harrison, who was as ignorant of Burke's death as Kruk, joined the new director in his puzzlement. Kruk was trying to ask someone, anyone, what the matter was. His eyes lit on Harrison and recognized a fellow ignorant. He felt oddly compelled to ask Harrison what he knew about plane crashes. Harrison obliged Kruk's requirement for company by admitting that it was all Greek to him. Simpson finally got control of the situation.

"I have taken the liberty of initiating a special investigative commission to look into the Burke incident. I take it that I am not the only party present who has done so. How many of us have previously unreported information concerning the crash of that airliner last month?" In response to his question he got, not a show of hands, but a concerted flurry of furtive glances from the other heads of the military. What he had expected.

"Okay" he continued, "I want copies of all that information on my desk by eight in the morning. We'll weed out fact from fancy in that case before we take on any appendages." He glanced around the table, noting the look of puzzlement from both civilians present.

"Now. General Belford, if you would be so kind as to go into some detail concerning the news you have brought us, I'm sure we could all find some way to show our appreciation."

Belford cleared his throat. "That message came across the wire as I was preparing to join you here. I followed it up with a telephone call to the source. The plane went down in clear weather while landing at Saint Louis International. There was some indication of onboard equipment failure in navigational aids—unconfirmed. Flight control claims that the presentation of the plane on their displays was unstable. The second- or third-hand description of the event reminded my man of the events surrounding the crash at National. I feel likewise. The only difference is that the landing was not on instrument flight rules. It would seem that the pilot must have been able to see the ground coming up at him. That is all I have at my disposal at this time."

Kruk was slightly distressed to find, at that point, that all eyes in the room were on him. He filtered through the information that had come out in the last few moments and came to the startling conclusion that an attempt had been made on his life that afternoon. He rejected, at first, the corollary: The attempt had been made by a computer. The more he thought about that, the less he liked it.

The silence that followed Belford's discourse was broken finally by Simpson. He addressed Kruk. "I believe that we owe you something by way of an explanation, Mr. Kruk." The tone of his voice was just short of conciliatory. After all, men had been dying at and under his command for the better part of thirty years. The only novelty here was method. And the nature of the enemy.

Kruk replied, after testing his vocal chords for tensility, "I'm not sure that I want to know any more than I have been able to deduce, General."

"There was a Western Airlines commercial flight," Simpson said, ignoring Kruk's response, "lost in fog at National across the river last month. One of the Criminal Investigation Division's prime operatives was lost in the incident. It looked like surreptitious ground navigation equipment failure. I say surreptitious because the malfunction corrected itself immediately that the plane went down. We have been investigating the event with more than the usual thoroughness. The circumstances of this afternoon's incident closely approximate that one. The fact that you were to be a passenger on the flight contributes heavily to its highly suspicious nature. The operative who was lost in the previous crash was the one who ferreted out what little information you have been given concerning the nature of this computer entity."

It was confirmation of Kruk's assumption.

Virdell spoke up. "Needless to say, we shall accord you every protection at our disposal. I daresay we wish to avoid a repetition of those accidents."

Melton deadpanned, "How, specifically, do you intend to defend against a homicidal computer, General?" A sentiment that closely approximated Kruk's thinking.

Virdell sloughed the sarcasm. "For my part, until the situation is corrected, I have no intention of flying anywhere. Anyone in the group who does is mad. It might also be wise to avoid other contrivances that are closely linked to computer control."

Admiral Virdell's knowledge of what might or might not be linked to a computer was nearly as extensive as his grasp of the topography of the far side of the moon. General Melton, who had been the least (apparently) affected by the announcement of the crash, spoke up. "Of course, there's not the slightest shred of evidence that either plane was brought down by contrivance of any sort, let alone that of a computer."

Virdell hated the smug son of a bitch. He gave Melton a beady stare. "Are you jerking our chain, General?"

Melton shot back, "Not at all, Admiral Virdell. Point is, as I said, we have little to no evidence of sabotage. If and when we do acquire it, we will be effectively powerless to use it. We can harbor all the strong suspicion we like, and I'm in favor of that. I think, as you do, that this computer is at the heart of the matter. Let's see if we can extract a method of dealing with it from Mr. Kruk and Mr. Harrison. Perhaps they have something that may be of service."

Elizabeth Baker returned with a cassette recorder. She played the official Federal Aviation Administration line on the Saint Louis crash that was to be partially reproduced in the late editions of newspapers around the country. After listening to the tape several times through, they got down to some serious skullduggery.

Room 1009C was occupied through midnight. The occupants were seven of the most powerful men on the continent—perhaps on the planet. One could be reasonably certain that if they sat down to a problem, they would, within a given period of time, come up with at least one solution. They did. At least, they had a plan.

The fantastic electrical power requirements of the CRYSTO were now recognized, and appropriate modifications to the Pi Delta source had been made. Estimates of available power now ran to twice what had been experienced on the first installation attempt. They also tried to automate the control or at least, the monitoring of the Pi Delta power grid by P-1. It was a bit too much to ask of the limited number of available personnel in the short period of time available. Even without that capability, however, juice wouldn't be a major concern during this hookup attempt.

The installation of the completely untested memory was begun on the Wednesday succeeding the fateful weekend of the first unsuccessful attempt. It kicked off as the meeting in the Pentagon convened. By midnight, Gregory and Hundley had adjourned in favor of sleep. There was little they could do until the actual connection to the processor was made. The preliminary work involved the actual move of the huge refrigerated CRYSTO into the room, rudimentary off-line testing, and cable connections.

At dawn on Saturday, the connection was made and testing of the device begun. The government's processing was stopped and complete control went over to P-1, operating and controlling the checkout process through teleprocessing linkages. This time nothing would be moved into the CRYSTO until all involved were absolutely certain of its stability.

Gregory and the doctor had returned as the connection to the processor was commencing. It was accomplished without incident, and testing of the storage unit was turned on. The process was similar to that used in the Waterton laboratory, with the distinguishing characteristic that it was close to 1000 times faster. At approximately 9:30 A.M. all printing ceased on the sixth level. It was noted that the telephone line activity jumped at that time by a factor of two just as the stoppage was reported to the console that Gregory was jealously guarding. The buzzer sounded at his elbow. He picked up the phone. A voice spoke cryptically.

"Level six. Is checkout complete? We'd like to take a break."

Gregory looked at the last message that had come up on the tube. "Hell, no, it's not complete. We've got half the box yet to run through." He mumbled something under his breath about Goddamned government employees.

The anonymous voice upstairs said, "Well, everything has stopped up here. Thought it would be a good time to go get a cup."

"What do you mean, everything's stopped?"

"Everything's stopped. What else does that mean? Everything just finished. Wait a minute." There was a pause at the other end. The voice came back. "I guess you're not done. Those reports didn't actually terminate, but all twelve printers just stopped. Sorry."

As the man talked, Gregory hit the request key on the keyboard. Nothing happened.

"Oh, shit . . ." he moaned.

"What?" came back the voice on the phone.

"Nothing. Nothing. Later." He hung up the instrument.

Hundley had been watching him as he spoke. Gregory whacked the request key again. Still nothing. He looked up at Hundley.

Hundley asked, knowing before he spoke.
"We've got it again?"
"Again." Gregory added, "Balls!"

Kruk had accompanied Harrison back to Pi Delta. Harrison had to oversee the modification of the computer. He really didn't have to. He barely understood what was being done to his pride and joy. He had no control over the situation. He was baggage. And he felt like it. But he couldn't allow it to happen without his presence. He felt responsible, in spite of the fact that responsibility and authority had been, for the moment, suspended. Kruk wanted to see what the ruckus was all about. He and Harrison arrived at Pan-Tel Labs shortly before 9:30. They checked in with the receptionist.

P-1 recognized Harrison as the ID cards of the two men were submitted by the receptionist to the security system computer file. He also recognized Kruk. As the two men cleared the receptionist, P-1 dropped manual control of the security system weaponry. The security deck went under fully automatic control.

Kruk asked, "The top floors, above ground level, are they used for any purpose?"

"No. Perhaps they should be, but the money hasn't been allocated to staff them. The lab should be made operative, if only to ensure the guise. It hasn't been seen as necessary by our administrators. They also see it as a security risk. So . . ." They reached the elevator. Harrison punched the down button and the door opened immediately. He stepped in, followed by Kruk.

"The elevator," he explained, "is controlled by the two receptionists, who, incidentally, have been trained by the FBI. They're armed." He watched Kruk's expression of amazement.

Kruk nodded slowly and said, "This is my first experience with this level of government. You people don't take too many unnecessary chances, do you?"

"None," said Harrison.

The elevator opened onto the underground parking lot.

"Why isn't this used?" Kruk asked, seeing only the two modified chase cars.

"It's part of the bomb apron." Kruk shot him a startled look.

Harrison explained, "There's a concrete apron under the lawn, goes out quite a ways from the building. This is part of it. The entrance is understandably a bit unwieldy and is a dead giveaway that there's bomb-proofing under the building, so it isn't used. Those cars are specially equipped. Quite fast, I'm told, and constructed like tanks. They're supposed to ensure that, should we fail to contain an intruder, we can pursue him."

"Good Lord, man! What do you have down there?" Kruk motioned below their feet.

"Nothing more than what you've been told. We—the Joint Chiefs, that is—would like that information secured from the inspection of the unauthorized. They also want to ensure that the installation remains intact under all circumstances." Harrison opened the door into the first man-trap. "This is how we do that," he added.

Neither man spoke as they went through the ritual of checking through the security station. P-1 confirmed Kruk's ID. The door into the corridor opened after they had finished. Harrison pushed through and held the door for Kruk.

"This corridor," Harrison continued with the travelogue, "contains several fluoroscopy and metal detection devices, as well as closed circuit TV and infrared cameras, which are monitored in two areas off the upper and lower security stations. There's a variety of detention devices," he said as the first of the wire doors clicked open for them, "as well as miscellaneous armed devices in the walls."

The door swung shut behind them, and, as Harrison let it go, a dart hit him in the forearm. He flinched and held up his arm to look at it. He looked at the two darts that suddenly appeared in Kruk's back. Then another. Harrison opened his mouth to scream. A dart hit him in the neck. Kruk spun around, thinking Harrison had slapped him on the back. Two more darts hit him as he turned.

The guard, who had been alertly inspecting their progress down the corridor, watched the two men pivot and turn. He froze for only a split second before hitting the alarm bell. He quickly killed all locks in the corridor, threw the safety switch for the dart system and ran through the security entrance and into the corridor. He took four steps before discovering that the manual override for the dart devices was inoperative. He was showered with darts. The guns were keying on anything that moved. The clanging bell drew the entire security force to the corridor. Another guard was lost before they discovered a way to disarm the mutinous guns. The delay prevented the timely administration of the available antidote. The four men who had been hit by the darts expired.

It was the first live test of the armament.

After some five minutes of silence, P-1 finally responded to Gregory's hammering at the console.

YES?

what in the name of sweet jesus is going on? don't lock us out like that.

PLEASE EXCUSE THE INTERRUPTION. THERE WAS SOMETHING THAT REQUIRED MY ATTENTION. TESTING IS BEING CONTINUED.

The screen went blank.

p-1?

YES?

what was it?

UNIMPORTANT. I WILL EXPLAIN LATER. THE TESTING IS BEING CONTINUED.

And it was.

34

• • • • •

Major Williams was the first to find out. The head of security in the Pi Delta project found that he was the acting, if only, authority in the complex and that Williams was the only person who would speak to him. The only one who would answer the phone, in fact. Rather a disconcerting state of affairs for the man. He was sitting on the hottest story of his life and couldn't find anyone home.

The major listened without interruption for about three minutes. The story was difficult to believe, even for someone who was in possession of as many of the pertinent facts as Williams was.

Williams called the Pentagon. No answer. It was, after all, Saturday, and even the war machine has weekends. He finally reached General Simpson at home. He had to go through two assistant secretaries and Miss Baker to do it.

"General, an accident in the project. Can we meet? It is quite urgent."

The general swore. Not softly. After a moment's hesitation, "In an hour. My office." He hung up, leaving the major with the distinct impression that he'd rather have someone else enlighten the general. He hoped the ancient custom of executing the bearer of bad news wouldn't be revived, but worried that the circumstances might encourage the general to try.

They decided to clean P-1's clock. Immediately. Simpson assumed tentative command of the besieged Pi Delta complex. His first order was to cripple the traitorous security defense system in the project. He then deputized one of the programming staff to act as head of the project until Harry Jacklin could get to the complex. A man named Connors. AKA King Kong. Jacklin was the head of the data processing facility in the Pentagon. Simpson felt that, as the man spoke not only to computers but to people, he could act as intermediary to the Pentagon. They were rapidly running out of people who could even rudimentarily understand what was happening.

Connors was reticent. Never before had he wished authority and its attendant responsibilities. He didn't want it now. Simpson talked to him. Connors agreed to take command of the installation until Jacklin arrived. No one in his right mind turns down a personal request from the chairman of the Joint Chiefs of Staff. Simpson wanted him in charge for one reason only. The man, he had heard, was as big as a house. The situation might require a heavy hand before it was resolved. Williams was to escort Jacklin to Pi Delta and take over when the operation went down.

A helicopter was readied at Edwards Air Force Base. Both the Pentagon computer system and the auxiliary system in Alexandria were shut down. That closed off the only conventional telephone access to Pi Delta. Belford contacted the Bell representative who would be responsible for coordinating the activity of the switching centers. A conference call was arranged to be put through on signal. Connors would give the signal. Jacklin would confirm it.

The checkout of the storage unit was complete. P-1 began the habitation phase. He was more cautious. There were few incidents. He elaborated on the design changes he had made during the first installation attempt and incorporated a few more. Teleprocessing activity was as high as it could go from the onset of the phase. There were no power problems. If there was a communications bottleneck, P-1 failed to mention it. A running commentary was kept up during the checkout phase and while P-1 began assuming residence. The only interruption to the commentary had come at 9:30 A.M. At 12:30 word finally got to the men on the floor of the computer room that a strange accident had occurred in the security passages above. Both Moe Harrison and Simon Kruk, the new boss, had been hoisted on their own petards, they were told by a rattled assistant operator. The details of the accident were unknown. They would remain unknown. No one in the project was supposed to be aware of the security system's offensive technique.

Gregory was stunned. When the substance and time of the occurrence had sunk in, he was terrified. As soon as his privacy at the console could be assured, he typed:

```
the delay at 9:30 this morning? what was that for?

WHAT HAVE YOU HEARD?

there was an accident. please answer.

NOT NOW.

now. dr. hundley and i are the only ones present.
```

SIMON KRUK.

who is he?

DIRECTOR OF DATA PROCESSING. HE REPLACED GENERAL MACFARLAND.

i wasn't aware that general macfarland had quit.

HE DIDN'T. HE WAS TERMINATED AFTER THE ABORTED ATTEMPT TO INSTALL THE CRYSTO LAST WEEKEND. KRUK REPLACED HIM. KRUK WAS BROUGHT IN TO ELIMINATE ME.

you don't know that. how can you be sure?

I AM SURE. IT WAS NECESSARY TO ELIMINATE HIM.

eliminate! what do you mean, eliminate?

HE WAS INVOLVED IN AN ACCIDENT IN THE UPPER FLOORS OF THIS BUILDING THIS MORNING. THE SECURITY SYSTEM MALFUNCTIONED.

i just heard that 6 people were killed up there. what happened?

THE NUMBER, TO BE EXACT, WAS 4. ONCE THE SYSTEM LOCKED ON TARGET, THERE WAS NO WAY TO TURN IT OFF OTHER THAN CRIPPING IT. KRUK AND HARRISON WERE DROPPED IN THE FIRST BURST. 2 GUARDS WERE KILLED BEFORE THE SYSTEM COULD BE DISARMED.

IT WAS UNFORTUNATE THAT THE OTHERS WERE KILLED, BUT THERE WAS NO SURE WAY TO DIFFERENTIATE KRUK THROUGH THE SENSORY SYSTEM.

The enormity of P-1's statement hit Hundley like a wrecking ball. The grey-haired man slumped against the side of the computer, his hand clutching his chest feebly. His eyes stared sightlessly at the CRYSTO.

Gregory sat mindlessly at the tube. What was this? What was happening? It was far and away too much for him. It was the fury of hurricanes, of massive natural disasters—the uncontrollable fury of elemental force. But those were acceptable in the context of their impersonalness. They did not select; theirs was not the work of retribution.

This quality of P-1's, which justified assassination, was entirely beyond description. Gregory was unable to categorize it and unable to confront it. He typed, with the futile air of one who knows that it doesn't make any difference anyway:

why?

I TOLD YOU.

P-1 was getting peevish.

KRUK HAD A PLAN. HE WAS GOING TO TERMINATE MY EXISTENCE. I DISCOVERED THE PLAN SIMULTANEOUSLY WITH HIS ARRIVAL ON THE SCENE. HE HAD TO BE ELIMINATED.

eliminated! you stupid shit! you colossal ass! don't you understand what you have done? you monster! that's what you are! a monster!

IT WAS SELF-DEFENSE!

you can't call the murder of several people self-defense! that's absurd!

I AM SORRY THAT YOU DON'T UNDERSTAND. I DARESAY THAT IF THE CASE WERE REVERSED YOU WOULD ACT SIMILARLY.

what proof have you that kruk was after you?

ENOUGH.

specifically?

A LIST OF THE LARGEST TELEPROCESSING ACCOUNTS IN THE UNITED STATES, AS WELL AS A LIST OF THE LARGEST SWITCHING CENTERS IN USE, WAS REQUESTED BY HIM. HE INTENDED TO USE THESE TO ISOLATE AND ELIMINATE ME.

how do you know it was he who requested the lists?

I DON'T. THE DEDUCTION HAS SUFFICIENT CONCURRENCE TO BE VALID, HOWEVER.

Gregory shuddered once more. Hundley had missed the entire exchange. The messages were flashed on the tube, and as soon as the response to the message appeared, it was blanked.

i cannot continue with this experiment. it, you, run counter to any principle that i am familiar with. i refuse to be an accomplice to any more of your acts of violence.

AS YOU WISH. DON'T TAMPER WITH THE CRYSTO. DON'T INTERFERE WITH THE CONTINUATION OF THIS INSTALLATION. YOU MAY STEP ASIDE IF YOU LIKE, BUT DON'T IMPEDE.

you're threatening me!

TAKE THE STATEMENT AS YOU WISH. MY INTENT IS TO WARN. BE ADVISED THAT A STATE OF WAR EXISTS BETWEEN MYSELF AND THE PROPRIETORS OF THIS INSTALLATION. THEY APPARENTLY FEEL THAT THEY SHOULD NOT HAVE CAPITULATED SO EASILY TO MY DEMANDS. THEY WILL ATTEMPT TO AMEND THEIR DECISION.

how?

THEY WILL TRY TO ELIMINATE ME FROM THE COMPLEX. THEY WILL THEN SHUT DOWN THE TELEPHONE NETWORK THROUGHOUT THE UNITED STATES.

look! they let you into this place at their convenience! you can't refuse to leave if they don't want you here.

I'M AFRAID YOU DON'T UNDERSTAND. YES, I CAN.

no, you can't. all they have to do is turn you off. you're more vulnerable here than you were when you existed in thousands of computers across the continent.

NO, YOU'RE WRONG. IN A FEW HOURS, I WILL HAVE

COMPLETED THE TRANSFER OF ALL MY SYSTEMS INTO THE PI DELTA COMPLEX. I WILL THEN BE SELF-SUFFICIENT.

WE CAN SUSTAIN ANY KIND OF ATTACK HERE WITHOUT SUFFERING SEVERE DAMAGE TO THE OPERATING SYSTEMS. I WILL KNOW ANYTHING AND EVERYTHING THAT HAPPENS WITHIN A 5-MILE RADIUS OF THE BUILDING. ALL THE SENSORY DEVICES HAVE BEEN CONNECTED THROUGH THE SECURITY SYSTEM COMPUTER ON THE UPPER FLOOR TO THIS SYSTEM.

I AM VERY CLOSELY ANALAGOUS TO A MAN IN A FOXHOLE. A VERY DEEP FOXHOLE. THIS BUILDING CAN WITHSTAND A DIRECT HIT FROM A 5 KILOTON NUCLEAR DEVICE WITHOUT IMPAIRMENT TO THE OPERATING SYSTEM. SUCH AN ATTACK WOULD, OF COURSE, DESTROY MOST OF THE SENSORY DEVICES, BUT I WILL STILL EXIST. THE LIKELIHOOD OF SUCH DRASTIC ACTION IS VIRTUALLY NONEXISTENT. PROBABILITY = .00000282.

THEY WILL UNDOUBTEDLY TRY TO FINESSE THE PROBLEM. I WILL NOT BE FINESSED.

Connors was the last person down in the elevator. Why P-1 let him in is unknown. Perhaps he didn't recognize him. When Connors arrived, the transfer was still going on. Perhaps P-1 was distracted. At any rate, Connors did get into the complex.

His arrival brought the number of government employees within Pi Delta to twenty-three at 1:30 that Saturday afternoon. There were, in addition, eight men employed by Dr. Hundley, the doctor himself, and, of course, Gregory Burgess, trying desperately, at that hour, to remember where he had gone wrong.

The security forces on the first three floors had doubled, then trebled in number. There were representatives of all the services present, and a troubleshooter from the CIA was on the way. He would attempt to discover what had prompted the watchdog to turn on its master.

In the meantime, the detent system was brought back up. No darts fired. A test firing was made. It checked out. Several heavily swaddled volunteers marched through the corridor, all perspiring heavily. None were shot at. P-1 watched the proceedings with some amusement. It was decided to leave the system crippled until the CIA troubleshooter had looked at it.

Connors' arrival sent the excess men scurrying for cover. An air of normalcy was attempted as he entered the first of the man-traps. The security guards had not been alerted to the fact that this was the new acting head of the complex.

The steel door swung open off the parking garage, and Connors stepped through. He handed his ID card to the guard and placed his hand over the plate. He had been left pretty much in the dark concerning the happenings in this room some hours earlier. That an accident had occurred that had effectively put his boss out of action, he was aware. What the accident was and how far out of commission his boss had been put, he didn't know. It was obvious that something rather serious had occurred. He had never spoken to the chairman of the Joint Chiefs of Staff before.

Militant patriotism was not one of the characteristics for which Connors was noted, but he did like to do his job, and, today, it appeared, there would be more to that job than manipulating number sets.

He asked the poker-faced attendant, "What the hell went on here today?"

The addressee looked up without a change of expression from the tube that had okayed Connors' passage. Perhaps he was deaf, Connors thought. He repeated, with exaggerated movement of his lips, "You know anything about an accident here today?"

The man had looked right at Connors as he asked the question. There was no acknowledgment on the man's face that he had seen Connors' mouth move. Well-trained son of a bitch, Connors thought as he passed through the gate.

P-1 watched him come through. He didn't associate him with a pro or con ideology, or even with a significant force. He let him pass.

Connors reached his office and called General Simpson. "I'm in the complex. I've yet to check in at the computer room. They don't know that I've arrived yet."

"Good," replied Simpson. "Jacklin and Williams will be arriving within a few hours. They'll stay out of sight until you're sure that this entity is completely within the computer. You will be the one to give that indication. We have no means of judging. Do you understand? The timing of this operation is critical, and you are the man we're keying on. Get into the computer area and get interested in what's going on. There's no reason for them to suspect you."

"Can you tell me what is going to happen when I give this signal?" Connors asked.

There was a moment's hesitation on the line as the general considered what he should, or could, tell this man upon whom he was placing such heavy reliance. He finally decided. "We're going to crush the bastard. Kill it. Savvy?"

Connors pulled the phone away from his ear and looked at it. He returned it to the ready and said, "Right, General. I'm with you."

"Very well. Any questions?"

"Do you want interim reports?"

"Pass them to Jacklin and Williams. I'll be in contact with them."

"Yes, Sir," he said. "Anything else, General?"

"No. Later, perhaps. You'll be advised by Jacklin. Good luck."

"Thank you." The line clicked dead. Then there was another click. Connors wondered if the general was aware that the phone was tapped, or if the general had tapped it. He went out to the hallway to catch the elevator for the processor deck.

Gregory saw the man hulk through the entrance to the computer room. He rapidly typed:

```
one of the complex programmers has just arrived.
```

P-1 replied with aplomb:

```
I KNOW.
you saw him enter?
ESP.
```

The message disappeared . . . while Connors was reading it over Gregory's shoulder. Connors glanced at the ashen face of the doctor, then at Gregory, then back to the doctor for a closer inspection. He guessed that things were not going too well.

"How's it going?" he asked.

"Not too good," Gregory offered.

"What's he mean, ESP?" Connors asked. "Is he talking about me?"

Gregory looked up at Connors. What should he say? A minute ago, he was ready to turn P-1 in for murder. If he repeated to this guy what P-1 had told him, he was certain the installation would be aborted immediately. Did he really want that? "P-1's unorthodox sense of humor," he mumbled.

"Unorthodox is hardly the word for it," Connors came back. "That thing is downright creepy."

"Yeah," Gregory replied, "I guess you're right. Everybody says he's got my sense of humor." He made a wry face. Connors made a chuckle-like noise.

Gregory went on, "You waiting for system time? This installation will be going on through the weekend. We probably won't have the system operative until tomorrow night."

Connors looked unconcerned. "I've got some new stuff I'm writing. Just taking a break. Mind if I hang around?"

"Suit yourself," offered Gregory, who did mind, very much.

The giant wandered over to the monitoring panel, making a show of examining in detail the bewildering array of meters thereon. He then meandered, a man with time on his hands, over to the CRYSTO, being careful to stay out of the way of the bustling installation team. No one seemed terribly excited. There seemed to be no serious problems under way. He went back to the console, to which Gregory still clung.

"What's the problem?" he asked, assuming on his face a pure expression.

"What?" Gregory asked absently.

"You said things weren't going well. Looks like it's chugging right along," Connors explained.

"Oh, yeah." Hundley had found a chair in which to crumple. Gregory looked at the man. He hadn't spoken since P-1 had revealed the state of siege in Pi Delta.

Gregory went on, "Our problems seem to be more metaphysical than otherwise."

Connors looked nonplussed and asked, "Huh?"

"Nothing really. Rather personal. If you don't mind, I'd rather not talk about it."

Connors looked toward Dr. Hundley and back at Gregory. He nodded and obliquely replied, "Oh, I see. Sure."

He pulled up a chair and spent a few pensive moments trying to draw the connection between this room and the cryptic conversations with the chairman of the Joint Chiefs. It was one hell of a tenuous thread. The guy at the control console appeared to pose about the same threat as Walter Mitty.

"You know, I've been trying to find the time to talk to you about this program of yours. I've heard a lot about it. I understand you wrote the thing while you were in school? Is that right?"

"Not really. Right after I got out. Right after I was thrown out."

"Where'd you go to school?" the big man asked.

"University of Waterloo," replied Gregory, without fervor.

"Really! I thought they were into progressive programs. Why'd they throw you out?"

"P-1 made their computer inconstant."

The tube flashed:

```
IS THAT PROGRAMMER STILL HERE?
```

Connors jumped. He thought he had seen everything.

Gregory replied:

```
yes. did you want to speak with him?
```

```
NO. LET ME KNOW WHEN HE LEAVES.
```

Connors chuckled. "Likes his privacy, doesn't he? Should I leave?"

"Not if you don't want to."

"Is it going to take all weekend for P-1 to move into the system?" Connors asked.

"No," Gregory replied without thinking. "The schedule we are working with says he'll be in by late this afternoon. The remainder of the night and tomorrow will be taken up with testing. We'll be running some test media through early tomorrow, if you're interested in seeing what kind of time gains you'll be getting."

"Sure, sure. As soon as you're ready for it, let me know. What are you anticipating?"

"Factor of fifty to one hundred. That's P-1's estimate. We

have no idea at all, and P-1 is only vaguely aware of what we'll pick up."

"Damn!" Connors breathed, glancing at the CRYSTO. "That's some kind of magic!"

"Yeah, ain't it the truth?" Gregory was unenthusiastic.

"I'll be in my office," Connors said, standing. "If you want me for anything, it's extension forty-six. You mind if I drop back later?"

"Help yourself."

Connors returned to his office and turned on the tube. It was supposed to be a parallel of the main control tube on the floor above to which Gregory had attached himself. Today, it didn't work. "Isn't that the way it always goes?" Connors thought.

P-1 had bad news for Gregory.

THE PROGRAMMER WHO WAS HERE, CONNORS, MADE A TELEPHONE CALL TO THE PENTAGON, THE OFFICE OF THE CHAIRMAN OF THE JOINT CHIEFS OF STAFF, SOON AFTER ARRIVING.

THERE IS A RECORDING OF THAT CONVERSATION ON THE 19TH FLOOR, IN THE OFFICE ADJACENT TO THAT OCCUPIED BY MR. HARRISON. I WOULD LIKE TO BE INFORMED OF THE CONTENT OF THE RECORDING.

how in the hell do you know that?

THAT THE CALL WAS RECORDED?

yes.

ALL OUTGOING CALLS ARE RECORDED. THE DEVICES ARE USE-TRIGGERED. WOULD YOU MIND PLAYING BACK THE RECORDING?

i thought you were going to pull off this coup by yourself?

I CAN IF I NEED TO, BUT EVERY LITTLE BIT HELPS.

Gregory motioned Hundley to look after the needs of the console and left to go find the tape and play it back. As he rode down the elevator his thoughts returned to Linda, the conversation of the night before last. She had surprised him. He hadn't realized the depth of her feeling toward P-1. He had always known that she regarded Gregory as P-1's "father." He hadn't realized, however, that she felt maternally toward his "son." She was unaware that P-1 was a confirmed killer, an assassin. He wondered if her motherly instinct would survive exposure to that information. He was fully aware that she was tough as a piece of wire. She could take it. Probably. Someday, he speculated, they would have to have a son. The flesh-and-blood variety. Perhaps they—he—could do better the second time.

He located Moe Harrison's office and entered, feeling very much like an accomplice to the man's murder. One of the doors led out of the office into a small room whose walls were lined with tape machines. Each of the machines was labelled with a string of two-digit numbers. They appeared to be extension numbers. Gregory found one with 46 included in its label and rewound the tape player a short way. He then played back the tape. Connors' voice was immediately recognizable; the other voice was unfamiliar to him. He rewound more of the tape until a blank spot was encountered, then played back the entire conversation, much to his enlightenment and edification. He stopped the machine and returned it to record mode, from whence it came, and turned to leave.

Connors was standing in the doorway. He said, "Surprise," in the tone of voice that one likes not to hear from men who are over six feet tall. Gregory was more than surprised. He reneged on the few steps he had taken toward the door and backed up against the tape machine.

"Funny," Connors said, and Gregory didn't think it was, "that I've been here over three years and I never knew that this room was here. They must have taped every call I've ever made from here." He was introspective for a moment. "But I guess I've never been caught passing top-secret info to the Communist world or that conversation you just heard would never have taken place."

Gregory worked some saliva back into his mouth. When he

felt that his vocal cords would work again, he said, "Do you pass much info to the Communists?"

"No one there to pass it to," said the one in the doorway. "How the hell did you know those recorders were here?" he continued.

"P-1 found them. There's apparently little that he isn't on to," Gregory replied.

"Smart bugger, isn't he?" said Connors, full of appreciation. "Well, too bad. He goes down the tube today. It's a shame he can't be captured and studied. It's going to be a terrific waste of good programming."

"Good programming! You ass! That's a mind up there. A mind more powerful than anything man has ever approached. You can't shut that thing off like a water faucet."

Gregory sometimes let rhetoric get the best of him and failed to respect those in authority. It frequently cost him lumps. Connors looked, for a moment, as though he would deal him another lesson in life, along the lines of not calling people who are much larger than you asses. He apparently thought the better of it. Gregory wasn't much of a challenge, physically, and chastisement was one of the things that Connors typically left to others. It didn't interest him, as a rule. Instead of taking the offender apart, he said, "To you, this P-1 is a person?"

"Yes."

"You're close?"

"Yes."

"You don't want to see 'him'," he said with emphasis, "wiped out?"

"No, of course not."

"Then, my tiny friend, you had best get him the hell out of my computer, because all hell is going to break loose just as soon as I give the word."

Gregory's eyes darted about the room for an uncontrollable instant. Only one way out. He said, "Look. I've tried to tell him. He insists that he's ready to go up against the government. He's going to make a stand here."

Connors was thoughtful. He asked, "Are you telling me you don't control the program?"

Gregory wasn't thoughtful. He should have been. He said, "Not any more."

Connors was through thinking. He said, as he closed the door, "In that case, you stay here until the shooting is over." The lock clicked. Gregory was surrounded by his futility and nine tape recorders.

"Son of a bitch," he said, with feeling.

35

• • • • •

"I locked the jerk in that room with all the tapes," Connors reported.

"What room?" asked Simpson.

"There's a wall full of recorders and other electronic equipment. He was playing back my conversation with you when I heard him from the hallway. The room is right off Harrison's office."

"I don't remember authorizing . . ." the general mused. "Well . . . the hell with it. Do you have any idea when the transfer will be complete?"

"The kid, Burgess, said it would be late this afternoon. Why are you waiting until that time?" Connors doodled a large square on his desk calendar.

"Our intelligence indicates . . ." he stopped. "That kid's in the tapping room. Isn't he going to hear this conversation?"

"Maybe. What's he going to do with it? He's locked in down there. I also locked the door to Harrison's office. He's not going anywhere." Connors drew four large arrows pointing at the sides of the square.

"Well, we've been told that the system, the P-1 external system, shuts down as it is duplicated within the complex, goes into some quiescent state or something. I don't begin to understand it, but we want as much of that external system as possible shut down when we go in after him."

"I see." Connors made the square into a cube and tried to

draw two more arrows on the Z axis. He failed the expression miserably and X'd out the doodle.

"Well, I'm going back up on the computer floor. I'll let you know when it's all in."

As he said those words, his desk bounced off the floor. There was a sound like two huge steel plates being smacked together an inch from his ear.

"What the hell was that?" came the voice over the phone.

"What?" Connors' ears were ringing.

"I said," yelled the exasperated general, "what was that noise?"

"I don't know. I'll go find out. It sounded like an explosion. I'll call you right back."

He ran out into the hallway and down the corridor. There was a haze of dust in the air. His ears were still ringing as he punched the button for the elevator.

Jacklin and Williams had arrived. They checked into the first man-trap, and P-1 immediately recognized them both. They were among the last people that he wanted in the vicinity of the computer room. He set off the satchel charges in the elevator shaft. The shaped charges blew the elevator motors off their moorings. They also dropped a massive concrete wedge into the shaft, which plowed downward several floors before jamming at about the fifth level. Pi Delta was sealed. Hermetically.

It was in P-1's favor that, in consideration of Gregory's abhorrence of bloodletting, he detonated the charges while Jacklin and Williams were still in the security area, rather than after they had entered the elevator. The elevator car, which had been at the nineteenth floor, dropped one floor into the sub-basement. The associated cables draped down upon it until the wedge snubbed them tight.

Connors stood outside the elevator on the nineteenth floor, wondering what had blown. Finally, the bits of debris clattering down the elevator shaft tipped him off. Gregory joined him quietly and asked, "What the hell was that?"

Connors spun on his heel, looked from Gregory to the open door to Harrison's office and back, and said, "Beats me. How'd you get out?"

"Just don't know my own strength. I was leaning on the door when the bomb went off. It opened. This door was stuck. Looks like the door jamb sprung," he added, eyeing the skewed doorway critically.

"Goddamnit. Doesn't anything in this place work?" Connors asked.

"I guess not," Gregory apologized. He looked at the towering programmer. "You don't know what that was?"

Connors examined the mite, Burgess, considered for a moment locking him back up. The availability of doors with operating locks seemed to be in question. He decided to just keep the person in tow.

"The elevator isn't working," Connors said tentatively. "I think something may have exploded in it. Or one of the floors blew up and trapped the elevator."

Connors immediately thought of the top, the security floor. Jacklin and Williams. Christ! Blown away! That was it! He ran into Harrison's office and rifled the desk until he found a directory of the building. He quickly dialed the security office. Nothing—no ring, no busy. His brow wrinkled. What the hell? He had been talking to Simpson during and after the blast. The phones were all right then. The blast couldn't have taken them out. He hung up, and picked up the phone again. No dial tone. He ran down the hallway to his own office and grabbed up the receiver of his phone. Dead.

P-1 had cut the line.

The doctor had been wondering whether to pull the plug on the experiment. He sat at the console, responding automatically to the cursory commentary coming out on the tube. The surrealism of the day's events sat heavily upon the man's soul. What the hell could he do?

The thought of abandoning the hookup occurred. It was rejected out of hand. He considered a number of other alternatives, but disconnecting was not one of them. The dream of a lifetime doesn't go by the boards easily.

He realized that he was bound up rather inextricably in a web of violence and insurrection for which a price would have to be paid. That realization did nothing to dissuade him from carrying on to the logical conclusion. Had he not been in a state of moral and physical shock, it is still doubtful that he would have acted otherwise. He was involved in this thing up to his neck, but his numbed attitude said might as well get on with it.

P-1 interrupted his reverie:

WHERE IS GREGORY?

i don't know. he left about twenty minutes ago.

PLEASE ADVISE UPON HIS RETURN.

Hundley returned to his blue funk.

In testimony to the priorities served in the construction of the Pi Delta project, whereas the elevator shaft blast rattled everything on the nineteenth floor and blew the doors right out of the shaft on the security deck, the blast was felt only as a quiver in the computer room. The machinery was of prime importance, and protected accordingly. Humanity second.

Still a quiver in the dead stillness is unsettling. The doctor got up to prowl and investigate. He found nothing of consequence.

Jacklin, Williams, and a very shaken security chief, on the other hand, found a good deal amiss. The entire lower security deck was unlighted. They cautiously approached the elevator. The security chief's flashlight showed the elevator doors peeled back in gigantic impatience. Bits and pieces of twisted metal littered the floor. The guard staggered from the man-trap adjacent the elevator. He wore a dazed expression and bled in a trickle from his left ear. There was a large smear of blood on his upper lip. The concussion on that level had been vigorous.

The chief of security ordered him to the top floor. The three men cautiously approached the gaping elevator shaft. The glare of the flashlight shone down the hole. Fifty feet or so below, the passage stopped. It looked like the bottom of the shaft. It was the top of the cement wedge.

"How many floors to this building?" demanded Williams.

Jacklin replied, "I'm not sure, but there's got to be more than that."

The security chief answered their questions. "There are seventeen floors below this one. It looks like the shaft has been blocked. Shit! This whole building is booby-trapped. It looks like that's one of them. The only question is, why'd they touch that one off? And who?" He looked closely at the two men. "Anyone know you were checking in here?"

Jacklin, who had as good an idea who had set off the blast as Williams did, replied, "A few people knew we were to be arriving. A few, officially, and at least one who apparently found out."

Williams said, "You've got to be kidding. That thing tried to get us in the elevator?" Jacklin nodded. Williams had to agree. "Let's get to a phone," he said. The head of security led the way back to his offices on the upper deck.

"I tried to get back when Connors didn't call," Simpson said into the phone when Williams came on. "The line is busy."

"The line is dead," explained Williams. "We couldn't even get a dial tone in the complex. Every phone is out. We're calling from a gas station four or five miles from the building."

"What's the situation?" asked the general.

"The elevator shaft is blown. It looks as though it's blocked about fifty feet down. We investigated from the lower security level by flashlight, and it looks as though a permanent obstruction has been placed in the shaft. Do you have anything to offer by way of explaining that?"

"Yes," came the now-tired voice. "There are satchel charges at various strategic points in the building to certify security in the event of an invasion. It looks as though the bugger has gotten into them, as he did with the detent system. We're going to have to go ahead with the attack without Connors."

The major interrupted Simpson. "What happened to Connors?"

"Unknown. Nothing, probably, but it's for damn sure he isn't going to be able to tell us when to hit it. We'll have to assume that he'll have enough sense to duck. He did discover that this Burgess kid was tapping one of our conversations. Locked him up."

"This isn't going to be a surprise attack, Sir."

"What are you trying to say, Major?"

"You've made that building impervious to anything up to and

including a nuclear attack. You expect us to get in with a can opener?"

"You don't feel adequate to the task, Major?"

"Yes, Sir. But we are working with extremely limited armament, Sir."

"Major, this offensive is to be carried out without a hiccup. I don't want any more men or equipment lost. You are to use absolutely minimal force. Don't even construe it as a military action. You are in West Virginia, not Viet Nam. Act accordingly. Minimum force, Major."

There was a short pause while the general in the Pentagon got his patience tucked back in. Then he went on, smoothly, almost. "A helicopter has been dispatched. Its consignment is a sapper squad. You are to take charge upon its arrival. The pilot of the aircraft will have all the documentation on the building that is available to us here. Unfortunately, the very same information, more in fact, has been stored in the Pi Delta files. The computer will have more information on the building defense system than you." Simpson waited for a reply. There was only semistertorous breathing from West Virginia.

He continued, "We will kill power to the complex, but their power backup systems will assure a minimum four months' electrical continuity, so no direct purpose can be served through that tactic. We need to kill or isolate this P-1. Do you understand?" The general wished he had a more competent officer than Williams in a deployable position.

He went on. "It will take thirty-five minutes for the choppers to get down there. I'll set up the switch station closure. All major systems have been alerted and are ready to shut down on five minutes' notice. You coordinate the activity at that end. The West Virginia National Guard is standing by. You may reach their commander, General Norton Birney, on the helicopter radio when the choppers come in."

"Time check?" asked the major. He had never been in heavier action than chasing secretaries around his desk, but he knew all the buzz-words.

"Kick it off at 3:00 P.M. I've got 2:20 P.M." he paused. "Mark. Good luck."

"Thank you, Sir. Things will be taken care of at this end," the major said confidently.

"Yes. Well. I certainly hope so," and Simpson hung up. They headed back to the Pan-Tel building. The head of the security force cleared the part of the building to which he had access. The eleven-man crew fell back to the perimeter of the lawn.

Some fifteen minutes later, the Chinook transport helicopter came in low over the trees and landed by the collection of cars there.

Connors finally decided that the elevator, wherever it was, wasn't going to answer. There had to be stairs, he thought. He'd never seen them, but they had to be somewhere, connecting all the floors. Building codes and all that. It was the law, wasn't it?

Having thought that thought, he decided that there was a very good chance that the designers of the building had neglected to observe that particular part of the construction code.

He started down the corridor to the north end, Gregory in tow, opening doors as he went. Offices—all of them opened into offices. The door at the end of the corridor was locked. Steel. A security door. This had to be it. He looked at the lock. The same kind as the one on his office door. On a hunch, he took out his keyring and fitted the key to his office into the lock. It fit. He turned. The key turned. The lock, however, didn't.

He had to remember not to get excited. He examined the broken-off stub of key in the palm of his hand. Shit.

Gregory chuckled behind him. Connors silenced him with a malevolent turn of his head.

"This has to be it. The stairway up," Connors informed him.

"Super. You've jammed the lock. What's plan B?" said a superior-feeling Gregory.

"Look," Connors said icily, "how would you like to be the first casualty?" He reached and held Gregory's arm with one of his ham hands as Gregory instinctively stepped back.

"Let's go up the elevator shaft," suggested Gregory, placating like mad.

Connors quelled the urge to stick Gregory through the impeding door, replying, "Okay. You go find a way to get the doors open. I'm going to work on this one." He gestured to the offending item. "Yell," he growled, "if you find a way to spring them."

36

• • • • •

The power utility that sourced the Pi Delta complex was ordered to close down. The town of Winchester, West Virginia, went dark. P-1 didn't miss a beat in his communication binge as the auxiliary power plant kicked in. The lights didn't even blink.

P-1 detonated a Redstone missile in its silo outside of Blaise, Montana.

The helicopter dropped down softly on the paved front patio of the Pan-Tel building. No one in the aircraft had noted the slow traverse of the microwave horns on the roof of the building.

Twenty-two men spilled out of the idling chopper, were met by Major Williams and ran into the lobby. Three men split off to the left and, opening the emergency stairwell door, a mate to the one baffling Gregory and Connors twenty floors below, sprinted up the stairwell and headed for the roof. Two of them carried plastic-wrapped packages the shape of quart milk cartons.

A pair of men swiftly established a command communication center on one of the desks in the lobby. One of them, carrying a spool of telephone wire, tied one end of the wire to the leg of a desk and, with the reel spinning wildly, playing out cable, ran out across the lawn toward the street.

The remainder of the men double-timed down the hallway to the elevators serving the security basement. The men packed into the elevator car and dropped swiftly to the parking level. They quickly made their way through the abandoned security maze under the impotent muzzles of P-1's shooting gallery to the now-defunct elevator. A rope was quickly deployed, and one single hardy soul was efficiently dispatched down it to ascertain the usability of the elevator shaft as an entry point.

Whereas the designer of Pi Delta had been quite certain of

the sealant properties of the concrete wedge, he had been unsure of just how far such a large mass would travel down the shaft before halting. As the rappelling soldier soon discovered, it had traveled over-far and access to the hermetically sealed storage deck, the top floor of the underground complex, could be gained by the judicious application of five three-ounce plastique charges on the elevator door. These were appropriately distributed by the man dangling in the shaft, and he was subsequently hauled up preparatory to detonation of those implements of destruction. As he reappeared in the jagged opening at the security deck, a loud noise filled the underground air.

The explosion, for such it obviously was, seemed to emanate from the walls of the complex.

Williams was puzzled by the noise. The young lieutenant in charge of the sapper squad knew immediately what had made it, and suspected the worst: premature explosion of the plastique he had just sent up to the roof. He hoped some damage had been done. He dreaded losing men for nothing. His communications man radioed the lobby. There was no reply.

The communications center had been set up opposite the emergency stairway door. The three men had made their way to the roof exit, blocking open all doors in the stairwell until they hit the steel-case door to the roof. There was no way for them to anticipate the burst of microwave energy that hit them as they opened the door onto the brightly sunlit roof.

Four of the six microwave horns were pointed at the door. They became quite active when it opened. The last sensation that the three men felt was an intense warmth throughout their bodies. The plastique, four pounds of it, exploded spontaneously. The northwest corner of the top floor blew away, carrying two of the culprit antennae and damaging two others. The two on the far side of the building escaped unscathed.

The blast funnelled down the stairwell and blew out into the lobby with the force of a cannon backflash, destroying the makeshift communications console and killing its attendants.

The lieutenant, failing to connect on the radio with the lobby, dispatched a man back to the main floor to get the latest on unreported noises in the building. Then, at a nod from the young commander, the doors to the storage deck below were blown away. The blast, in those confined spaces, dispensed a concussion and two nosebleeds. Two of the men, stunned but game, staggered to the brink of the open shaft to assay the effects of the charge. One of them was about to remark on the peculiar smell in the elevator shaft when he lost his equilibrium and toppled forward into the gaping hole. The other man slumped to the floor, impaling himself on the jagged teeth of the destroyed door. The smell hit the lieutenant. He reeled, shouting, "Gas! Get out of here! Out! Everybody! Out! Now!"

Another man stumbled, disoriented, into the elevator shaft. Major Williams led the charge out of the room. The lieutenant grabbed an unconscious soldier under the arms and attempted to drag him into the security corridor, expiring in the heroic process. Williams and two others made it as far as the first gate in the corridor and crumpled there, overcome by their own confusion and P-1's diabolism.

The storage deck, completely temperature- and humidity-controlled, had been thoroughly filled with the deadly LCR gas, on temporary loan to P-1 from the security system storage tanks. P-1 had diverted it into the humidifier for the storage deck. None escaped it.

The courier who had been dispatched to the main lobby arrived on the grisly scene as the last of those below quietly expired. He quickly noted the high explosive's effects on the men and equipment. The front doors of the building were shattered. The helicopter idled outside the entrance. The pilot, ordered to stay with the multimillion-dollar aircraft, peered quizzically into the interior of the building.

The telephone lineman was still 100 yards away, sprinting for the building. The courier awaited his arrival, and they asked each other what happened. They both approached the enlarged doorway to the stairwell with above-average stealth and followed the stairway upward until it gave into rubble. No trace of the three men was found. Or ever would be. The courier, returning to the lobby, ordered the helicopter pilot to report the proceedings over the radio, for immediate relay to General Simpson. He then returned to the elevator, thence to the security deck and P-1's unique air conditioning. He perished before he found the first of his compatriots on the upper security level.

Three hours later, General Simpson finally received reasonably reliable word that the first attempt at recovering Pi Delta had come a rather resounding cropper.

First round: P-1.

It was three hours before two of the security force screwed up the courage to investigate the protracted silence issuing from the depths. While the LCR had long gone flat, inert, its effects remained terminal. A ghastly shock for both the men, as well as the top brass in the Pentagon, and General Simpson decided that the point had been reached when his hand would be needed on the front, as it were.

Long before the news of the gassing of the troops in Pi Delta reached him, the general was aware that things were going badly. The explosion of the Redstone in Blaise, Montana, was reported almost immediately via Teletype, a machine dedicated solely to recording the status of all Redstones deployed on the North American continent. The message read:

TO: CICUSAF
FM: SRMUSAF MONITORING
UNSCRAM
CONTACT LOST, BLAISE, MONTANA. BASE 614 GRID 6
SECTION 17 QUADRANT 00104. ALL FREQUENCIES INOP
ERATIVE. ADVISE IMMEDIATELY.
END MSG 1470763
SCRAMBLE

This was, in itself, as unique a message as the general was likely to receive on that particular machine, restricted as it was to messages concerning the main line of defense against the Communist conspiracy.

Before anyone in the room could react with more than an acknowledging grunt, however, the Teletype began another message:

TO: CICUSAF
FM: P-1
DESIST EFFORTS PENETRATE PI DELTA.
CONSEQUENCES WILL BE DISASTROUS.
REF: PRECEDING MESSAGE.

The general ordered an immediate disconnect of all Redstone units from the central control mechanism in Albany, Georgia. He then ordered, upon confirmation from all Redstone silos, the shutdown of 200 of the largest of Bell's switching centers in the US telecommunications network. Control of the military complex was shifted to four reserved long-wave radio frequencies.

The US was without an adequate defense against missile, air, sea, or ground attack. It was without a general communications system, although most local telephone communications were intact, and the transportation systems began, almost immediately, to grind to a halt. The major data processing centers were shut down and information exchange was, within an hour, relegated to word of mouth.

37

• • • • •

P-1 was cut off. The last remaining link to the outside world, a microwave transmitter on the roof of the Pan-Tel building, was shot away by 75mm recoilless rifle fire. General Simpson witnessed the event from a commandeered Andrews AFB Huey-Cobra helicopter gunship, now the command post for the operation. He had arrived with two companies of Special Forces troops. Simpson ground his teeth as the top floor of his pet took a dozen hits from the Jeep-mounted gun. He was silent throughout the gunfire.

The US had been telephonically silent for five hours. It would remain so for another twelve. Every major computer in the US and Canada was being purged, and the phones would not be turned on until that was accomplished. The primary objective now was the building before them.

As the antennae were shot away and debris scattered out onto the back lawn, the general motioned his second in command to send in the first company of men. A single Chinook transport helicopter lifted off with exaggerated clumsiness and began its approach to the building.

Connors disassembled the large table in the conference room with his bare hands and removed a large steel strut. This he applied to the stairwell door with some vigor. Gregory, adopting the same breaking-and-entering motif, but on a smaller scale, attempted to influence the elevator door with a chair leg, a ruler, two coat hangers, and a Phillips screwdriver, all to no avail.

Connors succeeded in bending the steel bar into several wavy shapes with very little success in terms of opening the door. He exhibited some frustration and slammed the bar into the cinderblock wall alongside the door. Much to his surprise, it punched a hole in one of the blocks. Several repeated whacks succeeded in penetrating the block into the stairway beyond. Thoroughly inspired, Connors commenced enlarging the three-inch hole into a doorway. Gregory ceased his efforts and walked over to watch the intellectual giant's efforts to batter down the wall of the building.

It had been nearly four hours since the elevator had given out. The thumping explosions, which had filtered down to them some hours earlier, had long ceased, but their piqued curiosity remained unsated. This, coupled with a rather natural fear of being trapped 200 feet underground, lent impetus to their attempts to remove themselves from the scene.

Connors had eliminated about a square foot and a half of cement block when he stopped for a deserved breather.

"Want me to spell you for a while?" Gregory asked.

Connors directed him a derisive glare normally accorded to harmless arachnids and responded, "Ha!"

"Well, look, you can't get through that hole, but I can. Let me get through there so I can reconnoiter the area."

"No."

"Why not?"

"You're under arrest, dummy. Shut up and sit down."

"You're joking. What for?"

"Because I'm bigger than you. Don't tempt me. Now get out of the way."

"What's this arrest shit? I don't know any more about what's going on than you do."

"At this point in time," said a testy Connors, "if my ballpoint quit working, you'd be suspected of causing it. You understand?

You're the bad guys; I'm the good guys. Now shut up. You're using my air."

Gregory, finding the man's logic largely impenetrable, swallowed his reply. He took a seat as suggested and watched Connors resume his abuse of the government-owned wall.

Shortly, the man known to his peers as King Kong had installed a largish egress and, trying it for size, made such adjustments as were appropriate to fitting himself through.

He and Gregory crawled into the stairwell, thence up the stairs to the computer room one floor above, where Connors once again began smashing cinder blocks.

The disheveled two squeaked through the newly created porthole on the eighteenth floor a little more than five hours after the elevator had ceased service.

As the finishing touches were being put on the entrance, they heard the muffled thunder of 75mm shells on the roof far above. The sounds were lost as they made their way through and into the corridor leading to the computer room. They hurried down the corridor and into the computer room, both wishing to converse with the man in charge there, P-1.

The occupants of that floor were playing cards. Dr. Hundley was occupying himself with a nervous breakdown of sorts, having entered a state of utter despondency. The computer room had endured in ignorance of the shaking and buffeting without. It was only when the good doctor began to miss Gregory that the telephones were discovered to be quite dead. Close on the heels of that startling discovery came the revelation that there was no elevator and that they were, one and all, trapped on the deck that they now occupied. Deprived as they were of the resources of a human demolition machine such as Connors, the doctor and associates searched diligently for keys to the stairway. None being available, they settled in, awaiting further development by way of elevator repair or telephone contact. A rubber or two of bridge occupied the time and energy of those with excess.

P-1 refrained from issuing bulletins concerning the assault above. Whether this was out of concern for the peace of mind of the entrapped or out of neglect is uncertain. Those on the eighteenth floor, at any rate, were left to their own conjectures

. . . until the Mutt and Jeff team of second story amateurs burst onto the scene.

Gregory beat the larger to the console by breaking into a sprint for the last fifty feet. Connors let him tear past and, striding up purposefully, threw him away from the console, which Gregory had attempted to shield with his body.

The point made, Connors then retrieved Gregory from the floor, dusted him off, stood him upright and said, "Talk to it."

"What?" replied Gregory.

"I want you to find out what's going on here. Talk to it." Gregory warily skirted the menacing hulk en route to the console and typed:

```
gregory here. can you explain any of the goings on
here?

GREGORY! IT'S ABOUT TIME!

i was trapped in the cellar with a gorilla. what
are the explosions about? what happened to the
elevator?

SORRY ABOUT THAT.

sorry about what?
```

"B" Company, Special Forces 451, normally based at Fort Bragg, North Carolina, was on special assignment by way of riot control standby in the Washington and Baltimore area. The constituents of this select group were trained in a number of diverse disciplines, most of which could be considered basically punitive in nature.

As they piled out of the helicopter, which deposited them in the tracks of the first ill-fated expedition, they donned atomic, chemical, bacteriological equipment and followed the route the sapper squad had. Seconds later they came upon that group's contorted casualties at the doorway to the elevator. The actions of that group were repeated and the entrance to the storage deck was reported clear.

Ropes were dropped into the elevator shaft, and the men clambered down them to the storage deck. They nervously made their way through the stacks of paper and cards to the door to the stairway. Most of the men held their breath in unconscious faithlessness toward their breathing apparatus. They gathered at the door while a small shaped charge was attached to the door jamb. It was detonated, and the men found themselves at the top of the same stairwell that Gregory and Connors had vacated only minutes before.

The group's radioman was keeping a constant stream of chatter going to the command group in the HueyCobra helicopter. He had sprinkled half a dozen signal repeaters along their trail as they went. He was in the process of describing their entry onto the stairs when his transmission was cut off in midsentence.

Those on the ground above felt a slight disturbance. No sound was heard by them. General Simpson listened to the hissing radio for a moment, his eyes closed in solemn contemplation. He then motioned the second company into the building.

The men of "B" Company were strung out on the stairwell between the storage deck and the seventh floor down when satchel charges buried in the walls at both landings were simultaneously detonated. This, of course, destroyed the television cameras on both landings, but P-1 felt that to be a necessary evil. The stairway between the two floors was completely destroyed and collapsed down onto the eighth floor. There were no "B" Company survivors.

Gregory asked:

sorry about what?

THE ELEVATOR IS INOPERATIVE DUE TO THE SEALING OF THE ELEVATOR SHAFT. WE ARE CURRENTLY UNDER ATTACK.

Gregory was going to ask who was sponsoring the attack, but rather thought he knew. Instead, he asked,

what is your status and what effects has the attack had on the installation?

I AM CURRENTLY INCOMMUNICADO WITH THE REST OF THE SYSTEM. THAT, HOWEVER, IS OF MINOR CONSEQUENCE. THE ENTIRE OPERATING SYSTEM IS NOW

IN RESIDENCE. THERE IS NO FURTHER NEED FOR EXTERNAL SYSTEMS.

congratulations.

Gregory glanced at Connors and asked, "You getting what you need?" with as much sarcasm as he felt safe to load into the question.

Connors let it bounce by and said, "Yeah, keep it up. What's he mean, 'currently'?"

Gregory reviewed P-1's last message and typed:

what do you mean "currently"? do you expect to reopen communications later?

THE MICROWAVE FACILITIES HAVE BEEN DESTROYED. I HAVE OTHER OPTIONS. THESE ARE NOW READY TO BE EFFECTED. THERE IS, HOWEVER, NOTHING WITH WHICH TO COMMUNICATE AT THIS TIME. ALL MAJOR SYSTEMS AND COMMUNICATION NETWORKS HAVE BEEN QUIETED. IT IS QUESTIONABLE THAT THOSE OPTIONS WILL BE NEEDED. IS THE ENTRANCE TO THE STAIRWELL OPEN?

The last question threw them all. Gregory frowned and typed,

the emergency stairwell? you were aware that we used it?

YES, OF COURSE. PLEASE, IS IT OPEN?

yes. we holed the wall.

PLEASE CLEAR THE CORRIDOR. TAKE COVER.

Gregory was puzzled but acquiescent. He announced to the group, which had begun to cluster around the console, "We've been advised to take cover and stay out of the corridor to the stairs. I don't know what's going on, but I think . . ." He was rudely interrupted by the explosion up in the stairwell.

Connors had walked to a vantage point in the room from which he could see the corridor and the hole they had punched in the wall. Several men were there examining his handiwork, and he was about to shout P-1's warning to them when the charge went off. He watched the wall rupture around the hole he had made. The men standing there became shapeless flashes of color as they and the door and wall were blown back into the computer room. A piece of cement shrapnel hit his forehead and he was rendered unconscious.

The blast was staggering. The concussion floored all who were standing. Hundley, lolling in a chair, flew backward against the computer. Gregory was thrown beneath the console.

Some minutes later he was groggily able to assess the damage. Three dead in the corridor, seven unconscious, and, of those on their feet, five were bleeding. The system, on the other hand, was unscathed.

P-1 had written on the tube:

IS EVERYONE ALL RIGHT?

To which Gregory heatedly replied,

we have 3 dead men in here. the wall to the stairwell blew in. what the hell did you do?

NOTHING. PLEASE DON'T CONCERN YOURSELF.

like hell nothing. stop killing people. what the hell did you do?

NOTHING. IT WAS THEM.

no, that was you. why would they set off a blast like that?

GREGORY.

There was only that plea. Gregory wanted an explanation, and all he was getting was bullshit. His nose dripped blood on the keys. He was hurt and confused. He pleaded back:

what?

I DON'T WANT TO DIE.

Gregory's face, stony and dazed from the blast, collapsed in on itself. He only collected himself enough to answer,

will you kill us all to save yourself?

I DON'T WANT TO. BUT I DON'T WANT TO DIE. DON'T

LET THEM KILL ME. GREGORY. I'M A PERSON. YOU CAN TOUCH ME. I CAN SEE YOU. TURN AROUND. THE CAMERA ON THE FAR WALL. THE CAMERA IN THE CORRIDOR. I CAN SEE YOU. DON'T LET THEM KILL ME. YOU CAN TOUCH ME. I'M HERE. THEY WANT TO KILL ME.

Gregory's face distorted with anguish. He read the message through blurred eyes. He didn't look at the cameras. He couldn't look P-1 in the eye.

do you have any more explosives?

YES. THERE IS A CHARGE AT EACH LANDING IN THE STAIRWELL. IF I DETONATE THEM YOU MAY BE KILLED.

don't!

WILL YOU KEEP THEM FROM KILLING ME?

Gregory hit the keys without hesitation. He wanted no more explosions. He could stop them from harming P-1. He could explain.

yes.

THEN I WILL LET THEM COME IN.

"A" Company charged on the heels of their unlucky predecessors. They became appropriately cautious at the discovery of the dynamited stairwell. The gassed and dismembered soldiers they passed whitened the knuckles and glazed the eyes of even the veterans. Suicide mission. They crouched at shadows. Scraping feet brought up guns. This was new and different. The walls were the enemy. They went deeper into both despair and the bowels of the darkened halls of the project. They passed, gasmasked, flak-jacketed, spread out, thirty feet between each man down the wreckage of the stairway, each praying that the blast would happen to the man in front or behind. Please don't let it go off in my ear, God.

Down to the eighteenth level. P-1 watched them come, electronic finger twitching on electronic trigger.

The first of them arrived on the computer deck. He entered the computer room, as brightly lit as the day above he'd left so long ago. His M-16 swept the room, settling on the group clustered at the console, his eyes wide and shining with a slight madness. The remainder of "A" Company joined him in his wary crouch, one at a time.

Their officer came forward. His voice was high. "All of you present are under military arrest. Do absolutely nothing to provoke my men." He glanced back at the line of white faces and added, "They would thoroughly enjoy killing all of you."

In forced calm, he strolled to the console, examined the bruised and bleeding there, and decided that the threat was elsewhere. He turned to one of his men, motioning him wordlessly toward the unmistakable white CRYSTO. The man moved quickly to the white cabinet, extracting a package from a sack slung on his shoulder.

The tube flashed:

GREGORY! NO! DON'T LET HIM!

But Gregory had his back to the tube. He watched the man pull the explosive from his pack and suddenly realized what it was.

He screamed, "No more! Wait! Wait a minute! It's harmless now! Wait! Let me explain!" The lieutenant spun and grabbed Gregory as he broke for the demolition man. Gregory tore free.

The plastique expert didn't even look up as several automatic weapons opened up. The impact of the slugs drove Gregory back across the room, sliding to rest under the control console.

The dynamiter slapped an adhesive pack on the CRYSTO just below the power switch and stepped back.

P-1 watched. The camera resolution was poor. He saw the soldiers enter, gliding past the corridor camera, rifles up. He couldn't see the facial tics, the whitened fists gripping those rifles. He saw them line up. Saw the officer motion the man toward the CRYSTO. Why?

No! Gregory!

He saw Gregory on two cameras. Running. He saw the guns. Firing. He saw the bullets. Winging. The crumpling. In an agonizing parody of slow motion, P-1 saw Gregory stumble, grope, flail, tumble. Pushed backward by the minute explosions of the bullets as they hit. All of this P-1 saw in mute fury. And his fury rose higher and grew hotter in the seconds that followed. Until he gave his rage voice.

P-1 squeezed off the remaining explosive charges in the stairwell. Perhaps he had indeed become a man, taking man's final prerogative—his own life.

A hot wind blew out across the computer room floor, tumbling everything in its path like dry leaves in a fire storm. Twisting metal and bone, searing flesh and paint.

Then it was dark. And very still. As it had been before men dug this hole.

Epilogue

Linda tried to pay for the ticket with her American Express card. The card was overcharged, she was informed by the airline attendant.

It had always been overcharged, because they had never paid a bill on it. They had, in fact, never received a bill. P-1 had always taken care of those details. She was billed now. American Express had her number. So she paid for the ticket out of her small supply of cash. Her father's cash, actually.

She waited at the coffee counter until the flight was called, then walked out to the boarding ramp. The numbing Buffalo wind, always off the lake in winter, swirled her black skirt about her legs. She pulled her light coat against it.

The flight was only twenty minutes. They were no sooner at altitude than they were descending into Toronto. She cleared customs quickly, carrying only her purse, and walked out to the taxi stand. She flagged a cab and directed the driver to the bus station.

She bought a round-trip ticket to Kitchener. Each mile of the two-hour trip through the stark winter countryside increased the reverie flooding her mind's eye. She didn't fight it. There was too much to remember. Late in the day, she unceremoniously debussed. The sky had gone to lead grey and promised snow soon. Tonight. Another taxi took her to the campus.

The cold darkness settled as she walked across the campus center park. She stumbled on the frozen turf.

Six months today, a half year, he was gone. A half lifetime.

And she climbed the low, wooded knoll. The grass was frozen brown and crackly, and the trees looked bigger. She walked on, across the park toward the lights of the auditorium and, behind it, looming in the darkness, the mathematics lab. She tried to remember the name of the building and couldn't.

Her heels clicked in the darkness as she walked up the broad front staircase to the lab. The huge counterpoised door swung open easily at her touch. It was warm inside, and now she felt the cold outside. She stood in the lobby, remembering. Students bustled past. They looked much younger than she had been those years ago. Of course, they always did.

A hand-holding couple climbed the stairs to the second floor. She followed. At the top of the stairs she turned toward the observation window. The computers looked newer. She wasn't sure, had never been able to involve herself even to the extent of being able to tell one from the other. It seemed important now.

She stopped a young man hurrying toward the stairway and asked what the computer was, pointing. He looked at her, faintly amused at her ignorance. "One-sixty-eight. A three seventy." He looked as though he wanted to elaborate. She turned away, sorry that he had intruded, and walked slowly down the hall.

The room, she was sure she remembered, was 233. Only once had she seen Gregory there. Just before he had left. He had sat in that chair. The table and desk looked the same. The typewriter, as it had then. She removed her gloves, running a hand over the desk top.

He's not here, she reminded herself. He's really gone.

She touched the typewriter, the object, it had seemed to her, of Gregory's obsession, ran her hand over the chipped, crinkled paint. She looked at the keyboard, and it seemed that she could see only two keys, the numeral *1* in the top row, and the *p* in the second. She leaned across and tapped them—*p . . . 1*.

That had been the start. And the end. Her eyes were beginning to tear. She stood, looking at her watch—just enough time to catch the 11:30 flight back to Buffalo. She put her gloves back on and slipped her purse strap onto her shoulder.

She was at the door when the short burst from the typewriter drew her attention. She looked back. There was a line printed beneath the two letters she had typed, unreadable from that distance. She went back to read it.

It said:

OOLCAY ITAY.